Shade

NEIL JORDAN

Shade

JOHN MURRAY

HODDER HEADLINE IRELAND

© Neil Jordan 2004

Quotation from 'In Memory of Eva Gore Booth and Con Markiewicz' by
W.B. Yeats reproduced courtesy of A.P. Watt Ltd on behalf of Michael B. Yeats

First published in Great Britain in 2004 by John Murray (Publishers)
338 Euston Road, London NW1 3BH, a division of Hodder Headline

First published in Ireland in 2004 by Hodder Headline Ireland
8 Castlecourt, Castleknock, Dublin 15, a division of Hodder Headline

1 3 5 7 9 10 8 6 4 2

A CIP catalogue record for this title is available from the British Library

Hardback ISBN 0 7195 6186 8
Trade Paperback ISBN 0 7195 6187 6
Ireland ISBN 0 340 83485 4

Typeset in 11.75/14.75 Monotype Sabon by Servis Filmsetting Ltd, Manchester
Printed and bound in Great Britain by Clays Ltd, St Ives plc

Hodder Headline's policy is to use papers that are natural, renewable and recyclable
products and made from wood grown in sustainable forests. The logging and
manufacturing processes are expected to conform to the environmental regulations
of the country of origin.

John Murray and Hodder Headline Ireland
Divisions of Hodder Headline
338 Euston Road
London NW1 3BH

Dear shadows, now you know it all

W. B. Yeats

I

I

I KNOW EXACTLY when I died. It was twenty past three on the fourteenth of January of the year nineteen fifty, an afternoon of bright unseasonable sunlight with a whipping wind that scurried the white clouds through the blue sky above me and gave the Irish sea beyond more than its normal share of white horses.

Even the river had its complement of white. It was a rare wind, I knew from my childhood by that river, that would mould the waves into runnels of white foam, but it was a rare wind that day. I had studied those black waters as a child, sat on the bank of its smaller tributary with the hem of my yellow skirt between my chin and knees, because waves and all of their motions held a strange fascination for me. From the inkily silver reflecting surface, untouched by air, to the parabolas of ripples that would appear and then vanish, to the regular lapping of small pyramids of water, to the sculpted crests with their flecks of white. It was those the river had that day, and more. A good force five, a sailor would say. And George, who killed me, had been a sailor in his time.

George killed me with his gardening shears, the ones with which he cut the overgrown ivy on the house and trimmed the expanse of lawn, hedge and garden that descended towards the mudflats and tributaries of the Boyne river. He had large hands, gardener's hands, scarred in many places by the blades he wielded: shears, secateurs, lawnmower and scythe. He had one finger missing and a face marked with the memory of fires long ago. If one could have chosen one's killer, needless to say one would not have chosen George. One would have chosen softer hands, or more efficient ones, the kind of hands that you see in films or read about in books. Definitely five-fingered hands, that could smother easily, break a neck in one gesture. But life, as we all know, rarely imitates fiction, nor does it move with the strange efficiency of the films I once acted in. And if George's life had prepared him for anything, it was to deliver me a death that was, like the house, Georgian.

He held the shears to my neck in the glasshouse, and with quite spectacular clumsiness opened a moonlike gash on my throat. He mistook my loss of consciousness for death, then brought the world back to me while he dragged me through the roses, the world with its scudding clouds above. He watched the last of my blood flow into the muddy channel and augmented it with tears of his own. He decided against a watery grave and carried me like a lifesize doll to the septic tank, then realised I was still living while lowering me in. He spent one last energetic minute severing the head from the body he had known, in one way or another, since his early childhood. And so my last sight was not of sky, sea or river, but of his blood-spattered watch on his thick wrist, and the time on that watch read twenty past three.

Time ended for me then, but nothing else did. I can't explain that fact, merely marvel at the narrative that unravels, the most impossible and yet the commonest in the books I read in that house as a child. The narrator for whom past, present and to some extent the future are the same, who flips between them with inhuman ease. My Pip is my Estella and both are my Joe Gargery, and what Joe says to Pip I would say to George. What larks, Pip.

So there I am, aged seven, rocking on the wooden swing beneath the chestnut tree at the bottom of the sloping field that curved below the grass-covered manhole. There are Gregory and George, behind me or beneath me. I'm worried about whether they can see my knickers, then oddly not worried at all, staring at the tall, sad woman who is staring back at me, dressed in a grey fur coat, black beret and a pair of wellington boots. This woman is me, and they are my gardening clothes. I have an attitude of elegance, despite the tufted coat, I am smiling, despite the air of angular sadness, and I am my own ghost. I am glad I didn't know that then, glad the girl that I was could luxuriate in this comforting presence, this familiar, without knowing how familiar it actually was.

But I knew, when he finally deposited my remains in that septic sphere, replacing the covering of rusted metal, smoothing the grass above it with his bloodied nine fingers. I knew it all then.

You saw me play Rosalind in the school hall, George, I would have said if I could. But of course I couldn't and his name twisted into anagrams in whatever consciousness I had. George, Eorgeg, Egg Roe, Ogre, Gregory. Men have died from time to time, and worms have eaten them, but not for love. But men *have* killed for love, endlessly.

And when he dumped me into my excremental grave it was perhaps in the dim hope that the body he'd longed for would seep one day where all the old effluent seeped, into the river and thence to the sea. And maybe it was an act of flawed, bruised affection, that attempt to send me into the mouth of the river I had loved, and into the final embrace of that sea, which had seemed to all of us, since childhood, infinite.

To have carried me into that sea, to have lowered me into the scarfed waters of that river, might have been love, a love at least that Rosalind could have mused upon. But corpses don't seep like effluent. George, in fact, left me undiscovered in that undiscovered country, never to reach that sea or glimpse that shore beyond which is no other shore. He would be arrested, since the trail of blood and tissue would be as messy as it could have been. But forensics wouldn't exhume my body, he had seen to that. The plot beside my parents' grave in Baltray churchyard would remain unopened. And I would remain in a circle of old effluent within the sphere of a septic tank.

I look at myself, with eyes as preternaturally quiet as the eyes with which George looked at me that afternoon of scudding clouds, wind and murder. I could fear for myself, but fear will be singularly useless. The girl that I was will follow her course and nothing I, her familiar, could do would prevent it. But there's a comfort in her gaze and I'm trying to comprehend it. She is swinging, still, over the runnel of the larger river on that swing her father so carefully built her, swinging high, so she can see beyond the waters, beyond the dull green swathe of mud she will one day call Mozambique to where the white caps garnish the sea itself. I turn, to follow her arcing gaze towards the shore beyond which is no other shore, and her face comes level with the back of my head, and I feel the wind of life brush my dead hair into movement and I turn again and find myself looking directly into those wonderful eyes.

I can see myself in those eyes, my own reflection, retreating from me as she swings away, gaining on me as she swings back, and I realise the comfort lies in the fact that I am seen, I am seen and therefore am. I know it with a certainty I only came close to when he hacked the head from my body and was certain that death was coming, sweet easeful death, and the certainty is that I am, I exist, somehow, in those pools of luscious brown, swinging towards me and away, on the swing Dan Turnbull and her father built her, or was it me.

So her narrative begins, as it will end, with a ghost.

2

SHE HAD BEEN born in the house some time before the new
century, three years exactly, but her awareness of the sad presence coincided with the new era. Three years old, in or around
the year nineteen hundred, and her mother found her in the
curve below the large stairwell, talking quietly and intimately to
somebody who wasn't there. The sunlight came through the
bubbled glass of the tall convex window, and she sat below it in
the darkness, her doll clutched to her tiny chest, talking to
nothing in particular.

'Nina Hardy,' said her mother – for that was her name, Nina,
and Elizabeth was the mother's – 'whatever are you doing,
talking to yourself on the draughty stairs? Come down and have
your breakfast.'

'Can she come too?' asked Nina, and when her mother asked
who, Nina pointed to the nothing in particular she had been
addressing.

'Of course she can,' said mother, who was a woman wise
enough not to question the private world of children, and took
Nina's hand and led her down the stairs to the stone floor of the
kitchen, where the flags were cold beneath her bare feet, where
the whitewashed limestone arched above the deal table and the
range where Mary Dagge prepared her eggs. 'Now Nina,' said
Mary Dagge, 'here's your egges.'

She pronounced eggs with two syllables because she came
from the town nearby, Drogheda, where eggs were pronounced
egges. And when she placed the cracked plate with its blue
castellated pattern and its damp yellow pile of scrambled eggs

beside Nina, Nina divided it neatly in two, one for herself and one for her unseen playmate. And over the years to come Mary Dagge would grow accustomed to this division of spoils, to the portions of meals left uneaten on the right-hand side of her plate, to the sugar-coated sweets carefully shared with nobody in particular and to the conversations with shadows in isolated corners of the draughty house. For Nina was an imaginative child, her large brown eyes were pools into which one could sink, gladly, and the house was large, too large for an only child like her.

The house was on a bend of the estuary of the river Boyne, close to where it entered the sea in a small delta of mudflats. There were unkempt gardens leading to the river's tributary, over which a chestnut tree inclined, and her father attached two ropes to its sturdiest overhanging branch which he tied in turn to a small wooden swing. So Nina could swing, when the weather permitted, over the coal-black waters and glimpse the white caps of the waves on the ocean beyond, providing, that is, she swung high enough. There was a glasshouse to one side and a vegetable garden, the walls of which continued, along the roadside, to the banks of the river itself.

To be present at the beginning of a new century pleased her father, she could tell that instinctively, though she might not have known what the word century meant. But when she saw him supervise the riveting of the rope to the wooden chair of the swing, the rope spliced neatly round the piece of metal shaped like a tear-drop, the screw's thread beneath it fitting neatly into the precut hole in the wood, she knew it was part of a process that was exact and industrial, it was to do with metal and meas-urement and that this swing would be a superior swing to those built long ago. And when her father lifted her at last, placed her on the finished swing, and Dan Turnbull, who had screwed the final bolts, pushed her from behind, it felt odd to be swinging on a seat so new and to be staring over the water, at the face of the sad and lovely presence who was part of a story she would never know, that must have happened long ago.

Her father was old too, but so much in love with newness that his oldness fitted in, somehow, with every new thing. She could never imagine loving anyone more than her father, except perhaps her secret friend, during her more secret moments, but because she was secret that didn't count. No, her father was part of the world that declared itself as real and she loved him for it, as much as for his love of all things new.

And when he brought her to the shellfish factory he had built by the mouth of the Boyne river, on a late summer's day when the salmon were already leaping, to show her the new ice-machine, she loved him most of all. He led her by the hand into the low, stinking interior, pierced by the rays of the summer sun from the windows on one side, where the shellfish workers stood and touched their caps as he passed towards the sound of rhythmic clunking in the back. There were clouds like steam, but it was a cold steam, and the clunking had two causes, that of the engine-belt which rattled as it moved, and that of the great ice-blocks which hit the wooden base with a thump, shattered in clouds of that cold steam and shattered again under the force of the sledge-hammers which the shirtless men swung down. When he told her it would keep the shellfish alive and fresh until they reached the cities of England, it was impossible not to share his pleasure, though she was uncertain what this meant.

She was glad, if the truth be known, when he led her out of that hellish interior, but was happy again when he knelt with her by the river and watched its molten immensity flow past and told her once more the story of the river's birth. How the well at its source blinded anyone who was bold enough to gaze at their reflection. How a girl of surpassing beauty, with flowing locks like her own, came to wash her hair in it. How the waters rose, shocked at her beauty, how she ran to escape them and how they finally overtook her here, at the seashore near Mornington, deprived her of both her sight and her life. Her name was Boinn, so the river was called Boyne, after the name of its first victim.

There were long tendrils of seaweed beneath the water which rippled with the moving tide. And looking down on them, she could well imagine a long bed of hair beneath the shifting river, the young girl of surpassing beauty still beneath it, the waters perpetually washing her ever-growing hair. Looking up, she could see the obelisk of barnacled stone that sprang up where the river met the sea and was called the Lady's Finger. Beyond it was the ruined hulk of the Maiden's Tower. When sailors wished to enter the river's mouth, her father told her, they would shift their boats until the Lady's Finger was in line with the Maiden's Tower, then know they were at an angle to strike the bar. What strike the bar meant she had no idea, but a river whose mouth was guarded by the Lady's Finger and the Maiden's Tower and whose source was a young girl's hair seemed without doubt to be a womanly river. And the men who angled their sails through her, who pulled the fish from her in dark wet nets, who dragged the scallops, cockles and mussels from her seaweedy depths were lucky to have a woman of such bounty. She wondered were the drowned girl and her secret companion one and the same. But she decided on reflection that they could not be, since her ghost wore clothes that were of a later time and the clothes were never, ever wet.

~

Shade. Of a bat's wing, of a sycamore at noon, of an ash in thin moonlight, in the biggest shade of all. Nightshade. Shade of what was. I am that oddest of things, an absence now. A rumour, a shade within a shadow, a remembrance of a memory, my own. A stray dog forages with my wellington boot, buries it in the potato patch, digs it up again, buries it again.

George sits in his cottage in the grounds after the event and listens to the accounts of afternoon race meets on his radio.

There is a distant creak from the ironwrought gate by the house entrance as the postman pushes it open. The faint sound of crunching footsteps, as he wheels his bike down the curving avenue, stuffs a handful of bent brown envelopes through the letterbox which fall on the varnished floor. As the tide turns, the winds drop and the clouds quieten their movement, the white horses subside. A low, endless mackerel sky forms a backdrop to the falling sun. Oystercatchers pick their way along the mudflats of the estuary. A film of ice forms along the edges of the river. The blood on the grass grows white with hoar-frost. The world becomes a painting without me in it.

George rises from the car seat that is his only chair, walks out of his cottage leaving the door ajar, the radio on. He moves between the copse of ash and elder like a ghost himself. He wades across the river in his twine-tied boots, leaving elephantine prints in the mud behind him. The water reaches his neck, almost washes him clean. He makes his way along the other side of the river as the moon rises, picks mussels from the frozen shore, eats them raw. The words in his head are estuary, anglo-saxon, monosyllabic – mulch, shit, loam, earth. He lies face down in the wet sand and feels the brine seeping through his old tweed jacket with the leather elbow-patches. The casts of lugworms stretch away before his eyes to the rippled sand of the shore where the water laps sluggishly in the moonlight. If he could burrow his way into the sand beneath him, he would. If he could shed his coat, his flannel shirt, his greasy jeans and the orange twine that binds them, his flesh and the tissue that binds it, if he could shed the whole of him and throw it up as wet cast, he would.

He is beyond connective thought, but the words thrum through him. What covers the earth is mulch and decay and he has delivered the living to it. He has partaken in the savage order of things. And George now feels the murmur of renewal inside him. A spider crab crawls between his fingers and edges into a wormhole. A kittiwake squawks and he rises, walks along the

Mornington shore and the suck of wet sand beneath his feet changes to the crunch of broken seashell. Scallop, cockle, mussel, periwinkle, every footfall tells him of the necessity of death and how the earth needs its skeletons.

Mornington, Bettystown, Laytown, he covers each strand and wades waist-deep through the mouth of the Nanny river, a large hunched figure dark against the phosphorous glow of the breaking waves. He is on a journey back from reason, to the place he was released, St Ita's psychiatric hospital, Portrane.

It is morning when he reaches it. He walks from the shore past the round tower to the lawns with the red-bricked citadel of the asylum in the background. The nurses are arriving in their wrappings of stiff white. Beneath the barred window he once knew he stands covered in brine, sand, silt, any trace of the blood he spilt encrusted beneath it. He seems lost and wants asylum, in the old sense. Dr Hannon drives by in a black Ford car, stops and says, 'George, what on earth.' And George says, simply, 'Home.'

3

HER MOTHER, UNLIKE her father, seemed unexcited by the onset of the new century. The house was hers, had come to her through her father, Jeremiah Tynan, whose fortune rose steadily from the early days of the Drogheda Steampacket Company and who bought it with the profits gleaned from the first iron paddle-steamer, the *Colleen Bawn*, on the Drogheda–Liverpool route. He had died before the launching of the *Kathleen Mavourneen*, the largest steamer built for the Drogheda Steampacket Company, two hundred and sixty feet long, with a beam depth of one hundred and fifty feet and a gross tonnage of nine hundred and ninety-eight. But the fortune remained intact, indeed prospered, until the company was sold and the house passed to his wife and eventually his youngest daughter, by which time it seemed to have been theirs for ever. Baltray House, on the northern banks of the mouth of the Boyne river, with a view of Mornington, across the river, to the south.

His only daughter had been spared the vicissitudes of trade, had been educated at the Siena Convent on the Chord Road, Drogheda, founded by Mother Catherine Plunkett, grand-niece of the martyred St Oliver, for the education of young Catholic ladies. On her graduation she had travelled to Siena itself in the company of a nun of her mother's choosing and had there acquired, instead of a taste for the mysticism of St Catherine of Siena, a taste for the fine arts. In Arezzo she dutifully copied the Piero della Francescas, and later, in Florence, the Raphaels at the Uffizi and the towering marble of Michelangelo's *David* at the Accademia.

And there, in front of the *David*, she met a young English-man named David Hardy who was tracing, on his rectangular pad, everything about the statue but its marble penis. A conversation was struck up under the watchful eye of the chaperoning nun which was resumed two years later, after a chance meeting in the National Gallery in Trafalgar Square under the canvas of Velázquez' *Immaculate Conception*, Elizabeth Tynan having travelled to London to further her studies in the fine arts. There were tears streaming down his face and the reason for those tears, when she questioned him gently, moved her deeply. They were caused, he told her, as he dried his cheeks on the handkerchief she had lent him, by his feeling of utter inadequacy in the face of the perfection of the canvas in front of him, a perfection he could never hope to match. In fact the tears, she would learn some eight years later, when the son that had been denied him entered their lives, had quite a different source. But in front of the canvas, the serene beauty of the Virgin's face seemed a more than adequate explanation, and soon she was crying too. So he gave her back her handkerchief, and their fingers touched.

Indifferent artists both, their interest in Velázquez was soon overwhelmed by their interest in each other, and a courtship ensued, an irregular one, given that both were orphans in effect, the last parents on both sides having recently died, the mother in her case, the father in his. And soon the first of many trips across the Irish Sea began, from Liverpool to Drogheda on the *Kathleen Mavourneen*, now in the ownership of the British and Irish Steampacket Company in which Elizabeth, with her four brothers, retained a substantial interest. David Hardy, of sufficient means to be unembarrassed by his fiancée's estate, fell in love with the ship, the music of its name and, when he saw it, the thin, dun-coloured vista of the Boyne estuary which reminded him of nothing so much as the Flemish landscapes of Jacob van Ruisdael.

Perhaps he fell in love with it because he needed to, needed a home for his turbulent emotions, so radically different from anything he had hitherto known. That he was in love with Elizabeth was for him beyond question. And perhaps, again, he should have questioned that emotion, as to whether the long drama it was leading him towards was a symptom of the short drama he had left behind. But there is a third supposition, that this moment was fortuitous in the way few moments are, that he could bring whatever consolation was needed to the small-boned hand that he held in his. And when he leaned against the curved metal casing of the giant steam-paddle, placed his other hand around Elizabeth's thin waist and saw the obelisk of the Lady's Finger drift by, with the Maiden's Tower in line with it and beyond them both the long stretch of Mornington Strand, he felt that strangest of affections, for a landscape and country he had never seen before, never imagined he would see.

~

As night comes down again the radio speaks to itself in George's empty cottage. A weather-man predicts unseasonable sunshine. The amber lamp in the radio dial illuminates the frosted window. A pale wash of moonlight pencils each branch of the ash trees beyond. Sadness, if I could feel sadness, would be what that disembodied voice would evoke. He left it on, and the coming days of winter sunshine are broadcast to nothing human. As the night progresses and the moon moves and all the shadows of the trees move with it, it seems the calm the radio predicted has already descended. The winds that have blown for the last three days are bound for the Azores.

I should have read the signs, of course. George, like all of us, had his weather too. He had seemed restless because of those winds, obeying instructions other than mine. Instead of grass verges clipped, manure was spread around the roots of the black-currants and cherries in the walled garden.

'It is winter, George, the ground is frozen, why manure the frozen ground?'

'I'm doing what I'm told,' he said.

'I didn't tell you,' I said.

'No,' he said, 'what do you know about gardens?'

By the river's bank I had found a sparrow with its head cut off.

'Who would decapitate a sparrow, George?' I asked him.

'A mink,' he said. He pointed towards Baltray, where the mink farm was. But the head had been sliced neatly, as if with a shears.

'Maybe it was you, George, clipping.'

'Why would I clip,' he had asked me, 'in the middle of winter?'

Why indeed, I wondered, and forgot about it.

I had come upon him that afternoon, lying face down in the frozen grass beneath the apple tree.

'You'll freeze, George,' I told him.

'Maybe,' he said, 'but I'll warm the earth.'

'And I'm sure the earth will appreciate your efforts, George,' I said, 'but why not let the spring do it for you?'

'The spring needs help,' he said, 'the summer needs help too.'

'Are you an Adonis then, George, in overalls?'

'Who is Adonis?' he asked.

'Adonis revived the earth,' I told him.

'He was a gardener then?'

'Yes,' I told him, 'of a kind.'

'We used to lie here,' he said, 'just like this, the four of us.'

'Yes,' I said, 'but in the summer and the grass was high and we were children then.'

He raised himself at that and stood, awkwardly, as if re-entering his oversized adult limbs.

'You took my part,' he said, or I thought he said, and turned away.

'I what?' I asked.

And he repeated, over the blowing wind, 'You took my part.'

I stared at the outline his body had left in the crushed winter grass. I remembered the tiny theatre of the four of us beneath that apple tree in the long September grasses of my childhood. His part had been Touchstone, not Adonis. And he would strike me more dead than a great reckoning in a little room.

4

THE HOUSE, WHEN David Hardy came to view it – or it came to view him, for its approach was calm and silent as Dan Turnbull's handling of the grey mare that pulled them past the limestone pillars of the gates – seemed like a folly to him, an imitation of a civilised façade set arbitrarily in a vista that could have been the Azores or the Antipodes, or the Flemish estuaries in those paintings of Jacob van Ruisdael. There was a strangeness about it that never left him, the strangeness he felt when Dan manoeuvred the horse through the half-open gates, when the wheels of the trap crunched over the long-uncrunched gravel and swung round the back, which, to his mild surprise, he realised was the front.

I know now, of course, what he had left. How do I know this? It is the only grace of my state. I am everywhere being nowhere, the narrative sublime, a kind of mote in his eye as he rubbed from it the dust stirred up by the mare's hooves and saw the house he never expected to see, its lumpen limestone an affront to the lowland fields.

I would blame her, for many years, for a state of things engendered by him. His corduroy trousers, his tweed jacket, the military belt I loved to finger with its copper clasp, the linen shirt with its blue and red tracing pulled tight beneath it, the studded shoes that touched the gravel as he helped her out, all concealed something as banal and Victorian as a secret. And secrets, he should have known even then, will always out.

He took her elbow with an assurance that he cannot quite have felt. He concealed, because he had to, his trepidation, his fear even, of what this house might hold for him. She dismissed Dan with a nod and led him, by way of her elbow, the thin forearm pressed reassuringly on his thick, hesitant fingers, towards the door. She felt he was in need of reassurance and thought she knew why. He was in another country, the house was large and Mary Dagge, who opened the door, was all starch and unnatural whiteness.

Come into my world, she intimated, a world I promise will cloak you with delight. And he wondered, as he entered the shades of that interior, how the promise would be kept. They made love in the early afternoon on the large oak bed of the room they had decided would be theirs, and if there was a kindness in the low rays of the October sun that touched the bubbled window, the bedspread and her tangled stockings, there was an emptiness as well. He was a stranger among her familiar things. He had chosen to be this stranger, this journeyman. He wanted his journey to end here, but he wondered would it: would he always be a stranger here too, no matter how familiar this place became.

And then, maybe, or if not then, some time in that first month the child was conceived, another stranger in her body. And as it grew inside her, it slowed her movements, hampered that angular swiftness of which she was so proud, imposed a weightiness on her that she never quite forgave. He was overjoyed at the prospect of replacing that which he thought he had lost. But for her, child-birth and motherhood were an estrangement from her girlish self, a burden she never did repeat.

Two strangers, then. And the sense of strangeness released in him energies he never knew were there, energies he expended in, of all things, crustaceans. He loved to walk the banks of the rivermouth, on its Mornington and Baltray sides, hear the crunch beneath his feet of decades of scallop-shells. He loved to paint the fishermen as they pulled in their salmon-nets, listening to their talk as the oil-paint dried. He heard how they were flush for the season of the salmon run, then starved the rest of the year, noted the lobsters and prawn they flung back into the waters, began his first tentative co-operative, shipping ice-packed boxes of lobster, prawn, cockle, mussel and scallop on the steampacket to Liverpool. Liverpool's appetite for shellfish proved insatiable and the shipments grew, spread their tentacles to Blackpool, Southampton, Brighton, London.

Soon the string of fishermen's huts grew inadequate for the enterprise it had become, and a factory was needed which he financed, and so found himself, nearing the end of the old century, a surprised and surprisingly successful man of business. And soon he was rooted in this strange land, this strange house, as if he had been here for ever, the only hint of the life he had left being the tears that flowed occasionally from his hazel eyes, always unexpectedly, which he would explain to his young wife with the single word: Velázquez.

So Velázquez had become their word, for the eternal lost in the quotidian, for those lingering hopes one had but had to forget, those ambitions that were thwarted because of accidents, inability, or both. And, in the way of such words, for that moment when they had met the second time, and had known, within minutes of meeting, that they would be together for ever. That globe on the canvas, suspended in its dark background of dimly glittering stars.

And when she arrived, that's all he thought of, the child-virgin with the pinched face standing on the apex, utterly alone in the chilly universe. And when the doctor informed him that this child would be their last, tears were not an issue. He could not imagine this perfection ever being repeated.

She was carried into the house by her father, her tiny cheek resting against the white crocheted shawl over the rumpled corduroy of her father's sleeve. Her mother followed in a wickerwork nursing chair, carried by Dan Turnbull and two farm-hands, gingerly, like some exotic piece of china that might break at any moment. The house greeted her, as it greeted each newcomer, with a mysterious, unbreakable embrace.

Her eyes observed the house through a liquid prism, calm as pools of bog-water unruffled by any sentient breeze, disembodied as any ghost, carried by arms she was barely aware of through the front door into the yawning dark of the hallway, the oak staircase rising to the tall windows with their oblongs of grey Irish light. Her eyes closed at irregular intervals and the dark came in like a lake. They opened on a whim to see an entirely new vista, a nurse bending towards her in a different room, black hair brushing like wings off her face, sliding the bottle with India-rubber nipple downwards. The mother stretched in the verandaed room below her on the easy chair, wrapped in blankets, hand checking her vaginal stitches, father pacing the ground floor, now tinkering on the piano in the dining room, now sketching his sleeping wife with a soft charcoal pencil in the whey-coloured wash of light that seeped through those mildewed windows.

But his wife wasn't sleeping; she had closed her eyes against the need to meet his. Some exhaustion had entered her very being, some rage against the flesh, the skin, the tissue and bone of the animal in her that enabled this birth. She spoke when she must of course – yes my love, tired, maybe, I suppose I must be, tea, yes please – but her soul, her heart, whatever flower she gave to him was a bloody mess and was in hibernation.

The child's eyes opened in the room above and no effort of the suckling showed in them and she stared above the nurse's crow-black hair at what was not there. No cognition, no recognition. Just a stare.

An isolate child. Her name could have been just that: isolate, Isolda, with its connotations of tranquillity in aloneness. Dark pools of eyes, darker than her father's hazel, staring from his hand as he held her, in her mother's christening robe, above the stone baptismal font in the Siena Convent. Legend had it that they never blinked when the cold water trickled down her creased forehead. The shrunken head of Oliver Plunkett, sliced free of its body in Tyburn more than two hundred years ago, in its glass casket across the nave, could not have been more still. The eyes seemed designed for that too-large house, with its dark brown timbers, its damp limestone, its draughts and its shadows. When speech came, legend had it too, it came early, and always seemed addressed to someone else. They thought she had a lazy eye at first, the mamas and the papas always addressed to a point beyond their shoulders. But when they called Dr Quirk and he moved his finger in front of those brown orbs from left to right and saw them follow, they found nothing ocular at fault. And as they were blessed with ignorance of Dr Freud, who had, in point of fact, not yet begun to formulate his theories, they put it down to fancy and imagination.

They called her Nina.

~

The sky has clouded over and the pencil shadows on the branches have softened into a gloomy wash. The light on the window-pane is warmer now, the only light around. The onset of dawn can be felt before it is seen. The cough of a pigeon can be heard as it wakes, the wind seems to quicken and the dead leaves shift and somewhere beyond the copse of trees, the whir-ring of wings. After a patriotic tune on a thin organ, after a considered series of electronic beeps, the radio comes to life in the empty room with news of high and low fronts, of millibars rising slowly. And then the weak daylight comes. The night will retreat into shadow once more, into the dark spaces that define the bright.

George must have woken that last morning, turned the radio on and left it that way, found no milk in the fridge and walked through the crusted white fields towards the house. For I had come down, half-dressed, to the sound of banging in the kitchen and found the door open, a bottle of milk rocking on the pine table, spilling to the floor. A set of milk footprints traced the passage of his boots from the table to the door. I cursed them silently while I cleaned them and thought once more of ending his tenure as gardener, handyman and general factotum. Where are you, my Adonis, with your spilt milk and your bleeding sparrows?

And his words echoed in my brain, You took my part, as I went about my day, that day that ended prematurely when I came upon him two hours later in the glasshouse. The broken glass clinked around his boots as he emerged from the curtain of dead tomato plants. And he repeated the phrase I had first heard beneath the apple tree. But it wasn't his part I had taken. Heart, he said.

'You took my heart.'

5

Her mother, in the third year of the new century, decided Nina needed company other than imaginary. So she took the train to Dublin and visited, on Eustace Street, the Institute For Governesses, a grand-sounding title for the cramped fourth-floor room in which she interviewed lady after lady of the teaching classes. She settled on one, a Miss Isobel Shawcross, from the Kildare Shawcrosses, with a prim mouth and a carriage as straight as a pencil. The house was large, Mrs Hardy explained, Nina was quiet and given to daydreams and prone to fill the empty spaces with her imagination. What she needed was the kind of diversion an early education could bring. Miss Shawcross nodded, and in her nodding an understanding seemed implicit, an understanding of young girls in empty houses with large imaginations. There were references to be examined, fees to be discussed, but from the moment of that nod Mrs Hardy made her decision and Miss Shawcross found herself hired.

And found herself, one week later, drawn in a train over the Boyne river, with the mullet circling lazily in the waters below, a kingfisher skimming the waters, its wings blue over the alluvial flow which looked like nothing so much as the gathering froth on the glass of porter that Miss Shawcross was bringing to her lips. For the governess liked her porter, brown upon brown.

Dan Turnbull met her at the station, carried her many bags to the pony and trap. And his dark, wide-brimmed hat with the fisherman's hooks and flies dangling over the edge framed her view of the streets. She could have looked left or right and been free of this impediment, but Miss Shawcross's gaze was designed to mean business, and, meaning business, remained fixed on the road ahead. So the city quays were spooled to her against this dark foreground, like the lumpen mass of a projector against a cinematograph screen. They were mean, shabby and noisome, as she had of course expected. What she had not expected was the gathering charm, as the bustle of the North Quay modulated to the low swish of fuchsia hedges against the carriage wheels. There were splashes of red and orange against the irregular line of hedge to her left, since the fuchsia and the honeysuckle were in full bloom, and to her right were the tidal mudflats, the tilted masts of fishing boats at odd angles in the silt, as if they had been dropped from a great height by an unseen hand. The only sounds were the swish and crackle of the wheels against the hedge, the scraping of the mare's hooves and the drone of bees' wings round the fuchsia and the honeysuckle.

Miss Shawcross, who had an imaginative soul belying her rigid exterior, began to speculate on the new charge that awaited her and that act of speculation, assisted by the Guinness she had consumed, became a kind of waking dream. She saw an oval face with a fringe of curls, a bow-like mouth beneath large brown eyes, and the face moved towards her and away, drifting in and out of focus as if she, Miss Shawcross, far from being on a jaunting car driven by the fixture whose name she had forgotten up in front, was in fact on a giant, swinging pendulum. And her speculative faculties being so dulled by the Guinness, she let this dream occupy the whole of her for well-nigh twenty minutes and was therefore both surprised and unsurprised to shake herself out of it, raise her head to view an irregular driveway curve towards a grey limestone house with a girl framed beneath it, standing in the unkempt grass, staring at the approaching trap with those same unblinking brown eyes of which she had been dreaming. Dan Turnbull let the mare nudge her way through the wrought-iron gates. Laziness had long inured him against attempting it himself, and besides, he admired the ingenuity, the sheer persistence with which she pressed the dappled plane of her forehead against the metal, gradually widening the gap to the screech of rusted metal hinges. Good girl, Garibaldi, there we go now. Garibaldi was a man, he had been told soon after he had named her, an Italian patriot, but he liked the name, so Garibaldi she remained. And the dead weight of the gates scraped off the mare's broad flanks as she pulled the trap through. He could hear the slow, careful scraping of the hooves against the gravel, the metal hinged screech and a lightly snoring sound behind him, which he presumed was that schoolteacher sleeping, like a cow, half upright. The gate swung back behind to its half-open state as the mare quickened her pace, scattering the gravel. Nina watched from the lawn, the house behind her at first, then shifting to one side as they headed towards the forecourt. Dan raised his arm in a lazy wave, which Nina imitated, a look of scientific curiosity in her upturned face. She walked, then ran, then slowed to a walk again, following the trap around the grey limestone walls.

The sun to the left of the house, gently shivering fingers spreading over the orchard wall, illuminates Dan Turnbull, the horse and cart and the lady with the pencil-stiff back and the stiffer-brimmed hat, leaving the house dark behind it. The lady is standing in the cart now and the golden glow lends her an alarming theatricality. Dan kicks loose the wooden steps with his foot, holds her gloved hand and plots her delicate course down step after wooden step till her feet reach the gravel.

'This is Nina,' he says and yells, 'Nina. Nina!' His voice, brown and oiled like old tobacco, incapable of anything but warmth. 'How are you Nina, how are you.' His hands, like stooks of barley, their own smell, tobacco and engine grease.

I walked around the house, I remember, towards the dribbling horse and the woman with the dark hat. Dan kept calling even though I was walking towards him, but he was like that, Dan, he would repeat a thing even though you had already answered. He lifted me up with those barley-stook hands and I could smell the tobacco and he said, 'Here's the girl miss, Nina, here's your teacher,' and I knew even then that she wouldn't last long. Her dark brim dipped down towards me and she peeled off her glove and reached out her hand. Her breath smelt of malt and her nails were dirty, yet I took it.

'My tiny one,' she said.

~

An oil-tanker drags its way through the already open gates, trundles up the driveway and parks in the gravelled yard. It sits there, diesel fumes steaming from its rusted exhaust pipes, beeps its horn, waits, beeps its horn again and waits again. A barrel-chested man in blue overalls gets out and lights a cigarette. He calls George's name, George who ordered oil for delivery on this sixteenth of January, nineteen fifty. A radio bleeds from his cabin, a politician's voice talking about the rural electrification scheme and its implications for counties Roscommon, Sligo and Leitrim. He listens to the voice, the silence around it, smokes his cigarette to the butt and walks towards the kitchen door. He pushes it open slowly, calls George's name again. As his voice dies away, echoing through the empty scullery, he notices the purse on the pine table. He listens and when the silence seems absolute, he lifts up the purse, opens its clasp. He sees the wrapped notes inside but must think twice about it since he closes the clasp again, puts it down, walks back into the yard.

He walks down the path of packed mud towards the glass-house, still calling, 'Is there anyone there for Jaysus sake?' and only stops when he notices the streaks of red, frozen on the crushed grass, like deft calligraphy against the white hoar-frost. He follows them step by bloody step to the shattered glasshouse door, edges it aside and enters a warmer world, where the pale

27

sun works its magic through the windows and falls directly on the syrupy pool of copper-coloured liquid. He says nothing, stares with a child's curiosity and only makes a sound when he notes his own footprints: like George's in the milk, but russet-coloured with day-old blood, the broken oval of the sole with the minute squares of rust inside it. He gasps, an emphysemic sound, through lungs long ruined by cigarette-smoke. He seems to want to run but resists the urge. He lifts his foot instead, grabs his ankle with his right hand, twists his shoe to stare at the sole. He replaces it carefully on the unbloodied portion of the glasshouse floor, steps carefully outside and does the unexpected. He wipes his feet on the frosted grass, an automatic cleansing. He feels either tainted, implicated, or simply repelled.

Then he runs back up the pathway of frozen mud, through the low stone arch of the outhouses, jumps into the cabin of his oil-tanker which lumbers into life, spewing clouds of diesel as it performs a groaning turn and hauls itself out of sight, leaving a pale mist of fume, through which the façade behind gradually defines itself.

6

THE HOUSE THAT Isobel Shawcross entered through the back, by the kitchen door, was a big house, a very big house. And Miss Shawcross's first instinct was to make it smaller. She walked through it as though used to houses far bigger than this, infinitely more opulent, without the workaday scramble of its kitchen, the bicycle upturned outside the scullery door, without the irregular brass fittings of the ribbed stair-carpet that ascended towards those rectangular Georgian windows with their cubes of dusty light; as if she was used to houses infinitely more organised. And she sensed, though she can't have known it then, that this was a house whose irregularities consumed things: trinkets, penknives, cutlery, haircombs of whalebone and ivory, odd socks and shoes, letters, laces and lapis lazuli rings. She would lose things in this house, she sensed, but she could never, then, have known how much. She could never have known that the losses would extend far beyond the contents of those stout leather valises that Dan Turnbull heaved in, one balanced precariously on his oily crown, one beneath his oxter and the third pushed by his hobnailed boot over the flagstoned floor.

'Let me show you to your room, Ma'am. And Ma'am?'

Miss Shawcross turned, in the scullery hallway.

'Yes?'

'I haven't got three hands. Could you help me with that bag?'

She hesitated for a moment, and her nostrils did a birdlike twitch which Nina, and Dan, would remember as particular only to her. She bent then, took the valise in both hands and stood aside while he made his angled way, up the stone stairway, into the carpeted hall, up the wooden staircase with the high windows bleached by the afternoon light, on to the upper floor. There were doors to either side, all of them half opened, revealing further evidence of that disorder she had already divined. But her room when she reached it was a miracle of neatness. A smooth coverlet over a plain oak bed, a writing table by a window with a charming gothic arch.

'I'll leave them here, Missus.'

'Miss,' said Isobel Shawcross. 'Miss Isobel Shawcross,' she added, gazing out of the window at the white bundle swinging from the chestnut tree far below.

~

But now, in the present, in the time that moves at a constant measure, that neither speeds nor slows, at ten twenty-one on this sixteenth of January, a policeman passes through the sagging gates on a black bicycle. The white beard has all but vanished from the lawns, leaving such an even glisten of dew that it could be dawn again. It is Buttsy Flanagan from the station up the river beyond the docks and cement-works, the RIC barracks burned down in the Troubles and restored by the Civic Guards. He cycles slowly, as if unwilling to arrive. And having arrived at the circle of gravel behind the house scoured by the oil-tanker's tyres, he examines the scene slowly, with a methodical, almost disinterested ease. He notes the crushed grass, the footprints, the pool of dried blood in the glasshouse. Each breath emerges from him slowly, visible in the cold morning air, like a laboured question-mark. He knew George, knew Nina Hardy, knew George's sister Jane, but can no more connect the memories from his childhood with the scene before him than he could with a witch's sabbath. He remembers three figures on a hayrick, swaying on the back of an unsteady tractor in the late evening sunlight. He remembers the beautiful girl, the woman really, in the floral print dress, walking past the pennant of the eighteenth-hole green towards the tennis-club dance. He remembers the scent of heather and cut grass and the sound of a Percy French song drifting from the clubhouse. Oh the nights of the Kerry dances, oh the ring of the piper's tune, lingers on in our hours of madness . . . The conclusive line evades him for more than a minute, then, in the way of memory, comes just when he has stopped straining for it . . . Gone, alas; like our youth – too soon! He wonders idly how one sentence can contain so much punctuation. Then he hears the sound of a car chugging beyond the gaunt bulk of the house, and he feels relieved, that whoever has to plumb the realities of the scene before him, it will not be him. At least not him alone.

The car stops by the gates, deposits a policeman who closes them ceremoniously; his presence draws a knot of children coming home from school for lunch, whose presence in turn stops the milk van on its rounds, and a tractor carrying a mound of winter feed. By lunchtime the sun has broken through the clouds, the grasses are dry, the inquisitive crowd by the gates has grown and the lawns are progressively trodden by policemen moving with large, somnambulist steps. There are no raised voices, no eruptions of emotion and the tragedy, if tragedy it was, seems already to have happened a long time ago. Another car arrives, dispenses policemen who proceed to traverse the grounds the way the first ones did, while those who have already traversed stand stamping their feet in the cold winter sunlight, smoking, talking in lowered voices. Towards evening a third car arrives, an unmarked one this time, pushes its way through the knot of the curious, waits while the gates are opened, then crunches its way up the gravelled driveway to the back of the house, which is revealed to be in fact the front.

Buttsy Flanagan stands in the low arch that encloses the courtyard and recognises the utterly silent, bowed profile in the back seat. He sees a man emerge from the front, in a white hospital coat, open the back door, hold an expectant arm forwards. He sees George emerge, place one enormous fist in the crook of the white-coated arm. He waits as George is led towards him, moves to one side and walks with them, following the irregular trail of blood towards the glasshouse. He observes George's eyes, mute and uncomprehending, then follows again, when doctor and patient move, under whose impulse he cannot be sure, towards the river. There is a boat rocking in its concentric circle of waves, two policemen dragging the silt below with lead-weighted lines. George stares, his eyes sunk behind flickering lids, and stays mute. Then he disengages his arm from the doctor's, turns and shuffles slowly away. The doctor moves to intercept him but Buttsy shakes his head, rapidly, surreptitiously. They let George walk then, and let themselves follow along the curve of river, up the rough field of marsh grasses that leads to the copse of ash and elder. They follow him through it with difficulty, an irregular path through the brambles and the darkening trunks. The light is now failing and they hold their breath as they walk, anticipating some Armageddon. They hear voices beyond them, ghostly voices drifting tonelessly through the ash trees. A shape up ahead, the curved eaves of a cottage from a forgotten fairytale. The voices continue, unaware, it seems, of the sound of three approaching pairs of feet. Then George edges the door open with his twine-laced boot, pushes it open and the voices grow, in volume but not in tone. And George sits down on the scuffed leather car seat, places his head close to the vibrating fabric of the radio speaker and listens to the evening news.

7

IN THE HOUSE the light dies and the walls are scored three times by yellow headlamps as the cars depart. By the window upstairs someone stands, me perhaps, but there is no reflection and no breath on the glass. The window holds my eye for an age and then there is breath on the pane, small waves of it that fade and are wiped by a young girl's hand, that appear once more as she breathes again, wipes again. She is young and alone in this huge room, looking beyond the breathing pane now to the gates and the fields beyond, the traces of haystacks in them as it is late summer. So I am beyond her and she is here, she is me, of course, and over the gap of years I am amazed by her patience, her presentness and her calm acceptance of the fact that she is observed. A tell-tale clatter downstairs presages tea and her mother will call her down soon, but for the moment she's perfectly content, breathing on the pane, watching how the haystacks vanish in the mist of her breath and wiping it again to see them reappear. I am the figure she occasionally notices, her guardian angel or hidden sister. And tonight, when she is called down, she will make room for me beside her at tea.

'A plate for my friend,' she'll say.

'And what is your friend's name today?' her mother will ask.

'Emily,' she'll say, or Susan, or Sarah, for the names change with her mood, and her moods can be mercurial.

There'll be another at table tonight, she knows, tonight and many other nights, the stiff-backed woman with the vegetable breath who she knows already will gaze askance at her division of comestibles, her conversations with empty air.

But she forgets this worry as quickly as it came upon her. She has heard a sound, the scraping of the heavy front door off the limestone lintel, and she runs down, streaks from the stairs through the half-open door into his arms, knowing they will be open to greet her. He smells of fish, an odour that on anyone else would repel her, but not on him. He runs the shellfish plant down by the river's mouth, came from England to do it, why she doesn't know though she knows for some reason it's important to him: that he moved from a country she's never seen, that gave him his measured speech, to the one she lives in. And if she's lucky, after tea with her mother, Mary Dagge and the stiff-backed newcomer, he'll take her in the trap down to the river's mouth. And after a last check through the warehouse of ice, ice that always seems burning to her, quietly burning in calm clouds of steam, they'll sit by the low wall over the river and watch the salmon come in. And he'll once more tell her the story of the river's ghost.

She was observed, the next morning, by more eyes than were needed. She swung over the waters and could see herself swinging, from the high vantage point of an upstairs window. She didn't like seeing herself in this way; all she wanted to see was the river arcing below her, the dunes with the red-roofed cottage and the sea eventually coming into view. So she stopped swinging then, played with her hessian doll, walking it from the chestnut tree to the walled garden and back again till she tired of that too. She knew all was observed in this tiny world of hers, as her doll was observed by her. But a pair of new eyes had intruded, those eyes that appeared and disappeared at the upper window as Miss Shawcross transferred her clothes from suitcase to cupboard, and this new observer, she felt, would take some getting used to.

'She is our governess now,' she informed Dolly, 'and she will teach us things.'

'What things?' asked Dolly in that voice like a silken rustle.

'Oh you know,' murmured Nina as she walked, 'all sorts of

things, like how to sit straight at table and in what hand to hold the knife and fork.'

'She is the governess of eating, then?' asked Dolly.

'No, no,' said Nina who was alternately peeved and amused by Dolly's obtuseness, 'she'll be the governess of drinking too, of reading and writing and I do believe, of sums.'

'What are sums?' asked Dolly prosaically, for Dolly was mostly prosaic.

'Sums,' said Nina, 'sums. Well, sums are . . . Sums are sums.' And with that Nina walked into a shadow, bumped her forehead into a corseted stomach and found herself looking down at Isobel Shawcross's laced leather boots.

Isobel Shawcross took her smaller hand as if she had a right to. She bent down with a rustle of crinoline, and the smell of porter had been reduced to a faint whiff of barley and distant vomit.

'You were talking, Nina,' she said.

'Was I?' the little one said. 'How could I, since I'm here alone?'

'But I distinctly heard voices—'

The large hand held the small one tighter. It was ringless with brown spots and veins standing proud of the flesh.

'Perhaps you were talking to yourself?'

'Dolly, I was talking to Dolly.'

'No,' she said and began to walk her to the river, 'you were talking to yourself, Nina, because Dolly cannot hear, cannot reply. And from now on there will be a penalty for talking to yourself.'

'What's a penalty?' Nina asked, hoping that this woman with the mottled hands and the breath of vomit would somehow vanish.

'Somewhere between penance and punishment stands a penalty. And a penance comes in the form of prayer, a punishment in the form of bodily chastisement. So a penalty will come in the form of lessons. Learning. I am the mistress of your learning, and my first task will be this – to wean you from that world of imaginary things to the world of real ones. And each conversation with nothing in particular will be punished – or should I say penalised – with a lesson. And the lesson for today,' she said, 'is that Dolly is inanimate, Dolly is lifeless, Dolly is made of ceramic and horse-hair, and most pertinent of all, Dolly does not talk.'

'She talks to me,' said Nina.

'How? Does she whisper? Does she murmur? Does she moan? If you drop her in the river, does she call out for help?'

'No,' said Nina, 'but I'd know she needed help if she—'

Miss Shawcross plucked Dolly from Nina's arms then, and dangled her over the waters.

'Do we hear Dolly calling? For anything?'

Dolly returned Nina's tearful gaze with a mute stare.

She let her drop then, and a cry rent the air. Not Dolly's, but Nina's. Dolly hit the water with a dull plop. She began to drift towards the chestnut tree, where one long branch stroked the waters like fingers.

'Dolly does cry,' Nina whispered, ''cause I can hear her. She's crying 'cause she's wet.'

'That's you, Nina dear,' said Miss Shawcross.

And Nina howled, confirming that it was her after all. She howled with anguish and fury, at the hand that was gripping hers, pulling her back from Dolly's sodden form. The more she pulled, the more the fingers tightened, the louder her howls became.

'Crying will get us nowhere, Nina.'

But Nina howled louder, because she wondered which would break first, her heart or her fingers. Her fingers, she decided, so she brought her teeth down to the mottled fingers crushing hers and bit, and somehow still managed to howl. She heard a gasp of pain, then twisted like an eel and darted below the swing, grabbed the rope and reached out for her charge, trapped in the water.

'Here Dolly,' she said.

Dolly stared back.

'No, don't worry, I'm coming, I'm coming—'

And the waters shifted Dolly ever so slightly, free of the finger-
ing branches, set her moving out in the current once more. Nina
reached further. The rope slipped through her fingers and she
saw the water rushing towards her.

She hit it, sank, thrashed in a world of green bubbles and saw
Dolly floating cruciform above her. She reached up and grabbed
her, brought her face to the surface for air and they both now
cried as they sank again, and came up again, gasping.

And now Miss Shawcross was crying too.

Nina's feet, though, for all the drama of her thrashing head,
were placed firmly and safely on the largest root of the chestnut
tree beneath the river. She suspected Dan knew this, when he ran
down the long field with the gardening rake, stretched it out to
her to pull her back in. She suspected Dolly knew, for her eyes
and her ceramic smile seemed paradoxically peaceful, given the
peril of their situation and the pitch of Nina's screams. But she
was certain Miss Shawcross didn't know, for her cries, her dis-
tress, her regret, were heartbreaking to behold.

'My little one,' she cried, 'My little one.'

She was carried from the river by Dan Turnbull, deposited in
the arms of Mary Dagge by the house, wrapped in a white towel
while the bath was poured, and when the soapy water eventually
lapped around her, she lay and listened to the whispering of
adults in the hall outside. She was aware she had won something
in the war with Isobel Shawcross, governess, not the war itself,
not a battle even, but perhaps the opening skirmish. And at tea
that evening she wisely kept her bow-shaped mouth shut when
she heard the incident recounted. She noticed the omission of
certain crucial details, most notably the suspension of Dolly
above the water, and gathered from this that the details themselves were wanting, in some code of behaviour as yet unknown
to her that seemed to be the norm between governess and
governed. She sat Dolly on the table beside her though, and con-
spicuously added to her plate whenever she felt it necessary.

'She's hungry,' her father murmured, ruffling her hair, 'and why wouldn't she be, all that cold water.' And Nina nodded. They both were hungry, and why wouldn't they be.

Nina slept beside her doll that night as she did every night, and made a list of the stratagems needed to maintain their presence in each other's lives. Firstly, all conversations would be held in private, within earshot of nobody, neither Isobel Shawcross nor Mary Dagge nor Dan Turnbull. Not even, for that matter, her mother and father. The inclusion of her father gave her a pang of loss which she didn't fully understand. She knew her father liked conversation, with and about anything, animate or non-animate, liked stories, such as the one about the lady of the river. But she also knew Miss Shawcross was paid by somebody, probably by him, and it was better to be safe than sorry. Secondly, all glances, glass eye to real, all hints of complicity, of a shared world, were to cease, in public at least. At this Dolly's head fell forwards, ceramic head slumped on horsehair chest. But Nina was frighteningly insistent. The time would come, she said, when things would be as before; but until that time, in public, under the eyes of adults, and in particular under the eyes of her burping governess, Dolly would pretend to be made of ceramic and horsehair, and Nina would pretend that too.

Sleep came on then, the way sleep did, before she knew it and she dreamt, as she always did. She dreamt of Miss Shawcross on a seat by the bend in the river, *Magnall's Questions* open on her lap, Nina herself swinging above her as she dutifully answered her ABCs. The waters were rising, gradually, beneath her and by the time she reached P and Q, they were around Miss Shawcross's corseted waist. By the time she reached Z, Miss Shawcross was floating out towards Mornington while Nina still swung, but now over an expanse of unbroken azure. Dolly sat on a branch of the chestnut tree above her and developed a smile of satisfaction as Miss Shawcross's spread-eagled form, like a monstrous, corseted doll itself, sank slowly beneath the bright waters to where they both knew the seaweed mingled its tendrils with the dead Boinn's hair. And the satisfaction in Dolly's smile was of the kind that knew it shouldn't be there. Which is why it vanished when Nina turned towards her and said, to reprimand her, 'Tut, Dolly, tut.'

She awoke to the scent of pollen, to the sight of her father bending towards her in the late spring sunshine, muttering till she woke, 'What larks, Pip.'

'Who is Pip?' she asked for the umpteenth time, and again, of course, he told her.

'Pip, who loved Estella, lived with Bob and Mrs Bob and ate his vittles. Time to eat your vittles, Nina.'

She dressed, in the shafts of low sunlight that streamed through the window. And she padded down the corridor, through the wedges of bright that stood against the dark, down the staircase, against the huge streams of illuminated dust. Was there more sunlight then? So it seems, so it seems. And it seemed to Nina, in the battle between dark and bright, that the bright was for the moment winning. She clutched her mute doll between thumb and forefinger and when she entered the dining room, placed her hessian back against the wheaten-coloured pitcher that held the milk. Her father, already rising from the table, paused to kiss the whorl of hair at the top of her crown before he left.

There was silence, and the sound of decorous chewing from the other end of the table. Miss Shawcross sat there with Mary Dagge, a plate of Mary Dagge's eggs in front of her. Egges, thought Nina, and rubbed her sleepy eyes.

'Keep your hands,' Miss Shawcross said, 'to yourself. Keep your hands from yourself.'

Nina looked to her left, saw Mary Dagge rising, her eyes wide-open in an O of alarm.

'Like this?' said Nina, placing her wrists, like Miss Shawcross's, on the deal table, her palms turned downwards. She watched as a plate was placed between them, with a fluffy yellow soufflé of scrambled eggs. Egges, she thought again and felt a longing for times past.

'Yes,' said Miss Shawcross.

'How do I eat then, Miss?' asked Nina.

'Without moving the elbows,' said Miss Shawcross, 'with a knife and fork.'

Nina scooped egg on to her fork and her wrist moved upwards.

'You're spooning,' said Miss Shawcross. 'Don't spoon.'

'How am I spooning?' asked Nina.

'It's a fork, not a spoon. Use it as one.'

And Miss Shawcross demonstrated. The egg placed on the away curve of the fork with the help of the knife, lifted heaven-wards. Her mouth opened slightly, the fork entered, the mouth closed, chewed, barely.

Nina did likewise, imitating her perfectly. To her surprise, she enjoyed the act of imitation.

'And sit straight,' said Miss Shawcross.

'Straight,' said Nina. And again she imitated.

Nina found, through those next few sun-filled weeks, that there were lessons for every possible procedure in life, that for every act she had hitherto performed unthinkingly, there was a better, an infinitely superior version. She learnt to sit without crossing her legs, to walk without turning her feet outwards, not to speak without being spoken to, to keep her hands neither to nor from herself, to rise from her chair to a standing position with her back even straighter than Miss Shawcross's. She learned not to be Nina, indeed, to be quite another person who needed a name, a name quite different from her own. She decided on Emily as a name for this other she was becoming, and though she enjoyed becoming Emily, enjoyed pretending to be her, enjoyed learning

Emily's prim habits, she knew in her heart of hearts that she hated her. Emily learnt her ABCs, learnt her Bible stories, learnt her two times tables, always sitting upright in the small cupboard-like room Miss Shawcross had chosen as their learning emporium, but Nina longed to sit open-legged on Dan Turnbull's cart, longed to swing on the swing he built her with her dress blowing upwards in the wind, longed to pronounce eggs as egges. And Nina longed most of all to cross that curving rivulet and to join the two children who, lately, had come to sit on the other side observing her.

'Don't look,' said Miss Shawcross, who was walking her along the bank to demonstrate the differences between shamrock and clover. Emily, of course, didn't look, but Nina herself couldn't help stealing a glance. The girl's hair was a sunbleached blonde, her dress yellow, short and faintly tattered, and her feet bare. The boy beside her was smaller, squatter, and at that moment was observing the mud squeezing between his toes from the wet riverbank.

'Clover,' said Miss Shawcross, 'has four leaves and is common to all of the British Isles. Shamrock has three and is particular to Ireland.'

'Shamrock,' shouted the boy from across the bank. 'Shamrock shamrock shamrock.'

'Shut up Georgie,' said the girl.

'Don't look,' again whispered Miss Shawcross. 'Shamrock was used by St Patrick to convert the heathens on this island. He bent down and plucked some—' and Miss Shawcross bent down and plucked some, and said, 'three persons in the one God. Three leaves on the one shamrock.'

'But it's got four,' said Nina.

'No,' said Miss Shawcross, 'a shamrock can only have three.'

'It's got four and it's a clover,' said Nina.

'Clover,' shouted the boy. 'Clover, clover.'

'Shut up, Georgie,' said the girl.

'Well, if it's got four it must be clover, but shamrock has three. We're going back to the house now, since it's teatime. And don't look.'

And Nina walked back to the house, one hand in Miss Shawcross's mottled one, walking with Emily's gait but stealing a glance backwards with Nina's eyes. And Nina's free hand waved.

At tea that evening Nina wished, not for the first time, that Miss Shawcross was gone. An image crossed her mind as she ate her salted herring, placing it neatly on the downward curve of the fork and raising it delicately towards her mouth, of the governess lying placidly among the seaweed that rippled beneath her father's shellfish plant, like the maiden of the river, hair undulating with the water. The image vanished as soon as it came, like a ripple on the same water, obscuring the desired picture beneath, and Nina felt immediately guilty and asked Emily to take over. Emily did, and finished her meal without any untoward displays.

Afterwards Miss Shawcross wished, since it was Friday and her evening off, to visit the town of Drogheda. Dan Turnbull took her in the horse and trap. And Nina watched the bonneted head diminish as the trap passed through the gates, banished all thoughts of Emily and ran through the low archway, past the glasshouse, down the long field towards the chestnut tree. There she swung and let her skirts fly. She swung high, till she could see the sun shimmering over the sea, over the metal-roofed cottage that she noticed, for the first time, adjacent to the beach. Four or five children were tumbling down a sand-dune, running up it and tumbling down again. She felt a longing like a physical pain beneath her ribcage, she felt wet smudges trickling down her cheeks and realised she was crying.

'Why are you crying?' Dolly asked her, Dolly, who she had placed face down in the branches immediately above.

'Because,' said Nina, 'because because because.'

'Because you're lonely,' said Dolly.

'How do you spell lonely?' asked Nina, mindful of her ABC's.
'L–o–n–l–y,' said Dolly.'

'Maybe,' said Nina. She swung high again, and Dolly disappeared momentarily from view. She saw two children detach themselves from the fury of sand round the dune, running forwards. The girl with sunbleached hair and the boy.

'You want a brother,' Dolly intoned, as she came back into view.

'Why not a sister?' asked Nina.

'Because,' said Dolly, 'because because because . . .'

'How do you spell because?' asked Nina, anxious to change the subject.

'B–e–c–a–u–s–e.'

'Because if I had a sister,' said Nina, 'I wouldn't need to talk to you.'

'That's not fair,' said Dolly.

'Fair enough,' said Nina. 'And when I have a sister, I definitely won't talk to you. And no, that moany look won't help you. In fact moaning will only make things worse.'

'Who's moaning?'

Across the runnel of water, on the muddy bank now, the girl with bare feet in a thin yellow dress. The boy beside her, half her size, looking again at the mud oozing between his toes.

Nina let herself swing for a moment and decided Dolly could no longer be simple Dolly any more, she needed a name. And the name came newly minted, fresh from Miss Shawcross's Bible stories.

'Hester, who do you think?'

'Hester the doll?'

'Hester the whine, Hester the moan, Hester the pester.'

'Hester the pester,' the boy repeated. He shifted his position on the bank, to observe new emissions of mud whorl between his toes.

'So why is she moaning?'

43

'Oh questions, questions. You're worse than Emily.'

'Where's Emily?'

'Not telling.'

And Nina diverted her gaze and swung higher, concentrating on the blue line of the horizon and the small red-roofed house. Until she was surprised by a splash. She looked down and saw the equally surprised waters rippling with a brown body swimming through them, like a thin frog in a yellow dress. The feet found solid ground and the head splashed upwards and Nina's dress, as she swung, for she had determined now to continue swinging, brushed gently off the wet forehead with the plastered blonde hair.

'No, tell me, where's Emily?'

'All right, you're standing on her.'

The girl jumped to one side. And Nina, who seemed to appreciate this affirmation of her imagination, allowed the force of gravity to slow her pendulum.

'Sorry.'

'And Emily doesn't like to be trod on.'

'I said I'm sorry.' The girl shifted her feet. Looked down at the empty grass. 'What did I stand on?'

'Her shoe.'

'What's her shoe like?'

'Just like mine, actually.' Nina liked the sound of that word 'actually', and felt Miss Shawcross would have been proud. Then another word struck her, a word that put 'actually' quite in the shade. 'She's my twin, actually.'

'Sorry, twin.'

'Her name's Emily.'

'Sorry, Emily.'

Nina twisted clockwise in the swing, tangling the ropes above her, let Hester by the chestnut trunk come into view, let the whole world turn, and stopped by the thin girl in the yellow dress. She could see her ribs showing through the wet fabric.

'She'll accept your apology,' Nina said, 'but only if she knows your name.'

'Janie.'

'Janie, this is Hester.' Nina raised her eyes, looked into Janie's. Brown freckles around them, but the eyes were browner. 'I'm Nina.'

On the other riverbank, the boy began to howl.

'And who might he be?'

'That's George. Shut up, George.'

8

A TRANSFORMATION CAME over Miss Isobel Shawcross during the course of her first Friday evening off governess duties. It began in the lounge of the Old Court Hotel, with the consumption of a glass of Guinness and a gin chaser. The prim, stiff back gradually became a curved one, the decorous thin mouth acquired a downward turn and the pencil of lipstick began to spread towards the chin. After a fifth Guinness and yet another gin she made her exit from the Old Court Hotel, an exit most unlike her entrance ninety-five minutes earlier. The laced bootees didn't walk so much as clump down the wooden stairs, one hand steadying itself on the brass rail, her stomach seemed to precede her progress, the curve of her back following it like an inelegant version of the letter S, which she had so diligently drummed into Nina two days earlier. S is for saint, S is servant, S is for sofa, Miss Shawcross had intoned, neglecting to mention S is also for slither, for Shawcross, not to mention stomach. Her own began to burble as she turned an unsteady left out of the fine stained-glass doors of the Old Court Hotel and made her way down Shop Street, and a barely-suppressed belch announced her entrance on to the North Quay.

She was drawn by the sound of distant music then, and following it found the source was quite proximate to her unsteady presence, the illusion of distance provided by the yellow peeling façade of the quaintly named Star Of The Sea Music Emporium. She walked up steps, through a doorway, down an arched hall and found herself in a wooden rotunda where a small orchestra was playing a Viennese waltz and off-duty sailors were dancing

46

with Drogheda ladies. She sat by an empty table and ordered another gin, and as she watched the swirl of giggling bodies around her a brown mood of melancholy settled over her. This mood was somewhat tempered by the taste of the gin she had ordered and by the presence, hot on its heels, of one Randal Noyce, Merchant Seaman. He complimented her on her presence in the same establishment, remarked on how it raised the tone of the place which was, between the two of them, hardly a step above your run-of-the-mill house of ill-repute, and congratulated himself, indeed, on his fortune in finding a like-minded soul in such a cesspit. He enquired of her profession and, on her reply, displayed an absorbing interest in all matters pertaining to the education of young ladies. He ordered a succession of further gins for Miss Isobel Shawcross of, as he was pleased to discover, the Kildare Shawcrosses, and noted with pleasure how the collo-quialism of her speech increased in direct proportion to the number of gins she imbibed.

He asked her to dance and again was pleased to observe a defi-nite shift in her centre of gravity as she accompanied him to the floor. This shift became if anything more pronounced as the band exercised themselves in yet another version of the 'Blue Danube' and Merchant Seaman Noyce and Miss Shawcross exer-cised themselves in their version of a waltz. Mr Noyce being small, and a dapper waltzer, it was all he could do to negotiate the increasingly gravitationless bulk of Miss Shawcross round the floor. There was, to be sure, the fleeting pleasure of her ample bosom, now felt on the crook of his left arm, now on the right and occasionally even brushing off the tip of his chin. And this pleasure, Mr Noyce eventually felt, needed an environment more intimate than that of the Star of The Sea Music Emporium. So he invited her for, in his own phrase, 'a walk along the river,' an invi-tation which she readily accepted, looking forward to hearing, in her own phrase, 'the waters rowl.'

Once out on the North Quay, Miss Isobel Shawcross, of the

Kildare Shawcrosses, revealed herself to have an education and a repertoire that ranged far beyond the confines of *Magnall's Questions* and the King James Bible. She began a scandalous recitative version of 'Captain Kelly's Kitchen' which ran to seventeen verses, to the accompaniment of the slapping of river water and the creaking of steel hawsers. This lasted till Steampacket Quay where, in a disused shed behind Hope Mill, Miss Shawcross displayed a gymnastic agility most unsuited to ladies of the Kildare Shawcrosses, to any ladies whatsoever, indeed to all but Merchant Seaman Noyce, whom it suited fine. What suited him even finer was her rapid descent afterwards into the arms of Morpheus, a phrase of which the Kildare Shawcrosses surely would have approved as much as they would have disapproved the sight of her, legs akimbo, arms spread-eagled on a wooden palette. He left her there, snoring gently, among the broken barrels and damp wood shavings and an odour of old hops and excrement.

She awoke, forty minutes later. Befuddled by gin and sensuality, she instantly wanted more of both. She staggered out of the warehouse and made her way towards the sound of voices, which seemed to be coming from a licensed premises across the cobbled way. She could see a light gleaming, and now added to the sound of voices was the rippling music of a sailor's melodeon. She could see a round window like a porthole, a lamp silhouetting figures inside. She reached out to knock on it, found it beyond her arm's length, took one step forwards and fell thirty feet into the river below.

9

Nina woke the next day with the recently christened Hester close to her cheek. And the name proved durable, if only because throughout that Saturday she found she was quite free to say it at will. Miss Shawcross made no appearance at breakfast, though as it was Saturday she was under no strict obligation to. So Mary Dagge, for one, was not surprised.

'Would Hester like egges?' she asked, pleased to have free reign in her kitchen once more.

'Hester would like egges,' said Nina, 'and actually, Nina would too.'

'Sure we know Nina would,' chuckled Mary Dagge and spooned out two portions on Nina's plate.

Hester proved even more durable because after breakfast that morning Janie and George returned to watch the fanciful girl with the doll of that name on the swing above the river. The river divided them, a large, brown, swirling fact of nature, a fact of metaphor too, for the divisions that must needs exist between two ragamuffins from a tin-roofed cottage and a girl from a large limestone house. Hester chatted with the unseen Emily and the all-too-visible Nina and had acquired definite character now, with her Puritan bib and smock, her intolerance of questions and her refusal to answer to any particular logic. Hester now, simply and definitely, was.

'Hester the Pester Hester the Pester,' George intoned tunelessly to himself, his large blue eyes on the dark girl swinging, legs crossed and kicking, over the river. He watched Janie dive in again and swim towards her, who had already come to signify all the resonance the word beauty would convey when he came to understand it. Was she Hester, he wondered, or was Hester the doll? The swing idled back and forwards on its own now and the doll sat crooked in the branches above it, as if willing it to maintain its motion. For Janie had reached the other side and they were both sitting with their bare feet in the lazy current. He could hear words like nursery rhymes and was trying not to cry. He could see them clapping hands together, a sailor came to sea-sea-sea to see what he could see-see-see. He walked into the river then to be less alone, he felt the tears would take over if he waited any longer. He felt the muddy current round his knees, his trousers, his waist, at which point he warmed the cold in his loins with his own urine, and the current took him and there was brown all around him, a thick, comforting swirling world of brown, no up no down, in which he could have floated for ever had not four hands grabbed him and pulled him to the surface and he found himself on the muddy bank on the other side.

'Say thank you, George,' said the beauty with brown hair, wiping her muddy hands on her white dress.

'If it wasn't for us you would have floated out to sea, you would have drowned,' said Janie matter-of-factly, 'so you'd better say thank you.'

'Thank you Hester,' said George.

And the girl who was beautiful, although he didn't know the word yet, giggled.

'Don't thank Hester, thank me.'

'Are you not Hester?' George asked.

'No,' she said, 'and I'm not Emily either. I'm Nina.'

'Thank you Nina,' said George.

'You're welcome. Now let's get you cleaned.'

George saw her stand and walk towards the house. Janie immediately followed. So George followed too. They had crossed the river, in fact as well as in spirit, and he was dimly aware that different rules now applied. To George, a mass of brown mud from head to toe, to Janie, with her wet dress clinging to her. Perhaps even to the immaculate Nina, clutching her doll, who alone knew the way.

'I've got just the job for you, George,' she said, 'just the job for you.'

The phrase was Dan Turnbull's, which seemed apt enough for the business at hand. Apt enough too was Dan Turnbull's hose, threading its way through the limp tomato plants that seemed to exhale in rows in the greenhouse. Nina dragged out the hose, turned on the spigot and watched the India-rubber respond as if an invisible snake was coursing through it.

'Stand to attention, George,' she ordered. 'Like a soldier,' she added when she saw his mudcaked face puzzled by the concept of attention.

So George stood upright, his right hand frozen to his eyebrow the way he'd seen the soldiers do it in South Quay Barracks. And Nina circled round him with her cleansing spray which became a punishing jet when she pressed her finger to the nozzle. Which transferred the river's mud from George to the cracked panes of the glasshouse behind him.

'Do you know what Hester thinks?' said Nina dreamily, watching George's hair part under pressure from the hosepipe.

'Hester The Pester,' said George, his mouth hardly moving, military style.

'What does Hester think?' asked Janie, who was lying face down with the doll by Nina's feet.

'Hester thinks we might be friends . . .'

Dan Turnbull thought they must be friends. So after he had lifted Nina into the cart he had hitched on to Garibaldi, the grey mare, he lifted Janie and George too. He neglected to lift Hester, who Nina had left beside the India-rubber hose and the mud-splattered glasshouse. George surmised that she belonged to the house, the river and the chestnut tree and so couldn't come along for the ride. It was not, he decided, that she wasn't wanted on this journey through the fuchsia and honeysuckle hedges, with the low hum of bees drowned by the rattle of the cart's metal wheels, it was just that she wasn't thought of. There were indeed other things to think of, like the dark soft hair of the girl beside him, darker than the shadows of the brown cows standing in the fields, melting in the heat of the midday sun. Like the appeals of the children that ran from every cottage, begging to clamber on for the ride. But Dan wouldn't take them, would he. All Dan would carry was Nina, George and Janie, because he was collecting seaweed for the flowerbeds in Baltray House and hadn't room for more than three. 'So get off that trailer, Buttsy Flanagan, and crying won't help you, will it, Nina?' And Nina said no, crying wouldn't help one bit.

But the truth was Nina didn't take Hester because for once, on that Saturday morning, she had no need of Hester. She would have exchanged the company of Hester, Emily and whatever incorporeal friend she could ever imagine for the company of those two beside her on Dan Turnbull's cart.

Dan guided the mare towards the estuary mouth, where the large granite boulders broke away into scraps of fossilised stone, where the Lady's Finger pointed towards an invisible spot in the hot sky above, at the apex of the triangle of river and sea. Across the warm, lazy river was the random straggle of huts around Nina's father's fish factory.

Dan forked the seaweed that clung to the rocks by the water's edge, wet clumps of brine-smelling tendrils the colour of dried blood.

'That's hair,' said Nina.

'What's hair?' asked Janie.

'A woman's hair,' said Nina.

'Hester's hair,' said Georgie.

And Nina told them what her father had told her, the story of the spring and the foaming water and the girl who ran from it until she was caught by the waters here, at the mouth of what would become the Boyne river. And if the limestone tower was her finger, the seaweed must surely be her hair.

'Her hair,' said George, sitting on a rock at the water's edge.

'Yes,' said Nina, 'her hair.'

'No, her hair,' said George again, pointing down.

And Dan Turnbull thrust his pitchfork in the water below George and found it entangled in what indeed was hair, the hair of Miss Isobel Shawcross, governess, of the Kildare Shawcrosses, who floated to the surface like a flounder caught by a gaffhook.

~

The sun rises to more hoar-frost on the morning of the seventeenth of January. The fields are pure expanses of white and the sycamore by the gates is a palm of silver fingers appealing to the sky. A veil of mist lies inches above the frosted surfaces, curling round the sycamore and the black Ford car parked by the gates in which a lone policeman sleeps. A second car comes to relieve him as the mist disperses; men in uniform step out of it, stamp their feet, bang on the frosted window until the one who sat vigil awakes. They pour him tea from a flask and as the steam from their mugs drifts into the dispersing mists a third car joins them. Dr Hannon now emerges, leading George gently by the hand. Then behind comes Janie. The girl who was so thin and freckled has gained something of a stoop. She has a hat pinned to her greying hair, is wearing a black coat with a black fur collar, thinking the colour, perhaps, is appropriate to the agony of the occasion.

'Come on, George,' she says to her brother, 'tell the men now.'

But George has little to tell. His feet are sore from wandering, the laces in his shoes are missing and the leather edges have rubbed his sockless ankles raw. He complains about his heels as Janie moves him through the gates and the policemen follow at a distance, thinking any speech, perhaps, is better than none. They move up the driveway, at George's shambling, uncertain pace, round the courtyard at the back, through the arches round the outhouses. And George stops, in mid-stride, outside the orchard wall. He stares at the bare apple trees, as if remembering them bowed down with fruit. There is a slight, sad smile around the corners of his mouth, and his eyes are wistful. The group of policemen shuffle awkwardly behind him.

'Is it inside there,' Janie asks gently, 'somewhere in the orchard?'

'The orchard,' George echoes.

'Not the orchard, Janie,' Buttsy Flanagan says, 'we've checked the orchard.'

And George, as if in agreement, starts to walk again. Past the glasshouse to his right. Down the path of scuffed grass towards the river. And the procession follows.

George's eyes are pale blue, the colour of cigarette-smoke, and Janie's are brown. Time has not been kind to her eyes, to the lids above them, the circles beneath them, but there is still tomboy tartness to her face, an arresting slash of purple lipstick on the wide mouth, beneath the hungry hollow cheeks. In fact time itself has only served to enhance that waif-like, lost abandon. Even now, as she holds George's elbow, allows him to lead her towards the river, Sergeant Buttsy Flanagan is eyeing not the moving ripples in the river, but the pendulum of Janie's hips.

The grass beneath her impractical high-heeled shoes is scuffed from years of children's feet into something like a path. And where the chestnut arches over the river, the branch above it still with the ringlet of scar on its bark, the ground below it still empty of grass as if from the memory of thrusting feet, there George stops. His blue eyes mist up. He pulls a crushed packet of Sweet Afton from his top pocket and fumbles for a light.

'You want a light, Georgie?' Janie asks. The policeman next to her proffers it.

The match flares, the smoke curls up and the mist in his eyes turns to tears. He could be remembering his sister's small, half-naked body that used to swing like a knotted branch over that water, fall and float away as deftly as wood. The policeman, of course, presumes something else. He pictures George lowering an adult body into that water, with all the solicitude of deranged affection. He pictures the high tide carrying the body past the ruined shellfish plant, past the old breakwater, past the Lady's Finger, out to sea.

10

Dan turned the body over with his pitchfork once, then twice, and said to Nina in his lazy way, 'Nina, lead the mare over to that bank so she can eat some clover.'

'Clover,' Nina said. She was staring at a picture she had seen before but she couldn't remember where.

'Grass or clover, all the same to her, she's hungry. Georgie, Janie, give her a hand.'

He had the body turned by now, in a tangle of floating seaweed. He was hoping they wouldn't understand what they had seen.

'Will she eat shamrock?' Nina asked. She had the loose reins of the mare in her hand and was leading her away from the image she wanted to forget.

'She'd eat anything,' Dan said.

'Clover,' said Georgie.

Nina drew the mare's head down towards the grass and saw her lips curl back, baring long yellow teeth. She listened to the crunch of seagrass and shivered even though the sun was hot enough to make her cheeks burn. She remembered wishing her governess gone and wished now that she hadn't wished that. Because if all of her fleeting desires came true, she didn't want to think of what would happen.

'That was Miss Shawcross, wasn't it?' she said quietly to Dan, who jammed his pitchfork in whatever seaweed he had so far collected, and took the reins from her hand.

'Don't you bother your head about it.'

Dan lifted her first, then Janie and last of all George on to the cart.

'Is she drowned?'

'Drowneded,' echoed Georgie.

'We're taking you home now Nina,' said Dan softly, 'and I don't want you to bother with what you've seen. Leave that to the peelers.'

'She's still hungry,' said Nina, as Dan jerked the mare's head upright, and whipped her into a smart trot down the sandy road.

'She is,' said Dan, 'and I know a fine field of clover she can chew to her heart's content.'

'Where's that?' asked Janie

'Below the RIC barracks.'

She lulled herself into a dream as the horse trotted back, a dream scented with honeysuckle and clover and the smell of wet seaweed. In her dream the face turned over and over, the hair spreading out in the water like a scallop-shell. In her waking the river threaded its way above the hedges, a hot ribbon of silver. The sound of humming bees droned towards her from the hedges and away to the dunes and made common cause with both her dream and her waking. Whatever made this happen wasn't her, she sensed, but some part of her had seen it before it happened, so some part of her could at the very least have stopped it from happening. To know what was to come would be a burden, a terrible burden, even worse than knowing what was not to come. She would return, she knew, to the house, to father and mother and Mary Dagge, to her doll Hester and to a world without Miss Isobel Shawcross.

She tried to picture Dan's arrival at the peelers' station, sunlit swathes of green below the redbricked barracks, two peelers running towards them from the door, buttoning their tunics, serious, serious, all business. Dark glances towards her, the girl in the back, you, you of all people knew. But to her immense relief it wasn't like that at all. An officer in shirtsleeves was lazily clipping the lawns, Dan pulled the mare to a halt, handed the reins to

Nina, said, 'One minute now,' left them on the seaweed-smelling cart while he walked forwards, shook his hand and whispered.

'She's dead, isn't she?' said Janie.

'You think so?' asked Nina.

'Well, I don't think she was swimming.'

'Maybe she can't,' said Nina.

'Can't what?'

'Swim.'

The mare cropped at the grass by the roadside.

'Clover,' said Georgie.

'Stop saying clover,' said Nina.

'Grass,' said Georgie.

'That's better. Grass.'

Louder voices on the lawn then, two peelers walking fast down towards them. Buttoning their tunics, just the way she'd pictured, to her shock and disappointment, but not really her surprise.

'Make room there,' said Dan, and they clambered up, large laced boots and shining buttons. Dan thwacked the reins and drew the mare in a half-circle. She moved off unwillingly with the extra load.

'So where is she?' asked the first, fixing the last buttons on his greatcoat.

Dan shot the officer a disapproving glance.

'Across from the Lady's Finger. I'll drop off the childer first and take you there.'

'A bad business.'

'Maybe.'

So he left them by the gates to make their way up the avenue on their own.

'Don't be bothering your little heads, now,' he said. 'Nina will take you to Mary Dagge for your tea.'

The three of them walked over the crunching pale gravel, the death now unmentioned between them. To her two new friends, if friends they were, the sight of this gaunt façade was like another entrance, another house. They had seen its jumble from behind, the crumbling wall of an orchard, the long triangle of glass and rusted metal, the stone arch leading to the stables, but this looming thing, this dark rectangle with the sun now right behind its bunched chimneys, this was neither house nor home, church nor castle, this was some unimagined, unimaginable fact they would have to find new words for.

The large front door was ajar and Nina pushed it open with her shoulder. The sound of a piano, soft and measured, came from the living room. She held the door open for Janie and George and looked down at George's bare feet as he tested the tuft of the carpet, his splayed toes pressing it as if he expected it to ooze between them like mud. Then she walked towards the sound of the piano. George and Janie followed, stepping in her brief footprints in the carpet, fearful that the area outside them would indeed turn to mud, the kind of mud that sank for ever, that they would vanish beneath that red and purple leaf-shaped pattern, hardly leaving a ripple.

Nina walked over the varnished wood round the doorway on to a different carpet. George and Janie stayed by the door jamb, as if another carpet was more than they could negotiate today. Her mother wore a cream blouse, hair falling around her sculpted cheeks in an untidy but not unpleasing tangle. A glass with a lemon-slice held back the pages of *The Well-Tempered Clavier*. The pearly notes cascaded round her and she looked at her only daughter through a concentrated haze.

'Nina, you're a disgrace,' she murmured, looking at her stained white smock and her smudged shoes, then towards the door. 'And who are these two other disgraces?'

~

'Would he have placed her in the river, Ma'am?' the nearest policeman asks Janie in a low mumble, designed to be unheard by George.

'Did you put Nina in the river?' Janie asks George, her teeth clenched, her fist scratching at her watery eyelids.

'The river,' George repeats.

'Is she in the river, George?' Janie asks again.

'She's in the river,' says George, 'and the seaweed is her hair.'

'Not her, George,' says Janie. 'Nina. We're talking about Nina.'

'What was that about seaweed?' Buttsy Flanagan asks.

'We found a body once, when we were children, tangled in the seaweed—'

'Her hair,' says George.

'Isobel Shawcross,' says Janie. 'Check the coroner's records. She drowned.'

'The river took her,' says George.

'Took who?' asks Doctor Hannon.

'Took Boinn—'

'Who's Boinn?'

'Only one place the river could take her,' says a policeman. 'Out to sea.'

'You don't understand,' says Janie, 'he's confusing one thing with another—'

'Why did the river take her?' asks the doctor.

'For her hair—'

'Jesus Christ—'

'Let him speak—'

'She's not in the river, Georgie, is she?' asks Janie. 'That would be too simple.'

'Much too simple,' says George.

'Why did you kill her, George?' Janie says slowly.

'Kill who?' says George.

'Nina,' says Janie, and her closed fist scratches again at her eyelid.

'Didn't kill Nina,' says George. 'I killed Hester.'

'Oh Jesus,' says Janie and walks away.

'Hester?' asks the doctor. 'Who's Hester?'

They are being led to a conclusion and maybe George, with some defensive, fractured intuition, is leading them to it. Dr Hannon enquires about Hester, Buttsy Flanagan about Isobel Shawcross, George smokes one cigarette to its end and holds his hand out mutely for another. They walk back from the river as the light fades and a consensus is emerging from the interstices of their conversation, from what Janie can remember of their childhood narrative, from the dementia of her grief and her unwillingness to penetrate it.

And the conclusion when arrived at is, like all conclusions, the most convenient. That he lowered the body into the water with all the care of deranged affection, that the tide, which would have been high then, would have carried it past the ruins of the shellfish plant, past the limestone tower at the old breakwater out to sea. And besides convenience, there is a mystery to this conclusion, there is a pleasing poetry to it, the body never found, the lapping waters of an infinite, open grave, the sense that, whatever the warp-spasm that came over George, he deposited Nina, Boinn, Hester, in the arms of the river, in the body of the ocean she loved with some warped version of the same emotion.

So there would be, conveniently, no body to be dealt with, no visit from the State Coroner, no grave to be dug; and the sentence, when it came to be passed in Drogheda District Court, would be one of guilty but insane. There would not be even the inconvenience of a change of residence for George: the ward in St Ita's would become his prison, and out of his barred window he could look towards the same insane sea.

On the grassed-over cover of the rusting manhole of the old septic tank, they gather and drink coffee from a policeman's flask. He spices his cup with whiskey, raises the metal hip-flask towards Janie with an enquiring eye. She nods.

'A bird,' Buttsy Flanagan informs her, 'never flew on one wing.'

'Hester,' says Dr Hannon, 'was your . . .'

'Nina's doll. Nina's ghost. Whatever Nina wanted her to be.'

'Her familiar.'

'Yes,' says Janie, 'she became familiar all right.'

'And Boinn?' says Buttsy.

'Get a guide-book of the locality,' says Janie. 'You'll come across her.'

'A legend,' says Dr Hannon.

'Again,' says Janie, 'Nina's. And I think I'm going to cry now.'

The rusting cover of the manhole reads Twyfords Adamant and Janie's heel scrapes over it as she turns away and weeps.

I I

HESTER THE PESTER. Her inanimate eyes seemed to know it all that afternoon, seemed able to decipher Dan's whispers, when he entered and conferred with her mother, seemed able to interpret her mother's gasp when she held her mouth and turned away. 'My God,' her mother said out loud, then, 'Nina,' and she took her and wrapped her arms around her as Dan led her two new friends towards the front door. She would remember that holding, those arms stroking her hair, the comfort of being comforted, in years to come, when no comfort was forthcoming. She would remember the sound of her father's feet, the sight of him as the door burst open and the two of them held her, together. She would wonder what it would take to recreate that, the three of them wrapped around each other – the death of another governess, perhaps. She felt privileged by death that evening, as her mother and her father let her play with Hester till the sun went down, watched her with moist, attentive eyes, before accompanying her up to her room, to sleep.

Sleep, of course, was late in coming, for Nina if not for Hester. She lay there, thinking of cause and effect. She had wished her governess gone and now her governess was gone. She looked at the moon through the half-drawn curtains at the window, and wished it gone. But her wish had no effect: the indistinct half-globe stared down at her as if teasing her with its continued presence. She wished the curtains would close of their own accord, blocking out the moon, but of course the curtains stayed, limp and inanimate. She thought of Miss Shawcross's definition of her doll, inanimate, lifeless, ceramic and horsehair. For a moment she wished Hester gone, then instantly regretted it; but Hester remained, sleeping on the crook of her arm, in her Puritan bib and smock.

And then the light darkened imperceptibly on Hester's ceramic cheeks and Nina looked back at the window and the moon was gone, behind a thin strip of cloud shaped like an orange-peel. For an unending moment she was filled with a bottomless terror and wished the moon back again. And the moon indeed came back, as the cloud changed its shape from an orange-peel to a wisp of hair, exposing the half-finished globe once more. And although she knew the moon exposed itself independent of her wishes, she was still not certain that her wishes had no effect. If her wish cohered with what inevitably would happen, did her wish not in some way conspire with what would happen? If she had not wished, would what had happened have slipped into the realm of that which would not happen? And if, having glimpsed a vision of Miss Shawcross's hair under water, mingling with the seaweed, she had warned Miss Shawcross of the imminent dangers of water, would Miss Shawcross have still ended thus, under the limp seaweed in the waters of the Boyne? Or would she have dismissed Nina's inner world as adroitly as she dismissed that of her doll, now named Hester?

If she had wished, then, that George had not taken the course he did, would she rather than I be standing now by the upper window, observing, since observation is all I am, the lone police-man's breath on the cold air, his stamping feet on the hoar-frosted grass by the gates? Had she been at the left-hand window in the dining room on the first storey, could she have transferred her gaze to the pale light spilling in through the right-hand window, from a moon very like the one she wished away, spilling its light over the frozen fields? And since we are supposing here, as she loved to suppose, could she have seen the mauve *fleur-de-lys* of the wallpaper print of forty-five years ago, could she have followed that pattern to the door? Could she have walked to the accompaniment of distant piano music from downstairs, towards that door?

Time would be malleable for her in her world of supposition, so the formidable oak stairway would still be intact, the steps would even creak as she mounted them. The door to her bedroom would still be open, so she could enter, silent as the grave, and observe her young self sleeping at last, under the oatmeal-coloured blanket, the doll with its Puritan bib and smock on the pillow beside her. She could watch her own chest rise and fall, her bowed mouth half open, she could bend close and feel the warmth of her breath. She could wonder at her loneliness, her utter isolation, the kind of isolation that animates the inanimate Hester, that brings others, perhaps even me, into being. She could cease these suppositions then and look once more out of the window, see below her, instead of a policeman stamping his feet, blowing his cold fingers, wondering about the fact of murder, hares dancing in the moonlit fields between the haystacks.

12

Nina's mother, in the third year of the new century, came to acknowledge her imaginative world for what it was – loneliness. Perhaps because she herself was growing familiar with that condition. The days stretched out ahead of her like infinite extensions of the crossword puzzles she filled-in, drab, endless and somehow more real than she had ever expected them to be. Her husband returned home at six, then often left again at seven, to oversee the night shippings. Everything that was new to him, it seemed, was old to her, in this vast house where she had grown up, with this child whose imaginative world filled all the empty spaces. She slept late often, rose to find Nina already fed by Mary Dagge and realised her more ardent self was slumbering too. 'Nine across', she said to her husband once at dinner, 'Spanish Court painter'.

'Velázquez', he replied, but without the recognition she had hoped for. She decided then, to let that self slumber on.

And in the absence of Isobel Shawcross, she decided to leave her daughter's schooling to nature, Dan Turnbull and the 'two disgraces' from the cottage across the river. Nina would eventually learn to spell, with the same George and Janie, in the national school across the river, and would misspell one word consistently, leaving out the 'e': lonly. And when the mistake was pointed out to her, she would misspell it deliberately, claiming it looked more beautiful that way.

But for the moment she was left free, to substitute real friends for imaginary ones, to share their world, to adopt the townland dialect, so fivepence became fippence, a long walk became a dreadful foreigner. She would talk of silage and rides on the back of the harvester with Dan, of colly dogs that are whores for barking, and her bemused parents would see this lithe tinker grow between them. Her father would walk her through that long cathedral of steaming ice and hear her talk with the shellfish packers in a tongue that was, to him, near impenetrable.

Her summer became one long swathe of sensuality, a bathing suit beneath a tattered dress, whole weeks spent on the dunes that spread from the Baltray golf-course to the interminable stretch of empty beach to the north of the river-mouth. The cottages across the Boyne river from her father's shellfish plant became her second home: George and Janie Tuite in one, fifteen children spread between the other two. The blue and white horizon of the foaming sea was always perched, it seemed, over the three smoking chimneys, threatening to douse them entirely. Between those cottages and her parents' large, ungovernable house was the estuary swamp, a terrain of dried mud, of slowly creeping tides, of barely formed canals Dan Turnbull had chosen to call Mozambique.

Why Mozambique, they were never sure. But there were flies in Mozambique, Dan told them, flies, mosquitoes, and the fetid humours you get in flatlands below sea-level, so Mozambique it did become. And in Mozambique there were all of the estuary delights, crabs and kingfishers, channels and runnels, stagnant ponds, mudflats and seeping tides that rose at will, turning cracked black earth into mud that squelched and oozed between George's ever-naked toes. There were men digging for earth-worms in the early morning, mists like white hair clinging to the low ground, obliterating the dunes beyond, making Mozambique seem endless, men turning sand with spades, sever-ing a lugworm here, a ragworm there. And when the men and the mists departed, there were monsters to be found in Mozambique: a huge flatfish left in a runnel by the departing tide, flapping, gasping vainly for air with its whitened mouth; an eel slinking in

a stilled pool; multitudinous crabs; and one day a horned creature, up to its midriff in the soft mud, mud caked on its hair, its
tail, mud from the incessant flailing of its four trapped legs, mud
which dried around it as the sun rose.

They surveyed this thing for hours, a footless mound of hair
with two curved horns rising from it, wondering was it reindeer,
unicorn or seahorse, until Dan arrived and told them it was none
of those, it was Mabel Hatch's goat. He undid the muddied rope
from round its neck, slid it beneath its belly, avoided its jagging
horns and pulled. And they heard grotesque sucking sounds as
first the front legs, then the back ones emerged from their prison
in the sludge and the whole goat was up, unsteady on its feet but
standing free and readying itself to take a run at Dan. Which it
tried, but slipped and rolled again in the mud-caked earth, and
Dan said 'Enough so,' grabbed it by the horns and hind legs,
hoisted it over his shoulders and walked into the sunlight
towards Mabel Hatch's field.

And what she would remember for ever was not the goat stuck
in the mud but the horns, which seemed to sprout from Dan
Turnbull's bent head as he disappeared, silhouetted against the
light.

George walked in the goat's footsteps, his bare feet obliterating the cloven indentations in the mud. 'So, it was a goat, then,'
he said.

'No,' Nina answered, 'it was a unicorn.'

'Dan Turnbull said it was Mabel Hatch's goat.'

'Well, Hester told me it was a unicorn. What do you think,
Janie?'

'A unicorn,' said Janie, 'without a doubt.'

'So where does a unicorn come from?' George asked. He was
in a shifting, uncertain world, each question could be referred to
an entity that wasn't there.

'From the sea,' Nina answered. 'Hester thinks a unicorn comes
from the sea. And in the sea it has a tail like a mermaid, or a sea-

horse really, and when it reaches the land, why the tail turns into legs.'

'Legs,' repeated George.

'Legs, four legs. A tail for the water, legs for the land.'

And sure enough, the cloven tracks led right to the water's edge, where they disappeared into the inky current.

'A unicorn feeds on starfish,' Nina said, 'spears them with its horn, and that's what the horn is for. And when the starfish run out, a unicorn has to venture on dry land.'

'And what does it eat on dry land?' George asked.

'Eels,' said Nina without hesitation.

'Eels,' repeated Janie.

'Eels and starfish, the basic unicorn diet without which its horn falls off, the coat moults and it ends up looking like any old goat.'

'Goat,' said Georgie, 'you said goat.'

'I said like any old goat, didn't I Janie?'

'You did, Nina. And stop asking unicorn questions, Georgie, we're getting tired.'

So they ran from Mozambique to the Sahara, the Sahara being those large slopes of elephant grass which they tumbled down, dresses up to their shoulders, bloomers to the air.

'Close your eyes, George, and count to twenty,' Janie said.

'What if I don't?' he replied.

'Then the unicorn will get you—'

So of course he shut them on the instant, placed sandy fingers over his crinkled lids and began counting. And they ran fast and kept running until he was long out of earshot, until they reached that jagged line of rocks where the river met the sea. Janie pulled off her dress and dived and Nina followed suit and they swam out to the raft by the Lady's Finger and lay there for hours until the sun had dried their skins to a silken sheen, till they heard George roaring from the shore, an ancient bellow of agony and loss. And they turned their heads and saw a salmon fisherman comforting

69

him, though his grief seemed unstoppable. They dived back in and swam towards him, got close enough to hear the fisherman saying, there are no unicorns son, and even if there were they wouldn't take your sister.

'What was that, mister?' Janie said, stepping from the water like a mermaid herself, the sun glinting on every drop that clung to her thin body. 'What do you know about unicorns?'

'Where's the poor craythur's mother?' the fisherman asked.

'She drowned,' said Janie, 'she was swimming, when the unicorns took her.'

Janie held out her arms for George. But the one he ran to, clung to, was Nina.

That body, smaller than mine, a ball of muscle even then, clinging to my wet self for fear the unicorns would take me. I kissed his tears away and took his hand and said 'Georgie, porgy, pudd'n'npie, kissed the girls and made them cry. Stop it now.' But he couldn't, great raking breaths coursing through his lungs, his arms, his hands, his lips shaking for fear of a loss he couldn't comprehend, and when the fear was banished the tears kept coming, a delirium to be stopped only by its own exhaustion. It was the first of those moments when the world, its furies, its pains, its agonies overwhelmed him with a physical wallop. And as he grew the warp-spasms grew, until at last they lost the battle with his great hulking body and buried themselves somewhere inside it. But then he was small, tiny and afraid and I carried him, little Nina, big George, through the Sahara grasses, back over the mudflats of Mozambique to the curve of river by the swing and dipped him in. And only those waters seemed to calm him.

From the top window of the dead governess's room the phosphorescent sea is visible, the waves crashing with their insane regularity, the foam gleaming in the winter moonlight and the small row of cottages in the bowl of dunes beneath it. Two of them were thatched then and one, George and Janie Tuite's, had a red oxide corrugated metal roof. We came to share each other's homes, the anomaly of the contrast between the large limestone one and the miniscule one of pink-tinted whitewash being lost entirely on the three of us.

Jeremiah Tuite, who worked as pilot for the Harbourmaster, who would take us on his tug as he went to help the boats cross the bar, whose blue serge waistcoat had anchor buttons on it, came to view me, his 'little Nina,' as a cousin, a niece, a half-sibling of kinds, he found me so often beneath his corrugated roof. He smoked a pipe and drank porter in the Silver Dollar Bar. He swung Mrs Eva Tuite in a ceremonious half-circle each time he came home, as if he had just navigated to safety the *Flying Dutchman*. He would sit wreathed in tobacco-smoke, chair tilted against his pink-washed cottage wall, scanning the horizon for incoming vessels, then begin the race to be the first to meet it. His little Nina came to love that smoke, the peaty smell of it, came to love the sound of rain drumming off their metal roof, the taste of salted herring and potato cakes, if the rains persisted and she had to stay for tea.

And when the summer ended and school began, it seemed natural that the lacunae left in her education by the dead governess should be filled by the National School System. So she came to walk, with Janie and George, the three miles from her house to the National School on the Drogheda Road. The smell of sour milk would hit her from the yard, blending uneasily with the tang of urine from the toilets. She picked her way through the scraps of yesterday's bread, through the scavenging seagulls, her white shoes a perfect contrast to the grime. She found herself privileged there, in the dull green room with the high windows, the sunlight crawling through them, reaching only the upper walls; Miss Cannon, with a green plaid skirt to match those walls, leaving her free to dream, presuming the large house she came from conferred some prior refinement on her.

She was spared the strap and the ruler, the ruler which rained liberally on poor George's palms, his knuckles, his head, his shoulders. George got to know that strip of wood intimately, its edges serrated with the indentations of inches and feet, got to know its mood, its weather, its humours, always, it seemed, malign. 'Your place, George Ward,' Miss Cannon would loudly inform him as he stuttered through his *Viva Voce*, 'is not so much in this class as in the low field with your trousers in one hand and a lump of grass in the other.' The same field that Nina, Janie and George sat in after school, filling his copybook among the cowslips. But their neat girlish handwriting could never save him from the terror of recitation, his breath coagulating in his chest and his stutter rising gradually from staccato to the strangled lament of a dying swan. His broken syllables would stretch into one long single vowel, rising in his boy-soprano pitch to meet the whistling trill and crack of Miss Cannon's chosen instrument. The manuscript of his hands became an object of wonder after school, how two small lumps of flesh could carry so much scrawl – weals, welts, mounds of purple, streaks of broken, bloodied skin.

Nina would take one calloused hand, Janie the other and walk him down the lane to the low field among the haystacks. While Janie gathered cowslips, Nina would crush dockleaves and wrap them round his beaten hands and tell him Jesus Christ suffered more.

'Will you marry me, George?' she would ask him, spreading the green juice from the dockleaf like lipstick over his trembling mouth.

'Yes,' he would answer without hesitation, a blush like real lipstick spreading to his cheeks.

'You heard him, Janie, he said yes.'

'And that's a promise,' Janie would say, placing cowslips on each of her fingers. 'And if you break it, Hester will give you a whipping.'

'Does Hester give whippings?' George would ask.

'Yes,' said Nina, 'with her blackthorn stick. None of Miss Cannon's old rulers for Hester. In fact, here comes Hester now, she wants to be a witness.'

'What's a witness?'

'The one who says I heard you say you'll marry her and who'll give you a whipping if you don't. The one who says, now is the time to kiss the bride.'

'Who's the bride?'

'I am, silly. And now's the time.'

And Nina kissed him. On his green-smeared lips, on his green-smeared, calloused hands.

'Is that better, George?'

And George would nod. The kiss, he wanted to say, was almost worth the beating.

He grew attached to the after-school salving, to the kisses, to the hands that crushed the dockleaves, the fingers that placed them on his weals, the lips that brushed off each bloodied stripe, to the sight of her walking towards him from the house each morning, as he waited with Janie behind the metal gates. He would see the large door open, the mother bend down to kiss her cheek, see Nina emerge, oddly self-possessed, feet crunching delicately on the gravel, framed by the large, grey house.

'What larks, Pip,' she would say, like her father.

'What larks, Joe,' was his and Janie's answer, though they knew not why.

He walked barefoot for the first two months, September, October, then, when the November chill set in, inherited a pair of boots several sizes too big that left his sockless ankles raw. Nina found a pair of her own cast-off bootees and fitted them on his feet one morning in December, when the weals on his ankles almost matched those on his hands and the frost on the ground made walking barefoot impossible. Then he made his way over, the two miles to school in uncommon comfort, only to be surrounded in the schoolyard and pilloried mercilessly. Georgie Porgy what's the news, comes to school in girlie shoes. Georgie lashed out with his delicate boots and his fists which proved surprisingly indelicate, felled three of his tormentors before he was frogmarched by Miss Cannon to another, more comprehensive thrashing.

And thereafter a different George emerged, as if a chrysalis of soft skin had been shed, revealing a tougher, more impenetrable one beneath. His stutter congealed, during *Viva Voce*, into a monosyllabic mumble, his hands developed hide like leather and began to tire even Miss Cannon's indefatigable arm, and he grew into a child larger than most, immune to teasing, to his peers' contempt, still unaccountably attached to Nina's cast-off boots.

He wore them on the wran day, when they dressed him in one of Janie's smocks and carried him in a handcart from house to house with blackened faces and an imaginary bird in a furze bush. He wore them as the winter changed to spring, as the frozen earth on the road to school turned to mud again, as May approached and the mud turned to hard earth with a coating of fine dust. When his growing toes sprouted between the leathers and the uppers he wore them still; when Janie had cast off her own shoes and walked happily barefoot again, he wore them still; he wore them till all the stitching had shredded, till the soles had flapped loose, till the laces decayed and they literally fell off his feet. And only then did he go barefoot again.

'What larks, Pip,' Nina said, seeing the discarded bootees by the roadside.

'What larks, Nina,' he replied.

'You don't say what larks Nina,' Janie told him, 'you say what larks Joe.'

'Why can't I say what larks Nina?'

'Don't ask me, ask Nina.'

'Because that's not in the story.'

And Nina told him the story just as her father had told it, of Pip and Joe Gargery and of the larks they had when Mrs Joe wasn't looking, of the blacksmith Orlick, the convict Magwitch and the beautiful Estella.

'The beautiful Estella,' George repeated.

'Yes,' said Nina, 'in the big house behind the barred gates, with Miss Havisham and her mouldy wedding dress.'

~

The books frozen in their places on the shelves: *A Child's Garden Of Verses, Cautionary Tales, The Water Babies, What Katy Did, Lorna Doone, Little Women, Jo's Boys, Little Men, Hard Times, Great Expectations, Wuthering Heights, Jane Eyre*. The mildew on their spines dampens as the winter sun creeps through the window and ices over once more at night. Each frosted title acts like a lost perfume, whole worlds released in association. Matilda told such dreadful lies, it made one gasp and stretch one's eyes. My memories, frosted like theirs, as yet untitled. What larks, Pip. Miss Havisham, all her clocks stopped. Now that time has stopped do I remember, no, I read, as if within those frozen spines, the book whose ending I didn't write, written for me by one who hardly learned to write. I give it chapter headings, turn the non-existent pages, inhabit the story, delight in it, weep in it, die in it. But can I change the conclusion? Not a whit. The end began it and beginning ended it.

Then the freeze itself ends, with the mists and the white hoar-frost, and the bubbling spines of my library run with water. A proper Irish winter has set in. Rain is ever-present now, veils of it some days, torrents on others, and the ground beneath the copse of ash trees round the cottage becomes a swamp, with the plop and splash of water from the branches above. George's door stays open, sagging on its hinges, and the radio finally dies under the gathering damp. The chestnut over the bend of the river grows a permanent sheen, indistinguishable from the brown swirls of the water below. The house drips from the roof, the ceilings, moss and lichen flourish on the garden walls. Schoolchildren run past the bleak façade at evening, fearing ghosts and muttering prayers, but gather in the grey mornings to throw stones. The windows crack, split and shatter, glass splinters littering the sodden carpets, and the winds come through, shaking loose the doors, the wardrobes, lifting the mouldering rugs in undulating waves, whipping the linens from their shaken drawers, through the windswept corridors, like ghosts themselves. The shattered windows reinforce the haunted mien of the grey limestone façade, the children scurrying by it faster, mouthing charms their mothers taught them, sharing tales of the presence inside, female of course, in white, carrying her head sometimes, her intestines others, in a gown of blood-streaked white but never, it seems, in an ageing fur coat, in wellington boots and a black beret.

13

HESTER DIED ON a Saturday morning in September, mangled between the lathes of a threshing-machine, operated by the Bull Brennan in the fields that bordered the graveyard of the Protestant church in Termonfeckin. Her death was observed by Nina, George and Janie, sitting on the vibrating seat beside the rattling handles that were pushed and pulled by the gargantuan arms of the Bull, in an irregular rhythm and to a mysterious purpose, but one that kept the sheaves of barley trundling up the leather belt, grinding through the lathes, to be disgorged as yellow straw out of the right-hand funnel, chaff and barleycorn through the left. Dan Turnbull was shovelling the barley into sacks, five Brennan brothers were stacking the sheaves and Nina was staring at the leather conveyor belt, one long band of vibrating yellow on its way to the punishment of those wooden arms, like a mechanical hell constructed from giant versions of Miss Cannon's ruler. She didn't notice Hester slip, didn't hear her hit the belt, and when she saw her pink cheeks and green and white bib and smock among the yellow sheaves, she didn't cry out. She watched her with strange fascination make the shuddering journey up towards those threshing arms and was almost surprised to hear the panicked scream of George beside her.

'Hester!'

Dan looked up in mid-shovel, a halo of chaff around his saintly head. The Bull's muscular arms pulled two levers contrariwise and the threshing-machine slowly, agonisingly, began to grind to a halt. But not before Hester had completed her juddering crawl towards those mechanical arms, received the mother of all thrashings, found her head wrenched one way, her torso the other. Dan listened to the whine and grind of the thresher in its death throes, and when it finally fell silent saw the pieces of pulverised head fall from the hopper into the waiting sack, its broken ears mingling with the ears of barley.

He removed the knotted handkerchief that protected his head from the midday sun and laid it in the grass beside the sack of barley. He picked the tiny pieces out one by one and placed them in it. He walked around the machine, past the line of sweating Brennan brothers, and retrieved what remained of Hester's torso. He placed the pieces of shredded horsehair, bib and smock on the handkerchief beside the broken ceramic pieces of the head. He then took Nina from the Bull's enormous hands and noticed, to his mild surprise, that she wasn't crying. He lifted Janie next and last of all George, who was.

'Nobody's fault,' Dan said and repeated it, 'nobody's fault.'

'Humpty Dumpty,' said Nina. 'Had a big fall.'

'All the king's horses,' said Dan. 'All the king's men.'

'Couldn't put Humpty together again.'

'It's not Humpty,' said George, 'it's Hester.'

'But she's not gone,' said Nina, 'is she, Dan?'

Dan stared at the shattered pieces of doll and scratched his remaining hairs.

'She'd take some fixin',' he murmured.

'No, she won't be fixed,' said Nina.

'But she can be waked,' said Janie.

'Now you're talking,' says Dan. 'Pipes, whiskey and porter.'

So Nina wrapped up Dan's handkerchief, tying the four ends into a neat bow, picking up a broken piece of ash plant, inserting it into the bow and propping it on her shoulder, and began to walk across the stubbled barley field, for all the world like Dick Whittington. And they didn't find pipes or porter, but they found a china tea-set, and George and Janie had orangeade and biscuits while Nina swung out over the river beneath the chestnut tree, and emptied the contents of Dan Turnbull's handkerchief into the waters below.

'May she rest in peace,' said Nina.

'Amen,' said Janie.

'Amen,' repeated George.

'May she sleep the good sleep, may the river be her bed.'

'Amen,' repeated Janie and George.

'And when she dreams, may she dream only of us.'

'Dolls don't dream,' said George.

'Hester does.'

'How can she dream when she's dead?' asked Janie, for once wary of Nina's logic.

'When the dead dream,' said Nina, 'they dream of the living. If they're good, like Hester, they become our guardian angels.'

'And if they're bad?'

Nina thought for a moment, then shut her eyes, as if the prospect was too awful to contemplate. Then she opened them, and slowly, like a gathering wave, an expression of bliss flooded her face.

'What is it?' asked Janie, terrified by these transports.

'There,' said Nina, 'over the water—'

'Where?' asked Georgie.

'Open your eyes,' said Nina, 'her feet are in the rushes—'

'Who?' screamed Janie, her own eyes clamped.

'Hester,' Nina said, her voice somewhere between a breath and a prayer.

So she looks at me again, her only true familiar, and I realise again what a comfort it is, to be perceived. And I wonder was it me they waked with orangeade and biscuits, gave Hester as a name while the broken doll drifted, the ceramic cheeks descended slowly into silt, the shredded bib and smock, Puritan no more, drifted down towards Mozambique, got tangled in the bulrushes and the hair alone continued out towards the Lady's

Finger where it sank, eventually, down to meet the seaweed. Those eyes have said goodbye to childhood of a certain kind, to the whispered conversations with nothing in particular, the animation of the inanimate, the infinite present. They have a past now and memories, chief among them the memory of the broken doll, released from the knotted handkerchief, falling towards the water. They're growing into a colder time, where minutes won't last for ever but move, like serried stalks of barley, along a belt of sorts, leading to a particular end. Those eyes have no idea what that end will be, there'll be a journey, that's all they know, and on the journey a journeywoman called Hester, for want of a better name.

Three figures squatting beneath the chestnut tree, a miniature tablecloth spread out before them, miniature cups with orangeade and carefully broken biscuits. Two heads bowed, one head looking up with clear eyes, unafraid. Then George unclasps his bunched fist from his reddened eyes and looks up too. And he whispers, 'Hester'.

And though my name is Nina, two clear and sunlit syllables, and Hester is sibilant, all breath and nightshade, I can't complain, since any name is preferable to none.

II

14

AND THE HOUSE is now untouched by human hand. Children avoid the road at night and hurry past it in the morning, throw no more stones since every visible pane is broken. One night a fox comes through the sagging kitchen door, forages through the scullery for edibles, urinates on the piano-leg. I search him out. The yellow eyes, scouring for others in the shadows, that animal gaze, all instinct over sight, he pads in nightly, always more scraps to be found, more corners to forage in.

A vagrant pushes through the shattered window, cuts his arm on the broken glass, drinks the last sherry from the dining-room cabinet, sleeps on the damp, mouldy covers of my bed upstairs. A woman joins him, he rapes her on the kitchen floor, she flees, crying, bleeding. The police return, lead him off, place rusting padlocks on the gates, board up the broken doors and ground-floor windows. And the fox comes no more, there's just the choughing of pigeons and at night the flutter of bats. And from the road, through padlocked gates glistening with spring rain, the haunted aspect is complete.

Then one March day when the rains have stopped and crocuses have pushed their orange noses through the overgrown grass, when the pale sun has defined itself through the veils of cloud, a car drives up to the gates, a hackney turns a key in the rusting padlock, drags them open, drives on up the weed-festered gravel, swings round to a halt in the abandoned courtyard. The back door opens and Gregory gets out.

Forever young, his hair has greyed, his cheeks have hollowed but the naivety of step is exactly as I remember, the shoulders bowed by nothing but the air. He pulls vainly at the nailed struts fastened to the kitchen door, then walks to the outhouse, vanishes inside. He emerges with a hammer, begins to pry the nails from the boards with a sickening shriek of old timber against rusted nail. The dull clatter of boards around his feet, then the door is free. He edges it open with an immaculate, Jermyn Street shoe.

He is late, as always. Three months at least this time, and I remember again, as the sunlight pierces the kitchen's gloom, that there has been no funeral. Of course, no funeral, for a funeral needs a corpse and family, and my only family is here. He stands in the ravaged door-frame, filling it easily, one hand on the broken latch.

I can see him entering the same door when he was ten.

~

He was late then too, years late, the young Nina staring from the smaller doorway across the kitchen table with those wide, expectant eyes. Your brother is coming, they told her, or should we say your half-brother, and she wondered why they hadn't told her before. There is a creature like you somewhere in the world although you haven't met him yet. That slim pale boy standing in the doorway, case in one hand, the other in the hand of the hackney driver behind him. He had a nose for unkindness, she could tell that already, would smell it approaching at a hundred yards, climb into any cupboard to escape it, with his thick dark hair and the shadows in his cheeks like hers, mine. All that seemed different was his sex, male, and his eyes, green, they seemed to swallow the light – whatever little light there was in that kitchen, his eyes consumed it.

And the feeling she had, which I still cannot escape, which runs through the kitchen, ran through it instantaneously, like the sunlight, was of instant loss. She missed all the hours they hadn't spent together, the history they hadn't had, she wept inside for a past, for memories that had never existed. How can I remember you, never having known you? I could, we could, make it up, she tried to think; could invent a past, a book of hours for those nine years we hadn't known each other. For Nina was nine then, when Gregory was ten. And when Nina was ten, Gregory would be eleven. And Nina was no more now and Gregory was fifty-two. We have a lifetime to catch up, she thought. But somehow, even then, she knew they wouldn't. There would be a missing child-hood between them, no games of catch-up, and whatever lifetime they had would be strangely, dangerously askew, like no other.

'What's his name again?' she asked her mother, her mother who was not his, who was standing behind her, apparently casual, in the scullery corridor. She asked the question quietly, since she didn't feel she had the right to address him as yet. But he heard, all the same.

'Gregory,' he said, and stepped inside.

~

He walks in now, through the broken crockery and the fox-drop-pings and the flutter of pigeon's wings. He has either grieved his half-sister already or will never again grieve. He walks as if he's being looked at – as indeed he is, solemnly, observantly – around the wet pine table through the low stone passage to the front hallway. He climbs the stairs and stops to listen to every ringing creak. He walks into my bedroom but doesn't, of course, remem-ber it as mine. It is his father's, his new stepmother's, who after his arrival rarely left it till after noon. He looks without expres-sion at the wet, twisted coverlet where the fox and the rapist slept. He walks back into the corridor, opens the cupboard where once I told him, in a fit of malice, the dead Hester lived. He leaves the open door creaking and enters the room they chose to be his bedroom. I had kept, out of whimsy, want or some innate inabil-ity to change pertinent things, the same sturdy wooden bed he slept on, the same wallpaper with its boyish, sailboat pattern, the same photograph of him in cricket whites. He sits on the damp bed, looks at his younger self and smiles, grimly. He seems as foreign to his younger self then as he is to his younger sister, now.

'Nina,' he says softly, and I repeat the name so his voice echoes softly and comes back to him. He repeats it, 'Nina, Nina,' louder, so my echo comes louder, and he looks at himself in the mottled mirror of the wardrobe. 'Nina,' he says, and I am Echo again to his Narcissus and he lies on the bed and buries his face in the damp pillow.

There is a hint of sobbing in the air that must emanate from Echo, not Narcissus. Yes, I can hear sobbing but it is surely my own. Then he rises and his cheeks are damp so maybe the sobbing was his, but the pillow is damp with the mildew of three months, so maybe not. He walks back into the corridor, down the creaking stairs, and his Echo listens, catches each of his sounds, his footfalls, and throws them back. Then the piano makes its faltering sounds. The A and the D and the F and the D again, then the A an octave above. Echo gently doubles each slow, ponderous, broken note and recognises the piece, the Mozart Sonata in D. Three rapid trills. The B and the E and the G and the E and B above it. The playing grows surer, more forceful, and comes to full flood, no room for echo any more, like memory flooding back. The piano needs tuning, the pedals creak. But then, it always did.

~

She heard it the first night he came, and his playing of it seemed like a statement of kinds, a libation, a pouring out of what sounds he knew to the house, to his place within it. She was drawn from her room, quietly, down the carpeted stairs as the melody took flight. She stopped as the melody stopped, as he felt for a phrase and the melody tried to fly once more. Then it drew her again, to the curl of the banisters, where she could see him through the door, by the black, swanlike shape of the piano, his hands moving over the yellowing keys.

They hadn't told her because they couldn't, because they had no words. She understood that now, listening to the nameless music at the bottom of the stairs. And she understood the tension of the last month, the hushed voices in their bedroom at night, the sense of stilled argument, the frozen air in the kitchen at mealtimes.

'You have a brother,' her mother had said, walking her down before school to the gates to meet Janie and George. 'Or should I say a half-brother. He lives in England and his name is Gregory.'

'Who is his mother?' she asked, with a wicked sense of hurt in the question.

'I haven't met his mother, and your father hasn't met his mother for a long, long time. But she's sick, now, and she's troubled and the boy is coming here.'

'Were they married,' she asked, 'like you?' And she felt the hand let go of hers.

'No,' she said. 'Before your father came here he was a painter. They lead funny lives.'

'Funny,' she repeated, then thought for a while. 'What is a half-brother?' she asked.

'A half-brother,' her mother said carefully, 'is when one parent is the same and one parent is not the same.'

'Can I have a full-brother, please?' she asked, as she held her cheek up for the goodbye kiss.

'Perhaps,' said her mother, abstractedly. 'Perhaps.'

She had tried to imagine him, this Pip, this Dick Whittington, this Godolphin Horne, Ignobly born. She tried to imagine his clothes, his shoes, his complexion, his hands, his hair, his smell. She failed miserably. I have a brother, she scrawled on her slate at school, he has a different mother. There was a surprising poetry to the rhyme of those lines and she tried, having failed to imagine him, to imagine his mother. But she could hardly imagine his mother without imagining her father with her and felt oddly unfaithful imagining that. She pictured a woman by a twisting river, with a city behind it which she supposed was London. The woman was gazing at no-one in particular and the twisting river behind her was as if on a map, a map she then remembered she had seen, with pictures for the Houses of Parliament, for London Bridge, for Hyde Park. Where she had seen this map she had no idea, but the woman's face in the foreground was nothing like the face she knew best of all, her mother's. It was a thinner face with a different kind of sadness, with lank, blonde hair tied to one side. She imagined her father with this woman, walking through the oddly drawn streets of the map of London, past the fairy-tale towers of the Houses of Parliament, over the castellated entrance to Tower Bridge. She imagined her walking the same way her father walked, both absent-minded, the curling river behind them. She felt unaccountably sad then, and tried to think of her sick, in a large hospital ward, with a young boy by her side, a boy with a bag and a school blazer.

'I have a brother,' she had said to her father as they sat by the banks beneath the factory, watching a different river go by. It was meant to be a question, not a statement, but somehow it came out that way, flat.

'Yes,' he said, looking at the water. 'I have a son.'

'Why have I not met him?' she asked, and this time it came out as a proper question.

'Because sometimes,' he said, 'certain things are not possible.'

'Why has he a different mother?' Another question, harder this time.

'Because,' he said, choosing his words with unaccustomed care, 'I was young and . . . different I suppose . . . and I met his mother before I met yours.'

'You were a painter,' she said, repeating what she had heard, 'and they lead funny lives.'

'Indeed they do,' he said and smiled sadly, stood and threw a stone in the water. 'They lead lives in which they think everything is possible and they come to realise most things are not.'

'Not possible,' she repeated. She was puzzled.

'I was young, and wanted to marry, but her parents refused, even when the child was born. They disapproved.'

'Disapproved,' she repeated. She could never imagine anyone disapproving of her father.

'Yes,' he said. 'I was a painter. Painters lead funny lives. They sent her away. She travelled. France, Malta, India. He would never have come here, you need never have known, had his mother not become . . . ill . . .' He threw another stone, with his back to her. 'But he's coming, now. And I can't say I'm sorry, no matter what . . .'

He turned to her and lifted her up in his arms. 'You'll like him,' he said.

'How do you know?' she asked, her face close to his.

'Because,' he said softly, lifting her away from the river towards the road above the factory, 'he is more like you than anyone I can think of.'

She had wondered what he had said to her mother. I have a son. I was a painter. Before I met you. They lead funny lives. She imagined her mother by the curved window on the staircase, her arms around her elbows, turned away. She imagined the cold grey light coming through the window. She imagined the cold grey fingers wrapping round her heart. And she wondered would anything ever be the same again.

She had tried to keep her curiosity about this new brother mild, whimsical, abstract, otherwise her heart would have burst. Whether with the pressure of those cold grey fingers, or with the unbearable anticipation of his arrival, she could not be sure. She tried to prevent her need to know from consuming her like a growing flame. She tried to think of him as a new species of being, like the gnu or the ocelot, one she had never seen but heard rumours of from distant places. If she had been told his name, she soon forgot it, took to calling him Half-brother, and then, simply Half. And the name Half was suitably diffident, if also alarmingly engaging. For if he, Half, was one half, then she, Nina, was surely the other. Half is coming, she thought, Half is in London now but will one day take the train.

She found underneath her bed a jigsaw from her early days, of the City of London, complete with curving river, fairytale Houses of Parliament and castellated Tower Bridge, and realised where the picture of the city behind the imagined woman's face had come from. She rebuilt most of it one afternoon from Chelsea to the Isle of Dogs, and rose the next morning to finish it. She had reached Greenwich when the creak of the front gates sounded, and the crunch of hoof and wheel over gravel. She walked from her bedroom across the upper hallway and saw the trap, curving up the driveway, the anonymous figure sitting in the back. Half, she thought.

Through the tall windows of the stairwell she followed the passage of the hackney intermittently as it rounded the house. Half, she thought, will soon be whole. She lost sight of them then but heard the crunch and the creaking springs of the trap's halting, the whinny of the stalled horse. She raced down the last few stairs, through the front hallway, down the scullery corridors, then slowed her feet, walked with suitable nonchalance and stopped at the door into the kitchen. She could see him over the pine table, stopping at the threshold of the door on the other side.

'What's his name again?' she asked her mother.

'Gregory,' he said, and stepped inside.

She took him upstairs to his room with the new sailboat wall-paper and the smell of fresh paint and the wooden bed. He was tidy with his few things, the way she imagined an orphan would be. His case of scuffed leather was tied with a piece of string which he unknotted, opening the case across the bedclothes, meticulously spreading his clothes across the coverlet. She noticed a penknife, a piano-tutor and a clock left there, among the tangled braces.

'Did you take long to get here?' she asked him, with what she felt was the correct formality. She wanted to fill the air in the room with something other than his breathing.

'I took the train from St Pancras to Holyhead and the boat to Dublin and then the train again to Drogheda.' He pronounced it, she noted, Drocheeda. 'Then I was taken here.'

'Is that long then?'

'I would say it's long. A day and a night and another morning from Dublin.'

She relished those short English vowels and wanted to hear more of them. 'Is that the longest journey you've travelled?'

'India was longer.'

'What happened in India?'

'That was a boat journey all the way. It took two weeks, I think. We stayed with the Peels. They're Zoroastrians.'

'Zoro what?'

'Pharsee. It means fire-worshippers.' She could detect a hint of pride in his voice. 'They're English,' he continued, 'but they became Zoroastrian when they went to India.'

'Are you a Zoroastrian?' She could feel an inordinate amount of pleasure when the word emerged correctly.

'No,' he said, 'I'm C of E.'

'What,' she asked, 'is C of E?'

'Church of England. When I grow up I might be Zoroastrian. I don't know yet. Mother wanted to paint the fire-dances, and that's why we went.'

'Your mother's a painter?'

'Well,' he said, 'she hasn't painted for a while. She was, then, in India.'

She watched him open the drawers of the cupboards and place his clothes inside. She wanted to put her face to those shirts and inhale their smell. She wondered how much imagining she would have to do: London, Holyhead, Dublin and now India.

'Do you like your new house?'

'It's big,' he said. 'I'm not used to big houses.'

'Aren't the houses in India big?'

'We had a bungalow.'

And perhaps it was the word Zoroastrian that made her come out with it. 'The thing about this house,' she said, 'and I don't want to frighten you, but it's—'

'It's what?' he asked, and she could hear a hint of apprehension in those English vowels.

'It's haunted.'

He stopped his unpacking. 'So,' he said, and looked up at her. 'You're trying to frighten me.'

'No,' she said, and finally felt the freedom to walk inside. She sat down beside his shirts and things. She inhaled their odour, severe and fresh. 'She doesn't frighten anyone. Her name's Hester and she's always a little sad.'

'Does this ghost talk, then?' he asked and began his unpacking again. He gathered some clothes and moved to the cupboard, to get away from her, she felt.

'Dead people don't talk,' she said.

'So this ghost is dead.'

'All ghosts are.'

'I don't know,' he said. 'I don't know about ghosts.'

'She has no name, really.'

'No name,' he repeated.

'We gave her the name Hester,' she said, 'when my doll died.'

'Dolls don't die,' he said.

'Well, Hester did,' she said.

'You're trying to frighten me,' he said, 'but I won't be frightened.'

'No,' she said, 'I'm just telling you. Maybe so you won't be frightened. And if you see her, you're to tell me. That way I'll know.'

'Know what?'

'That we have the same eyes. George, Janie, Gregory, Nina.'

'Who are George and Janie?'

'My friends. Would you like to meet them?'

'Perhaps.'

'Would you like to meet Hester?

'It won't work,' he said. 'I won't be frightened.'

'Well, if you do see her, you have to promise that you'll tell me first.'

He took the clock from his case and placed it gingerly on the bedside table.

'Promise?'

He looked at her for the first time. She saw those green eyes, not the same as hers at all, but wonderfully present and hanging on her every word. She felt sorry for a moment that she had ever frightened them.

'I promise.'

15

H E SAW HESTER eventually, his Hester who was of course different from my Hester and different, so different, from
George's. Or he persuaded himself that he saw her, as I persuade
myself that I am seeing him. We create these unseens and give
them a kind of life, like St Anselm's God, that exists because of
our belief in it, because that belief after all is a kind of existence,
that perpetuates and remains when we are gone as I perhaps
remain now, persuade myself that I am listening to him finish his
Mozart sonata in the derelict, wet living room with nothing but
the broken panes of glass in the peeling window-frames to hear
him. I am no longer I, and he is as far from the young boy who
wandered the empty rooms, afraid of every shadow, every closed
wardrobe door, as I am from what I was.

But of course there is a difference. The difference being that
he can press those keys, create that ringing sound, the damp on
his cheeks which may or may not be tears can dry, and he can
stop, take out a notebook, walk round the house, make an inven-
tory of whatever artefacts remain unbroken. The Chinese vases I
bought in Kensington, the old oak bookcase with the mildewed
library, the marble table, the sodden, circular Persian carpet
beneath it. The hunting table in the dining room, the crystals
and decanters lying askance, the Gerald Brockhurst, the Jack
Yeats, the Lavery painting of Dún Laoghaire pier with the pale
blue of the evening sky and the darker blue of the evening sea
almost matching. Death is, of course, a series of inventories, of
abandoned possessions to be noted, redistributed among the
living. He has no wife, no child, so the line of my father's issue

will stop with him. He will be the sole inheritor of this stuff, this house and its gardens, lawns and fields, stretching down to the bend in the river. He will inherit me too, festering in my cesspit, and for a moment I am grateful that George left my corpse so cannily hidden.

He walks through the house for hours, filling his spiral-bound notebook. The Aga in the kitchen, the pine table, the tableware, the large four-poster in the room upstairs that I bought at auction in Kells and had restored in Drogheda. There is the safe, of course, which he won't yet discover, with its Erté bracelets, its scattering of pearl necklaces and cut diamonds. Then there is my office, with its typewriter, its copies of signed scripts, its awards, its posters, some valuable, some not. I can imagine the advert in the *Irish Times*, Saturday, on the Fine Arts page, public auction of the effects of Nina Hardy, actress, among the items on view . . .

I can imagine it but hope I won't have to see it, hope he will keep every item, every trinket, down to the spidery letters from Mr Bernard Shaw and the bustier I wore in that burlesque western. And like most of my imaginings, I imagine this will be disappointed in turn.

Gregory leaves, when darkness falls. All of the fuses are blown, the bulbs broken, he has no torch and a dead house at night is no place for the living. His headlights scorch through the window, traverse the walls once as the car departs towards the Wheel Inn where Albert Taffe, who played double-bass to his piano at the tennis-club dances, sits behind the desk with his cigarettes and his ever-widening paunch. They will exchange pleasantries, commiserations, memories of me in my lilac dress, Gregory and George in uniform already, with Janie sipping whiskey from a forbidden bottle as Bertie sang 'It's a Long Way To Tipperary' and the fight broke out between George and Buttsy Flanagan, no competition there.

Bertie perhaps will drink too much, recall the time he danced with me between sets, remember my long pale neck and my reddened lips, but will say nothing of the evening he walked with me on the newly laid golf-course, lay in the sand at the bunker of the seventeenth hole and put his tongue between my teeth, only to be stilled to rigidity by the sight of my purple brassière. 'You can touch it if you want.' But no, Bertie didn't, or couldn't, lost that cowboy swagger when he walked off-stage, drove his hands into the sand instead, and watched the grains fall through his fingers.

'Dreadful,' Bertie will say, 'only dreadful, a terrible thing, who would have thought it.' And Gregory will drink too much, but not as much as Bertie, renew acquaintance with the locals, his English accent gradually losing itself in the sough, the hum, the babble of talk. Worse things have happened of course in the intervening years: suicides, patricides, infanticides, new-born babies found in hayricks, Balbriggan burnt, not to talk of the South Quay Barracks. However my death will have the symmetry of detail, obey the tragic unities, of time, of place, of action.

But Gregory has long perfected the sublimation of emotion, the smoothing of it into a convenient shroud. He suffers only in his own time and in private. He suffered a war and rarely spoke of it, and now suffers a death and can barely speak of it. He finishes his whiskey and ginger ale, bids the company goodnight and makes his way, on admirably steady legs, towards the stairs with the wagon-wheel dangling from the ceiling. He mounts them towards the fourteenth and last room of the Wheel Inn, falls on the bed fully dressed and is instantly asleep.

Two hours later he is instantly awake again, the preternatural alertness too much alcohol can bring. He opens the window for fresh air, gazes across the fields at the distant house, framed by the desultory shapes of trees. He imagines for a moment I am gazing back at him, a pair of eyes behind the broken panes of glass, as restless, as unsatisfied as his.

And how can I explain my eye that is bloodless, fleshless, my sight that is constant, the dark that comes down and envelopes it but doesn't let it sleep? How I am everywhere and nowhere? The moments I have lived unwind before with the moments unlived, both numbered by the same clock. I am your perfect narrator, inhabit then and now, dance between both, am nothing but my story and my story seems already endless. There are rules to my condition but I haven't learned them yet, haven't learned to cross the river to the dull sea that laps beyond it, can see but not reach that window open in that hotel across those fields, those desultory trees, can sense those eyes that stare towards mine in that insomniac room. A grave would have done the trick in a vampire story, in a tale of horror like the ones I once screamed in, would have given this consciousness rest and finality, the blankness of non-being. But being I have and substance none, and this man's father was your father's son. And he closes the windows then and unlike me, his half-sister, finally sleeps.

~

Would half ever become whole, she wondered, as Dan Turnbull drove them, Father, Mother, Gregory and Nina, towards Drogheda. A Saturday, the morning after he arrived, and maybe, she thought, half already had become whole since she couldn't for the life of her remember a time all three of them had travelled together. He sat beside her in the back, Mamma and Father with Dan up in front, as Dan lazily nuzzled Garibaldi's ears with the riding crop.

'Half,' she murmured, 'that's what I called you, Half.'

'Half what?' he asked. His clothes were stitched and restitched, the elbows of his jacket reinforced with leather patches. He had a tweedy homespun poverty about him that was genteel and lonely all at once.

'Just Half,' she said. She wondered, glancing slyly at the uncut hair that tufted over his back collar, how much his mother missed him. She decided it must be a lot.

'You're my half-brother,' she said, 'not my whole brother.'

'If that's the case, then you're not my whole sister either.'

'Then neither of us is whole.'

'No, we're both halfs.' And she heard him giggle, for the first time.

'I would really hate to be a quarter,' he said, and it was her turn to laugh. She watched her father in front, the wind coursing off his greying hair, and knew he had heard their laughter and was pleased. Her mother beside him sat stiffly, apparently unconcerned.

She held her hand up towards him and said, 'Let's measure.'

'Measure what?' he asked.

'Hands, silly.'

So he held his hand up to hers and she saw how one fitted into the other, almost half the size.

'Half,' she said, 'my hand is half of yours.' Then she dropped her voice, to create a bubble around them in the back that they couldn't hear up front. 'I can show you something in Drogheda, if you keep being nice.'

'What can you show me in Drogheda?' he asked, and he still pronounced the 'gh' wrong, which made her like him even more.

'I can show you,' she whispered, 'the shrunken head of a saint that was chopped off by the English.'

'You're trying to scare me again,' he whispered back and she squeezed his hand to assure him she wasn't.

They made their way along the river past the warehouses and a smell of burnt butter filled the car from the margarine factory across the way.

'Does everything in Ireland smell?' he asked

'Probably,' she said, 'but I live here so I don't notice. What does it smell like to you?'

'Fish.'

'That's not fish,' she said, 'that's margarine from the margarine factory across the river.'

'Well, it smells like the fishmarket in Clerkenwell to me.'

Dan drew Garibaldi to a halt on the Quays and they got out and sure enough the air smelt of imminent rain and fish, and she wondered why she hadn't smelt it before. And Father took his hand and Mamma took hers and they walked down Shop Street to Gallagher's, where they replaced his overstitched jacket and his unevenly threaded trousers for smart new ones. Nina watched him with his hands held out while the Gallagher tailor marked his sleeves with chalk. She noted the fingers again, long and tapering, and when the jacket was back on the tailor's dummy and the tailor was making adjustments, she took his hand and slipped him out of the side door, across the street, into the vast gloom of the cathedral.

'Do you pray?' he asked her.

'No,' she told him, 'but I'm interested in martyrdoms.'

The cathedral seemed to whisper as they walked down the aisle but it was only, she noted, the murmur of prayers from the ladies bent over the wooden pews.

'You're a Zoroastrian,' she said, again proud that she remembered each syllable.

'I didn't say I was one. But I might be, some day.'

'Do Zoroastrians have martyrdoms?'

'I'm not sure what martyrdoms are.'

'Flayings,' she said, 'quarterings, boilings and decapitations. Like there.' And she drew him towards the centre nave where under the glass casket the small shrivelled head lay.

'It's black,' he said, 'like a pygmy.'

'It's only black,' she told him, 'because it's two hundred years old. And that's why it's shrivelled too. But the question you have to ask yourself is, if you were asked by Oliver Cromwell, do you believe in the Assumption of the Virgin Mary, and you knew they'd cut your head off if you said no, what answer would you give?'

'That sounds like a trick question,' he said, moving round the glass casket to get a better look. 'I mean, does it matter what you believe once your head is cut off?'

'It does if you're a martyr.'

'I thought if you're a martyr your head was already cut off.'

'Clever clever,' she said, 'I meant if you want to be a martyr.'

'I'm not sure I want to be a martyr,' he said.

So she led him back down the aisle and told him that if Miss Cannon asked him that question, his answer definitely was not the one to give.

They made it back to the draper's when the last threads were being pulled from his new jacket.

'Where did you two get to?' her mother asked, and Nina saw that she avoided his eye.

'We went to the cathedral and said a prayer,' Nina lied, 'didn't we, Gregory?'

'We did,' said Gregory. 'We gave thanks to God for my new family.'

Mother smiled tersely, caught his eye and looked away. Nina looked directly at him, hoping to catch him out in a smile, a giggle, an explosion of involuntary laughter. But Gregory returned her gaze with unsmiling lips, with expressionless green eyes, until his left eyelash fluttered down once, in a wink. And Nina returned his expressionless gaze and resolved to get him to teach her, as soon as possible, that fluttering wink.

George and Janie were waiting by the gates on the following Monday as she walked down with Gregory in his new jacket and trousers and his shiny shoes.

'This is Gregory, my brother,' Nina said grandly.

'You just got a brother?' George asked breathlessly. 'How can you just get a brother?'

'He was posted from England, weren't you, Gregory?'

And Gregory agreed, he had been sent from the depot for lost brothers via Royal Mail, arriving at our doorstep several days later.

'What's it like to be posted?' George asked, while Janie tried to kick him into silence.

Shade

'The worst thing,' said Gregory, 'is the taste of brown paper and the itching of the twine. Otherwise His Majesty's postal service is a perfectly fine way to travel.'

Janie laughed then, unwillingly, and George laughed too, although in a way that revealed he didn't really get the joke. 'You're a liar,' he said, 'you weren't posted.'

'I was,' said Gregory. 'And to prove it, I still have the stamp in my pocket.' He reached into his pocket and Nina wondered how he was going to wriggle out of this one, but his hand came out with a stamp between two fingers, which he passed to George. George examined the stamp with forensic concentration as they walked between the hayricks towards Miss Cannon's school. And once inside, as the class rose for prayers, Nina realised why Gregory would never have to face his martyrdom, when Miss Cannon excused him on the grounds that he was Protestant.

'C of E,' Gregory said. 'It's a different thing.'

'I think not,' said Miss Cannon, and so he sat while the class stood and sang their hymns to Mary.

'Why didn't you say Zoroastrian?' Nina whispered through the hymn. He smiled up at her and hissed, 'Because I haven't decided.'

They took him to the mudflats of Mozambique after school, and surprised a heron in one of the stagnant pools. With his new shoes sinking in the browning mud, he seemed as exotic as that bird with its long neck and its dangling legs.

'Nobody is posted,' George said, returning to the theme, 'I don't believe you were posted.'

'I came by boat and train,' said Gregory, 'but that's the way the post travels, so I was posted in a way. Posted, but not wrapped.'

'Who posted you then?' asked George.

'My mother,' said Gregory, 'licked a stamp and stuck in on my forehead and pinned the address to my coat.'

'What address?' asked Janie.

'My sister's,' he said. 'Nina's.' And as it was the first time he had used the word sister, Nina felt an inordinate pleasure, a pleasure that seemed to creep up on her the way the mud oozed through her barefoot toes.

Mozambique proved to be inadequately mapped for him; the conceit of the nomenclature he found pleasing, but inordinately broad. If you have a Mozambique, he told them, you need a Zanzibar, you need a Congo, you need a Sudan, you need a Nile, a Kilimanjaro, a Sahara and an Indian Ocean beyond it. They already had a Sahara, they told him, and so he named the beating waves beyond the dunes of the Sahara the Indian Ocean, the two runnelled canals that bordered the mudflats he called the Nile and the Limpopo, and the stretch of scrub with the waist-high bushes became the Congo.

'Explorers,' he told George, 'are quite specific about boundaries, and boundaries, once fixed, can never be altered.'

'So we're explorers?' asked George, with all the tentative hesitation of one genuinely entering new territory.

'You can be an explorer or a native,' Gregory opined graciously. 'It's up to each individual.'

So George elected to be native, a choice he regretted when he learnt the lot of the native was to carry the goods and chattels of explorers and spent the rest of the afternoon burdened with four schoolbags, Janie's, Nina's, Gregory's and of course his own.

'Is Cleopatra native?' Nina asked Gregory, since he had become a source of universal authority.

'Well now,' he sighed and stopped, and surveyed his vast and variegated kingdom.

'Cleopatra,' he said finally, 'is a native queen and thus occupies a different category.'

'Fine,' said Nina, 'then I'll be Cleopatra.'

'You can't,' he retorted, ever specific, 'because we haven't got an Egypt yet.'

'Yes we do,' she said, 'how can you have a Nile without an

Egypt, since the Nile runs into Egypt? So I'm Cleopatra and I'm going to look for Moses in the bulrushes on the banks of the Nile.'

So the boundaries that were to be fixed and never altered changed on an instant, and George found himself lumbered with an added burden, that of fanning Nina with a large dockleaf as she waded, dress held up above her knees, in her Nile, secure in the knowledge that her own fancy could sometimes match that of her new half-brother's.

16

Y ES, A GRAVE would have done the trick in a horror film. A
  funeral beforehand, plumed horses moving towards a misty
graveyard. And that Gregory has come for a funeral, a funeral
lacking its grave, becomes evident the next day as he drives up
once more to the sunlit gates with Brid, Emer and Granny
Moynihan. They have buckets and mops and bleach and floor
polish and a vacuum cleaner, which rattles in the boot. They
assault the house with a vengeance, and as Gregory retreats from
the gathering clouds of dust, Granny Moynihan mutters through
her whiskered lips, 'She deserves a proper house for a proper
funeral, God rest her soul.'

Brid Moynihan wipes the grime off a Moreau cupid, bought in
Francis Street, Dublin, restored in Aungier Street, the sculpted
glass flambeau long broken, replaced by a bare bulb and a
Chinese shade. She talks as she cleans, a fractured litany of
gossip, about the body not found, the brother returned, the
scandal in the townland when he first arrived, how the mother,
God rest her soul, was the one they pitied.

'No, the father,' retorts Emer, 'a nicer man never walked the
banks of that river, remembered kindly even now for the factory
he built there, the employment he gave, they were the good days,
of course, before all the trouble happened.'

'If he's remembered that kindly,' counters Brid, 'how come
they burnt it down?'

'Blackguards,' mutters Granny, now and then.

'It was the times that was in it,' Emer returns, 'they would have
burnt a pigsty if they could have, burnt everything from England,

except their coal. His only crime, after all, was being from there and living here, but then no-one in this house ever had a flitter of luck.'

And on that they're both agreed, and Granny most of all. Luck was never at a premium here, and the thought must be a gossip stopper, since Granny quietly blesses herself as she begins on the piano, and Brid and Emer move in blessed silence from the Moreaus to the pictures lining the walls.

But the house doesn't know it's cursed or haunted or that it never had any luck. The house knows nothing. The house simply endures, accepts the clouds of frenetic dust Granny Moynihan is raising with her dutiful daughters. The brick is lifeless and comforting for that too, the wallpaper merely hangs, grown bubbled, yellow, mildewed, and accepts being brushed to some semblance of its former glory as readily as it departed from that glory. The silver on the mirrors, mottled with time, reflects dutifully the shapes of the living who brush it clean and even gaze at it fitfully, tucking the mousebrown hair behind the reddened ear as Emer does now, having moved from the dustfree picture frame.

I could grow fond of this quality, this absence of being, this sense of objects quite denuded of association, as in a random photograph. This placid emptiness of things. The blue satin curtains don't resist when Granny Moynihan beats them with her duster, the greying paint on the woodwork doesn't complain when washed back to its former cream.

And had I even wanted to buttress the Moynihans' sense of the house as cursed or haunted, to topple that Japanese vase so it shattered on the marble fireplace, hear the silence descend, the questioning hushed and hurried – did you do that? I swear I didn't, you must have brushed off it surely, I was over by the window Mammy, how could I have brushed off it, mother of God between us and all harm, didn't I tell you – even if I wanted to, I couldn't. My being is as still, as unmanifest as the old oak hunting table, shining now, like the crystal that sits on top of it. But I can take something like pleasure in this semblance of newness, this restoration of the things I placed here to the cleanliness that was their former state.

And the thought strikes me, if thoughts can strike something such as me, that that old oak table, bought at auction in the Grange Estate after old Mr Huntingdon died, oval in shape, pitted with indentations of grain under the coats of varnish, that table has more substance than I have. It can gather dust and be swept free of dust, it can accept the weight of Emer's rear upon it, as she sits on it for a rest, wipes her forehead and says, 'Fag-break Mammy'.

'So what's the story?' Emer asks, igniting a Sweet Afton with a match, inhaling deeply, words emerging with the smoke from her capacious lungs. 'It'll go to Gregory, won't it, lock, stock and barrel? They were as thick as thieves always, the two of them, no room for third parties. Forget Janie, forget poor mad George who would have lain down and brayed among the hayricks to the full moon for her and probably did. Was there ever anyone else but her or him? There could be though, and now that I think about it, probably, is, a child somewhere.'

'What,' says Emer, 'you mean his?'

'No,' says Brid, 'hers. Like father like daughter. I mean no offence now, Mammy, but they don't live like you or I.'

'Actresses?' asks Granny Moynihan.

'No,' says Emer, 'Protestants.'

'She made her first communion with the lot of you,' says Granny.

'She may have worn the white dress and swallowed the host the body of Christ and all that, but that doesn't make her Catholic. Only showed she didn't care. All I'm saying is there may be a child in England, France, even America with some actor or producer boyo of a father. And if there is, that child'll give Gregory a run for his money.'

'How?' yelps Brid, breathing smoke if not fire.

'On the inheritance front.'

'Well, if there is a child swimming round somewhere,' says Granny, 'there's nothing like an inheritance to bring them up for air. But if you ask me, they'd all be well shot of this place, child or no.'

My only child, though, was him.

~

'Don't look now,' she told him, one afternoon in the piano room while he was practising his scales. 'But she's there.'

'Who?'

'Hester.'

And I am there, of course, always there, can see them both against the dark hulk of the instrument, the grey light of the window fleshing out their young figures. Gregory, dressed in trousers already too short for him. Nina, in a yellow cardigan and a green plaid skirt.

'The mirror.'

'Don't tell fibs.'

'I'm not telling fibs. Never about her. Just do what you're doing.'

'I'm doing scales.'

'Then keep doing scales. No. Come down here.' She squatted on all fours, crept beneath the piano legs. He seemed alone in the room for a moment, and terrified.

'Stop doing this.'

'I'll stop when you come down here.'

And he obeyed, of course, as he always did. Crept down, so close to her he could hear his heart beating.

'There,' she said, 'watch. Her feet.'

And the wind blew the dust on the floor, a silken sheen of it, from the mirror to the piano stool. The pitifully fair hairs on his arms stood up.

'Don't be frightened,' she says. 'She's a friend.'

'She's nobody.'

'How could anybody be nobody?'

'You're making this up.'

'Why would I make it up?'

'To frighten me. But I won't be frightened.'

She felt the hairs on his thin arms, like sticklebacks. She clasped her hand around his.

'Shall I shut up about her then?'

'Please.'

'But wouldn't you rather know what's there?'

'There's no-one there.'

'All right. There's no-one there. Get out from under the piano then.'

'No.'

'Why not if there's no-one there?'

'I like it here.' And his hand stayed in hers.

'All right,' he says, 'I give up. She is there.'

'So?'

'So? Tell me about her.'

'Her name's Hester.'

'You told me that. Tell me something different.'

'She wears a fur coat and a black hat.'

'So? It's cold wherever she is.'

'Is it cold here?'

'Not particularly.'

'So, she's here and she's not here . . .'

'Where would she be if she's not here?'

'I don't know. Home.'

'But surely this is her home?'

'Yes. Ghosts stay around when they die.'

'Where did she die?'

'Here. It has to be here. And there has to be a reason.'

'A reason for what?'

'A reason she's a ghost. Why does one stay around and not the others?'

'Which others?'

'All the others who died.'

'It'd be too crowded.'

'Ha ha. No, she stays because she has something to tell us.'

'What?'

'I don't know yet.'

His hand grew warmer in hers. 'Can we stop this now?'

'No,' she said. 'Not yet. Hester has a secret message to give you.'

'What message?'

'This one,' she said, and kissed him.

Under the piano, her lips touching his, I remember the boyish tautness of the mouth and the smell of surprise. The hairs on his arms all stood to attention. Like soldiers, like sheaves of wheat released from wind, like new-mown grass.

'Now,' she said, 'we have the same ghost.'

So he agreed to Hester, he admitted her, came to acknowledge her, and once having done so, being the studious, bookish English boy he was, he had to find a history for her. From the Empire period he imagined, given her description of the waisted coat and the hat that was shaped like a bonnet, but not quite. And they played together, with histories of their ghost, the inevitably sad and tragic circumstances of its untimely demise. When one ran out of details, the other gladly filled in.

The ghost was young, of course, young enough to be beautiful, thin of waist and delicate in complexion, always on the run from some unwarranted doom. Running from what, he wondered. From the forces of the Crown, she said, triumphantly, relishing the burr of history in the phrase she didn't fully understand. Lord Edward Fitzgerald, he decided, was the ghost's sweetheart, if Regency indeed was the period. They had been disturbed, of course, in the love-seat below the curved window, doing sweet-heart things, and she had run downstairs to distract their attention while out of the window and over the valleyed roofs he made his valiant escape. And many months later, after he had died of suspected suicide, an unwilling disembowelment with a rusty knife, she herself had leapt to join him from the window through which he had made his escape so valiant.

But if the period was Empire, he concluded, she needed a different history entirely. The ghost was an actress, he decided, who had travelled up from Smock Alley in Dublin for the Michaelmas festivities and was wandering round the corridors in preparation for her entry on to the small ballroom stage. As what, Nina wondered. And that was simple for Gregory. As a ghost.

Hester. The name itself suggested more urgent histories, like illustrated pages flicking over in a storybook. She had drowned crossing the Boyne when it was frozen over, the spider-cracks spreading in the ice beneath her high-heeled boots. She had died in childbirth, out of wedlock, was buried in a pauper's grave, had walled herself in behind the bricks of the coal-cellar . . . He invented litanies of deaths for her, none approaching the grotesque reality. And in school he drew wraithlike images of her on his slate during prayers, from which he was, being C of E, excused. Prayers to the Virgin, with which he is unfamiliar, to that tiny statue in the niche above the blackboard with her stiff plaster arms and her stiff blue cloak, pray for us who have recourse to thee. He confused them both, understandably, in his musings, his daydreams, two ghosts, both of them female, undemanding and both, apparently, everywhere.

But this was a new Hester, theirs alone, not George's, not Janie's, not anyone's in the whole breathing world. A Hester that belonged to the mist curling round the morning haystacks, to the pigeon's chuckle in the haybarn, to the owl's hoot at night, echoing round the house and the river. They attributed random events to her, unexplained events: a hen's egg floating in the well, a badger's pawprints on the front drive, milk turned sour on the kitchen steps, those rapid showers that swept across those flat fields, caught them unawares, drenching them only to vanish again. She became the cause and the repository of all lost things, socks, combs, pennies, stamps, laces, picture books, balls of all kinds – beach, cricket, golf and tennis, lawn and table, hurley and bat. She became the symbol, the embodiment of their uniqueness, their fraternity and sorority, their secret language.

The silences that fell over dinner, father lost in his glass of milk, mother sniffing distastefully at the whiff of dried fish, the gap that had grown between them with his arrival became a vast chasm that only Hester could fill. The space between the chink of cutlery and chomp of chewing became hers, they wedged eyes across the table and smiled complicitly at the unseen presence there. Her, me, or Hester. She would have approved, they felt, of the hours they spent in the barn, faces down in the prickly pile, her legs kicking his above. She was their game. Hester says, do this, do that, Hester says touch your toes, stamp your feet, Hester says hide and kiss me.

17

THE CATHOLIC CHURCH on the crest of the hill can be seen from the curved window on the upper hallway, with the graveyard beside it meandering towards the estuary wall, its granite spire tapering towards the grey March sky. Gregory walks up the grassed road towards it, his tan gaberdine flapping open on his shoulders, the buttons undone. The church door opens as he reaches the wrought-iron gate and a priest emerges, his small shape bent in a curve of vicarious sorrow. Gregory shakes his hand; he has made an appointment, he has been expected.

'Mr Hardy,' he murmurs, 'my condolences, a dreadful business even in these dreadful days. No, I didn't know her, she never graced St Agnes's with her presence as far as I recall, and ours is a small parish, a small congregation, I would have remembered. Perhaps she worshipped St Peter's in Drogheda or worshipped alone, no harm in that, no harm at all, who among us can cast the first stone. As to the issue of a service, a funeral mass, we would be delighted of course, privileged even, given her notoriety – no, wrong word that – given her stature, her reputation, her fame. What we need is her baptismal certificate and the issue of remains, now how can I put it, the issue of remains remains to be clarified, the Archbishop of course could guide us in this, there must be precedents, *requiem sans corpus*, an empty coffin need cause no offence, no scandal. No, the only scandal would actually reside in no mass, no service, no funeral rites, so of course, given the appropriate clearances, the baptismal certificate, the permissions, we will be happy to oblige . . .'

Stones in my coffin to give it weight, he wants a service to remember me, never religious my Gregory, C of E, how could he be, but afflicted with an almost Roman sense of duty, a pagan perception of the wastelands beyond this aching world. *Et in arcadio ego*, and I remember, of course, I posed for it once, the shepherdess by the massive gravestone, the skull peeping from the tangled, dying grasses round my sandalled feet and the muscled rustic below me gorging on a bunch of grapes. He wants to send me to that paradise but he doesn't know – how could he, his whole life spent in the pursuit of the quotidian – where or what that paradise is.

And then perhaps it's more subtle than that, more complicated. He wants to perform the rite in the oldest sense, as family, to remember me and even more, perhaps, to finish me, finally put me to rest. He could remember well that which he buries here, which he puts to rest in that tiny graveyard tumbling towards the river's mouth. He could remember it well in its purest, Platonic form. And as the priest moves into that dark interior, which seems to Gregory old, unshowy, plain but plangent, only one word comes to mind. Rest. So put me please to rest, my Gregory, bury the me you held inside you all those years – that gamine, thin, small-breasted teenage sister.

He walks inside then with the old priest, into the oaken interior, the wheat-coloured walls and the crumbling plaster. 'A donation,' murmurs the priest, 'yes, that would indeed be welcome, there are of course certain costs fixed by the parish but a donation over and above would be most gratefully received. The roof needs work, the flashing on the gutters needs replacing, a hard rain and a wind from the west and our little church weeps all by itself. And the rains, you can imagine, are considerable.'

Gregory leaves, blessing himself at the outside font with the wrong hand. He walks back from the church with a quickened gait. Something has been achieved although he's not sure what, the first spade in the grave has been turned, the ivy cleared, the coffin waxed and something done eases that ache, that scald of memory which he wants to quench and cannot. The church's spire sits behind his head like a conical hat, the fuchsia hedges of the little lane sprout either side of his shoulders like a bat's wings or a pantomime witch's cloak. The wind blows from the river, ruffles the water, darkens the grasses like a cosmic chuckle.

The dead are laughing. An empty coffin, an incense-burner wafted over an absent corpse, why wouldn't they be? But it's a forced laugh, the awful throaty wheeze of a joke badly told, the music-hall comedian sweating in the limelight with his rehearsed lines and his cackle that begs for a response in kind. The dead laugh because the ending's always the same, and, like the catastrophe in the old comedy, always comes when you least expect it. And the laugh is forced because, pinioned by the footlights in our sweat-odoured wigs and our bad make-up, we know the sad punchline before it happens. The laugh is bilious because we don't want to be these rancid comedians, we want all the innocence, the unknowing of that throng beyond the flaring limelight, whose laughter answers us in obedient waves.

Death envies life. It longs, weeps, pines, retches for that condition even at its bleakest. And as Gregory walks down the church lane with the ache inside him almost visible, I want to whisper to him, treasure the ache, the pain that seems as if it will never end, because the joke that you don't see coming is that it will.

Any feeling is better than none, my sweet, my unwhole brother. I could almost touch the penumbra of that ache as he walks on down, beneath the grey, quiet winter skies, towards his car by the graveyard gates. But it's not enough to ache, he must remember too. And so he drives towards the Drogheda Quays, underneath the viaduct, over St Mary's bridge, underneath the margarine factory, down that long road with the mulched river to his left now, and above him the bowed sycamore trees. We would cycle our bikes on weekends this way, the four of us, and only when we had reached this stretch, where the trees umbrellaed over the road and the sun danced through the shifting leaves, would we feel we were on the other side.

There are no leaves above him now, but bare brown spindles against the grey clouds. He passes Mornington and follows the road towards the river's mouth on the Bettystown side. The waves curl and do their pointless beating on the low stone waterbreaks. Our father's factory is a roofless ruin. He stops the car for the briefest moment and looks through the rusting girders at the trickle of water in the neap tide sludge. He drives on then, past the newly-fenced golf-course to the Maiden's Tower at the Boyne's southern mouth. Baltray sits low beneath the huge sky across the shifting water, smudges of dark green where the dunes meet the limp trees behind them, like those Dutch landscapes in the National Gallery. Those Dutch, as Michelangelo said, were only good for painting grass.

He parks the car in the crunching gravel, gets out, the shards of old scallop-shells beneath his boots. They are laced-up boots, not the elegant hand-stitched Jermyn Street shoes he wore yester-day. Shoes were always important to both of us. Fetishes, the portly young director told me in Gainsborough Studios, signa-tures of a hidden desire as he tried to get the camera below mine, below the high spindly heels he found erotic, in the hope it would take in the expanse of leg, the flare of skirt, the underwear above. And Gregory's boots now, neatly laced and polished, make their way across the broken scallop-shells, each step sounding like a crunched carrot. And I think, maybe it's true, fetishes – with him it was always shoes and hair, spit perfect, while the rest of him could happily look as if it had been dragged through a briar patch. The laced boots take him to the foul, shit-odoured entrance of the Maiden's Tower, and of course he shouldn't enter it but of course he will.

~

The Maiden's Tower, the Lady's Finger, the girl drowned in the
foaming waters. Hester. This estuarine landscape was populated
by dead women, Gregory concluded, all of them different, yet in
certain crucial details the same. Hester rarely moved beyond the
house and grounds, the Lady was buried somewhere beneath her
jutting finger, the girl was mired in the drowned seaweed. Of the
Maiden's Tower he knew nothing, other than that it rose from
the forbidden, Mornington side of the river. But he was determined all four of them would put this ignorance to right.

   The boat was lying in the shallows as it had been for months,
and it was a simple matter for four of them to drag it along the
dried mud, through the sand into the water. The oars were a different matter; they had to be stolen from the punts left abandoned for the long weekend by the salmon fishermen. George
walked along the water's edge, dragging a poacher's line through
the water, to which were attached, instead of poached salmon
bass, the two stolen oars. He slotted them into the rowlocks of
their chosen boat and lifted Janie on his back through the
shallow water, then Nina, while Gregory removed his shoes and
rolled his trousers up to his white speckled knees. George had
grown since Nina first met him by the chestnut tree, into something close to a youth, bigger than her, muscles already defined
on his chest. But as if his body still remembered its childlike
status, he kept his eyes cast to the ground, his shoulders bowed,
willing himself smaller. Once out on the river with the oars in his
hands, though, he felt instantly at home, and rowed with a fluid,
animal grace. He knew every current in that river by reputation,
through his father's hearsay, so he rowed them out towards sea
initially, to take advantage of the tide's incoming pull. Nina took
her shoes off, tucked her skirt between her knees, displaying her
smooth tapering calves to the wind and to the world.

   Nina told them the legend of the Maiden's Tower, how she was
young, dark and beautiful and waited each day for the return of
her lover from the wars.

'Which wars?' asked Gregory, ever specific.

'The Thirty Years War, the Ten Years War, the Half A Day War, I don't know, any old war. There are always wars, aren't there, George?'

And George agreed, as he rowed. Wars were a constant.

And Nina elaborated. How the maiden watched the seas each day from the parapet; how the returning ship was to show a black sail if it bore his dead body, a white sail if it bore his living one; how a black-sailed ship hove into view on the horizon and she hurled herself to her death on the rocks below; how, climbing the steps of the tower to the parapet, you can still hear her weeping. How the Lady's Finger, looming towards them now in the centre of the swirling river, was built in her memory.

'Why her finger?' asked Gregory. 'Why not her hand, her neck, her head?'

'Why not her knee?' asked George, moving his eyes from Nina's knees to the obelisk of the Lady's Finger. He guided the boat round it and let the current pull him towards the shore, and the Maiden's Tower.

'Because the Lady's Knee doesn't sound quite right,' said Nina. 'And because on her finger she wore his wedding-ring.'

They pulled the boat to the shore under the shadow of the tower and walked over the crackling shells.

'I would still like to know which wars,' said Gregory.

'What are the possibilities?' asked Nina.

'Norman, Jacobite, Elizabethan.'

'Norman,' said Nina and pressed her back against the Norman corners of the tower, as the summer wind blew fine grains of sand along her arms, blew her dress between her legs.

'He came over here,' said Nina, 'with Strongbow. He was an archer with a bow so rigid that only he could pull it and the arrows he fired were always strong and true. He saw her picking cockles by the river's edge, a barefoot Irish girl with the kind of beauty that stopped his heart. He drew back his bow and fired a different kind of arrow that stopped her heart. And he built this tower for her, to keep her for his pleasure, away from prying eyes.'

'What kind of pleasure?' asked Gregory.

'All kinds of pleasure,' said Nina. 'And, being Norman, his pleasures were violent, sudden and extreme. Because the Normans invented the mailed suit, the knight on horseback, rapine and pillage and courtly love. Isn't that true, brother mine?' she asked Gregory.

'And the Norman tower,' said Gregory.

'Now place your sturdy back, George, against this tower and let this lady effect her entry.'

And George, ever obedient, leaned his back against the tower wall and cupped his hands and held them out for her feet to hoist her up. She placed her hands on his shoulders, her foot on his hands and clambered up above him to where the steps began. She wandered into the gloom and heard the wind whistling down the curving steps.

'I can hear her,' she said, 'crying.'

'It's the wind,' said Gregory.

'No,' she said, 'it's the maiden.'

Janie clambered over George in turn and Gregory followed suit. He held out his hand for George, and as George grabbed it, scrabbling with his boots against the Norman stone, Nina tickled Gregory's armpit. George fell back down and muttered, 'Damn you, Nina Hardy.'

'The maiden's lover is away,' said Nina, 'and she finds herself torn. Should she admit this callow Irish youth, or keep up her lonely vigil? The maiden finds herself tempted.'

Nina reached her own hand down. He grasped it in his and Gregory held her from behind to bear his weight.

'Unhand me,' she whispered, as his barrelled shape made it into her arms, 'and consider my virtue. I'm Irish like you.'

There was blood on his cheekbone where the Norman stone

had grazed it. 'Let me kiss it better,' she murmured as if in apology, and she did. And he blushed as her lips met his cheek and the muscle in his trousers leapt with surprise. She withdrew her lips with a streak of red on them, like lipstick. Then she ran from him, as if propelled by an arrow, towards the light above.

"Hark! The maiden cried. Methinks a boat approaches—"

Thin stone steps curled upwards, softened by centuries of ascending feet. There were apertures every half-circle or so through which the sunlight poured, blurring the cut stone edges. She darted up them, leaving the smell of dried excrement behind her and wondering what she looked like from below, where she could hear their feet clattering, gaining on hers.

At the top the blast of wind enveloped her, wiping her clean of the fine down of sand. She lay down on the cold stone and heard a hum as if there were a bell-jar above her, a whorl of privacy and peace that left her below, untouched. She heard Gregory's feet and then saw the shoes he was so proud of, no longer immaculate.

'The maiden lies most days on the cold stone,' she said, 'pining for her lover's kiss.' She turned her head on the flagstone and saw Gregory above her, slowly-moving clouds behind his head, framed by the tower walls. 'She dreams of far-off castles and dusky maidens and wonders is he with one now.'

'One what?' asked Gregory.

'One dusky, sloe-eyed Abyssinian maid.'

'He's in Africa?'

'In the Holy Land, silly. Crusading.'

George's head behind Gregory's, then. Above them, blue, and the slowly-moving puffs of white.

'Lift me up.'

They both reached down. She gripped two hands, one long-fingered, delicate, one squat, like a spade. She pulled herself up like a straight rod, her hair dangling backwards. 'She stands on the parapet. She mistakes the white horses on the ocean for sails.'

The stone steps led up to a buttress. Nina mounted them, one by one. 'She grows bored with waiting, bored with watching.'

'Come down, Nina,' George whispered.

'Her lover pleads with her to come down. But her eyes stay glued to the horizon.'

George reached out his hand. She grasped it, leaned outwards, beyond the parapet. The wind scorched up the tower wall, blew her dress into a frenzy.

'And then she sees it. A sail. Unmistakably black.'

George pulled her towards him and she turned in his arms, her own arms crossing her breast like a bow.

'She can't help herself.'

And she couldn't, as the wind surged upwards, blew her hair around her face, turned her dress into a balloon, which she tried to smooth with one hand, the other holding his arm for balance, when she lost hers, swayed backwards and he reached out for her, too late, and they both tumbled into the mad air.

She could see herself falling, floating down like a dandelion pod, her troubled fantasy of tower and maiden unravelling in descent, her dress blown upwards in the wind, then reassuming its more proper configuration as gravity took over her upper body, George clinging to her, crying as he plummeted, the two long syllables that made up her name. She didn't recognise the name, though, she had become someone else, someone nameless, someone she didn't know, waiting for the sail, black or was it white, like the white sand rushing towards her, the wind pulling her hair backwards like a bonnet or a scarf.

She bounced like a broken doll, off the beautiful white sand-dune, and the sand hardly harmed her, spread out in a scallop, but George falling next did all of the damage, his knotty weight crushing her beneath him, his elbow shattering four ribs, his knee breaking her pelvis, his face whipping forwards to meet hers in a bloody kiss. They rolled then, raising a plumed feather of sand in the wind, and tumbled to a dead halt in one another's arms.

18

THERE ARE GRANITE blocks now stacked below the entrance where George let us use him as staircase, and Gregory climbs them into the gloom inside. The odour is the same after decades, though the light is different, wintry, and the temperature is cold. A breeze cuts down from above, and the apertures are barely defined by the dying light outside, almost a match to the darkness within. He climbs the indented steps and by the time he reaches the top, night has almost fallen. An endless stream of white caps dots the horizon and on the distant golf-course the last golfers are hurrying to the Captain's bar. The sand-dunes below have been shifted by the decades of wind and if I'd fallen now I would have bounced off the hard shale and died anyway. He walks the final steps up to the parapet and stands where we stood before the fall. He looks down at his laced boots and sees the sweep of the wall fall away below them. Then he hears the sound of another's feet and grips the buttress to steady himself. He hears a match flaring, the scraping of the red head off the sandpaper, and turns and sees the face behind the reddened glow inhale, brown eyes, the skin around them wrinkled with the years, small scurfed lips. He recognises the face from its earlier version and says her name. Janie.

'I could see you,' she says, 'I could see your car taking the road by the river, so slow that it looked like it was remembering. I come here once or twice a month, look out over the golf-course, over the river to Baltray, and indulge in the same activity. But what is it, Gregory, remembering? Is it revisiting the past in all its remembered detail, or is it trying to find that bit, that pivotal bit, we can't remember?'

'The latter, I would say.'

'Well, if it's that, then we use the wrong word for it, don't we? Trying for that bit we can't remember is not remembering, it's more like digging, gouging into the forgotten, asking why it is forgotten. And maybe it's forgotten because it needs to be, it's better that way. I like it up here though, like looking at the waves, the golf-course, the river, thinking of the black sail, the white sail, thinking of their fall from here, years ago, they almost died, could have saved us all this bother. And you could have called, Gregory, me of all people. You could have sent a polite note, Mr Hardy will be at home at the following hours, because, let's face it, it's not every day your brother murders your sister, is it?' She stubs out one cigarette, takes out another, holds the golden packet of Sweet Afton towards him. 'Do you want one,' and she adds the suffix, 'love?'

He takes one, though he doesn't smoke.

'No,' he says, 'it's not every day your brother murders your sister.'

'I walked him round the gardens,' she says, 'with the peelers and the doctor and asked him to give us a hint of where he had put her. And you know what, Gregory, it was the strangest thing. It looked like he was trying to remember too. Not where he'd dumped poor Nina's body, no – where we played by the river, where we swung on the swing, where we hosed him down when he got stuck in the silt, to remember everything but the bloody act of the day before or was it the day before that. And I've been trying to pinpoint the moment after which he never would get better, to remember it, I've been walking round here like a ghost revisiting, and I just can't do it. Was it here, when the two of them fell? Or after it, those weeks in the hospital when he grew like a bean-stalk? Or was it after, when he made the break with us, working in Keiling's fields with the dummies from Portrane? I got the schol-arship, remember, and your father did what he could, put me in the Siena Convent with Nina, and George became . . . George . . .

Or was it later when you both signed up, was it what happened in the Dardanelles? He never spoke about it, neither did you for that matter, how could you, you never came back. But he did, and he was missing a finger. Not the best move, maybe, with the way things were going. They gave him the mother and father of a hiding after they burnt the shellfish factory and he seemed strangely proud to receive it, walked around the townland with his battered face and his missing finger as if they were some kind of commendation from Lord Kitchener himself. But he was still George then, the George we knew, a damaged adult version, maybe, but still the brother I knew. We looked after him then in between his bouts of wandering, wherever, Lee-on-the-Solent, the South China Seas, but he always came back and at some stage, and I can't remember when, St Ita's Portrane became the only possible home from home for him. And by then I couldn't connect him any more to the brother I had. So, something happened. And I would love, more than the love of anything, more than the love of God, to know what it was. It got worse of course as the years went on, so that by the time she took over the house he was almost a boarder in St Ita's, and she took him, an act both noble and foolhardy, and ultimately, suicidal. Do you remember, Gregory, the times that he was right?'

'I do,' says Gregory and shivers. 'But is this the place to be having such a conversation?'

'Where else were you thinking?'

'Somewhere,' he says, and cannot help the cliché, 'a tad warmer.'

She is silent as he drives past the sand-swept golf-course, watching his profile against the lights of the cottages, against the darkness of the padlocked fairground. She can see the child she remembers there, like the faint imprint of the carvings they left on the chestnut tree. She shivers, as if the memory makes her colder, as he parks beside the rusting, silent cars.

'You remember,' says Janie as they approach the amber window-lights of the old thatched pub, 'the night Boxer Kavanagh took on five peelers after closing time?'

'I don't,' says Gregory.

'He of the seventeen children, by seven different farmer's wives, of the massive forearms and the breeze-block hands?'

'The life I lived here, Janie, seems like someone else's.'

The double doors of the pub swing open and they are inside, shivering, banging their hands together for warmth.

'An interlude,' he says.

'Interlude between what and what?' she asks.

'In the theatrical sense,' he says. 'Nina would have explained it better. A diversion, from what life was before, what it would be later. What'll it be, Janie?' he asks.

'Hot whiskey', she says, so he orders two, one for her, one for himself.

'I was Irish for seven years,' he says, 'and remember it as a diversion from a life that would have otherwise been ordered differently.'

'How differently?' she asks.

'Or a life that would have otherwise been ordered.'

'You seemed ordered enough to me,' she says, slipping the lemon from the drink through her teeth, 'but then you always seemed that, ordered to a fault.'

'Then why can I look on it like a dream, a dream of someone else's life with everything clearer than it should be?'

'If it's that clear, how come you don't remember Boxer Kavanagh and the five peelers?'

'Ever literal, Janie,' he says, and she laughs.

'I remember that laugh,' he says, 'and it is good to hear it, I remember it as clearly as the gap between your front teeth.'

She closes her mouth self-consciously and the laugh becomes a snigger. 'It was always her,' she says, 'always her could make me laugh, bend me over double, but the thing is I had to laugh, not because the joke was funny but because a laugh was what she expected. She'd put on that high-toned voice, come out with a quip or a quote and my job, pure and simple in the scheme of things, was to laugh at it.'

'The scheme of things,' says Gregory, 'what scheme of things?'

'I was smaller than her, slower than her, more timid than her, much poorer than her, less pretty than her. I was less, little Miss Less, in every possible way. That was the scheme of things, and so I laughed when bidden. But enough about me. Tell me about you, your interlude.'

'I never knew I had a sister, or a half-sister, till I came here.'

'Half-sister.'

'Yes. Two halfs, she said, trying to make a whole.'

'Did you ever make a whole?'

'Yes, for seven years. And you realise in retrospect, the inter-lude was in fact the play. These bits on either side, the before and after, your life, perhaps, but the interlude was where the drama was and everything else was . . . pale in comparison. I came to this country I never thought I would see, to this house I had never imagined to see, across the kitchen table the sister I never knew I had. And every moment after that, seven years of moments, all charged with the possibility of loss – loss of what you never knew you had, which you felt wasn't really yours, didn't deserve to be yours. I was a brother here, had a family for seven years, and when I left that life vanished, and whenever I came back, that life returned. It was only possible here, this townland, the sea, the river. And I got to thinking I had dreamt this life, the sea, the river, I had dreamt her and she had dreamt me.'

'You were her dream of a brother, you mean,' says Janie, smiling knowingly.

'Compliments will get you nowhere,' he says and tries to smile.

'No,' says Janie, way ahead of him, 'they never do.'

'You're laughing at me,' he says and she agrees, 'Yes, a little,' and leans over to flick that ash off his cigarette and touches his hand, gently, then strokes his finger, teasingly, and says, 'But really, enough about you, about my brother, nothing half about him, what was the point beyond which he lost it, retreated into that place of madness that would allow him to . . .' And she shivers, and sucks on her cigarette.

'I slept beside him till he got too big for the bed, he was the toddler, the little one with the blond hair and the nose that always needed wiping. And the reason you found me on the tower was I was wondering was that the day it all went wrong for him. The day he fell, with Nina. I remember looking down, they seemed to float, like those dandelion seeds we used to blow, float, until they hit the sand, and even when they hit the sand it didn't seem real, it puffed out around them like dust from a carpet-beater. Was that the day, I often wonder, when he changed from one thing to another? He came out of hospital, remember, six weeks later, and he'd sprouted, grown enormous, we couldn't call him little any more . . .'

~

She awoke in the hospital with tubes sticking out of her and a dim memory of the feel of sand on her cheek. A face bent towards her in the largest, whitest bonnet she had ever seen. 'Little girl,' the voice said, 'little girl, don't fret now, don't try to talk. You had an accident, you're in St Michael's Drogheda and all shall be well, very well.'

And of course talk was the first option she tried, making acquaintance with the metal braces round her jaw, twisting her body to make further acquaintance with the plaster round her hip and an agonising pain that made the white light burn whiter. The bonneted one smiled, as if pleased to receive such confirmation of her initial advice, then sailed slowly on through the ward on invisible feet. Nina closed her eyes, relaxed back into her multiple supports and tried to dream her way out of pain.

She came to again as another bonneted head, a black one this

time, her mother's, bent towards her. She smelt the odour of for-
maldehyde and fish-scales and recognised, behind her mother's
bonnet, her father with his greying hair tangled, his cap in his
hand, moist eyes reaching out to embrace her till his wife, her
mother, motioned him back.

'No, my love, don't excite her, the nurses said she shouldn't
move.'

'What larks, Nina love,' he said, 'what a fall, eh?' He clucked
his tongue and tried to smile, but she could see the tears interfer-
ing with the reassurance in his eyes. 'Georgie,' he said, 'is in the
boys' ward, hardly any the worse for wear than you are.'

Behind him, the dark shapes of trees through the oblong hospital windows, the grey-green walls and the shapes of those
bonnets moving, like large attendant butterflies. And behind him
another figure, motionless, staring blind, dressed in an old fur
coat, wellington boots and a black hat. Hello there, she thought,
you again, Hester.

And at night I can see her sleep, rigid in her casts and braces, her
head tossing in the millimetres left to it. I can see the flaws that
will develop in the adult face, the barely indented cheek, the tiny
scar above the left eye, the eye itself quite blind but moving with a
slow, lazy turn that would endear her to a public, those flaws that
mar the perfection, turn it into what is ordained to be beauty. I
had a real face, I was told, beautiful but real, which I always presumed meant not beautiful enough. The mouth was what defined
it though, full and downturned, with the promise of laughter at
its corners, a laughter deferred. Come Nina, I wanted to say,
mind how you go, walk out of here and change what will be your
history, choose, don't enter that turd-ridden megalithic tomb,
treasure your virginity, avoid those phosphorous-odoured lights,
see your father before he dies, love well but too much, take heed
of Rosalind. Don't take that boat to Liverpool, that train to
Brighton, beware those little accidents that will lead you to what

you will inevitably become, to me.

But she's sleeping now and a soft smile plays upon those lips, the smile for Gregory, for George, for Gregor-George. And even if I could disturb her sleep, I wouldn't.

~

George on the other hand lay sprawled in the boys' ward, the smell of stale sweat rising from his body, encased in blue striped pyjamas, the sheets twisting round his twisting body. He slept for six solid weeks, by which time she was up and about, casts off, braces almost gone, sitting by his bedside daily, waiting for him to wake. And when he emerged from that slumber, her damaged face was the first one he saw. He smiled as though he'd seen an angel, an angel with metal wires from teeth to earlobe.

'We fell,' he said, 'didn't we?'

'Yes, George,' she answers, 'we fell.'

'How far did we fall?'

'Till we hit the sand-dunes, George, and until you hit me.'

'I'm sorry,' he whispered, and reached out to touch her metal mask. 'Did I do that?'

'It was my fault, Georgie, all mine. We fell, like Icarus, like Lucifer.'

'No,' he said, 'we fell like Adam and Eve.'

'Theirs wasn't an actual fall, George, it was more like a fall from grace.'

She said this but she could see the theme was going to stick. Adam and Eve. They alone, among their peers, were of the fallen. They had fallen, moreover, together and ravaged each other's bodies in the falling. George, whose brief existence had heretofore been lived in the shadow of others, now had his legend, his fall, had tumbled from the Maiden's Tower with Nina Hardy, had punctured her maiden's body with his.

19

THE EMBERS ARE dying in the public house and Janie is on her fourth hot whiskey, cloves, sugar and a slice of lemon.

'His voice had dropped by the time he came out, down to something like a furry baritone, he had grown, sprouted, lengthened, broadened, he was too big for the bed, uncomfortable to sleep beside, and his size gave him a strange, misshapen dignity if there can be such a thing. And at school he'd fallen back so far, grown to the size where he could no longer fit in the desk, where Miss Cannon could no longer thump him, preposterous it would have been anyway, his hands could have crushed the ruler.

I don't know who decided he shouldn't return, Da, Ma, or George himself, but he got a job anyway in Keiling's farm, so walking home from school we'd see him, you remember, moving down the potato drills in a line with the labourers over from Scotland and the patients from Portrane. He'd give the bulk of his wages to Ma for my education and whatever he was let keep for himself he'd spend on clothes to imitate yours and Vaseline to slick his hair back and impress Nina. Yes, yours, don't tell me you don't remember, he could never wear them but he tried, did he try. Even down to the hair which he tried to grow like yours but it rose from his head like a brush which he tried to keep down with more Vaseline. So it grew uncomfortable, didn't it, we can't really deny it, Gregory. I was the scholarship girl, he was the day-labourer, you and Nina were the ideal that could never be matched. On his days off, hanging round your front gates or outside the shellfish plant, bouncing flat stones across the river, in his best clothes, waiting for a glimpse of Nina. I'd tell him,

George, don't let on to be so eager, but he would never understand, thought urgency and ardour would get him – what, I often
wondered, it couldn't have been romantic affection, even he
would have recognised that as ridiculous – no, it felt more like a
return, a need to go back to those childhood moments, when the
differences between the four of us were or seemed to be, for some
few magical years, non-existent.

He thought, if you will allow me to be so psychoanalytical,
that the more like you he was, the closer it would draw him to
her. And I thought, if you will allow me to be so bold and
forward, the more like her I was, the closer it would draw you to
me. So ours was a not uncommon delusion then, given we were
both a little bit in love with both of you, but in his case taken to
uncommon extremes. Though whether he ever got as close as I
did to you on that afternoon my father took the lot off to the
Laytown Races, and I crept with you into their bedroom to listen
to the rain drumming on the metal roof, to examine the intimacy
of my own undergarments, I cannot tell. Do you remember the
rain, Gregory, do you remember the sound of that rain?'

And it's raining when they leave the pub, a soft winter wash of it,
mottling his coat, which he holds over her with his left arm while
he searches for the car keys with his right. The wet dodgem cars
with their smiling faces glisten in the amber streetlights and
remind him of how much alcohol he has consumed.

'Show me the house, Gregory,' she says.

'I don't think that's wise,' he says, still fumbling for the keys,
as if waiting for the rain to sober him up.

'All proper now, love, are we? No, don't worry about Eros,
Gregory, she's long gone to sleep, but I would dearly like to see
inside, like to find out how much it reminds me of her. We're
visiting old ghosts, aren't we? Waking the sleeping dogs.'

'What sleeping dogs?' he asks.

'The ones that lie.'

'You mean,' he says, as he starts the car and the lights illuminate the rain-swept golf-course, 'we are emptying cupboards of
their skeletons.'

'Yes,' she says, 'all the old clichés. Old haunts with their
sleeping dogs and their skeletoned cupboards and their stones
unturned.'

She falls silent as the golf-course passes and the river comes
into view. She closes her eyes briefly around Mornington and
through Drogheda she snores, wistfully, it seems to him, and she
wakes again as the yellow headlights graze the gates, as the
wheels sough off the dampened gravel. The rain is heavy now
and turns them into diffuse wraiths as they huddle from the car
to the kitchen door.

'I loved this house,' Janie says, once over the threshold, 'and
everything in it, but wouldn't you if you came from a river-
pilot's cottage with a red oxide roof and slept four to the bed till
it became dangerous for the virtue of all concerned.' She takes
Gregory's arm as the door closes. 'With a roof that played per-
cussion when it rained. I got to know rain in all its varied moods,
my love, as I studied my Latin on the kitchen table. *Amo amas*, I
love a lass,' she says as she stretches up, tipsily, her heels in their
frayed stockings coming clear of the black lip of her shoe. She
kisses him, close to the corner of his mouth. She leaves her lips
close to his cheek and whispers, 'So can you pinpoint the
moment when it all went wrong, Gregory? When my dear
brother began to lose his marbles, when your sister became his
chosen obsession, when that summer play became a winter
frost?'

'We grew up,' says Gregory, pulling away from her, 'and maybe
that was all.'

'But isn't that the problem? We didn't. I suspect we just pretended.' She leads him by the arm through the kitchen door, into
the dark hallway, her head lying crooked on his shoulder. 'Where
do you work now, Gregory?'

'In Soho,' he says.

'Aha,' she whispers, 'what an adult-sounding place.' She walks him through the hallway, through the half-open living room door. 'And I suppose it is regrettable, Gregory, truly regrettable, this state of adulthood.'

'You're not making sense,' he answers.

'But I am,' she says, 'and I'll show you. Take off my coat.' And he obeys her, without question, undoes the buttons on the damp maroon cloak she's wearing.

'Carry me.' She drapes her arms around his shoulders and he assumes her weight. 'My brother carried you,' she says, 'carried you to safety across a burning desert.'

'I don't remember,' he says. 'I was wounded, unconscious.'

'But he does,' she says. 'At least he did once, because he told me. He assumed your weight the way an adult would a child's, left you unconscious of his gargantuan efforts and gave you life again. So lift me, Gregory, I'm nearing fifty and want to be a child again. And that's not lifting, you need one hand crooked below the knee to make me . . .'

'To make you what?' he asks, and his arm comes down and one knee crooks round it.

'To make me weightless,' she says, 'childlike and weightless.' She is in his arms now and he is swaying with her weight in the marginal light coming through the French windows.

'He said you called for your mother when he thought it was the end. So he answered you and carried on, like any mother would.'

'And I remember this couch,' she murmurs, as he rests her on it. 'I am drunk now, and I remember the velvet feel of this couch, the grassy smell of it, the dramas I imagined from it. There was a ghost, wasn't there, to observe our comings and goings? What did we call her?'

He slides to the floor and rests his head against her knee. 'Hester,' he says, as she strokes his cheek with her open palm.

'Yes, Hester. I was never quite au fait with Hester. What was the story? She died in childhood? Or of a broken heart? Or both, why not both, what a way to go.'

'The story changed,' says Gregory, 'as we did.'

'Of course. She was the doll, wasn't she, then the woman in white. Are you a child yet?' she asks, and strokes his lip with her finger.

'I'm getting close,' says Gregory.

'Then do you remember that day George saw her by the old manhole in the field by the river? I had pretended of course, pretended to see her, and do you know why I had pretended?'

'Why,' Gregory asks, as he must.

'Because I would have pretended anything to get into your world. And not just your world, but that magic circle between yourself and your sister Nina. That state of need, of belonging, of grace. So if I must see a ghost to gain admittance, well then, I've seen a ghost. But with Georgie, it was sadly different. We found him with a blade in his hands, what kind of blade, a secateurs it was, savaging a piece of wood. Pale and shaking. "Georgie," I said, "what's wrong? You look as if you've seen Hester." The cliché, you see.

"I have," he tells me.

"Was she wearing white?" I asked him.

"No," he says, "she was wearing black."

"George," I said, "you've cut yourself."

"No," he said, "I cut her."

And I wiped his hands, and sure enough, the skin was uncut. "So whose blood is it then?" I asked him, and he answered, "Hers." '

She presses his head between her open knees, into the folds of her skirt. 'Are we children yet, Gregory, have we banished the spectre of adulthood?'

'We can't,' he replies.

'But you do remember, you were there. We took him by the hand down to the river, me, you and Nina, and swung on the rope your father had tied to the overhanging branch of the chestnut tree. And when you pushed me I'd turn on the swing back and see him staring at the water, still gouging at the wood, and I knew something was wrong even then. There was a space between his gaze and what he looked at, and maybe I knew then that that space might never be filled. And I'm sorry, but I've drunk too much and I'm getting – what's the word? Maudlin. Is the word maudlin, Gregory?

'Reflective would be kinder,' he murmurs.

'Let me sleep here, Gregory, leave me on the couch and I'll be gone in the morning.'

She closes her eyes and lays her head on the brown velvet covering. And as he rises he seems almost disappointed. He takes off her shoes, lifts her legs and bends them underneath her.

'A blanket,' she whispers, 'would be nice.'

~

She walked out of the hospital, into the pale circle of cement that circled round the circle of green, with George on her arm, she with her somewhat new face and George with his new stare. Because he stared now, stared at a space in advance of the object he should have seen. There was an object parked on the circle that he should have stared at, yet he seemed not to notice it at all. It was a motor-car, and her father was proudly standing by its open door, his head encased in a motoring cap with earflaps like an airman.

'I thought Henry Ford should take us home,' he said, cranking the engine into juddering life, 'instead of Garibaldi.'

George kept his eyes fixed on the swinging door, and once he was inside, on the parallax of the hospital gates as they slid by the windscreen. The sun was strong that day, and left severe dark shadows, the windows of the shops on Shop Street were white with light and the tide on the mudflats of Mozambique were meandering strips of silver.

'No more jumping either, George, from any height bigger than your own,' her father shouted over the din in his kind voice, he couldn't help being kind.

'We didn't jump,' said George pedantically, 'we fell.'

'Well, no more falling then, because one is as bad as the other, isn't it?'

The cottage with the red roof came into view beyond her father's silhouetted head in the front of the car, the flat hot sea behind it. A gaggle of children ran forward to greet the new motor, Janie leaning at the door behind them, her arms crossed. As the children crawled over the steaming bonnet, Nina walked with George's hand in hers and deposited it in Janie's.

'Georgie,' Janie said, 'you're back in time for tea.' She used that bright voice that people use to intimate normality where it is noticeable only by its absence. And now he stared at the car, when it was leaving, at her face in the back window, barely visible through the running heads that followed in its pursuit. He let Janie draw him backwards into the house, his face still turned in the car's direction, now vanishing behind its sulphurous cloud.

And he became Nina's shadow for the rest of the summer. He would be there in the damp grass outside her window when she woke in the morning, would follow her and Gregory to the tennis-courts, collect the balls they missed and bounce them dutifully back towards them. When they swam out to the raft in the middle of the river's mouth, he would be the guardian of their clothes, against wind, rain and whatever prying hands might happen along. After a while the stare retreated, became a secret hiding-place from which he looked occasionally, but on those occasions she would always see it and know it was for her, and her alone. He reverted to his role of their willing clown, but was too big for it now – when she lathered his lips in lipstick, the effect was gro-tesque and unlovely, no matter how they tried to laugh it off. She would walk alone along the line of the tide and see his figure on the dunes behind, keeping pace, like some lonely Quasimodo.

'Are you the guardian of my virtue, George?' she would ask him, outside the gates, finding him still behind her.

'No,' he would say, then with a strange dignity, 'but I am your friend.'

'There are times,' she would tell him, 'when we need to be without our friends.'

'I understand,' he said, the haystacks gleaming behind him in the late August sunset, 'but she doesn't.'

'And who would she be?'

'You know,' he said. 'Hester.'

She felt a cold shiver inside her and realised things were stranger than she thought.

'Does she talk to you?'

'She tells me things,' he said, 'every now and then.'

'What things?'

'What you want, what you're thinking.'

'How could Hester know, when most times I don't know myself?'

'Because, maybe, she hasn't died yet.'

She stared at his blue open eyes and saw Gregory coming behind him, thinned by the fading light.

'Hester was a doll, George, and a game of ours when we were younger. She's gone now.'

'I wish she was,' he said.

But the next day was the last Sunday of the last weekend of summer and they acted children with a vengeance, perhaps because they weren't children any more. On the Monday they would be off to different schools; the old National on the road to Termonfeckin with the gulls and sour milk, and Mrs Cannon's ruler had done its best with them – though George would be off to no school at all.

She awoke in the morning and he wasn't there, in the dewy grass outside her window. The mist that curled like tobacco-smoke round the remaining haystacks seemed to accentuate his absence. She drifted into Gregory's room and sat at the end of his rumpled bed till he woke up. She liked the sound of his breathing, the way his pyjamas curled round his thin, lengthening arms. Most of all she liked watching him unobserved, unawake, as unaware of her as if she had never existed. She realised why she had misspelt lonely so consistently, as it was the condition she had endured without him. She felt pity for the girl she had been, the lonely girl who hadn't known she was lonely, and thought how odd it was to fully recognise a feeling only once it had vanished. She knew it now, truly, in retrospect and wondered did time always work like that, teaching us the truth of our condition only when that condition had ended. And then she felt a panic, like a sudden wave of water or a gulp of tears, at the thought that it might return. If it did return, it would be a more searing loneliness, one that knew itself, knew its word, its condition, knew its own history. The thought terrified her, stilled her into silence. She wondered what it would be like if he never woke up, slept like that, breathing peacefully, tangled under the bedclothes, for the rest of her days. Would that banish the fear of loneliness or make it worse, she wondered, and then he woke up.

The first tide was coming in over Mozambique, tiny runnels of water creeping over the cracked mud as if it would gradually consume the world. There was a horse there before them, a loose racehorse, hooves stuck in the mud, with purple and yellow racing colours, its saddle askew, foam dripping from its open mouth. George was standing by it, reaching out to touch its muzzle. When it whinnied George would pull his hand away, then reach out again, closer each time. Janie sat on a mound, her knees drawn up to her chin.

'It must have broken loose at the Laytown races,' she said knowledgeably. 'Run the whole length of the beach and got to here.'

'What about the river?' Gregory asked.

'It jumped in and swam across.'

'What about the jockey?'

'Threw him in Laytown. Or dumped him in the river. Either way, she's ours for a while.'

'He,' said George. He wiped foam from the horse's muzzle and whispered in its ear.

'What are you telling him, Georgie?' Janie asked idly and edged closer.

'Secrets,' said George. 'And mind his hind legs.'

'Can you share them with us?' Nina asked.

'No,' he said, and he seemed masterful for once. The muscles on his body matched the horse's, in solidity and weight. He whispered again.

'I heard the tinkers talk to ponies,' he said.

'What does it sound like?'

'Backwards talk. Lift me up.'

She cupped her hands for him the way he had cupped his hands for her outside the Maiden's Tower, and strained to keep them together as he hoisted himself up. The horse trembled when he sat on it, shifted its hooves in wide circles in the mud. George whispered again and it stilled itself.

'What do you think, shall I run her?'

'I'm not sure,' Nina said.

'Ah why not?' said Janie and gave the horse's rump a slap.

It reared several times, making great sucking sounds in the mud, and then it ran, and when it had made it on to hard ground it ran faster, jumped the ragged fence of barbed wire, vanishing beyond the dunes in a spume of kicked sand. They were left like three exhaled breaths in its wake and Janie screamed, out of fear or pleasure or both, and ran after it. By the time they reached the dunes, George and the racehorse were a small splash of white, like one curling wave in an otherwise placid sea. After a time the splash of white seemed to exhaust itself. It turned and moved back along the path it had traced, explosions of foam along the water's edge.

They walked down the sand-dunes towards the horse and the sea. There was no hurry now, he had not fallen again and broken more bones, the horse had not run riot and they were as spent as the horse must have been after its magical effort. Outlined by the glistening water like a diminutive satyr glued to the racehorse's wet back, the gentle wash reaching to his thighs, the horse turning slowly, rubbing its nose in the slow breakers, George seemed George at last, as if an ungainly chrysalis had peeled, leaving the stuttering and the stare behind, to reveal this almost elegant extension of the horse's mane. They waded out towards him and Nina felt the viscous wet clutch of seawater on her legs and her dress.

'Who wants a go?' he said, turning the animal gently so it faced them.

'Me,' said Nina, washing the foam on its flanks away with sea-water.

'You couldn't,' said George, and she was surprised by the authority in his voice.

'No,' she answered, 'but Gregory could. He's English, after all.'

'What's English got to do with it?' George asked.

'An Englishman's home is his castle. And his horse is his chariot. Isn't that right, Gregory?'

'Chariot?' asked Gregory, and Nina could hear the tremor in his voice.

'It's a saying.'

'I never heard that saying.'

'Or is it an Englishman's home is his horse? Either way, up you get Gregory.' And now she was surprised by the authority in her voice. Horses brought out the best in people, she surmised. 'Down you get, George.'

And George slid from the saddle through the lathers of foam

to the sand below the water. He leant his back against the quivering horse and cupped his hands.

'Come on, Gregory.'

And Gregory came on. He placed one foot in the clasped hands and George hoisted him up in one swift, deft movement. Nina watched him as he settled in the saddle, as stiff and elegant as a pencil, and decided horses definitely brought out the best in people.

'Will he take two?' asked Gregory, wrapping the reins round his hands.

'Why wouldn't he?' asked Nina, trying to assume an authority she didn't quite feel now. George leant back against the trembling flank, clasped his hands together and let Nina use him as a stepladder. She placed her wet shoe in his hands, her wet hands on his shoulder and lifted herself out of the sea. She sat down on this hard mound of wet leather, felt it shiver beneath her as if exploring this new burden, then felt it shift gently from foot to foot, so her legs were like butter-churns in the water, a sensation not at all unpleasant.

'Hold on to his belt,' said George, and she did, and thought perhaps if he'd told her to hang herself and her family, she'd have done so just as readily.

'What's it like when he gallops?' she asked him.

'Like falling,' he said, 'but never reaching the ground.'

She wrapped her fingers round Gregory's belt and felt the flannel of his underpants beneath it, the hard tiny scallops at the base of his spine against her knuckles.

'Are you ready?' she whispered.

'Yes,' he said, 'but how do I make it go?'

'Kick him,' said George.

Gregory tightened the reins in his hands in his hands and dug in his heels. The horse gave a kind of a whimper, but didn't move.

'Harder,' said George, and Gregory dug with his heels again. The horse shifted, splashed the water but stayed where it was.

Then George raised his right hand and slapped it hard against its rear, and it raised itself once on its hind legs and galloped.

She felt none of the pounding she had expected, more of a feeling of flight, a rhythmic rise and fall of the horse beneath her, and whether she rose or fell, the headlong rush kept her pressed against Gregory. So it must be falling, she thought, as George had said, her small breasts pressed against his shoulder-blades, her fingers dug into the belt of his trouserts, her chin dug into one side of his neck. The water splashed around them like spattered pearls and a yacht sailed by to their right, the red sail idling in the other direction, the sailor giving them a lazy wave. Come on boy come on boy come on she muttered like a tinker's mantra, and then the beach was at an end, they were coursing over the scutch and seagrass between the dunes and the farmland beyond it. There was a barbed wire fence and the horse jumped it, into a meadow full of August barley, and he pounded a flattening irregular path through the barley-stalks until a sound stopped him dead, and she fell again, sailed through the air with her brother this time, over the horse's bowed head.

This was a different fall, a more languorous one, and she would remember thinking as she sailed through the air, her fingers still clinging to his belt, if I have to fall, I want to fall with him. The thick barley welcomed them with soft, cushioned arms, parted before them and made a generous path as they rolled to a halt. She was on top of him, sneezing with the chaff in the air, her fingers still dug in the belt of his trousers, laughing with exhilaration, coughing with the dust, until the sound stilled her into silence.

It was the scraping of a stone off a scythe, one stroke upwards, one stroke downwards, and it continued, at its own deliberate rhythm, as if marking time for some dance about to happen. She looked up and saw sparks flaring against the yellow barley, sparks from the sharpening stone, drawn over the blade. The blade was dark against the sunlight and behind it she could see the outline of a large, bearded face beneath a cowl.

'Are you sorry now?'

Nina stifled her laughter and stared upwards. Whoever it was stood, framed by the dancing ears of barley, the scythe curving above the brown cowl of his head. Her eyes travelled down the brown folds that wrapped a sturdy body, tied at the waist with a smudged cord, to the fringes of a skirt, swaying gently over sandalled feet.

'For what, sir?' she managed to ask.

'For making a right haims of our barley.'

'Are you the devil?' she asked, for a reason she couldn't understand.

He laughed. 'No,' he said, 'but I'm in the devil of a bad humour. How will I explain this to the Abbot?'

'Tell him we're sorry sir,' she said, 'that the horse kept running and we couldn't—'

'The horse, was it?'

She turned away and saw the horse behind her, over Gregory's prone body. It was chewing lazily at the barley, a tremble, like the last breath of wind on water, running over its hide. There was a long black fist between the horse's legs, growing all the time.

'Is he dead?' she asked. The thought was as huge to her as the word was tiny.

'I hope not.' He dropped the scythe in the barley and the horse whinnied at the sound. He moved towards it and it reared, its hooves flailing over Gregory's head. She screamed, he grabbed the swinging reins, twisted the angry mouth towards him and whacked it in the rump with his free hand, letting the reins go with the other. It kicked free then, galloped through the barley, flattening another path. It jumped the fence, kicking sand up in clouds behind it, back the way it came.

He bent down towards Gregory, lifted him gently, turned his face towards the sunlight and pulled one eyelid open.

'What's his name?'

'Gregory.'

'Are you dead yet, Gregory?'

'Who's he, Nina?' Gregory asked slowly, eyes moving from one to the other.

'He's not the devil, anyway,' she said.

'No,' he said, smiling, 'I'm Brother Barnabas.'

He carried him then, through the waist-high barley, and Nina followed. Suddenly the terror struck her, after the event. The thought of death in this sunlit field seemed preposterous to her, unreal, but the very possibility made her shake. She heard the sound of sobbing, and realised it was hers.

'Are you crying, Nina?'

'No', she said, 'I'm just . . .'

'Just what?' he asked, holding Gregory's form free of the nodding eaves of barley, just in front.

'You're afraid of what I'll tell the Abbot.'

'Yes,' she lied.

'Well,' he said. 'There's time enough for that.'

The field rose towards a wizened tree and the barley diminished around it. There was a small round pool below with a lip of crumbling stone. He knelt at the pool, brought Gregory's head towards the water and dipped it in.

'Is the water cold?' he asked Gregory, who nodded. 'Can you see my face?' And Gregory nodded again. 'Can you stand?'

Gregory took a breath and he tilted him sideways, placed his feet on the ground. 'What do you remember?' he asked.

'I fell,' said Gregory, slowly.

'No,' he said. 'You died. The waters brought you back to life. Isn't that true, little Nina?'

'Is it?' she asked, and the thought frightened her more than any thought yet.

'Did you see angels?' he asked. Gregory shook his head.

'What a pity,' he said sadly, 'because they could have told you what to tell the Abbot.'

He reached out, took both of their hands and drew them

towards him. He squatted, so the brown skirt rose halfway towards his knees.

'We could tell him the truth, that Nina and Gregory rode a horse through the barley.'

'Do we have to?' asked Nina.

'We have to tell him the truth. But then, I suppose the truth is that the horse ran through the barley of its own accord.'

'It did,' said Gregory.

'And what will I tell him about Nina and Gregory?'

'Nothing,' said Gregory.

'We'll leave your field,' said Nina, 'we'll walk back along our tracks as if we never existed.'

'And maybe you don't,' said Brother Barnabas.

'Don't what?'

'Exist.'

'How could we not exist?'

'Maybe you're a dream the Abbot is having right now in the monastery garden. He likes his post-prandial nap. So why don't you run out of here before he wakes up?'

They ran, past the edge of the field of barley, and could see him penetrating deep inside it to where his scythe lay on the trampled ground, and the last sight they had of him was of the scythe flashing in the sunlight and his cowled head bending, up and down.

'So do we exist, Gregory?' she asked him, when they reached the shore again.

'No,' he said, his bare feet splashing in the water. 'Someone else is dreaming of us.'

'Is it a good dream then?'

He took her hand as he walked. 'It's an excellent dream of larks,' he said.

'Larks,' she said. 'What larks.'

I dreamed of that Abbot intermittently myself, sleeping in the walled garden of the monastery I never saw, beyond the barley field I did see, a rotund figure on a deckchair beneath a late-flowering cherry, the petals dropping occasionally and landing on his bald napping pate, since his cowl had slipped and was dangling behind him, in the hot, summer, bee-thickened air. He was the repository dreamer in the final circle of dreams, but was asleep himself so couldn't know it, and if the disturbance crept inside me, the unease I would come to know too well, the vacuity, I would console myself with the possibility that I was after all the dream of that unseen Abbot, and that my vacuity was his.

20

JANIE SLEEPS THE sleep of nine whiskies or was it ten, and dreams of the September morning she walked up the drive in the pearl-grey uniform of the Siena Convent. George had watched her roll her socks neatly round the edges of her bootees, and upon enquiring had been told that's the way the Siena girls wear them and what would he know about it anyway. George had agreed he would know little about it, and parted company with her near the gates and made his way towards the potato drills of Keiling's market-garden. Nina, Janie found when the front door finally opened, had her own socks stretched up above the knee. A debate had ensued as to which style the Siena girls favoured, to which Gregory, dressed in the grey flannels of St Lawrence's Grammar School, contributed nothing whatsoever. It was resolved by Mr Hardy, who proposed an elegant compromise, of the socks being drawn to just below the dimple of the kneecap, the knee, as Ruskin had once observed, being the signature of a young lady's beauty.

So George, as he moved among the potato drills with the line of day-labourers on a field above the Baltray Road, watched the trap make its way towards Drogheda, Gregory and Mr Hardy in the front, Nina and his sister Janie in the back, their knees decorously exposed to the September air. He noted the socks pulled up to just below the kneecap and concluded that was the way the Siena girls must wear them, after all.

And now Janie dreams, of Gregory walking towards the knot of youths beneath the brown castellated façade of his grammar school, with the careful gait of a heron picking its way through mudflats; of the mock-Gothic arch of the Siena Convent entrance, of the sheen of polished maple in the shady corridors, the smell of bleach and lavender, of Sister Annunciata in her white wimple and bonnet, the young novice from Mayo, Sister Camille, who walked them through the gardens holding both of their hands and who seemed as new to these hushed environs as they were themselves. She would squeeze Janie's hand tighter on some days, Nina's on others, and spend the next five years in an exquisite dilemma between the affections of both. She would share with Janie her memories of the road from Leenane to Louisburg, the bay with the frothing Atlantic below it, the curling booreen above it that led to her family's ever-smoking thatched cottage, of the bed that she so sorely missed, crowded at night with her five sisters. She slept now in an iron cot, curtained in blue and white check, with only the visitations of the unseen St Catherine to console her. She would share with Nina her devotion to the same St Catherine, the silent ecstasies that came to keep her company, advise her against fast dances, theatrical attendances and romantic novels while curling her fingers round the soft skin beneath her thumb. She would weep real tears before they left, come behind them in the dark corridor on the way to Mass as they passed the warm kitchen, kiss one and then the other, oh rapture, oh delight. And as Janie sleeps she wonders was anything in mature passion quite as good?

And George daydreamed, of Gregory, of Janie, but most of all of Nina, as he moved with the unwashed day-labourers in an irregular line along the ridged turnip fields. The daydreams almost made bearable the company he kept. Mostly outpatients from the asylum he would one day sleep in himself, they shifted with the unthinking regularity of cattle over the turnip drills, their fingers blackened from the wet earth, their boots gathering mud as they proceeded. The rains came down hard, but not hard enough to stop the work. It would take the thunder to do that. A great wail rose up from the line of the deranged and Keiling still kept them in check until the lightning flashed, and neither he nor his son could stop the rout. Towards the only shelter there was, the circular mound at the end of the fields, surrounded by a ring of blackthorn trees, where they huddled beneath the bare branches, and George alone ventured towards the grass-covered stone entrance and stepped inside.

A lintel of ancient limestone, the circular gougings etched in lichen, the dark interior illuminated by the intermittent lightning, the thunder-claps gaining on it until they met in concert, three or four minutes of soundful flashes. He saw a figure carved on the stone inside, a woman's head raised in an unearthly grin, her stone knees apart, her stone hands between them.

And when the thunder and the lightning ceased the others edged away from him, as if he was shadowed by contact with a world they wanted no part of. Which was fine with George, he adopted the mound as his refuge, ate his sandwiches in the interior gloom, watching them boiling tea-caddies beneath the blackthorn trees, silhouetted against the light.

In the spring his labour eased. He was given a shotgun to prowl the new-sown fields and keep them free of crows. He marked his day with the diurnal clopping of Garibaldi's hooves, bearing Nina to and from the Siena Convent, Drogheda. He waved from the wheat and barley fields, fired off a blast at the errant crows in a kind of greeting. He would walk home and as the sun lengthened the days, took to dallying in Mabel Hatch's barn above her father's fields, meeting one, two or all three of them there, as if the barn provided common ground between their childhood together and their days now, apart. His muscles were hardened now, his body had all the bulk of the agricultural labourer he was becoming, his blue eyes had retreated behind his wind-scalded, sunburnt skin. But all three of them were equal strangers in the new worlds they had entered, and the strangeness, if anything, increased their mutual bond.

They had a new companion here, a brown owl that flew in

occasionally from the golden light outside. And as two summers came and went, the brown owl stayed like a guardian angel, like their childhood ghost, their familiar, and George took to calling her, what else, Hester. 'Forget about Hester,' Nina said, 'she's long, long gone.' But no, George insisted, she was the brown owl and the brown owl was her.

The name seemed odd to Nina, like a shard from a world more properly gone, and she realised they needed new words, changed words, for the changed worlds that had grown around them. A whole new language. And late that September, under the tutelage of Sister Annunciata, she suddenly found it.

III

21

I PRAY THEE, Rosalind, sweet my coz, be merry.

The rehearsals began in the draughty, unused gymnasium, between the hanging ropes and the vaulting horse, dramatic exercise being deemed more suitable than gymnastic for the further education of young Catholic ladies.

Dear Celia, I show more mirth than I am mistress of; and would you yet I were merrier?

Celia was Janie's, a cipher of kinds, but Rosalind she claimed immediately as her own, more real than Nina was herself, than the ghost that intermittently haunted her. She would stay with her for ever and beyond, the mistress of her moods, consolation of her chosen profession, woman wise, woman heartfelt, woman witty, woman loving, perhaps loved. Through pretence, she realised immediately, Rosalind becomes herself since her own self is too multitudinous for any one expression of it. The girls of the Siena Convent played the boys' parts and the boys of St Lawrence's played the girls', both in their separate universes until a dress rehearsal before Christmas, awaited with as much trepidation as the meeting of the waters, where gender reasserted itself, male became male and female female with nothing in between.

'You are Jacques, all Jacques, make sure it's yours,' Nina told Gregory. But with his height and his measured diction, they put Orlando in his path. So he rehearsed them both, at home over the kitchen table, on weekends in the dripping glasshouse.

'They say you are a melancholy fellow.'

'I am so; I do love it better than laughing.'

'Rosalind,' she told him, 'in an ideal world would love them both. Don't you think, George?' she asked, George who, on his weekends off, they drafted in to play Touchstone and his galaxy of fools.

'A worthy fool, motley's the only wear.' Dan Turnbull's old jacket, too big for him and frayed at the elbows, a pair of oil-dosed trousers held up by his old school belt. 'Aye, now I am in Arden, more fool I.' His accent was now far thicker than theirs, his hands almost wholly scarred with agricultural blades. He sat behind the dead tomato plants and watched Gregory woo her.

'For now I am in a holiday humour and like enough to consent. What would you say to me now, an I were your very very Rosalind?'

'I would kiss before I spoke.' And she waited to reply until their lips touched.

'Nay, you were better speak first; and when you were gravell'd for lack of matter, you might take occasion to kiss.

'You saw that kiss, George?' she asked.

'I did,' he answered.

'Is it allowed by the presumptions of the drama?'

'Why not,' murmured George, 'any fool can kiss.'

'But Rosalind,' said Nina, 'pretends to be a beardless youth, who in turn allows the lovestruck Orlando to pretend he is Rosalind. So if Rosalind lets Orlando kiss her, won't the pretence be unveiled?'

'It depends,' said George, 'on what kind of kiss it is.'

'He's right,' said Nina. 'The kiss must be chaste and friendly, like a kiss between two girls.'

'Or boys,' said Gregory, 'since Orlando thinks she is a boy.'

'Boys don't kiss boys,' George offered, bringing the conversation to an odd conclusion.

'Let's leave the kiss To Be Determined,' said Janie.

'Another question,' asked Nina, her lips still close to Gregory's, 'if Rosalind pretends and Orlando kisses the pretender, who in fact is kissing whom?'

But the kiss stayed, in all its wonderful complexity, observed by George, who lit a cigarette behind the tomato plants. He had acquired the habit suddenly, in his headlong propulsion towards adulthood. He proffered the butt to Gregory, who sucked on it and asked him, 'How like you this shepherd's life, Master Touchstone?'

'Truly shepherd,' he answered, 'in respect of itself it is a good life; but in respect that it is a shepherd's life, it is nought.'

Gregory handed the butt to Nina, who sucked on it too, but coughed.

'In respect that it is solitary, I like it very well,' said George; 'but in respect that it is private, it is a very vile life.'

'Then why do you do it, George?' she asked him, unkindly, since she knew the answer already.

'Sir, I am a true labourer,' he answered. 'I earn that I eat, get that I wear, owe no man hate, envy no man's happiness.'

She was swinging beneath the chestnut after school, idly, like a child again, when she saw the freshly-scored lettering on the bark of the trunk. She tried to read as she swung, her head leaning backwards, face to one side. She deciphered one letter, then knew it all. If a hart do lack a hind, let him seek out Rosalinde. She turned, and saw the figure of George across the river, with Janie's copy of the play in his hands, still smoking.

'Did you write it, George?' she called.

'Write what?' he asked.

'That very false gallop of verses.'

'On the tree? Truly, the tree yields bad fruit.'

She swung for a bit and squinted her eyes and watched him, rising and falling, across the river in the fading light. He seemed a child and a man at once, as if he'd bypassed those awkward bits in between. Then his voice, quite soft, broke her reverie.

'There's someone behind you,' he said.

'Who?' she asked, though she felt she knew what his answer would be.

'He that sweetest rose will find must find love's prick and Rosalinde.'

'So it's Rosalind now. Not Hester.'

'So it seems,' he said.

'Is she beautiful?' she asked.

'No,' he said, 'not any more.'

'How can Rosalind not be beautiful?'

'She was once,' he said and threw his Woodbine in the water, where it sizzled and drifted down towards her.

22

JANIE WAKES, SLOWLY, the coverlet slipping from her body on to the newly-waxed floor. Her left hand reaches for her cigarettes before her eyes are open, her right hand scrabbles in her pocket for the box of matches and the crow's feet round her eyes crinkle with the pain of too much alcohol the night before. Soon a cloud of smoke wreathes round her, to be dispersed in turn by a rasping cough.

She walks through the empty house to the kitchen, where she fills a rusting kettle, lights the gas ring with another match and hears the tread of Gregory's feet on the stairs behind her. 'Have you got tea?' she asks him. 'And you may as well tell me now, did I embarrass myself last night?'

'Yes to the first question,' he says and hands her a tin.

'And the second?'

'I don't remember embarrassment,' he says, 'but then I don't remember much.'

The kettle begins its slow hiss and Janie fills a teapot with the dusty leaves.

'The purpose of the Irish funeral, my dear, you know what it is?'

'To bury the dead,' he says.

'No,' she says, and laughs bleakly, 'anyway, aren't we lacking a corpse? No,' she repeats, 'it's a social ritual of Byzantine complexity with embarrassment at its core. A time for endless handshakes, whispered condolences, intimations of impropriety, extremes of emotion valiantly kept at bay that release themselves as the day progresses. Building to an evening of raw conviviality where too much drink is taken as a matter of course, old sores are reopened, new ones found, enmities and intimacies erupt like water through a broken pipe and the dead one is gradually forgotten in a welter of new and unwarranted emotions.' And she smiles wryly. 'It will make you melancholy, Monsieur Jacques.'

He answers with another smile. 'I can suck melancholy out of a song, as a weasel sucks eggs.'

She leans on the table and touches his hand, lays her head achingly on his shoulder. 'Let me help you with it, Jacques,' she whispers.

'Orlando,' he says, 'I was her Orlando.'

'But,' she insists, 'you were always Jacques to me. So let me help you, with the melancholy, the food, the drink, the service. Let me help you choose the readings.'

'And what would you read, Janie?' he asks, in his voice already saying yes.

'Something of Rosalind's,' she says. 'How did it go?'

But these are all lies: men have died from time to time, and worms have eaten them, but not for love.

~

She was surprised by sentiment, that evening before the last Christmas break in the hall of the Siena Convent as the parents gathered in the corridors outside, as the scrape of hooves arriving and departing sounded from the forecourts. Janie and she had made each other's dresses, their version of Elizabethan, stitched and scissored from one of her mother's voluminous ball-gowns. She heard the shuffling of feet behind the stage curtain and drew back the gap to see George walking in, almost first in the hall, dressed in a suit he had bought with his farmhand's wages. He had memorised every word, she knew, sitting behind the dead tomato plants during their glasshouse rehearsals. And as the hall gradually filled, with those families from the town and hinterland whose daughters merited the attentions of the nuns of the Siena Convent, George sat apart, alone without family, quiet, preternaturally alert.

The red curtains bulged with the shape of youthful bodies, moving like a slow wind from left to right. A symphony of coughs and creaking bootstraps, the rhythmic scraping of chair-legs on parquet floor, the rustle of the cheap printed programme all merged with the gentle rattle of beads, as the bonneted nuns moved up and down the aisles, seating the latecomers, before sitting themselves. The lights were extinguished then, and an embarrassed hush fluttered through the hall and the curtains drew back to reveal Gregory on-stage in a pair of black stockings and a Robin Hood skirt, standing still and simple with that heron-like concentration of his, and speaking without any embarrassment at all.

She stood watching from the wings, saw the lights flaring from behind his knees, saw the upturned faces vanishing into a deep, delicious darkness. She saw they were no longer that uncertain, embarrassed group of midlands burghers, they were an audience.

I pray thee, Rosalind, sweet my coz, be merry.

She was surprised by sentiment, a sentiment as yet unknown to her. And, as when her new-found brother stood on the kitchen steps, she wondered where that sentiment had been till then. Janie smiled cheekily while delivering her first lines, as if it were a private game between them, and seemed as surprised as she when it was not Nina, but Rosalind who answered. Rosalind, who was not quite her, but more than her, who existed for two brief hours in the glower of the footlights, the whorls of dust raised by their buckled feet, in the smell of stale sweat and greasepaint. But she did not so much exist in those two hours, as become illumined, her existence was a prior fact, endless, and for two brief hours Nina was privileged to give it being. She acted, that is to say she pretended, and as she pretended, she became. The rush of feeling

Rosalind gave rise to in her moved her at points to tears, yet to her surprise, to her delight, they were tears she could turn on and off at will, weep with and enjoy the act, the principle of weeping.

'Love is merely a madness,' she told her brother, 'deserves as well a dark house and a whip as madmen do; and the reason why they are not so punish'd and cured is that the lunacy is so ordinary that the whippers are in love too.'

Not so much feeling as sentiment, sentiment informed, cultured, refined by the expression of it, one is at feeling's mercy, she realised, but one becomes sentiment's partner; and she spent two hours as Rosalind in a state of illuminated partnership, of ecstatic surprise.

~

'I'll always remember her,' says Janie, her head still perched precipitously on Gregory's shoulder, 'in the costume we cut from the purple gown her mother wore to the Meath Hunt Ball, when she turned and said to me, what was it – dear Celia, I show more mirth than I am mistress of. I was startled, even shocked, fully prepared to giggle my way through the whole thing like a bad school recitation, knock over a cardboard tree or get my hair caught in the paper leaves of the forest of Arden and laugh at it all on the journey home. But the speed of her reply almost floored me, the certainty of it, the poise in her movements as she said it, and there was someone else, I realised, on the stage beside me. Not Nina, not Rosalind either, nothing as novelettish as that, no, the spectacle I was witness to was that of her becoming, but becoming what? Help me here Gregory, you were there too in your Robin Hood outfit – becoming this thing, this other that stopped you in your tracks, made you laugh one minute, cry the next, as if the Nina we had known was just a ghost of the real one. And here it was, the real, it had been dormant all along, sleeping, like Snow White, or like in one of those vampire films she did, sleeping in the coffin of herself.'

'It was the character she loved,' Gregory says, 'Rosalind and then Viola. I saw her as Viola in *Twelfth Night*, some theatre in the West End I can't remember which, and she said to me afterwards in that bar by the Seven Dials, that they were both cousins, Rosalind, Viola, half-sisters maybe. And I remember thinking, what a beautiful idea, the same family that populates the plays. Touchstone by that logic would be Falstaff's illegitimate son, Edmund would be the darker twin of Jacques.'

'Family,' says Janie dreamily, 'what happened to it? Never remembered to have mine.'

And Gregory takes that as cue perhaps that their reveries have ended, lifts her head gently from his shoulder. 'Are you perfectly sure you want to help, Janie?'

'It would help me,' she says, 'if I could help you. We could wake her, together.'

~

If I were a woman I would kiss as many of you as had beards
that pleas'd me, complexions that lik'd me, and breaths that
I defied not.

But she was a girl, not yet a woman, a girl-woman perhaps, and could see Gregory behind the wings and could imagine George somewhere in that ocean of dark faces when she made curtsey and bade herself farewell. The curtain came down, or more exactly jerked across in incremental movements, behind it the spectral shape of a white nun's bonnet, and the applause began before it had fully closed. She heard applause, but to be more exact again, she heard an outpouring of whoops, boots hammered off the parquet floor with a strong undertone of handclapping beneath it all. And the nuns drew the curtains back again the minute they had touched to reveal her in mid-curtsey, the rest of the cast lumbering into a phalanx behind her. She felt a sudden crush of emptiness, as if whatever had filled her for two hours had left, like air escaping from a deflated balloon.

The curtain came across bringing dark and then a different kind of light, and that was the beginning of my envelopment in light itself and the darkness that surrounds it: footlights, arc-lights, toplights, keylights, each of them blazing out from their own cone of darkness, sculpting a cheek, filigreeing a hair, caressing a lip, piercing an eye, generally mine.

We blundered round in the darkness behind the heavy curtains until they pulled back, and where there had been a pit of gloom, an unseen audience was a group of clamouring parents and beaming nuns, among them my own, but no George. And the character was gone, quite suddenly, lifted from me by invisible hands with no sense of release; it was hovering somewhere, in the wings, maybe, like a ghost itself, awaiting another manifestation, another embodiment, another performance.

And maybe they are the most enduring spectres, the ones who survive without any particular life, wait patiently in a kind of death to be inhabited by the next actor who comes along. I remember Rosalind as a series of colours, a riot of smells, a host of stratagems, an intelligence I could never have matched, but once inside her I was glad to be that luminous mind, that well of kindness, that ironic, affectionate muse. Then she went, and that was that.

There was tea and scones afterwards in the beeswax-odoured refectory. My parents were there, my mother florid in a bowed hat talking to Sisters Assumpta, Bonaventura, Catherine, Camille, and I could see among the sea of faces Janie's parents with her and Gregory, but again, no George. And when we made our way home in my father's motor which proceeded with all the delicacy of a herd of buffalo down the Baltray Road, and we passed Mabel Hatch's haybarn, I saw a figure standing inside among the hayricks which I knew had to be him. The motor stalled and started again and before it resumed its journey I asked to be let out, to have the benefit of the fresh air and the walk home along the river. I kissed them both, and Gregory, and they drew away from me with a lot of engine noise and steam, and I turned to the haybarn and walked inside.

'Is that Touchstone?' I asked, hoping there was humour in my question, but finding none.

'No,' the answer came from the upper hayricks, 'this is George, the hayrickmaker, the turnipsnagger, the walking scarecrow, who earns what he eats, gets what he wears, owes no man hate, envies no man's happiness.'

'Did George enjoy the evening?' I asked, climbing up the hayricks towards him. There was a broken panel in the barn behind him through which the moonlight showed. I could see his head, utterly still against it. And I realised, with a sudden twist inside my stomach, that he was my only real, my only pertinent audience.

'Yes,' he said, 'George found it mighty altogether. And the kiss was mightiest of all.'

'So,' I said, sitting beside him, 'we solved the problems of the kiss.'

'You did,' he said, 'because you were someone altogether different. Gregory now, he was still Gregory, but Nina was no longer Nina.'

'So Rosalind kissed Gregory?' I asked him.

'As it should be,' he said.

'And can Rosalind kiss George?' I saw his large head, inscrutable in the moonlight, the broken wooden wall of the barn behind him.

'She cannot,' he said softly, 'but maybe Nina can.'

So I leaned over and up and kissed him and his lips were above me now, the reverse of the way they had been as children, always below, and they were broad with the skin peeling and the breath that came from behind them was shocking in its adulthood, its immediacy, because in other ways, particularly in the trembling of one lip against the other even as I closed them with mine, they were still, more than anything, a child's. I remembered the lipstick I had smudged upon them so wantonly, and raised my arms up to feel what had become of the blond curls, but there were none, there was the rough feel of the shaven nape of a neck which pulled away, and he looked at me directly, and then above my head.

'Look,' he said, 'at what's looking at us.' I turned and saw a brown owl perched on the beams below the wooden cathedral of a ceiling, and there was a low owly hoot and the wings flapped open and the owl flew over us, out through the broken wooden wall towards the moonlight.

'She'll remind me of you,' he said, 'when I go.'

'Where are you going?' I asked him.

'To the war,' he said. 'There's a war in Europe that pays better than Keiling's farm.'

23

'THERE WAS A calm,' says Janie, 'before the storm, wasn't there, Gregory? The lengthened evenings as the last school year ended and the longest of them all, the dress dance in the tennis club, when we could think of no-one to invite but each other. I decided, after endless reflection, to invite none other than you. Nina had options, she always had, but Buttsy Flanagan's breath smelt, she told me, and Albert Taffe, she was certain, would step on her toes. So she decided to ask my dear brother George, whose breath didn't smell, but who was equally certain to step on the toes of the red shoes she had bought from Quirk's on Church Street.

His preparations for the evening were careful, and immense. He scrubbed himself for days in the copper tub in the kitchen, as if multiple baths were necessary to clean off the grime of Keiling's pea and potato fields. He used whatever earnings he had saved to rent a suit from Quirk's. If there was to be a perfect evening, as perfect as the long lost ones in Mozambique, he wanted this to be it.

He came home around six on his bike, took one final bath and presented himself to me in his rented suit, his shoulders almost bursting the seams. I was amazed to hear him ask me what I thought and I noticed one small detail amiss. His face scrubbed clean and raw, his hair slicked back with oil, his sleeves too short of course, but what ruined it were his nails, long, thick and uncut, coatings of earth underneath them that successive bathing hadn't removed. I got out my scissors and clipped them and cleaned beneath the cuticles as much as I could, and he set off on his bike.

"Don't be too early, Georgie," I pleaded, "there's nothing

worse than that," but he assured me he wanted to take the long road round.

You arrived then, dressed in your father's evening suit, as the sun was going down over the dunes. My father was sitting on the small wickerwork chair outside the front door and bawled at me, his pipe still stuck between his teeth. Time, Janie, he said. I could hear the scrip scrape of Garibaldi's hooves on the shingle and remember thinking it should have been a clip clop. I was fixing the rose to my blouse in the tiny kitchen and my mother was fussing with my hair. She knew nothing of course would come of it, it was only the tennis-club dance, and was whispering to me, don't get any ideas, but with the excitement of someone who couldn't help but imagine them. Ideas, that is, of her youngest daughter being married to a son of Baltray House, questionable though his birth might be.

And you shook my father's hand, you exchanged pleasantries about the weather, grand evening for it, he said as if some ancient, untouchable rite was about to begin and you said, in your polite English vowels, grand indeed, Mr Tuite. You pronounced it tweet, not tchute in the local way, and my mother smiled at me, inside. She let the idea take hold of an old-fashioned courtship, and smiled at me in the mirror and said, your gentleman's here. Stop it, Ma, I said, he's not mine and he's not even, in all probability, a gentleman. But there was no stopping that smile, that I knew, and so I kissed her on the cheek in the way I knew she loved and went out to meet you.

Georgie by that time would have been on his bike, creaking his way down the avenue towards your much, much bigger front door. Your father met him there, your mother, stepmother or whatever the correct term is, watched from the upstairs window, I know because Nina told me. And Nina walked out without any fuss or ceremony, clapped your father on the back and threw herself over Georgie's crossbar. Off we go then, Touchstone, she said. And I know that because he told me.'

~

He was wearing a borrowed or a rented dress suit, and underneath the smell of mothballs I could detect the unmistakable whiff of heather, that peaty gorsy smell that came with him in summer. In winter it was damp and turnip-skinned, but in summer it was always the smell I remember from lying on my back in the prickly heather and staring up at the marching clouds. His chin touched the crown of my head as he cycled, came down with the pressure of each pedal, and I knew it was squashing the corsage my mother had picked and I had hooped round my bound hair, but I didn't really care. His arms were like two steel hawsers on either side of my shoulders and his knees came up and down like pistons, moving the bicycle relentlessly forwards. All I could think of was an agricultural machine like the ones they now threshed wheat and barley with, the one that ate Hester and crushed her, but a machine designed to balance me on its lap, with one purpose only, to move me as safely and as quickly as possible to the tennis club in the village of Baltray. An agricultural machine that, having gotten me to the entrance, would tilt itself to one side and balance the bicycle part of itself with an iron grip as I got off. That would transform itself into a two-stepping, lumbering approximation of dance once the band struck up. A dancing–agricultural machine then, with the promise of, in the event of any offence to the dignity of my person, a quite terrifying pugilistic machine.

So there was a muscle-bound dignity to George as he cycled to the clubhouse, balancing me perfectly, even elegantly on the bar of his bike, stopping by the knot of local dress-suited toughs outside the entrance, quietening the sniggers in their noses with the mere fact of his solidity, his size. He would have carried me over the dusty gravel and deposited my new shoes on the boards inside, but I was afraid those stilled sniggers would erupt into snorting laughter and the pugilist in the machine by my side would be suddenly switched on. So I linked my arm through his and nestled his elbow underneath the swell of my breast in that lace-fringed dress. And we walked, in a kind of erotic union, over the dusty crunch of the gravel to the boards inside.

If there was a dignity to George outside, there was almost a hauteur to him inside, as he took my hand in one of his, placed the other round my waist and guided me round the floor in a perfect three-step as the band played the Anniversary Waltz. I glided between the shuffling boots with my dancing machine and the toes of my red shoes survived, miraculously untrodden.

'Where did you learn to dance, George?' I asked him, and he answered, 'I practised with Janie.'

~

'We swapped partners of course,' says Janie. 'Don't tell me I'm the only one that remembers those delicious few hours where everything seemed possible. Anyway, we swapped partners, danced with other admirers and of course, in the *ronde* of exchange the moment came when brother danced with sister, half-brother with half-sister. We had practised in the kitchen at home, my father playing polkas on his seaman's melodeon. I got so entranced with the success of my tuition, the mechanical per-fection of the steps I had taught him, that I allowed myself to forget for a moment about you, Gregory, and when the tenor stopped singing 'Oh The Night Of the Kerry Dances' and the shuffling stopped, you both were gone.'

'I fixed the corsage on her hair,' says Gregory, 'I tried to make the honeysuckle stand upright but they were crushed beyond repair. I did better with the rose, it had a kind of indestructibility about it, and I inhaled the perfume I had got used to in my seven or eight or was it nine years there, and I told her she put all of the others to shame. She said the problem with the flowers was they had no air. So shall we give them air? I asked her, and she said, why not. We walked outside the crush around the door and headed towards the bunkers where the air was keen and the sand was fresh and white.'

~

I lay on the bunker of the eighteenth hole and he brushed the sand from my pale stockings. It glistened on the fabric like tiny diamonds in the moonlight and he would clear one knee and I would laugh and turn and turn back, the other knee now covered in tiny diamonds which he would clear too. The band was playing the Kerry Dances gone alas like my youth too soon, and I lay down then, my hair spread out over the white sand, daring him to do what he wanted, which I knew was to take his hand and place it on my cleavage while undoing the buttons at the top and bring his lips down towards me, oh to think of it, oh to dream of it fills my heart with tears. Would there be others, I wondered, who would move me as much as him? And I hoped there would, but somehow knew there wouldn't. And I realised there was another function latent in George, he was a preventative machine, there to stand between me and my half-brother, to absorb all this feeling welling inside me and to prevent an eruption.

'Do you remember Brother Barnabas?' I asked him, 'and the horse that crushed the barley? – It sounds like a jig or a reel that the band might play, the horse that crushed the barley.'

'Yes,' he said, 'why do you ask me that now?'

'Because,' I said, 'he told us we didn't exist, we were the dream of the Abbot in the monastery garden. We can only exist this way,' I told him, 'in the dream of someone else.' I brought my lips close to his and could see the blond downy hair on his neck but I didn't kiss, or couldn't.

'Is that tragic or comic?' he asked me.

'I wish it was comic,' I told him, 'but I suspect it's tragic.'

~

'So you both vanished,' Janie says 'during the song about the Kerry Dances, through one of the small green doors at the back. To do what? Stand and look at the purple sea? Hold hands like brother and sister and walk along the long dune grass whose sharp points would have tickled her knees, the underneath of her dress? I wanted to be the one walking there, you understand that, Gregory, feeling the prickly grasses probe between my knees, my hand under your hand, your hand counting the fingers. It was a quite innocent desire, but God, did it flood me with a warmth I didn't understand. I looked at George beside me sipping his lemonade, and the awkwardness of the dancers behind him, and could see then how wrongly shaped it all was, like a puzzle that had only one solution, but the solution was impossible of course, the pieces of the puzzle dragging towards their only possible fit, the impossible one. And then she came back in with you on her arm and the band started up and we changed partners and it was apparently all right again.

And when we walked home, George holding the bicycle by the side of the trap, Nina stretched across the seat, her head angled back, looking at the world upside down, you and me walking, my arm in yours, along the moonlit river, it was still possible to imagine, wasn't it, that everything would be all right? That we would have normal lives, whatever normal meant. But in the early summer of that year it would have meant a clerkship in the carriage office for me, marriage one day maybe, children. A cottage and smallholding for George, marriage, maybe one day children. And for you and Nina, a continuing life in Baltray House at least.'

~

I remember the trees going over my head, the leaves rustling with the cool breeze that came from the river, like a long bowed umbrella, the soft, still expanse of mackerel sky beyond them with the moon somewhere beyond that, unseen, but brightening the clouds. The feelings I had were gentle ones, as gentle as that sky, we were the four of us part of the same feeling. I remembered Sister Camille telling us about the fifths of Ireland, five provinces, *cuige*, she called them, but there were in fact only four, Munster, Leinster, Connacht and Ulster, and the fifth was the unity the other four made. And I thought that would be as apt an account as any of us, four of us, but in fact five, the fifth was all of us, or the spirit that bound all of us. And I allowed myself to dream of that fifth, that spirit, and thought of Hester again, she was the one, the unseen fifth, only there when all four of us were together. A mad thought perhaps, but no madder than what the future in fact held, far more comforting, maybe even more true than the reality.

I held the handlebars on George's bike and then when that became too much of a stretch, the crook of his arm. 'I don't want to grow up,' I said.

'You're already grown up,' said Janie.

'No,' I said, 'I'm not, and neither are the three of you. And if any one of us grows up it will be irrevocably tragic.' I laid back my head and watched the mackerel sky moving beyond the leaves of the trees and thought how much I liked that word 'irrevocably.' It sounded like the clop of Garibaldi's hooves, like the gentle swish of the reins that Dan stroked over her back, it sounded like a word that Nina would have relished sharing, long ago, with her dear and only Hester.

24

'POOR CATHOLIC BELGIUM,' says Janie, walking from the living room towards the kitchen where Brid Moynihan had left a week's grocery supplies and an electric kettle, 'remember Poor Catholic Belgium?'

'I remember Lady Day in Slane much better,' says Gregory.

'Poor Catholic Belgium,' says Janie, 'haunted Sister Camille so much she quite forgot her passion for poor me. She could see herself martyred by the Hun bayonet in the ruins of Louvain, the murmur of her voice turned into the mutter of novenas, in the kitchen, the corridors, the garden, the sacristy. The act she imagined was rape, though of course she never said the word, the sexual act so far sublimated it hardly existed in the real sense. In the broader imaginative realm it became a tide, a tide of blood, spreading to our virgin shores, threatening our virgin petticoats, her novitiate woollen drawers, though whose world was about to be ravaged? It wasn't mine, it was yours and Nina's, your father's—'

'What I do remember,' says Gregory, 'is Lady Day in Slane. The Volunteers had their stalls in the field of the demesne with all the pipe bands playing. The Marquis of Conyngham bellowing from the platform and that little Dublin politician next to him. Dan Turnbull took us out on the trap for the afternoon and George cycled alongside Garibaldi, tried to keep up with her trot. All the pilgrims round the Holy Well with bottles and cans for the water. There was a stand behind the platform and George saw the sign there with the magic figure, seven shillings: he didn't care about King and Country but he cared about that, much better than

Keiling's farm, three squares and a cot, boots and khaki thrown in. But I was primed already because I believed, you see, I believed with your Sister Camille the stories of the slavering Hun and the nuns in Belgium, and I knew my time was up here anyway, my childhood was about to be over, better end it quick.

There was a pencil tied on a piece of string to the green-baize table and a captain in uniform handing out bottles of porter, and we both signed and drank and tasted the dark bitter foam for the first time. And I put my arms around him and hugged him then, there was an odd satisfaction to the predicament we had both embraced, like we had embraced each other, again for the first time . . .'

~

But when the class of 1914 said their goodbyes on a hot June day in the quiet garden of the Siena Convent, the tide of blood that was threatening their virgin petticoats seemed very far away indeed. Nina, who had won first prize for elocution, a hand-bound copy of the poems of George Herbert, took her leave of Sister Catherine – two and then three kisses on both cheeks – and assured her she would always remember their walks in the garden together. She could see Janie, sitting on the twin chairs underneath the magnolia, swinging her feet, one foot entangling itself now and then round the calf of Sister Camille, who leaned close to her, proffering one more cup of tea. She could see her mother and father through a long range of bonnets, both ecclesiastical and secular, bending the ear, as they say, of the principal.

'Acting,' Sister Catherine whispered, 'would not normally be a profession I would have considered as remotely appropriate to a Siena girl. But I was stage-struck myself once, Nina dear. And I have a friend in Dublin, Ida, Ida Lennox, whose mission is to change the perception of the theatrical arts. You have a God-given talent, Nina dear, and perhaps what we need to do is place it in safe hands . . .'

Nina pinched her arm, gently, as another bonnet edged round hers. 'Mother,' she said, and Sister Catherine stopped her sentence, turned and saw, not her Reverend Mother, but Nina's, Mrs Elizabeth Hardy.

'Hasn't she bloomed, Sister Catherine?'

'I think so,' said Sister Catherine, shy as ever.

'We place our seedlings in your green hands and you bring them to flower.'

Sister Catherine blushed and her small hands retreated into her voluminous sleeves. 'We do our best,' she said uncertainly.

'Her brother hopes the Royal Irish will make a man of him.'

Sister Catherine saw Nina's eyes look downwards, like sinking moths. 'He's enlisted, then,' she said.

'And maybe his absence will make a lady of her?'

'I'm still a girl, mother,' said Nina.

'Yes, love, of course. My little Nina.'

She heard the sound long before she saw it. A dull throbbing in the summer fields, like a distant rumble of thunder unwilling to explode properly. Then she saw the puff of smoke as the sound grew louder, edging its way through the hedgerows, as if a toy train was busily puffing its way through the fuchsia. The sun glinted off a helmet and the thing appeared on the Drogheda Road, with a sidecar attached, leaving a trail of grey exhaust, both wheels raising dust from the summer-hardened surface, heading towards the gates at the speed of a horse on a steady canter. She ran from the upstairs window, down the oak staircase, and when she made it to the front door saw it trundling down the avenue towards her, more slowly now. Its balance seemed suspect, weighted to one side, the bulk of the driver threatening to crush the diminutive sidecar to the left. Then it reached her, shuddered to a halt and the driver pulled off goggles and helmet and revealed himself to be George, in khaki.

'She's pulling to the left,' he shouted at the figure of Gregory, behind him, emerging from the sidecar.

'Then counterbalance her. Lean to the right.'

'Yes, sir.'

'You have to call him sir?' asked Nina, walking down the steps.

'No,' said George, 'He's in the ranks like me. Shilling a day.'

'Then why the sir?'

'Because he looks like a sir. Even in a private's uniform.'

'Will you take sir and me for a ride, then?'

'On the pillion or the sidecar, Nina?' George asked her. 'It's up to you.'

'Don't you have to call me Ma'am?'

'No, Ma'am.'

'The pillion, then, Private George,' she said. 'We'll leave sir to the comfort of his sidecar.'

And he did look like a sir, she thought, as she moved to the motorbike. George took her hand, first removing his wing-shaped leather glove. Is everything to be different now, she wondered, gloves, goggles, titles, cognomens. Then she sat her bum on the pillion, tucking her dress beneath her, and felt George's iron back underneath the khaki greatcoat and realised some things would always be the same.

'Brace yourself, Nina,' he muttered. He raised his body and brought all of his weight down on the kick-starter and the thing roared to trembling life. 'And here we go, hold tight,' he said, and she felt it kick into movement, swaying slowly towards the gateway, through it, gaining speed along the riverside.

Speed seemed to complement them, to define them. Departure was best, she thought, with no thought of arrival, maybe they were destined for flight. And this, she realised, was far more interesting than the horse. The horse was all sweat, strain, effort and excretion. This was the future, a mechanised roar, a trembling of metal, a rattling of constituent parts, a ballistic and a

balletic trajectory, utterly new, roaring through the old dusty
fuchsia hedges, her arms wrapped round him for safety, into
some possibility of a future. They reached Drogheda in no time,
roared down the empty dock road, about-turned at the bridge
and headed north towards Clogherhead. George sped through
one-street villages, past a marquee festooned with conscription
posters, into the harbour with the smell of wet mackerel on the
drying air. There was a grey frigate visible on the horizon
heading for Carlingford Lough. It looked to Nina like a child's
drawing on an innocently drawn seascape, the only barely alive,
threatening aspect to it being the smokestack which uncurled
from the funnel, into a billowing, internally expanding black
cloud.

'You didn't have to join,' said Nina, staring at the glistening,
slapping mackerel in the fishing-boat below.

'No,' said George, 'but if I didn't join I would have had to keep
snagging turnips.'

There was a long-toothed conger eel twisting among the
mackerel. A fisherman speared it with a gaff hook, chopped its
tail off and then its head.

'I can't imagine a war,' she said, watching the black blood
spout over the ship's deck, on to the mackerel below. 'Can you,
Gregory?'

'No,' he said, 'it's not my job is it, to imagine a war.'

His voice sounded adult to her, but when she turned and
looked at his face, it seemed as young as ever.

'And who will look after you, Gregory, when you're fighting
this war?'

'Will you look after me, George?'

'I'll look out for you. Don't know I can look after you. Never
fought a war.'

'Look out for each other,' said Nina, taking them both by the
arms. There was a cold breeze now, coming in from the sea. 'Will
you promise me you'll both come back?'

They ate grilled mackerel, a halfpenny each, down by the boats. Her question was rhetorical, or must have been, since neither of them answered. Gregory talked of the itching of his boots, the discomfort of his khaki trousers, George of the distributor cap on the motorbike engine. Gregory said the fight was for civilisation, George said he had heard it was for Poor Catholic Belgium and Nina found it hard to visualise any of it. It was as if there was a black pit in her facility for daydreaming, her imagination, and they were both descending into it, rapidly, on a motorcycle and sidecar.

When they tired of the pier and the sight of gasping mackerel, they mounted it again, George spurred it into action and they took a circuitous route home. He wanted to show them the tomb of the woman of the river.

They reached it at sunset and the motorcycle headlights threw a cone of sulphurous light on to the low circular hill and the phosphorescent cows in the field beyond. Gregory was out first, lifted her gallantly by the waist and deposited her on the soft earth. George lit a cigarette and laid his chin on his crossed hands over the handlebars and the softly purring engine. She took Gregory's hand and walked towards the low hill at the dim end of the cone of light, surrounded by the oddly illumined Hereford cows. Their white patches gleamed against their patches of brown, vanishing into the gloom beyond, the last rays of the evening sun glancing around their nodding heads. Gregory's long thin fingers seemed an extension of hers.

'He's smitten,' he said, 'and that's why he's going.'

'So it's not the King's shilling?' she asked.

'No,' he said, 'it's you, love.'

'Love,' she said, 'you called me love, that's not allowed.'

'With you then, Nina,' he said.

'But he's Touchstone,' she told him, 'and a Touchstone smitten by a Rosalind is a dramatic absurdity.'

'In a comedy,' said Gregory. 'Maybe not in a tragedy.'

'Tragedy or comedy, Rosalind still loves Orlando.'

The yellow light on Gregory's hair shimmered and she heard the low rumble behind her and realised George was gunning the motorbike slowly forwards, following.

'Are you talking about me?' he asked.

'No,' said Gregory, 'we were talking about the difference between comedy and tragedy. People laugh in one and cry in the other.'

'And people live in one,' said George, 'and die in the other.'

'So let's make sure,' she said, 'we make ours a comedy.'

'What does that mean?' asked George.

'It means you both come back.'

The round hill was now up against them and he spun his front wheel slowly, raking the arc of white over the patchy grass, the few bare thorn trees, a goat with raised horns staring back at them from what seemed to be the perfect arc of the hillside. And then she saw them. Two cantilevered blocks of stone supporting a transept on top, the circular whorls etched in them that seemed, in the harsh contrast of the headlights, to have been carved yesterday.

'What are they?' she asked.

'The entrance,' said George behind her.

'The entrance to what?'

'To her tomb.'

She walked through the grass which was dampening by now. A cow shuffled to her left, into the cone of light and out again. The goat stared from above, as if hypnotised. George moved the bike behind her till it illuminated a gloomy passageway, beyond the standing stones, inside the perfect hill.

'Whose tomb, George?'

'You know.'

'Tell me again.'

'The woman of the river.'

'Boinn.'

'We boil our tea in there, when it rains.'

'So this is Keiling's farm?'

'Part of it. The vegetable part. Turnips, parsnips, potatoes.'

She tightened her hold on Gregory's fingers, to draw him in. But he disengaged them.

'Coward,' she whispered.

'No,' he said. 'I don't belong in there.'

The stone passageway gleamed in the headlights, the whorled carvings on each side as if scratched by a giant child. Like George, she thought. Beyond it, a circular gloom. She walked inside and saw her huge shadow dancing ahead of her. Another shadow gained on hers and she felt his breath on her neck.

'So you belong after all,' she said and took his hand, and was shocked for a moment at the strength of it until she realised it was George's. He held her hand hard, as if expecting a withdrawal.

'So Touchstone eats his vittles here?' she asked him, beginning again.

'When the rain comes down, when the potato drills turn into a swamp, when it's hardly worth continuing. Which seems like every day. I sit here,' he said, 'and think of you.'

They had reached a perfect half-circle, like a stone colander.

'Where,' she asked. 'Where do you sit?'

'Here,' he told her and reached out for her in the dark, lifted her bodily and placed her on a stone with a small seat-like indentation.

'I can't fit,' she said, 'and if I can't, I don't see how you could.'

'They were smaller then,' he said.

'P or Q Celts?' she asked.

'I don't know,' he said. 'I don't know about Celts.'

'There's one,' she said, 'who doesn't care about her P's and Q's.' She could see a woman, carved into the stone wall, her grinning face upturned and her knees pulled apart, her hands between them. 'Is she doing what I think she's doing?'

'What do you think she's doing?' George asked, and there was a new tenderness in his voice.

'Touching herself,' she said, and drew her knees together.

'Why would she be doing that?' he asked.

'She's an ancient Irish goddess and has a well between her legs.'

He withdrew his hand from her and she could see the large shape moving backwards.

'Don't go yet,' she said.

'A well?' he asked.

'Yes,' she said, 'a well that gives birth to a river.' And she reached out and felt his calloused hand and drew it towards her.

'That still doesn't tell me why she's . . .' He stopped, as if he didn't have the words for the stone hands on the wall carving.

'Maybe,' she said, and could feel the large hand on her knee now, 'she has to help the river on its journey.'

'How so?' he asked, breathing hard.

'To make the water flow,' she said.

She could feel his hand, unstoppably travelling towards her now, and she opened her knees again and put her own hand over his and helped him on his journey. Why she was doing this she wasn't sure, she wasn't sure of anything, only that he and her half-brother would be gone soon to a darkness she couldn't imagine, and the impulse felt strong, larger than her, larger than the woman on the wall who seemed to move her hands as George moved his and whose knee trembled as her knee trembled and it didn't feel like stone, far from it, it felt like water, a trickle of it first and then a slow moving river that bent as she bent and shifted as she shifted, and shifting, that was the word she'd heard for it, did you shift him, yes I shifted and he shifted me. And he must have shifted her because the woman was nowhere to be seen, only the circular stone whorls of the ceiling, she was on the cold floor, George was above her and she gave a soft cry like the one the owl gave in the barn that night, among the upper hayricks.

She closed her eyes then and it was like sleeping, but it was not sleep, for she felt him moving from her and could hear his boots, scraping softly off the stone floor. Soon the scraping stopped and another scraping began, by the entrance.

'Sheila-na-gig,' he said.

She heard the voice, echoing in the cold, delicious ancientness of the tomb. She turned her head and saw Gregory walking towards her, silhouetted by the headlights near the entrance.

'Sheila what?' she asked softly. She drew her knees to her chin and adjusted her clothing. There was a damp patch near her bum.

He raised his arm so the shadow of his finger fell on the stone carving behind her. It traced the open mouthed head, the spread knees, the clutching hands.

'Sheila-na-gig. It's a Celtic goddess. Disgraceful, don't you think?'

'Is it?'

'But then what would I know. I'm not a Celt.'

'Where's George?' she asked, rising.

'Isn't he in here?'

'No. He left.'

'Well, he didn't come out. I waited, you see. I waited for a long time, till my absence seemed beyond the bounds of . . . delicacy . . .'

'Is there another way out?' she asked. She smoothed her dress with her hands.

'But then is there anything delicate about Touchstone?'

'George,' she said. 'His name is George.'

'And did you resolve the issue?' he asked. 'Is it to be comedy or tragedy?'

Then the light shivered on them both and the motorcycle outside the tomb roared into life.

'There must be,' she said, 'another way out.'

The light wheeled off them as the motorcycle turned, positioning its rear towards them as they exited. She noted the whorls of its tracks in the grass like the whorls in the stone lintel of the entrance. George sat with his back towards them, patiently, keeping the engine alive. She chose the sidecar for the journey home, leaving the pillion and the comfort of George's waist to Gregory. They said little and the goat bleated from the top of the hill, as if to emphasise their silence.

The wind coursed through her hair on the journey home, as if the journey was one of air through her tresses, not through the glinting cottages of Slane, the dark streets of Drogheda, the moonlit low tide on the glittering wetlands. George wheeled to a halt in the gravel by their doorway and for some reason she hoped her mother was not up to greet her.

'Till tomorrow then, Private George,' said Gregory, dismounting.

'Goodnight Nina,' said George softly, as if Gregory didn't exist.

She rose from the sidecar and kissed his dusty cheek, beneath the leather goggles. 'Goodnight, George.'

Inside, the house was quiet. Her mother sat in the living room mixing a brandy and soda.

'You missed dinner,' she said.

'We had mackerel on the pier,' Nina answered, 'in Clogherhead.' She heard the difference in her own voice and hoped, obscurely, that her mother couldn't hear it. And, just as obscurely, she knew Gregory could. She walked through the hallway which seemed to shrink away from her, as if every angle, every plane, every parallel, bowed at her approach. She walked into the piano-room, with Gregory like a silent shadow behind her. She sat at the piano and began to play the Mozart, and when her memory of the Mozart failed, the bits of Schubert that she knew. Then her memory of the Schubert failed her in turn and she listened to the sound of the piano dying.

'I waited,' Gregory said.

'Did you?' she asked.

'Yes. I waited till it got too cold and I thought if you don't come out I'm going, and I went to go in but heard something that made me think I shouldn't.'

'Shouldn't what?'

'Shouldn't go in. Any further. But I could see your shadows on the wall, over the carvings. Then I walked back out.'

'Ah.'

'What? What does ah mean?'

'It means – Gregory, you're crying.'

'I'm sorry – I feel—'

'How do you feel?'

'The way I felt when I came here first. When I saw you first.'

So she rose and put her arms around him and drew him down on to the small heart-shaped sofa and rested his head on the white skin between her neck and where her dress began, the dress that was still damp round the bottom, the white skin that would be brown in a few weeks, the first few weeks of real summer, and told him not to cry, reminded him of the days they had had, days on the white blowing sand, days round the tennis-court, days on the dunes, on the small canals of Mozambique.

'You don't understand,' he said, 'what you gave me was what I never had, you gave me a childhood and now it's over.' And then her mother walked in.

What she saw was Gregory in Nina's arms on the heart-shaped sofa, a child in everything but size, his lips on the delicate hollow beneath the nape of her neck. Her mother stopped momentarily in the doorway, her head to one side like a questioning bird. Her lipstick was smudged around the edges of her mouth in a way that gave her shock the appearance of a smile. An amused smile, as if a blemish had been exposed in a garment that she knew was flawed all along. She held the paper in one hand and a chewed pencil in another.

'Consecrate with oil?' she asked, with her mouth but hardly with her eyes.

'Anoint,' said Nina.

'Anoint,' she repeated. Then she scribbled in the clenched paper, her eyes darting from the crossword back to Gregory, now standing, his hand disengaging from Nina's. 'I think it's probably best, after all, don't you, Gregory?'

'What is best, Ma'am?' he asked.

'That you'll be leaving soon. It's an ill wind, as they say, a very ill wind. That blows no good.'

25

IN MABEL HATCH's barn, I lay on the straw up near the top by the broken wooden wall looking out on the moonlit summer fields. And the hares danced, they definitely danced among the haystacks below. It had become the font of their going, their goodbyes, but I was alone there, enjoying my aloneness, wondering about that circular mound in Keiling's field, that *mons veneris* where the stone woman tickled her own stone groin. I heard a footstep below me and saw a uniform walk in below me. 'George?' I asked the uniform and the uniform answered 'yes', and this other George walked towards me, towards the uneven strawy steps the hayricks made, all on their own. He was lighter, this George, more delicate, more a Gregory than George, but Gregory needed to be George tonight, needed to be all that George had been, and this need added a solidity to his voice, added a weight to his step in the caked, straw-covered earth below.

'Is George coming up?' I asked.

'Does George normally come up?' he asked in turn.

'He does sometimes, sometimes he doesn't, sometimes he's up here and I come up to him.'

'Well then,' he said, 'George is coming up to you now.'

And there were shadows everywhere but on the outside, outside that broken rectangle of wood, so all I could see was the uniform, the uniform shape and the promise of the man beneath, wearing it.

'George,' I said, 'you're late.'

'What time did I say?' he asked and I answered, 'I don't remember but whatever time, this wasn't it.'

'I'm sorry', he said.

'So you should be,' I said. 'Sit down there now George, with your back against mine, I don't want to see your face this time either.'

'This time,' he said, sitting down, 'what about the last time?'

'The last time I didn't see your face George, and you know why I didn't want to see your face.'

'Tell me again,' he said, 'why you didn't want to see my face.'

'Because, you know, I wanted to imagine you were Gregory.'

'Why did you want to imagine George was Gregory?' he asked and I could feel the rough hairs of his uniform collar against my neck.

'Because then I could kiss you George, the way I would have kissed Gregory.'

'The way you would have kissed Gregory what?'

'The way I would have kissed Gregory if he had not been Gregory, if he had not been my half-brother, if he had been another called George.'

'Can you kiss and not see?' he asked softly.

'Yes,' I said, 'if you close your eyes and turn your head a half-turn and reach your hand around to mine and bring it to yours.'

And he did that. And I felt his lips, the delicate ones, and his cheek, the downy cheek, and it was all like a membrane of water, any minute ready to burst.

'Can George do this, then?' he asked, and his hand travelled from my chin down my neck to the hem round my front.

'Did he or can he?' I asked.

'Did he?'

'He did and he can,' I said and it became like a game then, a game called Did George: did George do this, do this, do this, that and that. I said 'That's what he did, just that, again that, but never so well, never so artfully. Are you remembering this, George?'

'Yes,' he said, 'I know with certainty I will never forget this.'

'Good,' I said, 'because it can never, ever happen again,' and the straw was around us now, if we wanted to be hidden we had ample means. The straw was under my arms, my knees, worrying the crack in my bum, the chaff in my mouth then, I ate it like manna, it was wet and dry at the same time, wet but left me thirsty, wet but left me dry somehow, and then I heard the owly cry again and listened for the beat of wings and then heard them, and opened my eyes in time to see the brown owl flying over him, above him, whose face I miraculously didn't let myself see. And I turned my face away and saw through the broken beams the hayricks outside, the moon playing on them and the hares, the hares were gone and the taste of the chaff had turned dry and ashy, all of a sudden, inside my mouth. I felt the uniform retreat from me, slide itself back down the impromptu stairs the hayricks made, and wondered if the man inside it was crying the way I was.

26

L IKE MOST EVENTS, though, their departure did not have a clear beginning and an end, a definable moment which they could isolate and say, that's when it happened, that's the way it was, the way I will remember. The summer days drifted, the heat-haze grew in the fields, the golfers plied their mashies and niblicks up and down the untamed course. Gregory and George arrived and departed, as if they both had grown into mechanical extensions of that motorcycle and sidecar. They sweated in their uniforms but kept them on, returned for day-long marches round Baldonnel, rifle practice on Richmond Hill, a two-month bivouac in the fields near Londonderry. Seven shillings each, with meals, bed, boots and clothing.

And one day on the Baltray side of the river, across from the fish factory, George picked out from a small rocky pool four oysters the swirling water had left behind like an afterthought. He prized the shells open with his army knife and offered one to each of them, Gregory, Nina and his sister Janie. When they declined on grounds of taste, of the dull, brackish water in which he found them, he ate them himself, tilting the open briny shell towards his lips and swallowing the contents.

'You are barely civilised,' Janie said.

'An asset to any battle for civilisation,' said Gregory.

'What could be wrong with them?' George asked. 'They're only oysters.' But on the fourth mouthful he gagged, coughed and began to choke. Nina slapped his back till his face turned blue, then Gregory took over, with harder, manly strokes across the broad expanse of khaki.

'Can't lose you, George, Kitchener needs you,' he said, and George coughed one last time, spat up whatever inside the shell had choked him. It rolled in the dry sand, gathered a coating of fawn, wet as it was, with his spittle.

'Ugh,' said Janie, disgusted by the whole procedure. But Nina watched it roll across the sand, back into the pool from which it came. She saw it gleam there, beneath the water, reached down her hand and rippled it back and forwards and drew it up again.

It was small, imperfectly round, with glints of turquoise beneath its creamy surface, unmistakably a pearl.

'You're full of surprises, George,' she said.

'Here,' he said. 'Consider it yours.'

'You swallow shellfish and spit up pearls.'

'Shall I try it again,' he asked, 'eat half of the riverbank and make you a necklace?'

'No, George. One is more than enough. To remember you by.' She inserted it in the stitching at the hem of her dress.

'You'll lose it,' Gregory said.

'No,' she said, 'I'll stitch it in tonight.'

As she stitched it in, alone in her room, not in her dress but in the lace hem of her peacock-blue shawl, she noticed the chestnut tree bending, in the evening light, over the roof of the courtyard outhouses. The branch parallel to the river, dipping under a considerable weight. She finished her stitching, rolled it in her fingers under the lacy hem to see it was secure. Then she left the window-frame, and emerged minutes later, crossing the courtyard, her white dress itself pearly against the dying light. She walked underneath the archway, past the glasshouse, down the long field towards the hulking figure, rocking on the swing beneath the chestnut tree.

'You came to me tonight,' George said.

'I was in my room,' she said, 'how could I?'

'I don't know how, but you walked across the fields and you got your feet wet and you knocked on my window and I climbed out and we walked across to Mabel Hatch's barn and listened to the rain falling on the roof.'

'It's not raining, George.'

'I know. I fell asleep. And in my dream you came to me.'

'Is that the first time I came to you?'

'Yes,' he said, 'but there will be others.'

'How do you know?'

'I don't know, but something about the way you looked at me when you were bending over me and your hair fell on my face. An owl flew in one end of the haybarn and out the other. A brown owl. And I thought, if you come to me like that, on the odd night, it won't matter. The brown owl will fly over us occasionally and the rain will drum off the roof and if I can't have you, at least I'll have this.'

'What will you have?' she asked him.

'I'll have the other you. And nobody can do anything about the other you, it will always be there with the river and the mudflats and Mozambique.'

'And let us not forget Mabel Hatch's haybarn,' she said.

'Did you stitch in the pearl?' he asked.

'Yes,' she said. 'I stitched in the pearl.'

And she held up the hem of her shawl for him to feel it, and he eased his swinging as his large fingers turned it round and round in its lace bedding, and she thought what a fine job Dan Turnbull had done on the swing all those years ago that it still could bear the weight of what he had become.

They left the next day.

~

'We came to the quays to wish you off,' says Janie, 'having no idea there'd be so many, khaki uniforms twenty deep along the quayside and the band playing "God Save The King" and that little politician, Redmond wasn't it, giving a speech from the raised platform and the other crowd dropping their banners of protest from the upper window of the Seamen's Union building. Her father, your father, held both of our hands and her mother said, My father built that ship, built the quay that holds that ship, what was its name, the *Kathleen Mavourneen*.'

'He was in love with her,' Gregory says, 'I knew that when he walked up the gangplank with me and refused to look back. He said if he did look back he would never have gone. And he said he knew Touchstone can't love Rosalind, knew it was a dramatic absurdity. And I know I treated his emotions with a frivolity that he must have found contemptible, because, to tell you the truth, I envied him for having any coherent emotions at all. I had none then, or none that I could understand. I was leaving a place that had given me a childhood, and given me whatever manhood I would ever have, and as I was standing there and the boat drew away I couldn't help wondering what was it that had turned the stuttering boy I met into the kind of man he was now. All I knew was that he loved her in a way I wanted to love her, but I knew of course that I couldn't. If Touchstone loving Rosalind was a dramatic absurdity, Orlando loving Rosalind would be a dramatic obscenity.'

~

Something curdled inside me, on the quays with the *Kathleen Mavourneen* pulling away and the band playing. I put it down to loss or grief, but it wasn't them, it was simple nausea. I leant down and threw up in the water and no-one noticed, every eye on the ship heading out to the Lady's Finger, and I remember thinking, does grief empty you out that much? It was a presence, this nausea, call it grief, an active presence I didn't want to recognise, and when I knew what it was, it left a bloody shock I never wanted to know again. Like my mother that way I suppose, I had my unmentionables, among them pleasure, the swoon on that stone floor was so intense with the stone woman and her hands between her knees. And it was around that time I came to hate my mother, I knew obscurely there was that inside me which would cause me to hate her. I took his side in all of the silences, there were never arguments, only silences, arguments would at least have had some objective existence. I took his side, his retraction into the abstract gentleness with which he would confront even unexpressed unpleasantness. If there had been love there, and there must have been, in Florence, in Trafalgar Square, the arrival of my half-brother, his full son, had dealt with it with scientific, exact precision.

IV

27

'LIVERPOOL TO BASINGSTOKE,' says Gregory, 'where we marched for a month round the Hampshire fields, dressed in kit for the Western Front, dripping with sweat in the May sunshine, until one fine day we were given pith helmets and open-necked shirts and we knew we were going East. By train to Devonport then, where they packed us on a coal-steamer and set out into the Bay of Biscay. We watched the dolphins follow the coal-ship's wake in the moonlight and knew our direction only by the gathering heat. The sun was too hot on deck and the air too thick in the hold, even the metal walls sweated. Everywhere men and the smell of men, stripped to their khaki shorts, playing twenty-one with the sweat-riddled cards, asking, where are we going?'

There is a sound like a distant train. Gregory's eyes sink from Janie's face, down the curve of her arm to the smoking cigarette and the kettle behind. He lays his fingers over the spout, feels the burgeoning steam.

'A woman called to visit,' says Janie, 'a month or so after you'd left. Ida Lennox, sent by Sister Catherine from some Dublin dramatic society, with a prim straight back and more airs than the west wind. We had afternoon tea in the shadow of the chestnut tree, a hamper open on the grass. Mary Dagge bringing fresh tea down from the house, me buttering the warm scones and Ida Lennox talking about the theatre.

"I want to change the perception of the theatrical arts in the world at large," she said, "and get society to realise that, far from being a mere doorstep above streetwalking, acting is a noble aim for any young woman to aspire to. And you, my dear, with what I've been told are your obvious, even resplendent talents, should be placed in the care of His Majesty's Prison Service if you consider anything else as a career . . ."

I looked at Nina after she had left. "Who does she remind you of?" she asked me.

I was surprised, I remember, at the flatness of her voice. "Who?" I asked and she said, "you won't remember."

"I might," I said, and saw her looking at the swing, gathering mould over the water.

"Shawcross," she said. "Miss Isobel Shawcross."

And I knew something was wrong with her then, but I didn't know what.'

'We steamed from Cyprus to Alexandria to fight the Turk in the Sinai desert,' says Gregory. '"What's wrong with the Turk," George asked, "what did he do to Poor Catholic Belgium, what have we got against him? I miss home, I miss Mozambique."

"There's a canal here too," I told him, "bigger than anything at home."

I wrote his letters for him. Dear Dada and Janie, I wrote for him, it is hot here and we are at dock in Alexandria waiting to fight the Turk in the Sinai desert, but mostly drinking sweet tea in the marketplaces, the tiny streets go on for ever and if it wasn't for the woven thatch they string above them the sun would be unbearable. I have seen two hundred million flies and my body has been host to most if not all of them. We have been told today we are not to fight the Turk in the Sinai desert but in a place they call the Dardanelles.'

~

She was doing her crossword in the kitchen, sitting over a plate of Mary Dagge's scrambled eggs, her heavily chewed pencil in her left hand.

'Colloquial stomach,' she said, as if nothing at all had happened, as if he had never been there, as if he never had left.

'Belly,' I said, as if nothing had happened too. Father was bending over her left shoulder, pouring a steaming stream of tea.

'The Laytown Races,' he said, 'I thought we could pay them a visit, horses running on the strand at low tide.'

'When is low tide?' I asked.

'Four,' he said, 'would you enjoy it, Nina?'

I nodded, and looked at her to divine what she knew, but saw that her face, if I watched it for a century, would reveal nothing. 'Would you enjoy it, mother?' I asked her.

'I would enjoy,' she said, 'whatever you both enjoy.'

He poured tea for me and kissed the top of my forehead with that abstract kindness of his. 'So, let's go.'

So the horses were arcing along the beach, raising spray, the jockeys' colours bright like toy soldiers against the metal sea, the tick-tack men and the bookmakers' stands all in a bunch by the hard sand. But that didn't interest me. What interested me was the marquee on the green behind with the sign that read *The Tragedy Of The Colleen Bawn*, Playing Nightly. And while they watched the horses, I walked to the tent and made my way inside to the smell of damp canvas and crushed grass.

There was a girl on a raised wooden stage, lamenting her undoing at the hands of a gentleman. There were painted flats behind her depicting a thatched Irish cottage in a landscape of bog. I watched the girl, and despite her stiff gestures and her mannered delivery was soon engrossed in her story, her impending death in the unseen lake behind the cottage. And I thought this was a use to which I could put this useless body of mine.

The girl was pale with a pimpled face and an English accent which she disguised in the thickest Irish brogue.

'You can't be here,' she said, 'I'm rehearsing, we don't start till eight.'

I looked at her pale thin face with the pimpled forehead and liked her immediately. 'I'm sorry,' I said, 'I just wandered in, I'm not here for the horses, I'm a student of acting.' I liked the way that sounded, a student of acting, and the way it caught her attention. 'How long are you here for?' I asked.

'Three nights,' she said, 'then it's over the river to Baltray and then back on the boat to England.'

'What's the play about?' I asked her.

'An Irish girl who's undone by an Irish gentleman,' she said. 'The opposite of me. I'm an English girl undone by an English gentleman.'

~

'"Hellespont," I told him, "Troy, the Aegean islands. Where Odysseus built the wooden horse and Achilles took the arrow in the heel. Gallipoli. There's a narrow strip of water that leads all the way to Constantinople. They want to force it."

"Penetrate it," he said.

"Yes," I said, "into the womb of the Black Sea. Think of it in erotic terms. The thrust of the Royal Navy. Into the seraglio. The Ottoman Empire. Asia Minor. The Orient."'

~

She sat among the odorous crowd on the unsteady benches and saw the rouged faces perform their little drama with a singular lack of intent, a laziness that she found strangely attractive. They seemed to take the drama as read, the death of the Colleen Bawn as a fact that they merely had to refer to, hardly emote, and no amount of histrionics could have enhanced the crowd's rapture, the crowd's engagement in the life, the death, of their sullied heroine. She realised she would love such an escape, into a life other than her own, nightly, any life, and she would love the anonymity the constant travel in those caravans would bring. Her face was pale enough, she realised now, not to need any greasepaint, and after the performance she walked amongst them, till she found the same girl, door open, illuminated by oil-lamp inside, struggling with the cords of her *bustier*.

'Let me help you with that,' she said.

'Why thank you love,' the girl muttered and then saw her in the mirror. 'You again,' she said, and lifted a cigarette with her free hand from the butt-filled saucer in front of her.

She heard her father's voice then, calling from outside, 'Nina, Nina love,' and she stopped what she was doing, made her good-byes, left and closed the door behind her. And she could see the trap among the caravans, the rancid moon behind it, Dan Turnbull in the front, her mother in the back, her father beside Dan.

'Nina,' he called again, in that sad worried voice, and she wondered what day it would be that she would break his heart.

28

'I REMEMBER HIS letters,' says Janie as the kettle boils over and she scours the pot with the scalding water, then throws in the leaves, 'in your handwriting with his syntax, an oddly comforting juxtaposition of elements if I may say so, you two had become the one creature at last, elegant yet unlettered, the occasional erudite word sitting like an awkward jewel among the plain and pithy sentences. I read your own letters with Nina, and no matter how well expressed I could never quite see what was at issue. But those of Gregory—George, if I can call your union that, had the simplicity of direct depiction, direct speech, that allowed me to visualise. I could see the blue Mediterranean, bluer as he said than the cornflowers that grew round the turnip ridges in Keiling's Farm. I could see the islands edging past the coal-ship the way the clouds edged past the Mourne Mountains or the chestnut tree when we lay in the dried mud at the trunk and looked up at them, sometimes for hours. I could see the coal-ship then edge past the islands to reveal the isthmus surrounded by the floating pots and pans of His Majesty's Royal Navy. Each battleship belching smoke, I think he wrote, or you wrote for him, like a primus stove.'

~

The pearl, the pearl, he seemed born to find glories under rocks, to pull fistfuls of Kerry Blues out of the wet earth, to find the mulch beneath a seashell, he chewed the flesh of that oyster and spat out that pearl, left me that pearl and I sewed it in my shawl as I promised I would. I thought of the speck of sand deposited by the river, growing slowly inside the horned shell, how long does it take pearls to grow I wondered, longer than whatever else was growing. We were lost, temporarily, without the two of them, the two of us, Janie and me, considering our futures.

Ida Lennox brought me to Dublin, asked me to consider acting as a future. I listened in the concert rooms to the girl reciting *Hiawatha* and curtseyed myself, did my own recitation, *Francis Farrelly* by Percy French. But of course it was impossible, my mother wouldn't countenance it, and underneath the pig-iron bridge by the Customs House Ida Lennox kissed me and left me her card, please consider, and that was when I expurged again, into the brown waters of the river Liffey this time, I would have preferred it was the Boyne.

'Are you all right my dear, are you ill?'

'But no,' I told her, 'it will pass, it seems to.' On the train back I felt weak and light-headed, supine and giddy at the same time. It was Mary Dagge who noticed first, the breakfast I expelled on to the kitchen floor. By her sudden stillness I could tell something was wrong, terribly, irredeemably wrong. She stared at me in her maid's bonnet for one interminable moment. Then a swallow flew through the open door from the courtyard outside and she took it as a blessed release from the issue at hand, grabbed a mop and whirled it round the kitchen like a dervish, at the swallow, or was it sparrow, until she caught it a full-force blow and it bounced against the range and fell on the flagstones beside the vomit. Let me clean that up, she muttered, grabbed the pail, doused the mop in the greasy water and swept the regurgitated breakfast and the stunned swallow–sparrow out the kitchen door on to the gravel outside.

'How are you, Nina?' she said, her face turned away, and it was odd, she'd never called me Nina. Miss, girl or child were her particular terms of endearment.

'I'm fine,' I said, 'never better.'

'No,' she said, 'Nina, I've known you since you were born, I've nursed you through influenza, measles and scarlet fever, and I know enough to know this is not what anyone could call fine. Has someone been at you, child?'

And her head was cocked sideways as she said this, as if she couldn't bear to take the answer, and my mother came in at that moment, saved me for once, or saved me for the moment. Her nose was twitching like a King Charles spaniel. 'I get a whiff,' she said, 'whiffy in here, Mary, has the dog been sick?'

'Yes, Ma'am,' said Mary, 'that hound has been chewing grass again.' And I knew the subterranean awfulness of whatever was at issue then, if Mary Dagge could blame a dog for my vomit.

'Do the crossword with me, Nina?' she asked, mother that is, and I sat beside her as she chewed her pencil and Mary poured her tea. 'Strung, around a barrel,' she asked.

'Hooped,' I answered.

~

'Poetry,' says Gregory, and he sips at the lip of the china, feels the scald on his mouth and blows it cold. 'I took it down as plain poetry, and I can remember him now on the deck at evening in Mudros Harbour rocking back and forwards as he dictated, Dear Dada, dear Janie. But they were all poets then, before the thing began, subalterns thumbing through their school *Iliads* at dawn, wondering where on that broken line of pink mountains in the distance was Thermopylae, banishing the dust, the heat, the steaming turds in the Aegean sea with their scented imaginings.'

'And you,' says Janie, 'didn't you write?'

'No,' he says, 'I didn't, I wrote through him maybe, and that was enough for me, besides, who would I write to?'

'Nina,' she says. 'Or, God help us, me?'

'I was back to where I'd started,' he says, 'before I walked over the gravelled back yard with my case tied up with twine in my hand. Among a mass of men, one among many, there was a comfort in knowing this is as individual as it ever gets, and the years in Baltray I realised were an aberration. This isolation, this me, this lone consciousness among a crowd, this was the norm. Besides, you get closer, and I don't know how to put this, you get closer to them than you've ever been, and it's a closeness that demands nothing of you, demands no other contact than the knowledge that the condition is shared, of being one among a mass of rubbing shoulders – yes, how are you mate, don't have to tell me, I know, I know. Most of them would die and something in me sensed that, suspected perhaps that he would die too, but for some reason I never thought of myself among the chosen, though the irony is that I would have died in the end, if not for him. So I had left, absolutely and definitively, and if wasn't for what happened, Janie, I would have never come back.'

'She had changed too,' says Janie, 'and maybe that was why. She changed when you both left. I couldn't understand it, but it was that odd feeling of one world having finished and another having not yet begun. I had thought it would bring us closer – there was so much we could share now, you know, the world of girls about to be women, women saying goodbye to girls. But she went alone to Dublin to see that actress Ida Lennox who reminded her of her drowned nanny. I felt hurt I remember, the trip to Dublin would have been more than grand and would have implied we might have shared a similar future, or at least talk about our dissimilar ones. What future was there for me? My father, bless his heart, had petitioned the Harbourmaster for an apprentice clerkship, no opening for a girl, although my fine copperplate handwriting was as fine as any boy's. Marriage maybe, or some post in one of the houses? I could have been Mary Dagge, Gregory, or my version of Mary Dagge. But we had that summer, I had hoped and longed for that summer between us, me and Nina, and I had imagined the murmurings about our mutual futures we would have shared, hoped for the talk about shared hopes. But she had withdrawn into a distant shell like the oyster George had opened with his teeth, and there was no opening for me, I wasn't let in. So I lost your sister in a sense, that summer.'

~

I walked along the shore, the other shore, down along the carpet of dead shells by the water's edge to the factory. It was almost empty now. The market had dried up, most of the young men enlisted, and my father was downwind of the smell of rotting shellfish with paints and an easel before him, in a corduroy jacket, smoking a pipe. He was standing as he daubed, the brown river in front of him, the few boats, the Dutch landscape on the other side. He seemed not to have a care in the world.

'I know I am an indifferent painter,' he said, 'and I know I can never capture precisely what the landscape before my eyes means inside my eyes, so to speak. But the question is, Nina dear, why doesn't my lack of talent impinge more on my enjoyment of the activity?'

'Maybe it distracts,' I said, and curled myself beside his feet on the warm round stones. 'Besides, it's beautiful to me.'

'Distracts from what?' he asked.

'From thoughts of war,' I said, 'of Gregory out there, wherever he is.'

'And George,' he said, 'not forgetting George. There have been wars since this river invented itself, but the river flows on regardless.'

'So,' I said, 'that's what the river did, it invented itself.' And a tug passed by creating its own wake like a knife through the placid waters and Janie's father waved from the wheel.

'That's the question,' he said, 'did Boinn invent the river or did the river invent Boinn?'

'If one was there before the other,' I said, 'there's no question about who invented whom.'

'But the spring was there before the girl looked at her reflection,' he said.

'But the spring was not yet a river,' I replied.

'Aha,' he said, 'there you are, we have a conundrum.' He daubed in the brown ribs of seaweed beneath the surface of the water which looked like lady's hair.

'Have you something to tell me, Nina?' he asked.

'No,' I lied. 'What could I have to tell you?'

'Something about your life, now that your brother is gone.'

'My half-brother,' I corrected him. 'But if I ever had something to tell you, would you punish me for it?'

'No,' he said, 'but I would certainly listen.'

'Is the factory finished?' I asked him.

'It's in abeyance,' he said, 'the King pays better wages than your father.'

'And how will we live then?'

'The way we have always lived,' he said. 'The factory made its money long ago, its continuance is more a matter of charity than anything else. So if they want to fight, let them fight, I will paint.'

'Talk to your mother,' he said as I turned to go.

'Why,' I asked him, 'why do you say that?'

'Because,' he said, 'you talk to me but less often to her.' And as I walked off over the carpet of dried shells, I wonder, did he sense something, did he sense the tiny seed the river had deposited in me that would grow to be a woman herself. All this growth, birth and death, I thought, why can't things just be frozen in the moments we perceive them, like a perfect picture, understandable and unchangeable? And I walked on away from him over the centuries of oyster-shells and cockle-shells and mussel-shells and scallop-shells that had made his fortune and grown pearls of their own, pearls forgotten now, growing somewhere still, underneath the surface of the brown water. Dan took me back in the trap and Garibaldi, who alone of all creatures should have stayed Garibaldi, brown and unchangeable, was coated I noticed with a fine sprinkling of grey hairs I'd never seen as a child. So she was changing too, I thought as he walked then trotted, slowly, with a laboured wheeze.

'She's not much left in her, this beast,' said Dan.

'Has she not, Dan?' I asked.

'No,' he said, 'almost time for the knacker's yard.'

'If she died,' I said to Dan, 'my world would be quite dead, do you know that, Dan?'

'No,' said Dan, 'you only think that, Nina girl. Another horse would take her place and you'd get used to it.'

29

'THEY CALLED IT musketry, though the guns we fired were now machines. They called us fusiliers, though the fusillades came from the ships behind us. They called us infantry and sent us to a beach where walking was an impossible dream, where movement was measured in inches. But they conspired,' says Gregory, 'to make it glorious on the morning we assembled in the old Scottish collier, and listened to the marching bands, their anthems growing distant under the slow chug of engines as we drew away. There were ocean liners for the brass and battleships, destroyers, more coal-ships than I could count. We dragged tows behind us and had gangplanks trussed to the collier's sides, like spiders' legs caught in a web. A storm seemed to threaten and then died away as the sun went down and the moon came out and we made our way through the quietening sea. It was impossible not to believe that something glorious, whatever glory meant, could not emerge from so much effort in concert, such a massive movement of men, of ships and of arms. But what glory meant, we would come to realise later. It meant death for somebody other than oneself. But at that time it seemed an abstract, as the coastline we were bound for defined itself glumly in the moonlight, a thin pencil of darkness, of suspect promise, the shattered hulk of the fort on the promontory, above the beach.

The tides were hard, of course, it was more than a river and less, far less than a sea, Asia looming from the cliffs on one side, Europe on the other, and this runnel of water, this massive, dark and turbulent Boyne running in between. We could hear the gunfire from the other beaches now, the flashes of naval artillery were lighting the sky, but that only served to augment the quietness here. We were in a cocoon of the strangest kind of silence, the distant clatter and boom seemed to isolate and flashes looked like a red faraway thunderstorm. We clambered into the smaller boats and were separated, George was across the water from me now, dragged in the wake by a metal hawser. I could see his head illuminated with a score or so others against the rippled moonlight on the surface which signalled the turbulence below. Then the gap-toothed outline of the fort of Sedd el Bahr loomed behind him and all recognition was gone. I watched the dark lip of the shore, when I could see it behind the coal-ship towing us, and the ship killed its engines and the sailors rowed us towards the beach and I don't think I have ever heard or felt such unnatural stillness.'

~

My mother was walking down the avenue with two sticks in her hand. 'Come Dan,' she said, 'and you too Nina, there's a new game we must learn, it's called golf.'

'Isn't golf for men, Ma'am?' Dan said gently, drawing Garibaldi to what seemed a welcome halt.

'It's Saturday,' she said, 'which I've been reliably informed is ladies' day.' She took Dan's hand and climbed, or clambered up. 'This is a putter,' she told me, holding up one of the sticks, 'and this, I've been told, is called a niblick.'

Dan left us at the first hole and she inserted a wooden spike in the ground and placed a white ball on top of it.

'One addresses the ball, Nina,' she said, 'and one draws back and swings.'

And she swung, with a rustle of skirts and a dangerous rush of air from the metal club and a dull twonk sounded. I saw the tiny spot of white rise in the air and bounce along the green sward, which, she told me, was called a fairway. I took my place and swung, and saw my own ball sail beyond hers into an outcrop of longer grass, which, she told me, was called the rough.

'We walk now, follow the balls,' she said, 'which is the point of the exercise.'

'And the point of the exercise is?' I asked.

'Exercise,' she said, 'the ballast of fresh air, the movement of the limbs, the quickening of the blood, the pulse. You are too pale, Nina, and since he left you have been pining, avoiding the sunlight, moulting in your room. You have a whole future before you, my dear.'

'And can you see it?' I asked her.

'See what?' she answered as she reached her own ball and addressed it again. Three swipes this time and a mess of earth clods around her before the small white thing bounced on its awkward way.

'My future,' I said.

'No,' she said, 'I can't see your future any more than I can see my own. At your age I went to Italy to study and met the man I would one day marry. And maybe you will marry one day, but until that day you have a life to live.'

'So, that life stops with marriage?' I asked her.

'Mine did,' she said, 'which doesn't mean yours has to, all the more reason to think about it now.'

I had reached my ball in the long grass and cut the grass around it with swipes of the niblick, as if it was a scythe. Then I swung and the ball sailed into the air and bounced delicately up a small incline on to a plateau of mown grass she called a green.

'Good girl, Nina,' she said, 'you have a talent for this. So have you thought,' she continued as she walked forwards after her own white ball, 'of further education, the professions, medicine, nursing, a spell in the college of art?'

'Acting,' I said. 'I have thought of acting.'

'Acting what?' she asked.

'Acting,' I repeated, 'on the stage.'

'No, Nina, no,' and she was peremptory and certain, 'acting is for mountebanks and fallen women. No daughter of mine could ever act.'

Well, I thought, but I held my counsel and watched her chop her ball on to what she called the green.

'We aren't without means, of course,' she said, 'so it's not as if you have to survive by the sweat of your brow. I would have rec-ommended a tour of Italy in the company of one of the Siena nuns if it weren't so hazardous to travel.'

'Now,' she said, 'here is where we relinquish the niblick and rely on the putter. Place it between your hands,' she said, 'like this,' and she stood behind me, placed both arms around me and I could feel her full breasts against the small of my back, I could hear the rustle of her skirts, her breath on the small hairs of my neck. 'A gentle swing,' she said, 'on the same plane as the grass itself,' and she swung my arms back and the club touched the ball, which rolled forwards, hesitantly, towards the hole.

'I feel faint, mother', I said, and I turned and the retching came again which I tried to stop and I swayed to the left. And she held me and a stream of liquid gushed from my mouth towards her surprised face, and then darkness came.

~

'I kept looking at the transports ahead of us as they reached the beaches, wondering when the fusillade would start and wonder-ing which of them was George's. But there was nothing except the dull crump of the hulls hitting the shingle below, the plash of boots into the water and the sound of a thousand feet wading. And so I thought, against all logic, that we would land unhin-dered, all the firepower had been drawn towards the unseen flashes and the distant thunder a long way to our left. I saw them wade towards the shore, their arms in an upstretched V, their rifles parallel to the water between them. I couldn't make out which was him.

There was a crush of transports now, an impatient queue

anxious to reach that nondescript shore, and suddenly those who had reached it fell as if they had tripped across an invisible wire and the water churned as if hailstones were raining across the surface to the lines of men wading with their guns above their heads in their arms like a V, and the guns went flying as the men went down and the transport ahead of us, whose gangplank had just descended, dipped backwards in the water with the weight of dying men. Then the sound came and I heard the fusillade and knew why we were called the Dublin Fusiliers. We were protected by the transport in front, but it wheeled to starboard to protect itself and exposed us to the streams of hot metal from the dunes and the fort above.

A wall of men staggered backwards, with no sound other than a gasp of surprise, and the tonnage of dead bodies pushed me to the floor and slewed the bloody vessel to one side. I tried to crawl free and felt others crawling over me as those who could clambered over the falling bodies and threw themselves in the water. The floor of the transport was wet then and I staggered in the liquid, thought it had taken water, then realised it was blood, and I did the same, I clambered over that steppe of groaning flesh and threw myself seawards.

My pack pulled me down of course, I had been told it would, and as it took water it dragged me down further. I struggled to free myself from it, I panicked as I had been told I would, and then I found, to my surprise, that my feet were on a bed of shale and broken seashell not unlike the one below my father's factory on the Boyne. This fact amazed me for some strange reason, how familiar and how strange, but of course, any shore will be like any other shore. But the shock of the familiar made me stand, made me rise slowly, and my head broke the water, which I realised couldn't have been deeper than four feet.

The sealogged pack almost pulled me backwards once more, then I bent my head forwards, kissing the water, and began to walk towards the only place I could, the shore. There were bodies

Neil Jordan

around me, some threshing, some dead, and the dead ones took the bullets as well as any sandbag and I pushed one with me, in front of me and felt it jerk as it took each bullet, saw the water spout or maybe the blood from the corpse, but it was my floating sandbag, my own dead anonymous protective angel, and I knelt as the sea grew shallower and finally abandoned it and ran. I ran towards a mound of dune which was spitting with awakened sand, behind which twenty other shapes were cowering, and I cowered there with them.'

~

I remember that terrible silence on the green when I awoke, flat out on the grass with my hair spread around me like the Lady of Shalott. She stood above me with the niblick in her hand, the metal club of which she seemed to want to bury in my skull.

'Mother,' I asked, 'what is it?'

She seemed unwilling to reply, and the silence spoke instead for her, that terrible silence through which I could hear a skylark singing and her breath heaving.

'Your father,' she said eventually, 'can never know.'

'Can never know of what?' I asked her.

'Of your condition,' she said. 'Who was it?' she asked, again after an age of that silence and the skylark singing. 'Him,' she answered for me, 'your half-brother, oh my Lord, oh my Lord.'

Then even the skylark's song faltered and she filled the silence by saying, 'Get up, you bitch.' I tried to rise and reached my hand out to her for help, but she stayed still, immobile with that terrible quiet, so I grasped the putter and used it as a stick to rise. I walked away from her, three-legged like a cripple, and after another of those moments she followed behind.

~

'There were dead bodies like colonies of sleeping seals everywhere along the shoreline, and a whole carpet of bodies in the

212

sea itself, some of them moving, most of them not. The sea rose and fell beneath them,' says Gregory, 'causing the carpet to rise and fall with it, less like a carpet, more like a blanket covering of seaweed, and it was coloured khaki, something like the colour of seaweed, and the sea underneath the khaki was red. Further out towards the flaring battleships the moving sea of bodies diminished to what seemed like infinity, and I remember thinking, there are not enough bodies in the world to cover that distance. And I realised the shapes in the distance were the carcasses of fish that were brought to the surface by each boom. The shells flew above us with a sound that was like a woman's skirt being torn, and crashed on the fort beyond, a huge cloud of dust and shrapnel billowing in the air. And then as the cloud diminished, the thousands of tiny flashes sparked again, and the sand spat and danced and any one of us whose head had risen above the dunes out of curiosity or bloody-mindedness got bloodied and went down. And I remember thinking, it is still early morning, can't be later than half past seven.'

~

The silence that I walked in now was deep and interminable, broken only by sounds that served as a dramatic emphasis to it, the sound of her feet crushing the grass behind me, her niblick dragging behind her feet, her voice, which continued on the same train of thought like a broken soliloquy, saying, actress, of course, what a perfect profession, actress and whore, but he can never know, you see that don't you, he must never even suspect so go, please, inhabit a flea-pit in Montgomery Street, some music-hall in Brighton but go quietly and quickly, leave a gap of silence to explain your absence and write then, write after nine months or however long it takes, you're no daughter of mine but I won't deprive him of the angel he imagines, just don't ever disabuse of him of how he needs to think of you . . .

~

'My hearing must have gone,' says Gregory, 'because from then on I remember it all in silence. A huge old collier pushed through the burning boats and the bobbing bodies towards a pier of barges they had strung together, stretching from the pink sand round the shore out into the bloody water. And the gangways fell and the men poured down them and we were given a respite, because the sand above my head stopped dancing and the water spumed towards the barges like some god was pissing down on them, all the fire of course was concentrated there, took less than seconds to reach them. And the bodies on the barges fell left into the sea, the bodies on the gangplanks fell backwards, making a carpet of corpses for the ones who came behind to clamber over. I knew then I was a coward, because whatever they were doing I could never have done, and in the end even they couldn't do it, since they gave up the attempt. The collier began to hiss steam and draw back like a huge and useless dragon, dragging the gangplanks with it, spilling out the corpses in a bloodied half-circle as it turned. But I was seeing it the way they didn't see it, flat, from behind, plain horrible, and if I had been them I realised I would have done the same, an hour before had just done the same, pushed the only way there was through the falling bodies, forwards, since there was no going back. But I was a coward, we were all heroic cowards, moving like lemmings in the only direction allowed us, towards the waves of fire.'

~

She hit me once before the clubhouse and I fell into a mound of sand which she had told me was a bunker. I got to my feet, spittle and sand mixed in my mouth with the taste of vomit, and I said, 'Mother.'

'Please don't call me mother,' she said, 'I have no daughter.'

And when we reached the house the silence was even vaster, though there was a wind now, rattling the shutters, a big wind which seemed as if it would continue for days. I went to my room where the wind augmented the silence, and after what seemed hours Mary Dagge came up with a glass of milk and a sandwich on a tray.

'What a thing,' she said, 'what a terrible thing, Nina. Now you have to eat, drink this milk, eat the sandwich, and when they're all asleep, I'll take you, I know a woman, a tinker woman who can do something.'

'Do what?' I asked her.

'What's necessary,' she said. 'Don't think you're the first, this happens in the townland, there are ways and means of dealing with it and it won't be pretty, but there it is.'

30

'WE BEGAN TO dig', says Gregory, 'since there was nothing more worthwhile to do. Ships wheeled in meandering circles behind us, tows full of shapes that seemed to be kneeling, sheltering from the fire until you realised, no, they were dead, jammed against each other, half-upright on their knees as if in some kind of prayer where they'd fallen. We knelt too, digging with the cloven-shaped spades from our packs, and made what I'd always dreamed of making on the dunes back home, a trench. We dug down until we could stand upright, we packed hard the walls of sand and reinforced them with driftwood sleepers, we dug sideways till we hit the hard rock where the cliff raked underneath the sand, we dug forwards, tunnelling underneath towards the Turkish side. We packed the sand we dug in sandbags and piled them on the top to take whatever they were firing at us. We dug like moles, burrowing into the sand to take whatever comfort it could give, and when we could dig no more we slept in the sandy bed we had dug for ourselves.'

~

I must have been asleep. Mary Dagge woke me, saying come quietly now, quietly. And she led me through the darkened house, as silent as it has become these days, down the stairs, through the hall, into the scullery, out the kitchen door, and there she had Garibaldi tethered to the trap, the bridle tied to the boot-cleaner. 'Get up there Nina,' and her accent had broadened, she was about country business I sensed, talking the way she rarely talked with us, and I got up. She held the horse hard by the reins and whipped it smartly and the old creature jumped with the shock, used to softness as I was. Where did all these hard knocks come from, her ears seemed to ask, pricking backwards on her flat griddled skull. Over the gravel with the wind blowing, so if they heard anything above, it was not the hooped wheels crunching off the gravel, it was the storm blowing. Why was there a storm? It seemed appropriate, too appropriate to my mood, ridiculously apt – I remember thinking the whole process like a cautionary tale, the summer leaves flying off the branches far too early, swirling around Garibaldi's pricked-back ears. Then the moon made an appearance as if it had to, as if it was required for this tale, a warning to all maidens young and fair.

'Where are we going?' I asked Mary Dagge, and she answered, 'Mabel Hatch.'

'You said a tinker woman,' I remember saying, 'Mabel Hatch's no tinker.'

'Some call her Mabel Cash,' she told me, 'one of the rare occurrences of travelling women that strike roots. Of the Clare Cashes,' she said, 'her father was Roustabout Cash, had women from here to Lisdoonvarna, knew how to deal with every ailment that affects them, and don't worry your head now, Nina, Mabel will see you right.'

~

'I awoke,' says Gregory, 'to a fine drizzle curtaining my face, turning the sand underneath me into wet clay. It was night and whatever fires had been burning on the ravaged boats had been long extinguished. There was a distant glow from the *Queen Elizabeth*, a strange movement from the sea, as if a beaded curtain was shifting with each wash of the tide, and the beads were bodies, of course, still uncollected. They would bloat over the next few days, the tide would retreat and leave them beached and sizzling in the hot sun, the tide would advance again and collect them, moisten their dried khakis and the dried skin beneath them until they shrivelled eventually, into something as insignificant as dried fish.'

~

In Mabel Hatch's house – a long way from her barn, who would have thought it – she had a steaming bowl, towels dipped in mustard and a bicycle pump which she dipped in a jar and pulled, it made a sucking sound I remember. She loosened my skirts and put hot towels round my tummy, a poultice she called it. She gave me a cup to drink, it tasted salt, tart salt, and I lay back my head on the straw feeling drowsy.

'That's it,' said Mary Dagge, 'sleep if you feel like it,' but it didn't feel like sleep, like a dream had while half awake. And I felt something cold between my legs, it was the pump, I tried to rise but Mary Dagge stroked my forehead, saying 'Hush, Nina, hush,' and I heard the sound of the sucking pump but it was blowing now, vomiting something over me in me, and I cried and she said hush, and I twisted from them both but my legs were wet.

'Does my mother know you're doing this?' I cried, and they both said, 'wisha no love,' in that country way, and the way they said it I knew she did.

'Take me home,' I said to Mary Dagge.

'Yes love,' she said, 'it's finished and we'll see tomorrow did it work.'

'Did what work?' I asked, but I didn't need the answer. I knew.

31

'I LAY THERE in the soft rain wondering which of them was George; it seemed impossible he'd made it, but then my comprehension was limited to the trenches we had dug and the score or so bodies that slept around me. For all I knew there could have been aerophagii roaming the beachhead, monsters chewing on the flesh of dead platoons. Mine was shattered and lost, I recognised none of the faces around me. I thought of the pearl that George had found in the river, extracted from the oyster-shell with his teeth, and hoped Nina had kept it, since it might be the only remembrance the three of us would have of him. He seemed more dear than life to me then, and looking out at that carpet of waterlogged bodies, a symbol of what was best in life, of what had been extinguished. I had survived and wasn't sure I wanted to, I lived like the tiny spider crabs that scurried round my boots, the bloated worms the soft drizzle was bringing to the surface in the dampening sand. There would be flesh for them to feed on, spilt intestines to swim in, dead arseholes to penetrate, those corpses over the weeks would live with maggots, worms, ticks, lice, with those huge bulbous bluebottles that seemed specific to those beaches. But whatever was George in each of them was dead. I remembered the boy that was pilloried at school, I remembered the crushed dockleaves Nina wrapped his battered hands in, I remembered his face behind the dried tomato plants reading Touchstone: sir, I am a true labourer, I earn that I eat, get that I wear, owe no man hate, envy no man's happiness.'

~

Mary Dagge sang softly on the way back, to the greying horse, not to me. She sang a lullaby about the windy castle at Dromore, about how those inside were safe as houses, or as castles I suppose the phrase should be. And the winds were dropping now as if they'd played whatever their part was, and the moon sat on a long vista of cloud the way the moon does after bad weather, you wonder how you can see it, sitting on the circles of cloud and not behind it, but there it was. She helped me up the stairs, kind again in that country way. She said, 'Where's your brother now, child, on the way to the Dardanelles?' And I tried to picture them both on a large metal ship like the ones that used to strike the bar by the Lady's Finger, but on a different sea, under the same moon maybe.

The house didn't seem to want me in it, I could feel that, the opposite to the way it is now, it won't let me go, and I wasn't sure I wanted to be in it any longer. I don't know why when I recount this I become the girl I was then, the breathy girl in a river of events, all the distance vanished, grief maybe, loss, so strong I can't separate myself. She said, 'Sleep, child,' like a spell and opened the door to my room, the room too that didn't seem to want me in it, and I could see through the window the sun was whitening the moonclouds over the curling river, over Mozambique. I took off my clothes, wet below, and felt my body didn't want me in it either, I felt my nightgown didn't want me in it, and so I got between the sheets naked, as Mary Dagge would have said in that country way, as the day I was born.

32

'I MUST HAVE slept again,' says Gregory, 'because I was awoken
by a hand on my shoulder and a pith helmet near my face, muttering something about an advance. He scurried down the trenches
we had dug and woke them one by one. It wasn't daybreak yet but
there was enough light in the sky to show the battleships, the
Queen Elizabeth like a black cardboard cut-out against the palest
dark behind it. Then the guns began to roar and I must have had
my hearing back, because the sound seemed all around me, like a
giant bell, booming, circular, whirling from one ear to the other.
We stared up from the sandbags and over the next twenty or so
minutes saw the fort above us disintegrate. It seemed to become its
own volcano, spewing clouds of dust and smoke from within its
bowels, geysers of red flame shooting upwards as each new shell
hit, eventually wrapping itself in a shroud of black through which
we could see nothing. Then the firing stopped and the cloud stilled
and there were no answering crackles of yellow, as if everyone
inside it must be dead. There were feet then, clambering over the
top, and I followed them, and was amazed to see, all over the
beach, squirming figures like our own emerging from invisible
dug-outs. We were everywhere, like ants gone to ground, scurrying
into the sunlight. How, I wondered, do these pockets of battered
humanity become an army again? But that's what they were, an
infantry of thousands of feet making for the cloud that twenty
minutes before had been the castle. We staggered up the rise and
into the cloud-fogged piles of ancient masonry. There were bodies
fused into the shattered stone, pulverised with the dust, bits of
bone and khaki mixed with the shattered brick, but no resistance.

We made it through the pall of smoke into the village behind, and there it was a different matter, they let us plough down streets then emerged from broken doorways to fire from behind. I fired blindly and jerked that bayonet four times into resistant flesh and became amazed again, this time at how simple savagery was and how long it took the recipients of it to die. Then, I felt a thud in my arm and went over through an open doorway, and lay there staring at a pot bubbling in an empty room, a wood fire beneath it. I got the smell of vegetables and spices and felt a hunger like I'd never felt, realised it was a day since I'd eaten. I heard the sounds of the cleaning out in the street behind me, the dulled cries and the pop of rifles, saw the low embers beneath the bubbling pot and realised somebody had left it, a meal interrupted. I edged myself forwards on my good arm and used a blackened piece of wood as a ladle and began to eat, the scalding liquid dribbling down my chin but the taste so good after that I didn't care. *Taajin*, I learnt to call it later, a rough broth of vegetables and lamb. And my eyes must have become accustomed to the dark because then I saw her, a girl, huddled, almost part of the shadows, as if she'd been there for ever and would never move again, braided hair and a ring of medallions round her sweating forehead. She stared at me as I continued to eat, and I tried to smile to reassure her that I meant no harm. She smiled back, a flash of white teeth from the shadows.

I got to my knees and felt in my pockets for a coin, a trinket, anything to pay for what I'd eaten, and I found one, a penny, covered in my own warm blood. I flicked it across the floor to her, and her hand spun out, and she caught it neatly. She bit it with her teeth, hoping, probably, that it was gold.'

~

I dreamed of the pearl, I remember, as large as the moon itself, lying in the round concentric mulch of the oyster's flesh, I was inside the shell and the pearl was as big as it could possibly have been. The swathes of colour, pink and delicately purple and white, shifted as I shifted my head. The oyster's flesh was around me like wet seaweed, shifting groggily the way seaweed does when the tide is turning, and I stretched my hand down to touch the pulpy mass and it parted to reveal the face of Isobel Shawcross with pearls in her open eyes.

I saw myself dreaming then, the enormous pearl outside the window sitting placidly in the purpling sky, and I saw my face below, my naked body under the sheets which were turning red, and I realised my body had a certain kind of beauty, although it still didn't want me in it. I could have left that body, I felt, left that body to its own devices, but as it had that certain kind of beauty I decided it might as well be put to use, as if it was suddenly someone else's body, not mine. And it went on that way, me dreaming of me dreaming, the pearl outside the window slowly vanishing in the reddening sky.

I awoke properly when the sun was going down, and the sheets were caked with sweat around me, or with something of more consistency than sweat. I felt I should wash but couldn't face the corridor, the silence that would be in the house for ever now, and so I lay quite still, thinking of this body, no longer really mine, and the uses to which it could be put. I heard the sounds of the house going about its business in the silence, and when the silence became unbearable I put on the clothes I had worn last night, the stiff clothes, soiled below. I waited until the silence around was quite complete, and then wrapped the shawl around me and walked down the stairs, outside.

~

'The bullet had nicked my shoulder, there was more blood than damage, and as I lay back and tried to undo the gory buttons, I heard a scuffling on the floor behind me. I turned and saw her crawling towards me, the coin between her teeth. It must have reassured her because she helped me bind the wound, undid my buttons, smiling all the time, whispering in that language she seemed to assume I understood. I ripped strips off my shirt and wrapped them round, her hennaed fingers held the knot while I tied it. The words were gutteral and vowel-less, but seemed infinitely kind, coming from her childish mouth.

"Thank you," I said, which seemed the only suitable response. Then I backed out into the street and saw her in the darkness of the room, huddling back into those shadows as if she would stay there for ever.

The fury was dying. There were bodies again in the street, like ritual petals scattered wherever we went, mainly Turkish ones this time, bootless, mounds of wadding wrapped round their pitifully scarred feet. Sallow-skinned faces, covered in a fine blowing dust. Some of them were living, not bodies at all, they were moaning and an officer walked down bayoneting the live ones as he went.

I was put to cleaning Turkish trenches outside the village, while the thing progressed towards a hill beyond, small figures running towards the distant barbed wire, lines of them that became gap-toothed as they went. Whatever the outcome was I was beyond caring, tired beyond belief. The dead here had been caught *in situ*, there was a horrible domesticity to the cooking utensils beside empty ammunition boxes, stale bread and olives. We grabbed each corpse and rolled it towards an outer trench which we filled with sand after we had filled it with bodies. We dug latrines and cleared the piles of faeces out since they seemed to have shat close to where they stood. By the time the moon came out, a white empty thing, we had the trenches fit for a new set of British corpses. And I watched them fill with live men who knew they could be dead tomorrow.

I was sent back then, to the beach from which I'd come, told to find my unit of the Dubliners, a fruitless task since it had been obliterated in the first ten minutes. What was left of the moonlit fort was crowded now with mules and transports, huge towers of supply crates growing arbitrarily. On the beach beyond I could see the boats unloading, there were jetties built, a whole ramshackle city growing on the tiny beach, men naked in the water washing themselves. And the shoreline was cleared of corpses, there were barges piled high with them, chugging out towards the hospital ships. Where are you George, I asked myself, where are you?'

33

THE MOON WAS coming up again and the haystacks sat in the fields as if they would always be there, but I knew of course that come September they'd be gone. I walked down the road, along by the river in the direction of Janie's, I would tell her, tell her it all I thought, and then it, whatever I was going to tell her, shifted inside me like a wallop and I sat on a bank of grass above the mudflats of Mozambique and felt my dress getting wet again. A horse and cart clipped by and I wrapped myself in my shawl like a travelling woman, and when the figure on it with the stove-pipe hat said grand night, I returned, the way Mary Dagge would have, grand night indeed.

I got up and staggered on towards Janie's, I felt I had to tell her. And outside Mabel Hatch's barn another wallop happened, and rather than fall on the road like an animal thing I made my way into the dark inside. I heard the owl hoot and then go still as I entered the dark, and the dark came clearer to my eyes, I could see the shadows of mounds of straw and the irregular ascent they made high up towards the broken wall. I was aware a passer-by on the road, by the river, could have seen a figure lying on the lower straw, and so I climbed up, out of sight of the road, slowly. Every step was another slow wallop.

~

'I found my trench, the trench we had dug the morning of that day, and pushed aside the dozing bodies to make room. I settled my pack down and my shovel and rifle and felt my left-hand sleeve stiff with the dried blood. I climbed out again and made my way to the bloodied shore, and was wading in the water when I saw a figure out there among the others, naked like them, but bigger, much bigger, bending with a pith helmet in his giant hands, filling it with seawater, pouring it over his cropped hair. I recognised the hands, I couldn't have mistaken them.

"George!" I shouted, and he turned, the moon and battleships behind him, the water dripping off his naked body, and he walked towards me then, held the pith helmet over his privates, then let it go again to embrace me, and said, with that crushing simplicity of his, "No larks here, Pip." And the salt water ran down his face like tears.'

~

I lay on the upper straw in the barn and waited for the owl to hoot one more time. One more time would do it I felt, would draw the thing out, would stop whatever was staining the shawl beneath my knees, the bale of hay below that. The yellow straw was silver in the moonlight and was turning a dull sea green below me, spreading all the time. And then I heard the low purr of wings and the brown thing flew over me once more and out of the triangular aperture where the moon was. That did it, I felt, whatever animal thing was happening was over now, and I remembered the stone woman in the circular passageway with her hands pulling her knees apart and me guiding George's hand to mine. And I thought, that's what her knees were open for. It wasn't the birth of the river, it was the birth of this.

It was in my wet shawl, it had been inside me, it had a shape I didn't want to see, a tiny form I didn't want to feel, and so I wrapped the shawl around it. But I knew even then the less I saw of it, the more I would remember.

I got to my knees slowly and felt the bale beneath me shift and slide, and I slid down with it on to the bales below. I fell on my back and it fell on top of me, the wet shawl with the part of me inside it, a pearl, I told myself, a precious, bloody, dead pearl, and I wrapped it, getting wetter all of the time. I slid down then on my wet bum, down bale after bale to the strawy floor. I wanted to be back, for some reason, in some place I had felt happier, by the chestnut tree or near the glasshouse. And so I walked back down the empty road along the riverside through the copse of trees, out past the glasshouse to the orchard wall.

And there, in the orchard, Dan had left his spade by the rusty gate. I took the spade and went to where the earth was soft and I dug. I dug the deepest hole that I could dig in what I would call my weakened state and put my shawl in there for ever and filled it up again. And then I walked down the long field to the river, and underneath the chestnut tree I entered the water and swam. Not so much swam as floated. I would happily have been found there in the morning with the stains of death all over me, but the water did something, the river always did something as I was to find through the years, it washed me clean, and the pull of the tide left me back eventually where I had started, underneath the swing and the chestnut tree.

So I climbed out again and walked to the house, and if anybody met me and asked why I was wet, I was swimming, of course, just swimming, and if they asked why, in your clothes, I would have asked back, what, you think a girl should swim naked?

~

'I stripped by the rancid beach while George put his clothes on.

"I'll mind them for you, Greg," he said, as if we were at a bathing spot in Bettystown.

I waded out into the hot sea and washed the grime off what used to be me in the pink foam. I knew nothing would ever be the same again, watching those huge plates of black metal out against the horizon waiting to spew their fire once more. I felt the dull pain as the salt seeped through the bandage, into the hole in my arm.

"Are you hurt?" I asked him.

"No," he said, "it doesn't hurt much."

"What doesn't hurt?" I asked, and turned and saw his hand come up to his face and realised he was missing one finger.

"Don't laugh," he said.

"How could I laugh, George?" I asked him.

"I don't know how," he said, "but it does seem funny." And he reached into the pocket of his tunic and drew something out, something small and pink that curled like a radish. "My finger," he said, with a dulled bemusement. "We were moving up the cliff-face, I reached up to grab a ledge and a bullet took it. It landed at my feet."

"You need to sleep, George," I said.

"I know," he said, "and so does my finger." And he laughed, and I laughed too because I knew he wanted me to.

"Shall we bury it?" he said, as I walked back towards him, shaking the drops from my naked body.

"Why not," I said. I dressed then, pulling my rancid trousers over my wet legs, buttoning my shirt that was stiff with blood and sweat, and George found a discarded bayonet, stabbed at the sand with it, gouging out a hole with his good hand. He placed the pink radish-like thing carefully inside, then covered it up, stamped the sand with his feet and stabbed in the bayonet once more so it protruded like a cross.

"Here lies my finger," he said, "which lost its little life some-where near the beach, beneath the fort whose name I can't pro-nounce. May it rest in peace." Then he blessed himself with his bad hand and the dried bloodied stump seemed not to bother him at all. He looked up at me with those eyes and it was hard to tell whether he was laughing or crying. "Have you anything to say, Gregory?"

"Yes," I said, and bowed my head. "I want to pay homage to George's little finger, whose service to King and Country has been mighty and immeasurable, which finger died in the heat of battle in defence of Poor Little Belgium on a beach in Turkey.

This finger paid the ultimate price and joins the ranks of glorious dead on these shores from Achilles to those thousands of poor souls around us as yet unburied. Amen." '

~

I changed in my bedroom and walked down the stairs, carrying my wet clothes in a bundle, down the avenue with the crunching gravel, through the gates and along by the silver river. I threw my bundle in the water, and I walked with no object, just to walk, just to feel my useless body moving of its own accord along the pitiless road. I knew the road had no pity, just as the house would have no pity, as my mother and Mary Dagge would have no pity, and the only one who would have pity I could never tell, and that would be my father.

So I walked away from him, putting so much distance between him and me that I would never have to hear the sound of his breaking heart. I walked until the house had long disappeared behind the hedges and the hayricks and the broadleafed trees, and kept the river to my left with the graveyard by Mornington across it. And when the spires of Drogheda came into view, and the masts of the boats like spires themselves, I saw the round yellow light of a porthole come into view with a gangplank above it. I stood by that porthole and looked down at how the yellow light seemed to make the lapping crests of water below even blacker. I could have taken one step in and found myself looking at the hull of the boat from the crush of water below. But I heard a sound then, the lowing of cattle from the ship above, and I decided to go wherever those cattle went. I walked up the manure-caked gangplank, and on the deck I could hear nothing but the creak of the ship and the moan of cattle below. There were bales of straw stacked below the funnel, and I crawled up them like I had crawled in Mabel Hatch's barn and I wrapped the loose straw around me and fell asleep.

~

'The trench was full of sleeping bodies so we burrowed into the sand above it like crabs. Or more like worms perhaps,' says Gregory, 'the kinds of worms that leave their sandcasts on Baltray strand, ragworms, lugworms . . . We scraped the ground with our knives and wormed our way in, leaving the displaced sand like casts above us, facing the Turkish line, ready to catch whatever bullets they fired our way when the sun came up. It felt as if the earth was our only comforter and there was a sweet protection in being so close to it, not even an oilcloth beneath us. We belonged to it and only it, it would protect us and if needs be bury us, embrace us, turn us once more into itself through the agency of what we seemed to be, worms. I was asleep within minutes and when I woke the hot sun was climbing above us and there was a burning in my left arm.'

~

When I awoke the funnel was spewing smoke above me and the sun was streaming through it. There was a girl standing by the mass of rivets with her arms crossed, looking down on me. I couldn't see her face for the smoke but I heard her voice.

'What do we have here,' she said, 'a stowaway? Oh no, it's the girl from the Laytown races.'

And I recognised the voice of the Colleen Bawn. 'Are we moving?' I asked her.

'No,' she said, 'we're waiting for the engines to warm up. I never got your name.'

'Rosalind,' I lied.

'What are you running from, Rosalind?' she asked.

'Nothing,' I said.

'You like sleeping on cattle feed, then?'

'No,' I said, 'but I've got no alternative.'

'You better come down,' she said, 'and have some breakfast or they'll send you back to nothing.'

~

'By eight o'clock the guns were going again from the sea behind us, and we crawled out of our burrows into the trench where we re-acquainted ourselves with our kit. George opened a tin and we ate the meat together, it was in a warm stew of suet and water and tasted like nothing I could remember. We were told to kit up and walk forwards which we did, though if we had ignored the order I don't know what they could have done since it came from no officer we knew, and besides, we hardly knew each other. But we walked forwards because that was why we came here, we had a dim memory of our purpose, and what were we there for, if not to walk blindly on to an unknown beach, across ridges of shale and scrub, through unannounced and unexpected red poppies, towards an opponent who only revealed himself in distant puffs of smoke. Maybe they had been cleared out by the bombardment, maybe they had fled, because we walked unopposed now, up small stony slopes that seemed hardly worth the effort.

We gained height gradually and made it to the ridge where I could see the whole peninsula – lines of men stretching away to the left and right, thousands of them, an endless plain in front of us, four or five broken stone columns jutting into the sky and beyond them what someone told me was a village. I could see the bright colours far to my right, red and blue – or was it gold? – of the French troops, miles away like small toys, images of what I had always imagined were soldiers, small emblazoned ants walking forwards and every now and then one of them would tumble backwards and vanish from view.

So there was firing down there, we could gather, but from where we were the only thing to stop us was our own tiredness and thirst. Thirst more than tiredness. We could have sleep-walked on, eyes half-closed, feet moving forwards in the half-remembered imitation of the act of walking, but the thirst blinded us to anything but the need for a drop of the water we were leaving behind us. They had runners carrying cans of it from the beaches, but the further we moved the less of it reached us, until around noon we just stopped, like mindless donkeys who could move neither forwards nor back but could only stand, struggling for breath in the punishing heat.

They came at us then, from somewhere in the leafless bushes beyond, one of them waving a sword of all things. And we probably would have let them cut right through us, when a shell whistled over and exploded above them leaving pulverised pieces of the flesh of fifty or more, a pall of white smoke, an echo that rattled from the gulley to our left and the distant groans of the men still alive, in a language that was unintelligible. But we understood well enough, they were dying, and that sounds the same in anyone's language.'

~

She brought me down below, past the merchant seamen waking up, to where the cattle were shifting in their pens and her companions were sleeping on their rolled-up tent canvas against the portholes. She poured a pitcher of cold water for me to wash myself in and as they woke, one by one, the questions came.

'Are you in trouble, Rosalind, the kind of trouble she's in?'

'What kind of trouble is she in?' I asked, and the older one with the straw-blonde hair rubbed her belly and laughed.

'The kind of trouble that shows,' she said, 'the kind of trouble that'll have her off the boards in a month's time.'

'No,' I said, 'I'm not in that kind of trouble, I'm not in any trouble at all, but I want to do what she does.'

'What do you want to do that I do?' she asked, looking at me with her clear blue eyes.

'Act,' I said.

34

'WE CRAWLED FORWARDS then through the groaning to an empty trench which they must have left. We settled ourselves in there and the more adventurous among us took up sniping positions and fired at anything that moved. George's hand was now a mass of pus as if he had dipped it in custard, and my shoulder was no better, the wound bubbling away in its own juices in the heat. Neither of us could hold a rifle but we had two good arms between us, his left, my right, and we were put to moving sandbags from the back of the trenches to the front.

The stretcher-bearers came as the sun was going down and two of them got hit by a blast; one died immediately and the other crawled above us groaning, a great hole in his chest. We were told to take their place, one-handed stretcher-bearers, and we lifted him on it and scurried with it back the way we had advanced all day, sideways, bent like crabs. At the beach now there were rafts with piles of wounded on them, pulled by other boats with piles of the same. We lifted him on the raft we could reach, said nothing to his curses in that fine Birmingham accent, and as the raft pulled off I had an idea.

"You're wounded, George," I said.

"If I'm wounded, Gregory," he said, "then you're wounded too."

"We're both wounded," I said, and pulled away my coat to display the bandaged arm, and we made it through the water to the raft and crawled on up, and saw the one we had carried had stopped cursing in his Brummie accent and was quite still now, already dead. The boat pulled us out to sea, to where the battleships still breathed their smoke, and then the moon came up and they stopped. We edged past them slowly, we drew alongside an old cattle-ship, and the business of winching them up began, one by one on the bloodied stretcher, until the ones who walked were left to clamber up the ladder by the side.

Up on the deck there was a blanket of what looked like yellow straw on the ground, until I lay on it in the only space I could find and realised it was dried horse and mule manure. We were on an animal transport that had been improvised into a hospital ship. But the improvisation was minimal, the men lay like worms on the dried turds, the only relief being a procession of orderlies going from one to the other with panniers of water. And when my turn came I opened my lips and drank what I could, then lay down and slept.'

~

They gave me tea and beans and a fried egg cooked on a small paraffin stove.

'We might have use for you,' said the blonde one, Ethel, lighting a cigarette. And what use it was I would soon find out, as the other girl grew bigger in the bed beside me. I graduated from washing and stitching costumes to taking her place on the boards, since I stayed small as there was nothing to grow big inside me. So I drank the tea and ate the egg and beans as every rivet in the hold began to shudder and the cattle bellowed and the gangplank was cranked away on its chains.

'Where are we going?' I asked Ethel, as the dockhands outside began to diminish in the porthole.

'Liverpool,' said Ethel, 'where else did you think?'

'Will you excuse me then,' I said, 'since I want to see the country that I'm leaving.'

~

'What still amazes me,' says Gregory, 'was the lack of any logic. I could see the hospital tents on the island from the ship's deck,

I could even see the nurses in their white uniforms and their bonnets like miniature tents, but we sailed right past them with our accompanying cloud of flies and bluebottles, all buzzing round the festering wounds on the open deck of that ship in the heat of the sun.

"Why don't we land?" I asked the orderly who cleaned the pus from my shoulder and injected it with quinine.

"Orders," he said, "to take you all to Egypt."

So we watched the empty hospital tents and the idle nurses retreat behind us.'

~

I climbed up to the morning air to see the town shifting slowly past the smoking funnel at the back, the small pilot tug in front of us with Janie's father at the helm. I could see the smoke from his pipe curling like a question mark over his cap, and the question the smoke seemed to ask was would I ever see them both again? The tall warehouses by the docks drew past me and the RIC station above the sloping lawns and the dotted shapes of cottages, then the small tributaries from the river we were on, one of them that curled round the grey limestone shape that I was leaving for good. The sun glinted off the glasshouse and the chestnut tree was tiny against the water, a small doll's umbrella, so small I couldn't see the swing below it.

Were they looking for me, I wondered, searching every room of the grounds around? Of course they would be, maybe even calling the peelers to help them in their search. I would write, I had decided, when I reached Liverpool, explaining nothing but that I was safe. Then there was Mozambique and Mabel Hatch's barn and the red roof of Janie's cottage. The Lady's Finger drifted by, the granite curve at the top so close I could nearly touch it, and the Maiden's Tower was to my right with the Bettystown strand curving away, and I wondered was she still there, a ghost of her, watching the ships of another era come and go. Then the line of the Irish sea, as quiet as tea in a teacup, and the only odd thing was the sound of the cattle lowing from below.

~

'They took us back to Alexandria, where we'd started from, an improvised hospital in what used to be a brothel. I lay on the floor in a tall room with one window high up in the almost conical walls and listened to the low moans of pain around me, not too different I supposed from the moans of pleasure that must have filled the place. My arm was better within the week and George's hand was saved the indignity of amputation. It was soon entirely functional with just three fingers and a thumb.

We were given a week's leave then, and wandered round the souks and market-places, round the working brothels where the hordes of squaddies drank warm beer while they waited for their turn. We were shy ourselves and didn't indulge, an odd innocence when you consider what we had been through. Then we were sent back on another cattle-ship, full of volunteers from the Tenth Division, Irish, eager to stick fresh bayonets in Johnny Turk; we listened and said nothing. Another landing on another bay. We kept our heads down this time, knew the wormlike procedure in the sand, saw them mown down around us like new-cut grass again, felt the crushing heat again, the flies, but kept our water cans full.

It settled into a routine then. They weren't moving and neither were we, and the new faces either vanished or something inside them vanished and they weren't new any more. We'd try to sleep by day and swatch off the flies, and at night go on with the business of living, scurry down to the beaches for water, walk back like pack mules carrying whatever they'd give us. At intervals there'd be another push, we'd get the word and off across the ridges at dawn, with the sun behind us shining in their eyes or the mist if we were lucky, and when the sun dispersed, whatever advantage it had given us, it would begin again, the fusillade of small dull pops, the whirring like the wings of a small bird, or the tearing of the air above us and the silence, then the boom, the groans of whoever took it. We stuck together, the two of us, learnt to embrace the sharp stones underneath our boots. I heard the rending of the air once and with the boom felt a kick in my back like a mule and was thrown six feet sideways, then felt nothing. When I woke the sun was gone again, there was a beautiful calm to the moonlight, pale curtains of mist over every ridge. I rubbed my back and shoulder and could feel the tiny incisions of shrapnel all over the khaki. I turned on my back and could see the Pleiades above through the thin night haze. If I had died, I remember thinking, it could not have been more peaceful.

I lay in that delicious absence of effort, of any need to move at all, for hours. But I suspected I hadn't died, there being a corpse to my left and the sound of groaning some distance away from me which soon, mercifully, stopped. There was a smell of thyme. Then a figure walked through those delicate mists, dispersing them as he walked, huge steps over the outcrops of thyme, and I recognised nine-fingered George.

"Couldn't you have come later?" I asked him.

"No," he said, bending and lifting me in one easy move. "Why would I come later?"

"Because," I told him, "it felt like peace." '

35

Dear Janie, I am in Liverpool, moving towards Wales, please give the enclosed letter to my father. Sister Catherine said acting would never be remotely appropriate for a Siena girl, but here I am, acting the part of the Colleen Bawn, Eily O'Connor, not Rosalind by any means but sufficient to the day the evil thereof. Eily is thought to be drowned in a lake by the hunchback Danny Mann, but comes back to life by the good graces of Myles na gCopaleen, Myles of the Ponies, if you don't remember your Irish which I for one hardly do. I hope to see you some day, in England if you ever get here or in Ireland if I ever get back there. Meanwhile, thinking of you and your brother and my brother too. Your dear friend, Nina.

~

'There was a hill,' says Gregory, 'it had been taken and abandoned and now had to be taken again. We could see the low sweep of the land down to the dry salt-lake behind us, looping like a pearl necklace towards the beach and the sea. We never knew why we were moving, what we were moving towards, sometimes we didn't know where. But when we were told to go, we went. There was waist-high grass or barley or wheat with clumps of flowerless gorse and they were throwing so much at us that the ridge caught fire, all the grass and gorse bushes burning, flames licking over the flinty ground in a lazy sweep and then the smell of burning flesh, of the ones that had dropped, the cries of the ones still living, burnt alive. And as the smoke rose up it made a curtain, I fell into a trench and the flames licked over it, the smoke filled it, I would have died there, roasted, asphyxiated. I had lost George somewhere up ahead and I grabbed a trench shovel, so hot it burnt my hands, and I crawled out again, beat my way through the smoke and flames with the red-hot shovel and I found him there, the biggest shape lying there, burning, all of his giant length burning. And I pulled him towards a small hollow where the flames had exhausted whatever vegetation there was, and as the flames and smoke died down the bullets again found whoever was unlucky enough to be visibly squirming there and finished them off, and maybe it was better that way.

Then finally the sun went down and the guttering hillside grew quiet except for the cries of those left there, still alive. George was one of those, his face unrecognisable. I wormed forwards through the ashes to collect the water cans of the dead ones and brought them back, poured whatever I found through his roasted lips. I could see his eyes then, lashless, eyebrowless, pleading, and I knew they were pleading with me to somehow end it for him. I couldn't, though pity churned in my stomach like sour milk, and I did what I knew even then would haunt me, what he could never thank me for. I brought the shovel over, turned his body so the charred seat of his trousers lay on the broad flat of it, I grabbed the haft and dragged it like a sled, down the charred hillside.

The moon was up by the time I had left the smoke behind. He must have been unconscious because all I could hear was his laboured breathing through burnt nostrils. I reached the salt-lake and pulled him across the flat, leaving a crabbed trail in the salt behind me. The cracked salt beneath me reminded me of the cracked mudflats of Mozambique when the tide was out, but these were saltflats and a dirty white: memory and comparison were like a negative photograph – what had been dark was light, what had been light was dark. I made it through the loop to the sand and dragged him to the water, looking for a hospital boat, and saw one out there, pulling away. And I took him in my arms and managed not to fall with the weight of him and walked into the water, and I swear as the seawater lapped over his body his body sizzled and steamed. He moaned then, with the pain of the saltwater, and the moan was like a dying swan or a swan that wished it could die. The boat heard him and stopped its rowing and waited until I reached them. Two orderlies reached down and unceremoniously lifted him in. I stood there, waist deep in the water as it drew away, and wondered what malignant destiny had left me there, apparently living and apparently unharmed.'

'They searched the townland for her,' says Janie, 'for a week or so thought she had died, till the letter arrived. And I walked up to the house that seemed so empty, without her, without him, found her father alone in the glasshouse with his leather gloves on, head down among the tomato plants, and gave him the letter.

"Tell me anything you know, please Janie," he said.

"She's in Liverpool, moving towards Wales with a theatre troupe," I said, "I only know what she wrote, maybe there's more inside there."

And he opened the letter in front of me. I could hear the slow drip of the hose and the sound of the paper tearing, the sound of his glasses coming out of his top pocket. And he read with that strange stillness that seemed to imply a death of kinds, and maybe for him it was. He seemed to age as he read it, two pages it was, in her neat handwriting, always better than mine.

"Thank you, Janie," he said finally, and folded it neatly, placed it with his glasses in the top pocket of his frayed gardening coat. "I've lost them both," he said, and turned back to the tomato plants.

And I walked back out round the side of the old house, and down the drive I saw her mother coming towards me, two golf clubs in her hand. She was wearing a winter coat, I remember, though it was still summer, late summer but still warm. She must have known I had news, but she passed me without saying a word, and from that I could only presume that whatever news I had, she didn't want to hear.'

'I found it difficult to die, though, ironically given that there was nothing but death all around me. There was no more push after that. The heat subsided, the summer was nearly over. I longed for the insane order to come, to walk blindly towards the bullet that would finish me, but no such order came. The Tenth Division left, went to Salonika I was told, but what was left of our division stayed, first there, last there. The swallows curved in arcs above us, the stench and the flies subsided, and the place became almost beautiful. There were rumours everywhere, exhaustion had congealed us into a very specific kind of torpor, an awful autumnal splendour wrapped the whole peninsula which made even dying seem ridiculous. Generals came and went, surveyed the few of us left from the first landing. A motor-launch came off the *Lord Nelson* and it was rumoured the old walrus, Kitchener himself, was on it. I saw a glint from a pair of binoculars above Anzac cove, rumoured to be his. I trained my rifle on it, imagined I saw those famous moustaches through the heat haze way beyond, thought how simple it would be to squeeze and wondered would it feel like vengeance. But I lacked the courage and realised there was one sensation I would never fully know.'

~

She played Eily as she grew bigger beside me, and I played Grace until she grew too big to play anything, then I played Eily in her place. They forgot about Grace, reduced the play to exclude her, and if it didn't make sense nobody cared since not many were listening anyway. There was a hall in each of those Lancashire seaside towns to accommodate us; we left the marquee behind us in a Liverpool warehouse on the biggest stretch of dockland I had ever seen. The pier stretching out to the whipped green sea with the circular end to it, the wooden boardwalk a cathedral of lights – I had never seen such delicacy, such vulgarity, such much-ness, so to speak. Crowds everywhere, late summer crowds, girls my own age with men in uniform, arms linked, the electric lights playing on their faces like reflected water. I walked arm-in-arm with Eily, Maggie was her real name, and felt against my elbow the strength of her hardening belly. The comedian at Margate, after the warm-up to our show, tried to touch me in the wings. His hand on my belly, heading downwards. I bit his ear until it bled and he couldn't dare let out a scream.

'Woah, woah, missus,' he said, 'it's not the end of the world.'

'Isn't it?' I asked him.

I could see Maggie through the flaring lights in the voluminous skirt that hid her condition. Samuel was the father's name: Samuel and Margaret, she would say like a litany, Maggie and Sam. He was a beekeeper in Somerset awaiting her return: she would stop off there and have the baby, leave the troupe while it moved to Brighton. We met two soldiers on the pier and allowed them to walk us down the boardwalk twice and a stop for ices.

'At Passchaendale,' the dark-eyed one told us, 'you could hear the guns roar long after they had stopped.'

'I can hear them still,' the blue-eyed one told us.

'So what's it like?' I asked.

'The sound?' the blue-eyed one asked.

'Do I detect an accent?' the brown-eyed one said. 'Irish?'

'Irish,' I said, 'but tell me what's it like. I have a brother over there.'

'Like the end of the world,' said the brown-eyed one, and I thought of the comedian and his hand on my belly. He held my hand on the way back and tried to kiss me under the eaves in the street. I turned my head this way and that and then let him kiss me anyway, and thought of Gregory.

'Where's your brother?' he asked me, making conversation.

'He's with the Dubliners,' I said.

'They're not in France,' he said, 'they're in the Dardanelles.'

'Where are the Dardanelles?' I asked him, and added, since it felt more like conversation, 'when they're at home?'

'Near Constantinople,' he said, 'fighting the Turk.'

36

'STORMS CAME, TOOK away the piers on the beaches, flooded the trenches. We crawled out of them to save ourselves from drowning and saw the Turks across the ridges do the same; we could have picked each other off like wet rats but there were other things to think about. Then the snows came, gentle at first, a dusting of white over the whole peninsula. Blizzards then, and the temperature plummeted, blackened hands and faces, we burnt everything we could find to warm our frostbitten fingers and began to miss the flies and heat.'

~

We moved further south towards Wales, and the towns got smaller and the halls now were parish halls, where stern revivalist meetings happened of a Sunday and where a pregnant leading lady could cause a true scandal, so I took Maggie's place and got the part of Eily. Maggie restitched her costumes for me, tucked them in at the waist and complimented me on what she called my demeanour.

'You could go far,' she said, 'with a carriage like that, with looks like that.

'What do you mean by carriage?' I asked her, and she answered, 'I mean a way of walking, I mean a certain poise that the real divas have.'

'What about you,' I asked her, 'won't you go far?'

'I'll go as far as Somerset,' she told me, 'I'll have the baby and Sam will marry me and we'll settle in a cottage and sell honey to the apple farmers.'

She didn't know about my happenstance and so whenever I asked to place a hand on her belly and feel the life inside, my tears would perplex her.

'Why are you crying?' she would ask. 'I'm the one who should be crying, the fallen woman, the girl undone.'

'There are other ways of falling,' I told her, 'I'm something of an expert in all of them.'

At night sometimes I could feel the tiny feet kicking from her soundly sleeping body beside me. How could she sleep, I would wonder, with so much life going on inside her? But she was easy-going, Maggie, things that would have bothered others didn't bother her a bit; she was part of the grass that grew and the world that turned and she woke up each morning like it was her first. Her first day in a whole new world. I would reach out in the darkness and place my hand on her stomach, feel it shifting under the flannel nightdress, and her hand would reach up and hold down mine. She would press her fingers between the gaps in mine and both of our hands would rub her stomach gently, her asleep, me soon to be, because the feel of her skin was the only thing that would bring tiredness on.

Sleep seemed an unreachable comfort without her beside me, without that large pod within which the seed was growing. I felt emptier than the emptiest thing, emptier than a seabed from which the ocean had retreated, emptier than the dried mudflats of Mozambique at the lowest tide. There were dried tears behind my eyes, parched by the emptiness and sometimes, with the comfort of her hand on mine, came the comfort of them flowing. I would cry then, and feel the velvet curtain of sleep and oblivion descending.

~

'In December it grew mild again and the word spread round that we were finally leaving. We kept up a pretence of occasional sniper fire, pretended sorties into their lines which they pretended to repulse. At night the lines of men would snake down to the beaches, the boats would fill and push off silently, leaving those of us behind to fill the gaps. We crawled from trench to trench, from ridge to ridge, positioned unmanned rifles and set them off with tripwires. If they noticed the difference they didn't pretend to care.'

~

Old men and young women in those coalmining towns, all of the young men gone, the collieries still, the miners digging in some tunnel under Flanders. Trenches have to be dug, a widow told me, and who better to dig them than Welsh miners? The crowds in the halls made a sea of black bonnets with the occasional soft cloth cap over an ancient face. The long beach at Llandudno reminded me of home and a fisherman with his long black rod stuck in the sand told me on a clear day you could see the Mourne Mountains. I felt sadness then, plain sadness, and realised the emptiness was turning into something more concrete. I thought of the approach to the Boyne and the Maiden's Tower and the Lady's Finger and my father's factory on the shore. And I learnt a lesson that would stand with me for forty years, forty years of being something other than what I was. I put that sadness to use on the stage that night, in a tiny, cramped mineworkers' union hall. It was hunching there behind the theatrical flats, waiting for me, a diminutive hunched succubus of loss, curled like a sad child, an accumulation of dust behind the lights, a penumbra, someone else's ghost. I have no existence, it seemed to say, make me live. And I took it with me and walked on-stage and put that ache inside me to work. I was the Colleen Bawn with an ache inside her, I pleaded for my poor, pathetic life with all the anguish of my genuine loss. I could use my own wounds, I realised then, as props, as supports, as emotional sluice-gates, and I could see their effect in the rows of rapt female faces in front of me. I could create my own wounds if I needed more, as the parts, the emotion, the occasions demanded. I would create more wounds, a wound for each new part: wounds of anger, bitterness, jealousy, resignation, rage, since sadness and loss were only part of the picture. I would become a St Sebastian of wounds until the biggest wound of all would put a kind of end to me. And as the play ended and the applause grew around me, I knew I would never properly know love, and never have children.

~

'We laid bombs in the latrines and set them with delayed fuses. On the last night a low mist hugged the ground and we could see the moon glowing through it like an expanding penny. We unwound our puttees and tied them round our boots, broke everything we couldn't carry and made our way down the hill towards the beach, where the small red torches flickered to guide us towards the waterline. We waded through the water and clambered on the boats with as much silence as we could manage. Behind us a kind of fictitious battle sputtered, a blast from a shit-hole covered the empty trenches in excrement and a desultory flash returned fire from the other side. It was as if the whole event had never happened, had been an imaginary fight against an imaginary opponent with imaginary ordnance and imaginary dead. And as if the bones we had left covering the hillsides had been dreamed in some nightmare that was now ending. As if the dream, in that contradictory peninsula, had been dreamed in the daytime, and this quiet, water-lapping night, illuminated by desultory booms from the battleships, was our waking.'

~

I knew the baby was coming before she did, in a small town on the Severn estuary; it would be an estuary child like I was. We had a late supper of fried kippers and left the rest of the cast to their night of bottled Guinness and cider. I helped her upstairs and said, 'It will be tonight, can't you feel it?'

'No,' Maggie said, 'I can just feel the weight of me, the appalling sowlike weight of me. When did I become a sow, Nina? And where is that bloody beekeeper that left me like this?'

'He didn't leave you, you left him,' I said, 'and didn't you tell me he's waiting in Somerset? Come on now love,' I said – I had the English argot now, love, sweetie, darling – 'lie down and sleep and wait to see what happens in the morning.'

But it didn't happen in the morning, did it, it didn't wait till morning. It happened that night, around half past two I awoke and the bed was wet. 'My waters have broken,' she said, and her stomach was heaving. I put my hand on it and could feel the shudder, the almighty tightening of some inside muscle, and I ran downstairs and found Ethel in a clinch with Myles na gCopaleen among a sea of empty bottles and cigarette butts. 'Get a doctor, Ethel,' I told her, 'it's happening.' 'At last,' she said obscurely, then made for the door.

I ran back upstairs, two steps at a time and found Maggie sitting up in bed with the tiny ecclesiastical window behind her.

'Hold me,' she said, and I sat behind her and placed both hands around her stomach. Her knees were spread apart like the stone woman and her hands were digging into mine. 'Oh God,' she said and she shuddered again, and then time slowed and the blanket slowly filled up with red and the shudders were the only time, the hard flesh on her stomach heaving with them, like a great clock that would strike and leave an echo in her body, a series of ripples, while she caught her breath until the clock struck again. But it was an odd clock with no regular rhythm. The beats gained on each other, came closer together until there was nothing but beating, and she rose on her knees and with a huge outpouring of herself gave a cry that came from where the clock struck, and her stomach heaved once more and something was over.

I heard a tiny cry, and down in the blankets, among the mess of blood and other stuff there was a tiny thing, a succubus like the bent form my own sadness assumed, but this was moving, this was a child, and I knew it was a boy. I lifted it, it was attached to her by part of her insides and it was squalling with life. She took it from my hands and the door opened and Ethel entered, behind her a doctor with his tall hat and leather bag.

'Leave it to me,' he said, and Maggie answered, 'No, no, don't leave it to him, I want her, I want Nina.'

'Get me a bowl then,' he said, 'Nina, is it?'

And I slid off the bed, and went to the bathroom and washed my bloodied hands and filled a ceramic bowl with fresh water.

I went back in and Ethel was doing what was her answer to every conceivable human situation, she was lighting a cigarette, and the smoke was curling and the small baby was crying and the doctor was separating it from her. I put the bowl down and he placed the baby in my hands and said, 'Wash it now.' I washed it clean of blood and brown as he took instruments from his bag and attended to her; more blood spurted but Maggie didn't seem to feel it. Her head was towards me, looking at me, Ethel behind me and the child in my hands in the bowl. 'Samuel,' she said.

~

'We boarded a steamer from the lighters and one huge last explosion shook the bay. A geyser of sparks as if from a volcano spouted above the mist, and I thought of the men who must have died beneath it, the scattered limbs and the groans in that universal language. The battleship behind us fired two salvoes even on its curve out of there, and I saw the bodies of dead fish come to the surface again, as they had on our arrival. I wandered over the deck, they were cheering everywhere, hugging, embracing as if something, God knows what, had been won. I cheered too, it would have been indelicate not to. We were survivors after all, and that uncertain element called life had been preserved in us. The dark purple line that retreated from our boat held the bones, buried and unburied, of those who should have been us and among those innumerable bones the bones of George's finger.'

~

We made our way towards Somerset and little Samuel grew, daily it seemed. We were hardly actors now, more a family round the two of them. But one day of course it happened, a small town perched above a shabby bay. We passed a field on which a forest of small houses seemed to grow, tiny eaved roofs outlined against the sea behind.

'Whatever are they?' asked Ethel, and I didn't even have to search for the answer.

'Beehives,' I said, and I knew baby Samuel was going from me.

The horses stopped and Maggie stepped down with her bundle in her arms and kissed me on the cheek and said, 'Goodbye Nina love, I'll always remember.'

'Remember what?' I asked her.

'You, love,' she said.

She walked towards the beehives as if she knew they were her home, and over the hill, outlined against the blue sea, came her other Samuel, a medieval hood and shawl draped round his head and shoulders, covered in a gently moving curtain of what I knew were bees. She stood before him holding her bundle, and the bees made a cloud around his head and he didn't move, or couldn't, because of the swarm around him. And the horses moved off and I took a last look before we rounded the corner of the road, and saw the two of them standing there, as if they would stand there, mute and unembracing, for ever.

~

'The island had tents in rows up the hillside and more than twenty-seven battleships out in the harbour, I counted them. It was hard to walk without an automatic stoop, without bending under the nearest available cover, sliding crabways in expectation

251

of a bullet through the skull. I bought oranges and lemons from the Greek kids who clustered round us and asked everywhere for word of George. I wandered round the hospital tents and examined face after bandaged face. Many Georges turned to me when I called out the name, Georges with many different surnames, many different wounds, Georges with limbs removed, legless, eyeless, some of them even speechless, but none of them was him. I squeezed oranges into their lips and sucked them myself then, down to the rinds, and within a week had exhausted all of the tents, all of the Georges in them and, it seemed, all of the oranges. Then I took a boat to Alexandria.'

37

THERE WERE TWO piers in Brighton, an East and a West, and we settled into the Cadogan Music-Hall beneath the promenade with the hotels like ice-cream parlours. And while I played the Colleen Bawn at night, I walked between the piers by day, along the shingled beach with the huge girders holding up the boardwalk and the music and sounds of wintry gaiety coming from above. The emptiness came back, but it was an emptiness beyond me now, surrounding the diminishing crowds like a mist, keeping me cocooned outside it, observing. The ladies with thin spindly shapes coming towards me with the evening sun behind them, the old gentlemen reading *The Times* behind the windbreak provided by the sea wall.

I kept to myself, was somewhat disenchanted by the troupe now that Maggie was gone, kept thinking of her and baby Samuel in their home by the beehives, were they happy, were her expectations fulfilled. In my heart of hearts I knew they probably weren't, that the last thing the good beekeeper expected was the return of this Somerset girl with a newborn child. But I didn't know the mores of Somerset, nor the mores of Brighton. All I knew were the mores of Eily O'Connor and Myles na gCopaleen, where her unexpected return from the cold waters made everybody unaccountably happy. The crowds were dwindling now at the performances, we were like a bunch of circus animals about to be confined to winter quarters.

'November and it'll all be over,' said Ethel, 'and where do you go to, love? London, back to Ireland? Drogheda, Dublin?'

And I was pondering this question, how this other family

would be gone and what would I do for a substitute, when the cinematograph man came.

He had seen the show and wanted to make what he called a one-reeler, *The True Tragedy of the Colleen Bawn*, and admired my style of acting, thought it perfect for his purposes, for what he called the pictures. And after the final night, when the count of the audience was less than the count of the cast on-stage, he took over the stage and set to work. We rehearsed in the empty wintry hall, where he reduced each scene to a series of wordless tableaux, gestures in front of the painted flats, which he had painted and repainted as he needed. Then he cut the play in half, excised the comedy and retained the tragedy, since tragic emotions, as he told me, were easier to replicate in a series of simple balletic gestures. He removed all of the lights from the ceiling and pointed them sideways and straight in our faces, turned them off and on, moved them and turned them off and on again. He created whole imagined landscapes with swathes of shadow. Then he brought in his wooden box with the winding handle and set to work.

We would enact each scene until he was happy, then he would move the box and enact the scene again. I found the reflective gaze of the lens a more comforting audience than the hundred or so faces that used to stare up at me each evening. I could imagine anyone behind there, any eye observing, but the only eye I ever caught reflected there was my own. What a perfect state of narcissism, I thought, what a benign mirror, and I remembered, of course I remembered, the tale my father told me, of the girl who gazed at her own reflection until the waters rose and became the river Boyne.

We did the drowning scene with the only water available to us, the lapping sea underneath the West Pier, where the great umbrella of the pier above us created a shadow to block out the sun. He sat on another boat, cranking his box, two oarsmen beside him to keep his boat abreast of ours, and with the fairground music rattling above I beat my breast and tore my flowing locks before I sank finally, underneath the freezing waters. So I died then, and came back to life again on a deckchair perched on the stony shale, with a mug of cocoa and a blanket around me to keep me warm.

'Come to London,' he told me, lighting his pipe, tightening his Norfolk jacket around him, like a scientist or a geographer, nothing like a man of the theatre. There's a career for you there, a great one, the Bush Studios are doing three and four reelers.'

'Gladly,' I told him. 'I'll go anywhere but home.'

~

'All of the liners in the world, and the coal-steamers, all of the metal that could float, it seemed, had gathered in the harbour at Alexandria, and the Arab dhows with sails like curved knives flitted between them, laden almost to the waterline with whatever they could sell. I bought a melon from one of them and sliced it in four pieces as I walked down the gangplank, and the juice ran down my chin into my shirt. The sun dried it almost instantly. I threw the pieces to the dogs that scavenged on the dockside and made my way to the Medina, where the wattled covering between the walls of the narrow streets provided some shade. There were soldiers everywhere, most of them damaged in some way, and I enquired of the damaged ones about the hospitals and began a three-day trek through the converted schools and army barracks and whorehouses, among the beds that lined the sweating walls and the nurses' starched white bonnets, looking for any word of George. I returned to the ship each night, to the hammock where I lay among a thousand others, tried to sleep and most of the time failed.

Then on the third day I was walking through the souk and I saw a figure ahead of me through the mounds of slowly moving donkeys laden with every conceivable produce under the sun. Both arms were bandaged and there was a scarf of some kind wrapped over the head but the size and the gait, that loping walk, were unmistakably his. I called his name and he didn't respond, he quickened his pace which told me that he'd heard, was trying to escape me, but there was no escaping in that crush. I saw him duck down a side-alley and followed him into a tiny street full of gold-beaters, tiny wizened men with hammers and sheets of the metal spreading out on blocks beside them. He turned left again, down a smaller alley, if that were possible, so narrow two people couldn't walk it side by side. And the alley ended by a small open door with a clutch of beggars outside, all pock-marked, shrivelled limbs reaching to brush off my hands, limbs that were stumps without hands.

"Give them money," he said, without turning round, without removing that scarf, "give them what you can, because they expect it. And follow me, if you want, into where I live now."

I emptied my pockets of coins and saw them scramble for them, scraping them on to begging bowls clutched between their teeth. He walked inside and I followed.

He was in an indigent house, an almshouse of some kind, and I could see figures with deformities that grew, as we climbed the stairs, into shapes that were barely recognisable as human.

"Leprosy," he said, "and don't ask me why I'm here, I'm here because only here it's possible to think of myself as fortunate." He ducked into a tiny room with a barred window, hardly big enough to hold him; there was a mat on the floor and everywhere the smell of excrement. I bent and entered, and he removed the scarf, and I could see then the skin pulled like a chicken's neck across what had been his face. I could see the skin of the hands like the discarded coat of a lizard, almost transparent, with the bones showing through.

"They tried to put me on a boat back to England with the others," he said, "but I wouldn't go. I stayed on in the hospital till they needed the bed, and then I wandered the markets until I found my way here. Here I can be Touchstone, and envy no man's happiness. But sometimes I think, Greg, if you don't mind me saying, that maybe you should have left me by that burning bush. I could have died there, not happily, but dead would be better than this. And sometimes I think, no, I should be alive because at least alive I might see your sister Nina's face again. But then if I saw her she would have to see me, and I can't countenance that thought, and I go back to thinking you should have left me on that hill to burn with the bushes. All those bushes are dead now and so should I be. And I go through both thoughts, from one to the other, and then I go through that doorway and down the stairs, and I see that among these at least I am fortunate. And I think of something else which is a rare relief, a blessing of kinds, the only blessing I get these days. So I stay on here and think I might end my days here. What do you think, Greg?" '

~

There was light day and night in the Bush Studios, great arc-lamps of it, no escape from it and I could see hints of the memories of what I used to be in the sparks that crackled round those carbon rods, I could see the succubus that had left me somewhere in the dark behind those lamps, the wheeling dust and the black studio wall. I came to understand those primitive peoples who believed the camera ate the soul, and I wanted it to eat mine whole and entire, and give me back another one, an artificial one that could be eaten in turn by whoever came to view me of an afternoon in a darkened hall when the projector whirred and the image flickered on the white sheet that was the screen. I wanted it to take my set of memories, of the river, the house, the swing beneath the chestnut tree, of Gregory's arrival with his twine-wrapped case, of George playing Touchstone behind the dead tomato plants, Janie thrusting out of the river water with the wet dress clinging to her tiny breasts, of the ghost that thrilled all four of us, Hester crushed to powder by the threshing machine, of the owl that hooted in Mabel Hatch's barn and the pearl, most of all the pearl. And the camera took them gladly, drew them into its plane of vision and demanded other memories of me, memories that left me quite unburdened, like a marionette twirling in an artificial clock, free but for the mechanism that moved her, and quite, quite empty.

He would smoke his pipe behind the cranking camera, with his stick and his Norfolk jacket, and when the roll had ended would walk forwards and place his hand too low about my waist; in time I got used to that too. I got used to all sorts of things: to the carnal round a motion picture demanded, pulling my stockings back on in the dressing room while the lover of sorts dressed with his face to the wall, watching the way the silk curled round my thin knees and thinking, One more time, and I was wrong about that one too. I was far from home and would stay far from home, and if anything of me returned it would be that other version, the one the roll retained on its acetate. So there, Mozambique.

~

'I received your letter,' says Gregory, 'and you told me how Nina had made her debut in moving pictures of all things. How you wondered was your brother dead or alive, and if alive he should know his father had died while piloting the *Kathleen Mavourneeen* in the September storms. His boat had gone down beyond the Lady's Finger; he had misjudged the point of entry. The seas were so high, and the spray so obscured his vision, that he hadn't seen the Maiden's Tower to get his co-ordinates right. There was to be a funeral, and if George was still alive they would delay it until his return. And that letter did the trick.

So I led him from that lazar house in Alexandria and brought him back once more into a kind of life, on to the last of the shipments returning home, from Salonika this time, the remains of the Tenth Division heading towards home leave and dispersal to another front. He wore an Arab djellabah with a hood and kept the scarf wrapped round his face, but the skin was growing again, returning him to some recognisable semblance of what he used to be. And on the boat there were so many like him that he came to feel at home, let the scarf fall, let his oddly touching visage be viewed by others, meet the sunlight on the long days steaming through the Mediterranean, round Gibraltar towards the Bay of Biscay.

I received your last letter when we berthed, with the scrap of an announcement from the London *Times*, an advertisement for the Scala Cinematograph, announcing ten showings daily of the seven-reel motion picture entitled *Sherlock Holmes and the Scarlet Lady*, starring Adrian Penrose (Magician) and Nina Hardy. He kept the cutting in his damaged hand on the train journey to London. I walked with him from the train through the vast, windowed station interior, where the light pushed through stacks of smoke that seemed to have acquired the permanence of pillars, barely glimmering on the sea of khaki caps that shifted and jostled and pitched a head-height below him. And there, as the red-bricked sooty cathedral of St Pancras spread out before him, I realised he would never be right.

"Is this the city, London?" he asked me.

"No, George," I said, "this is the station, St Pancras. London is outside." And I took his hand with the scrap of yellowing newspaper advertising my sister's cinematic debut and led him out of the turreted exit into the sprawling mayhem of King's Cross, where he seemed to realise the word city didn't have enough dimension for the vastness that he was encountering. He had seen the tops of smoking houses, acres and acres of them, on the journey from Dover, but as he would see a moving picture-book unravelling past the carriage window. This was real, this was moving, this was noisy, this pushed him out of its way, steamed, spewed smoke, this held more terror for him than the burning hillside in the Dardanelles. He pulled the scarf back over his face and told me he felt a pain like the drip of molten metal against his temple, he was unsure whether the roar was

259

emanating from his own ear-drums or from the tempest of directionless life around him. He seemed to long for a hint of nature he could recognise, and stared through the railings at the sooted tufts of grass between the tracks below. He heard a starling twitter from a leafless plane tree and saw a policeman raise his hand beneath it, saw the traffic stop as if by magic, and saw the vast crowd begin to shuffle from his pavement to the one opposite. He followed, knowing nothing else to do, and I followed him. And then, above the slowly bobbing heads, through the window of a stalled omnibus, he glimpsed Nina's face. Fixed to a curving wall, with the word HOLMES emblazoned on her forehead. I took his hand and led him towards her, revealing more and more as her image came clear of the omnibus. Eventually she loomed above us, the whole of her, bent into a half-loop around the curve of the building, the steps and the Italianate entrance of the Scala Cinematograph beneath her.

I remember little of the performance, but I do remember George, sitting beside an Egyptian column, his face happily shrouded in darkness, staring at her face on the screen, flickering, appealing, leaning down towards him in an attitude of benediction.

"I can see her," I remember him saying, "and she can't see me."

But why now? Why now? the caption said. A gentleman in a top coat and glistening hat twirled his stick, contemptuously, it seemed to George, because he asked me why didn't he seem to like her.

"He is the villain, George," I said, "he's not allowed to like her."

Then she was walking away, down a shadowy street. She turned a corner, walked into a fog and emerged by a river. It was a large river, George whispered to me, three times the size of the river at home. It had barges and sailing skiffs and a crescent moon in an unaccountably bright sky. Then she was there again, terrifyingly large, her eyes and mouth downcast, her face framed by a mass of black curls. She tumbled forwards towards us, so close that George reached out his hands to catch her. But his hands were singularly useless, as she was already in the river, floating towards one of the barges, the crescent moon reflected in the water beside her.

"Is she dead now, Greg?" George asked me in a kind of story-book terror.

"No," I told him, "she's not dead, George, it's only an illusion."

And afterwards I walked him into the daylight again towards another train station, Euston, this time.

"I can see her then," he said, "and she need not see me."

"Yes," I told him, "any time this film plays you can see her and sit happy in the dark in the knowledge that she cannot see you."

"But do they have such films at home, Greg?" he asked me.

"They will," I assured him, "they most certainly will."

And I bought his ticket and led him through another cathedral of smoke and grime and placed him on the train and asked the khaki-clad squaddies beside him to make sure he made it with them through Liverpool to Dublin where I told them his sister Janie would be waiting. And the last I saw of him was as the train drew off, his large head turning backwards in the window, the steam obscuring it in progressive bursts, and the steam was kind to his damaged face, softening it into something like what it used to be.'

~

They had finished my make-up, a solid cake of white with a thin pencil of purple for my lips, they had brought me into the huge swathe of light the sun poured through that wall of glass when the camera whirred, and I was pushed into the miniature of Harley Street and the magician pulled me this way and I pulled myself that. And I realised I was always aware of the surrounding crowds; no matter how blinding the light, how loud the noise, I could have counted the observers without a second thought and spotted an intruder across a score of them. Eyes, that was what it was about, eyes: I was being watched, and a new pair of eyes had joined the familiars. I looked out for this new pair of eyes as I pulled away and was pulled back, as my hand went to my forehead and away again, and at last I saw the outline of the khaki cap against the bare brick studio wall.

I knew it was him, though demobbed officers often passed through – we were the fairground attraction, the mechanical wonder, an invitation to the Bush was prized by government ministers, for God's sake. I knew it was him immediately though I couldn't see his face, couldn't see anyone's face, I was blinded by light as usual, and my grief and terror reached biblical proportions until the gathering was happy and the cranking arm on the camera box stopped.

I walked forwards then, in my costume of the last century, a ghost in everything but physique, and I passed the lights and my eyes accustomed themselves to the gloom behind. I was told a costume change was needed by the wardrobe mistress, but I walked on by her to the thin figure in uniform, smoking by the studio door.

'Gregory,' I said, 'it is you, isn't it?'

'Yes,' he said, 'who else?'

And I ran and he caught me by the open door and twirled me and said, so familiar, so unnecessary that it seemed redundant, 'What larks, sis.'

V

38

Dear father, I am never coming back. This is not because I don't love you, which I do, or mother, which I suppose I must. It is a daughter's duty to love a mother, so I will continue to do so, or try. No, I am never coming back because that was what was requested of me. My brother came to me too late for me to see him as my brother. So I will change myself, my home, my life, I will become someone other than your little Nina, become Rosalind, become Cordelia, become Lady Macbeth, who knows. I have left the best part of myself there and so, in some way, will always be yours, Nina.

How can I imagine another's pain? One's own is all there is. But there it is, in front of me now. He stands with Janie among the tomato plants in the glasshouse and folds my letter neatly, places it with his glasses in his top pocket and says, 'Thank you Janie', and turns back to the tomato plants, 'I've lost them both.'

There is a green mould which clings to the green leaves of the tomato plants and it covers him gradually during that afternoon. After Janie leaves, he moves among them slowly, painfully tying every sprig with burgeoning fruit, and when he has covered the whole glasshouse he begins again, retying them, changing their position on the wooden lattice. The summer's sun beats down and is exaggerated through the panes, his frayed jacket and collarless shirt amplify the heat in turn, and rivers of sweat run down his face but do nothing to stem the coating of green that gathers on his skin. And he emerges when the sun goes down, into a late sunset, a pink mackerel sky covering the townland from the river's mouth. His face is covered in that dusky green like a death mask, and he meets her by the entrance to the house, she had been cutting roses, she has her arms full of them.

'We have lost our daughter,' he says.

'No,' she says, 'we have no daughter. Nor son either.'

He goes upstairs and pours himself a bath and I can see him in it, lying in the old lead receptacle with the lukewarm water flowing from the taps, naked as I have never seen him, the jagged shoulders and the sodden line of hair in the centre of his sunken ribcage, the veins around and above his knees standing blue, almost clear of the skin. And perhaps this is the story I have to tell, the one without me in it. He lowers his head under the greenish water for what seems an age, longer than a living being could stand it, and then raises it again and breathes out my name.

'Nina.'

~

'Did I exploit her?' asks Gregory rhetorically, and then gives himself the answer: 'I don't think so, I hope not, but we were like two orphans alone in that huge metropolis. I was unemployed and unemployable, one among half a million demobbed soldiers. I had a grandfather in Surrey, I wrote hoping for some recognition or assistance, but got no reply. We were walking through the National Gallery in Trafalgar Square and I saw our reflection in the glass window of a huge canvas, I forget which one, and I saw her for the first time as others must see her: willowy, with that natural elegance, a true Irish rose. I saw me beside her in my tattered military greatcoat and saw immediately what others must think of me. And that's when I asked her to lend me money, enough to take me to a bespoke tailor's to make myself presentable and present myself as, of all things, her manager.

Those early pictures were made out of chaos and paid for in chaos. I began to put some order in her business. I became her shadow, a shadow as elegantly constructed as possible, the inter-preter of her deepest desires. I took to referring to her in the third person: Miss Hardy requests, Miss Hardy doesn't do, Miss Hardy would like. It allowed me the illusion there was some dis-tance between us and created in others the illusion of inaccess-ibility, and it was all illusion after all, let's face it, one I could make sure we both profited from.'

~

And so Gregory became my manager and confidant. We con-structed a unit that was unbreakable, unshakable, uncomfort-able, unsound. He exchanged his uniform for a Savile Row suit and found it distressingly simple to forget the mayhem he had experienced. We thought of changing my name – I was changing everything else, why not that too? – and would have done it but for the moderate fame the *Colleen Bawn* brought me. So the name stayed, Nina Hardy.

Studios were glasshouses then, whole walls and roofs of glass designed to let the sun illuminate the hothouse plant inside, chief among them being me, the Irish Rose. There was one they'd set up in Shoreham, near Brighton, and we made picture after picture there, in a purpose-built glasshouse ten times bigger than the glasshouse at home. And we played Orlando and Rosalind, again, no George, no Janie, no tomato plants, just the sun pouring in through that cathedral of glass when it shone, and when it didn't, we supplemented it with lamps to get an exposure. By the sea a row of cottages or bungalows, some things had changed immea-surably and others not at all. We could travel down on the train from Brighton or London to our new glasshouse, and we con-structed around us different versions of what we had left, we replaced you both with a succession of others. I would introduce my paramours to him for approval, he would introduce his to me. We held each other's lives in erotic suspension, a pattern that stayed with us like a smoking habit. I could gauge the time each young thing from the provinces would preoccupy him as accurately as a doctor would a fever, I could tell when the temperature would rise and fall, the virus depart and leave us back where we started. I supervised his love-affairs as he did mine.

'Does she stir you?' I would ask about a young ingénue actress.

'How long would you give her, sis?' he would ask.

'Two months,' I would reply, and deal with her tears in exactly two months' time.

39

To say the house grows quiet in my absence would be to humanise it, and houses, as we know, aren't human. They may, though, have human qualities, and this one does have me. So, it grows quiet, there is no escaping the presumption. The war has ended and another kind of war begun. The shellfish business loses its impetus and my father keeps the sullen workforce going till the pretence at business seems pointless any more, but he can't quite bring himself to close down the factory. He is spared his agonies of indecision by the sight of flames one night from the upper bedroom and knows instantly their source. They had burnt the RIC station, most of Balbriggan and half of the big houses round. He rides round there with Dan Turnbull and sees a figure, face wrapped in a scarf against the flames, vainly trying to quench them with water from the river. 'Let it burn, Georgie,' he says, and all three of them stand ankle deep in the water as they watch the walls fall in, the ice-machine melt in the heat.

So George has returned. I see him at night round the hayricks like a dog that has lost its master, the burns on his face always covered with a scarf. He senses a presence inside, a ghost, a malingerer, remembers the Hester of his childhood. Or else the thought of fire comes to consume him, afraid that after they'd burnt the factory, they'd come for the house. He stays intermittently in his parents' cottage, which Janie leaves each day for her teacher-training course, claims his disability pension, becomes suspect in the townland for taking the King's Shilling: it is not the time, we have to understand, to advertise such a stipend, what has been up is now down, what was down is now up. And they come one night with the rags and cans of petrol, and George is waiting for them behind a haystack with his father's shotgun; he lets off two blasts and retreats inside, closing the gates behind him, so they have to content themselves with burning the hayricks instead. Janie, cycling home from the station, sees the orange glow and thinks they've finally done it, Baltray House has gone the way of all the others. But she meets Georgie by the avenue, the sparks falling over his face like yellow snow. She sees the pride and the gathering lack of reason in his face and leads him home by the hand like a giant child, telling him he's got to stop this, they'll not let him off lightly, leave that sort of thing to the peelers. But of course, the peelers had been burnt out too.

~

'Lovers,' says Gregory. 'The term seems ridiculously French, though of course it's not. Love, I can't think of a more Anglo-Saxon verb unless it's fuck or shit, all nouns too, I might add, English and direct. But lovers, the plural seems French or Latin somehow in its propensity for drama. Yes, she had lovers and I supervised them, I regarded it as my filial and managerial, even dare I say it my dramatic duty. And my duties went like this: approval, in those languorous initial stages. Some of her choices were impossible, let's face it. Those burly prop-hands, those immense electricians, they reminded me of George, which is maybe why she flirted with them and why I ensured, like a well-meaning Iago, that all she did was flirt. I discovered the class system, you see, a mathematical precision in its organisation that was quite missing at home, and I had my own uses later for those ersatz Georges. No, her choices had to be above all of use, had to advance the cause of the Irish Rose and her imprecise shadow, me. Intervention, then, in the latter stages when I could see the need descend on her, the sense of belonging inappropriate to those English verbs, love, fuck, shit. For courtship, engagement, marriage, those impossibly French nouns, had to remain just that, impossible. For both of us.'

~

The director with the drying skin knew he would sleep with me that evening. He was wearing shorts because of the heat in whatever glasshouse it was, Lime Grove, I think, in Shepherd's Bush. I tried dress after dress to satisfy him, knew each time I disrobed he could see me in the wardrobe mirror and knew that he knew that I knew. I crossed Piccadilly with him that evening in a taffeta skirt, felt his shoe underneath it at dinner and glanced at Gregory across the table and knew that he knew. I let him remove it from me later in his quarters above the fish restaurant and remembered that scaly smell from my father's factory by the river. It seemed as appropriate as the smell of semen that covered my chest before he had even removed my stockings. And there, I thought, I was wrong about that too.

40

THEY COME BACK some nights later; not for the house, but for George, who still keeps vigil outside the front gates. They give him what is colloquially called the mother and father of a hiding. It takes seven of them, with hurley sticks and pickaxe handles, given his size and his strength. His blood spatters the hayricks and they leave him there with the owls flitting round him. And he crawls inside the gate, where my father finds him in the morning, drives him to the same hospital where we both recovered from the fall. He is bandaged and plastered, a much larger version of the broken child that lay there. Janie visits him with her mother, and sees in his unfocused eyes how some retreat has begun inside him, he is becoming one of the malfunctioning, inarticulate ones.

He emerges six months later, his shoulders bowed, his burnt skin pale and whey-coloured from confinement in plaster. And my father, sitting alone in the kitchen at night, hears from outside a distant, rhythmic creak, as a tree-trunk would make in a hard, steady wind, but when he walks out into the courtyard there is no wind, only a breathless evening with a moon barely hidden in concentric circles of motionless cloud. The rhythm is still there though, like the creaking of a leather halter off a horse's straining neck, and he follows the sound through the arch, past the glasshouse, down the lawns, and before he sees its source, knows it comes from the movement of the swing he constructed all those years ago. He moves down the grassy field and sees the huge shape, hunched on the seat, moving gently, silhouetted by the water.

'George,' he says softly as he comes behind him.

'Hush,' says George, 'you'll send her away again.'

'I would never want to do that,' says my father softly, and places a hand on his shoulder.

'No,' says George. 'If a hart lack a hind, let him find out Rosalind.'

'You should be home, George,' says my father, 'in your bed.'

'I can't leave her here,' says George.

'Yes, you can,' says my father, 'she'd want you to sleep.'

'Would she?' asks George with a child's innocence, and places his huge hand on my father's.

'Yes,' said my father, 'every boy needs sleep.'

He leads him by the four-fingered hand, off the swing and across the grassy hill, to the road by the river, past Mabel Hatch's barn to his father's tin-roofed cottage. And his idiocy proper begins there, a spell for three months in St Ita's, Portrane, by which time the new Civic Guard is formed, and George on his release is apprehended outside the Bettystown Funfair in a fracas with a strongman. Three nights in the Drogheda cells and my father, for George's safety as much as anything else, gets him employment as a merchant seaman, Drogheda to Liverpool first, then to Ostend, Rotterdam, and each spell of leave for George ending in incarceration of one kind or other. He travels further – Marseilles, Constantinople, Hong Kong, Macau, Australia – and the gaps between the spells at home grow, and Janie gets a teaching job, and the barred room in the Portrane asylum comes to seem like, whenever he revisits it, home.

~

'I had my own ghosts,' says Gregory, 'my reasons, if she had married I don't know what I would have done. I can remember that evening I arrived in the kitchen with my case wrapped in twine and she, or was it me, invented the fiction that I was posted from England, posted as what? As a gift, of course, to her. If I had anticipated such a sister, such an equal in everything but sex, it could have been different maybe. But a life began for me then, another life, and the thought of it ending felt like an end for me too.

I traced my mother's grave to a small churchyard in Surrey, which I visited and saw her name on the brown gravestone already covered in lichen. Annabel Martin. In the village beyond, with its spire and smoke curling in the September air – it was September I remember – there was a house, a substantial house I assumed, substantial enough for Sir Henry Martin to exclude her and me from its favours. I wondered for a mad moment would that have been my name – Gregory Martin – but it seemed impossible, two first names and no surname, and I realised I became what I was when I walked into that kitchen and saw her, Nina Hardy. I was Gregory Hardy and didn't know what I would have been without her. I was her gift, I was in her gift, as she was and would always be, in some way, in mine.'

~

When did I come to hate them, those artificial dramas with their chases, their stunts, their pratfalls, their flouncing, sweating period dresses, their simpering close-ups, their manufactured mystery and suspense, their light and shade? I think around the time they broke up the houses of glass and photographed the events in the great soundproofed stages. And maybe what I had liked had nothing to do with the river of black and white that ran through the cameras, but the glasshouses themselves, those cathedrals of light with the sun pouring through from ceiling to floor. In those glasshouses I was never too far from our game of pretence among the sweltering tomato plants, the four of us swapping affections like sugared sweets. When they shattered the glass and built the walls and brought in the lamps with their sparkling carbon, I began to hate the presumption of those lights, the darkness behind the halated glow. I could see my lost succubus there, wheeling in the dust behind the carbon arcs. I came to agree with those primitive peoples who believe the camera is sucking out the essence, the soul, the succubus. It was no longer me, moving in the caked make-up, the costumes stiff at the armpits from someone else's sweat. It was her, a person I didn't know any more, called Nina Hardy.

And that's when I thought I should have changed my name, called myself Isolda Birtwhistle or some such pretension, because at least the separation between us both would have been complete. I came to hate the reduction of meaning to whatever way she crinkled her face when the lights blazed, the camera turned. I wanted true artifice, not this artificiality, Rosalind's artifice. And that's when I said to Gregory, we have to stop this, I have to do the stage. But the money was too good, I realised, for him at least, and my reputation stank too much of this fairground wonder.

And at the same time I came to realise that Gregory's affections were not really, or not exclusively, fixed on the young blonde ingénues around me, the make-up and costume girls, but on the barrel-chested prop-boys, the electrician hefting that lamp, the muscles on his biceps twisting into cords. 'Do you miss George, Gregory?' I asked him. 'Sometimes,' he answered, 'I pine for him.' And I came to realise the game of desire we had played in our garden of Eden, our first glasshouse, was far more complicated than I had ever imagined.

Mr Shaw effected my release, came to the studio one winter's morning on a quasi-regal visit, to view the source of this new phenomenon that was filling the picture houses, promising me a play that was like those pictures, one hundred percent talk. I had tea with him in Adelphi Terrace, sandwiched between two ladies in mourning black where all three of them expressed implicit approval of his 'new Irish Rose.' We followed them to Malvern where he swam each morning in the pools, his beard preceding him in the water like a duck's nest. I played Orinthia in *The Apple Cart*, to everyone's approval but that of Mrs Patrick

Campbell, who had once been, it seemed, his old Irish Rose. His septuagenarian affection proved as thrilling as that of any nineteen-year-old and his jealousy even more compulsive. He followed the production to London and for two hundred and fifty-eight days plied me with advice on performance, diction, deportment and style. I was to be the last of his intellectual romances, he warned, so I must humour his ardour.

'How better can I humour it?' I asked.

'We are due to spend time,' he said, 'in Italy, Lago di Como. You must join us.' He seemed proud of the way he pronounced those prolonged Italian vowels.

'Can my brother come too?' I asked.

'*Il suo fratello*?' Again the same pride, the lips forming the O out of the oatmeal beard. '*Certissimo.*'

41

M Y FATHER PAINTS, sketches relentlessly, the riverbank, the Lady's Finger, the Maiden's Tower, the water beneath it, he hints at a girl beneath the ripples. He paints his wife gardening, on the summer and the autumn lawns, hoping for a glance at his endeavours, a word of appreciation which never seems to come. She lets the Meath Hunt occupy her winters, the golf-course her summers, gardening and crosswords everything in between. He embarks then on a sketching tour of the antiquities of the Boyne river, starting at the well at the foot of the hill of Carbury, where Boinn ran from the rising waters. He sketches each ruin first, from Carbury Castle to Monasterboice to the Maiden's Tower and the Lady's Finger, then begins an assiduous depiction of the megalithic remains: Newgrange, Knowth, Dowth, each detail of those ancient interiors. The project grows from winter to summer, summer to winter, its scope expands. He begins sketching a series of dramatic tableaux, starting with the mythic, the retreat of Boinn from the river's waters, ending with the historic, the rout of King James's forces by King Billy, William of Orange at the Battle of the Boyne. He flirts with the idea of publication by the Meath Historical Society but realises, at his present rate of progress, it may never be finished.

~

The lake was dark, darker than I thought water could have ever been. From the terrace of the old hotel above one of its corners we viewed its immensity and entertained ourselves with stories.

'I can imagine a cast of characters,' GBS told us, 'confined to this hotel, unable to face the gathering gloom in the world outside, with nothing else to pass the time but narratives of each other. Each narrative ends in one of the parties' demise. So the audience shrinks, story by story, to an audience of one, a soliloquy which concludes of course, in an act of *auto da fé*.'

'Is there a metaphor there?' I asked.

'No,' he replied, 'nothing as vulgar as that, what in the end is fiction but a way of passing the time? You first, Nina Hardy.'

'Can I be last?' I asked him.

'A suicidal soliloquy would hardly suit you,' he said, 'a sentence, by the way, the sibilance of which hardly suits this beard of mine.'

'On the contrary,' I told him, 'I would dive from the castellated wall here into those insanely dark waters below and wouldn't find death there, I'd find another kind of life.'

'What other kind of life?' he said with prosaic petulance. 'There is no other kind of life.'

'I would find,' I told him, and I only told him this to trouble him, 'a monastery garden with a riderless horse, an old Abbot asleep underneath a moulting cherry tree with a pair of sinewy feet in sockless sandals and a beard large enough for bees to make a hive in.'

'What does this Abbot do?' he asked me, his eyes flickering with recognition.

'He dreams,' I told him. 'He dreams of me.'

He took me rowing on the lake towards the town of Bellagio, but barely made it from the shoreline.

'Why an Abbot,' he asked me, 'why bees in his beard?'

'Because the Abbot is old,' I told him, 'and the bees do his pollination for him.'

'Does this Abbot ever wake?' he asked.

'If he did,' I replied, 'what existence would I have?'

He raised the oars on the rowlocks and perched them on the

gunwale of the boat so the lake's water dripped on my face and my dress. How odd, I thought, that the dripping water isn't dark after all.

'Forgive me,' he said, 'if I have husbanded my resources so frugally that when the time comes to spend them, they have quite dried up.'

I kneeled, then, on the gently rocking boat and leaned forwards between his tweed-covered legs because I knew he wanted me to. I pressed my bosom on his bearded chest and placed my own lips against his pursed, leathery, literary ones.

'Can I let you in on a secret?' he asked softly, and the Irishism of the phrase sounded odd in his timbre.

'Let me in,' I said, as softly.

'I do dream of you,' he said, 'and with your permission, would like to continue.'

'Don't stop,' I said.

~

Another riderless horse clops down the avenue one summer's afternoon, foam drying round its mouth and its sides heaving. The horse we rode through the monastery barley field must have long become horsemeat, but this one followed the same route, throwing its rider before the finishing post, throwing arcs of spray down the long beach with its bridle swinging behind it, leaping the small crumbling wall by the Maiden's Tower straight into the river with its leaping salmon. My mother stands up from her flowerbed, throws off her gardening gloves and walks to it, stroking its trembling sides, hushing it into silence. She knows horses, whispers arcane phrases into its pricked-back ear the way George once did, and for a moment I think she might mount it, take her husband on its back and leap through the fields of barley to the monastery garden where the Abbot lies in the afternoon heat, under the moulting cherry tree, dreaming of all of us. But no, of course not, she calls Dan

Turnbull, and Dan leads it by the wet reins down to the reconstituted RIC station, where young Buttsy Flanagan, Civic Guard, strokes his beardless chin and wonders whence it came.

~

He had a dream, he told me, that I was in *Twelfth Night* at the Lyceum, and I understood that this was less a dream than a desire, an arrangement he had already mooted with the management, and found myself walking down the Strand with him expounding on the character of Viola. Viola, cousin to Rosalind, surely, both of whom, through an odd alignment of parenthood, were second-cousins to the melancholy Jacques. So I began rehearsals and wondered where Viola had been all my life. Viola, with an even more complex predilection for disguise than Rosalind, loved and lost her brother Sebastian, last saw him lashed to a mast, holding acquaintance with the waves, on the seas off Illyria.

Prove true, imagination, Oh, prove true, that I, dear brother,
be now ta'en for you

He had himself chosen the youth who played Sebastian and chosen well, he was my fictive brother after all, long feminine lashes leading like fans down to alarmingly sculpted cheekbones. Jonathan was his name, Jonathan Cornfold; he kissed me in the empty stalls when he thought the cast had gone, and what's this, I thought, as his cock stood to attention in his sequinned tights.

'What's this?' I asked him out loud, as I ran my fingers down the sequinned shaft.

'An exclamation-mark,' he said.

'Are there exclamation-marks in Shakespeare?' I asked.

'Yes,' he said, 'the text is full of them.'

'It will have to remain,' I told him, 'a question-mark for the moment, until I have need of exclamations.'

I asked the bearded one before the opening night about the function of punctuation in Shakespeare. 'In Shakespear,' he said,

managing even to pronounce it without the 'e', 'the iamb provides its own punctuation.'

'No exclamation-marks,' I asked him, 'let alone question-
marks?'

'They are Victorian addenda,' he told me, 'to a torrent of language that otherwise might crush its readers.'

Viola, however, with or without punctuation, was about to be
crushed. 'What if I let myself love him, Gregory?' I asked in the
house in Regent's Park, where the leaves were turning brown in
the quarter-circle outside.

'Even worse,' he said, 'what if he lets himself love you?'

'Would that be so bad?' I asked. 'Would things be that different?'

'No,' he said. 'An apple, cleft in two, is not more twin than
these two creatures.' He took my hand as he quoted, parted my
fingers with his.

'Please,' I asked him, 'this time, leave me on my own.'

'No more larks then, sis?' he asked.

'No,' I told him. 'No more larks.'

I was everyone's Viola that opening night, my bearded abbot's in
the stalls, my brother's in his box, my Sebastian's in the wings.
But I allowed myself the fantasy, as an actor must, that in reality I
would be the latter's. Whoe'er I woo, myself would be his wife. I
expunged all punctuation from the text and let the iambs speak
and let the language crush me.

And so it began, the brief dance with desire, the lights became
kind again, those footlights wrapping his body in a sheath of
white. His entry in the play was late, but I was filled with anticipation for that presence, Viola in her boy's disguise, wooing the
bride that by the play's end would be his. Tempests are kind and
salt waves fresh in love, and the tempest built throughout the run.
The winds that coursed down Catherine Street outside the theatre
to the Strand, it was May I remember, they lifted my skirt and his

overcoat, he held mine down and kissed me. We joined Gregory in the Savoy for drinks – a certain femininity in their gestures, I was warned of course, I should have known, but theirs was a free-masonry with signalled gestures known only to each other.

'Are you sure it's him you want, my dear?' my half-brother asked when my fictional brother had left.

'What a question,' I replied, 'what presumption, Greg.'

~

'I fell,' says Gregory, 'and unlike George, I fell without her. It was an inverted fall, a fall from grace and a fall into grace, into the arms of her Sebastian. I had kept this destiny of mine at arm's length for years. I had used her presence to confine it to what I had hoped it was, a tendency, an occasional weakness for the callow youths that tended the costumes, for the rough diamonds that humped me much in the same way as they humped the lamps. But with him I felt something and I knew that it was different.

Because he looked like her, maybe, those long lashes and the declining curves of cheekbone, he looked impossibly like the brother she could have had, and playing her brother, he imitated her. She didn't see it coming, I could tell that, no matter how I tried to warn her of it, he imitated her for me and me for her, I sat with her in that room full of mirrors in the Savoy and he sat between us, a mirror for both of us.

"Are you sure," I asked her, when he had gone on some pretext of an errand, "that he is the one?" And she chided me gently, before she left too. We watched her then, from upstairs in the room I had booked, emerge from under the metal awning on to the Strand, the spring breeze whipping her coat round her ankles, and I couldn't feel sadness or guilt. All I felt was a miraculous rightness as he turned to me and gave me that which should have been hers. That long, slow afternoon of pleasure. You are playing with us both, I told him after it, and yes, he admitted, I have been, but the game is over now.'

42

W HEN THE SUMMER heat closed the theatre, we three siblings took a trip to Torquay, walked among those equatorial trees.

'This can be our Zanzibar,' said Gregory, 'a companion to our Mozambique.'

'Mozambique?' asked Jonathan.

'Yes,' said Gregory, 'my sister and I invent whole continents without the need to move.'

'Sounds alarming,' Jonathan said.

'No,' said Gregory, taking both our elbows, 'no need for alarm whatsoever.'

On the old brocaded bed in the hotel that seemed to want to tumble down into the metallic sea, in the afternoon, afterwards, I watched him as he slept beside me. Sleep came on him on the instant as it does to the innocent, the guiltless, and I thought I had been wrong about my brother, there was no vying for affection, but that both of us made a family that this guiltless wonder could join. I said as much to Gregory as he played the piano in the empty ballroom: Mozart, the childish round of fractured notes that never seemed to end, that could be interrupted for a word, and then resumed as if it had never stopped.

'I owe you an apology,' I said, 'I was wrong, there was no what do you call it, intent. So there, Greg, I'm sorry.'

'Never never,' he told me, 'apologise.'

So I went walking through what he called Zanzibar, the ash trees melting in the un-English heat. Like a girl again, I hung from the slim trunks of trees to help my journey down and I glimpsed the silver sheen of the water's surface through the hot green, still and almost tropical, and made my way down, balancing, trunk after trunk. And I saw the boat, moving gently by the rock, untended, two figures through the moss-covered trunks, biscuit-coloured skin against the silver water through the green. I sank my fingers in the moss and felt as if I was moving the tree-trunk past me, though it was I that moved past the trunk, to see them both, knee deep in water, one brother's arm against the other's shoulder, the other snaking down to find his trunks, to caress that exclamation-mark. Be you his eunuch, and your mute I'll be. He heard me then and turned. They both turned. And what he didn't say was, What larks, sis.

~

'If there is a judge,' says Gregory, 'in the court of love, she sat out in that melting sea among her affidavits and saw the three of us, Nina up among the trees, Jonathan and me standing in the water beside the rowing boat, and as Nina turned and clambered back up through that moss the scales of her justice tipped against me. And if there is a judge in the court of love she has the face of my dead mother and she sits wheezing in the dead heat in a rattan chair, which is the only memory I have left of her. She sits in permanent session and measures each breath, each promise, each betrayal and each possibility. I would no longer be my sister's manager. I would set up shop in Soho, Gregory Hardy Associates, Theatrical Management, and my associate was him. I would thrive of course; I had my father's effortless head for a business I hardly wanted. His career would founder, his only real talent was for sodomy. But he had a gift, if I can call it that, for bookkeeping and for simple, plain companionship, and my only defence would be that we endured.'

~

There was a train steaming by the small station with the blue and yellow eaves, and Gregory was shifting from foot to foot when I asked him to tell me that it was love or something like that, because anything else would be unforgivable.

'It is', he said, and I kissed his cheek and I hoped for his sake that it was. It has taken us a long time, I told him, to grow up. But can adulthood be so bad? I got on the train then and as it drew away became someone different; the difference was subtle, but for ever, and acute. Gregory waved and I turned my head around and didn't feel like waving back. But someone else did wave, raised her hand as if everything that had passed was just a play, a play whose outcome didn't matter much. Nina Hardy waved. And the train drew her through those sleepy, summer southern stations to a future without him.

She and I. We are not the same at all. She waved as if it didn't matter much. I turned from the window so he couldn't see my streaming tears.

~

'You were wrong,' Nina Hardy told George Bernard Shaw, 'about the punctuation.'

He was sitting in the walled garden of his country cottage, in the late spring heat, dressed in a three-piece tweed suit with bees, of all things, buzzing round the apple blossoms. 'Shakespeare,' she informed him, 'was all exclamation.'

'I will soon be dead,' he said, 'and am sure I will discover I was wrong about most other things too.'

43

WITH DAN TURNBULL'S death they realise they are truly alone. The house seems immense without him, the gardens and the grounds untenable, the shadows concealing the ghost of a child that will never speak. And when they realise, finally, how truly alone they are, some thaw begins between them. It happens unexpectedly: leaving Dan Turnbull's funeral mass she takes his hand, suddenly, as the coffin moves past towards the churchyard. He feels the hand in his, the wedding-ring, the paper-thin skin above the bones he had wanted to console so many years ago.

They begin gardening the same patch together that afternoon, Dan's vegetable patch. She is by the strawberry bed and he comes behind her with a trowel, kneels, and clears the weeds for her.

'Thank you, love,' she says, and the word, like the touch, is so unexpected it brings tears to his eyes.

'She's not coming back, I've known that for years, I realise that now.'

'No,' his wife says, 'and perhaps it's my fault.'

'Who would have thought,' he says, 'childbirth could bring so much trouble?'

'She left us on our own,' she says, 'because she imagined it would punish me.'

'And has it?' he asks.

'Not any more,' she says. 'And I realised this morning, all I ever really wanted was you. I wasn't good at mothering. But I was good at loving once, wasn't I?'

Shade

Happiness, however limited, confines them even further. She moves into his bedroom, the tiny one facing the estuary and they shrink the house to it, it seems, and the stairs between it and the kitchen.

The old quilted bedspread moves at night with their bodies beneath it in a ritual that seems ancient to them now, so long unpractised. He's a stranger again, he realises, in a house he hardly knows, and strangest of all the body he moulds with his veined hands.

'We'll take a walk tomorrow,' he says, 'down by the shingle and count the oystercatchers on Baltray strand.'

'They are uncountable,' she tells him.

He falls into her arms one autumn day, in the garden – where else? – and of course she cannot hold him. She tries, but turns, and he tumbles into the hollyhocks, destroying whole swathes of them, pulling her down with him, as if in a vain effort to be heard. He never finishes his last word to her. He manages the V and the S of the second syllable, and she has to intuit from them the name of a Spanish court painter with nine letters. She knows the name already, and knows also that he is dying.

Mary Dagge helps her with the still-breathing frame into the house. The wheelbarrow was nearby, without it how could two old women manage? But manage they do. They get him across the garden, scouring two heavy wheel-marks in the new-mown grass to the steps, then lift him bodily inside and place him on the chaise-longue while Mary Dagge rings Dr Henry.

She spends the next hour beside him, listening to his breathing, hoping for another word. But none comes, just the gradually decreasing pressure of his hand on hers. And for a time it is as if none of it had happened, any of it, births, betrayals, departures. They are in the Accademia again, looking at the marble *David*, and she is thinking of him, imagining his absence already, the absence she remembers from the days in Florence to the afternoon in the National Gallery in front of the Velázquez. By the time Dr Henry arrives he is dead, and she knows those hidden parts will be hers for ever.

~

She was in America when she heard the news, marooned there because of the war. In the Ambassador Hotel in downtown Los Angeles, a bellboy walked through calling, oddly, for a Mister Hardy. She stood on instinct and walked towards him and accompanied him through the huge ornate foyer to the telephone booth, where she heard Gregory's distant voice at the other end, for the first time in eighteen months. When he gave her the news of the death, it was not as if she had already known, but as if she had already experienced the loss.

'What should we do?' he asked. 'Go back, go home?'

'Yes,' she said, 'I suppose we should, but I don't know how.'

'We have to,' he said, uselessly.

'Yes,' she said again, 'I know we have to, but how will I travel?'

'One of us must go,' he said, 'and I suppose it must be me.'

'You?' she asked, knowing already, despite what promises he made, he would not keep them.

She visited the Chapel in La Brea in the sweltering heat and tried to imagine what the weather was at home. Windy, she decided, with the white caps spreading from the sea down the mouth of the river, diminishing to sculpted crests of almost black where the estuary rounded the field below the house. She tried to think of a word for those dark crests. Obsidian.

44

BY THE TIME she made it home, her mother had died too. The war had ended. She had spent it in America, having little choice and less appetite for a transatlantic crossing. Her ship had to wait outside the Boyne estuary until the tide was ready and she felt almost sick with pleasure and dread at the same time. She could see the Lady's Finger prodding from the blue with the low dull green of the wetlands around it, the haze of smoke that was the town behind it. Then the foghorn sounded even though there was no fog and the cattle-dealers smoked their cigarettes and pressed against the rail, and the Lady's Finger came ever so slowly closer, with the Maiden's Tower behind it, and the captain knew, as her father had told her so many years ago, that it was time to strike the bar.

There was a black Ford car waiting for her at the wharf and a driver in a grubby peaked cap, who took it off as he shook her hand and replaced it as he reached for her bags and left her standing, as the cattle were prodded from the rear of the ship towards the waiting lorries. He drove then, through the brown sludge that they left in their wake, down the road towards Baltray House.

She was shocked, initially, by the outcrops of cottages that surrounded it, small council dwellings in rows where there had been fields and hayricks. The grounds were intact, though, the fields, the gardens, the chestnut and the copse of trees to the left of the bend of the river, the combined impact of which was enough for her to consider this return to the milieu of her childhood justified.

She had bought out Gregory's portion of this, their only inheritance, and could remember with the clarity of an ache that afternoon in Brown's Hotel, Piccadilly when they signed the papers in the company of that small loquacious man from Gill and Company, Solicitors. She had paid far more than the market value to avoid any rancour. There was tea in china cups, good tea, which she appreciated after five years of American coffee, and she remembered thinking, watching Gregory's long fingers wielding the solicitor's fountain pen, how much she appreciated the nearness of those fingers too. And in the wood-panelled bar, the only sound between them being the rustle of parchment and the scraping of the nib of that fat-barrelled Parker pen, she could see their mutual future with an aching certainty.

There would be no acknowledgement that they were releasing each from the other, finally, like two tugs that had plied the same waters for years, tied together. He would plough on through whatever ocean he found himself in without any further recourse to her. For he would never visit, he had told her that, and she had no reason to disbelieve him. She had looked at his immaculate suit and his handmade shoes and tried not to wonder what his life was like now.

And on the street outside, as they had said their goodbyes in the mid-afternoon traffic and crowds, she cried. It took a moment like this, she had told him, and she lied, to bring the reality of a death home to her. And he had hugged her and said, 'I know sis, but, onwards, eh?'

And now, some thirty years after she had left home, the black Ford car purred in the forecourt as she wandered through the glass-riddled kitchen, poking away broken milk bottles with her laced bootee. She could have taken a plane from London to Dublin, but had preferred, for sentimental reasons, to go by rail to Liverpool and take the run-down ferry. She wanted to arrive back here the way her father had, through the brown alluvial silt of that river. For if there had ever been home for her, she knew this was it. Take me in.

Her name was now recognisable, her face less so. She had

flitted between theatre and film like a moth flitting between two contrary lamps. She had been lucky, she would admit that readily, had managed a fruitful and lucrative career with a modicum of embarrassment and had revealed of herself, in the course of it, nothing whatsoever.

The real Nina Hardy was known to very few. And the real Nina Hardy now walked through the ruins of her childhood home and gathered, from the stench of spilt alcohol and urine, that it had long become a venue for late night drinking sessions. But the damage, she surmised, was limited and much less offensive to the senses than the changes her mother had made in her absence. Polka-dotted wallpaper, flame yellow paint, mock-oak veneer, three decades of fads, fashions and fittings were mouldering, rusting, peeling, mildewing and generally rotting on the floors, windows and walls. A broken radio sat, unaccountably, on the living room floor, wrapped in the same cobwebs that spread over the blotched surface of the grand piano.

She lifted the wooden cover and pressed the faded ivory keys and was surprised by the fullness of the sound. Was surprised too, by her memory. She played the first few bars of the Mozart sonata and found her fingers reaching, automatically, for the development of the theme. I cannot, she thought, cannot have remembered it all, but the house, clever thing that it was, drew it from her. And as it filled up with music, childlike music indeed, played like a child, she knew with a certainty that had hit her several times in her fifty years, that she had, at last, at the very least, done the right thing.

45

THE DRIVER OF the black Ford car heard the music and remarked to himself on the contrast between the elegant woman who had entered the ruined house and the childlike music that emerged from it. He had recognised her face of course, her profile was burned in his memory like a Victorian daguerreotype, but was discreet enough to pretend he didn't. He knew the purpose of her visit too, remembering a column in the property section of the *Irish Times* with her photograph and a photograph from across the fields beyond, of the grey pile in the forecourt of which he was parked. And when the music stopped and she emerged again through the sagging kitchen door, he didn't jump to attention and open the rear door, because something in her way of walking, in the slow scrape of those chunky heels across the gravel, told him her visit was far from over. He admired her figure in the rear-view mirror, the trim of fur round the shoulders, the neat-fitting black beret atop the blonde, elegantly greying hair. She was one of those, he concluded, whose lives are not like yours or mine, who exist between the lines of society columns and gossip magazines. He had seen her half-undressed in a film the title of which he could not now remember, but could remember how at the age of seventeen she had seemed the essence of womanliness to him. So he averted his eyes, with a slight, secret shame, when she tapped at the window and told him she would be thirty or so more minutes. And when she turned her back to him he allowed himself the luxury of a direct glance, through the breath-misted side window, at those hips whose full glory he had relished at the age of seventeen in the

Fairview cinema in a film the name of which he could no longer remember. They travelled, with not a noticeable swagger, through a small group of outhouses, by a broken glasshouse, down long untidy lawns towards a chestnut tree, which bent over what he presumed must be a river.

The half-circle of once whitewashed outhouses bends or slopes into a passageway, and the gravel underfoot gives way to cobbles as the sunlight is shadowed for twelve footsteps or more, and the untidy slope of green comes into view with the glasshouse to the left, all of the panes broken, what else, how much to repair them but what matters, only money after all. The dangling stalks of long dead tomato plants, could they possibly be the same, the ones behind which she rehearsed her Rosalind, hart to the hind, full of leaf then, with a dead green mould that coloured her cheeks and fingers. The mud is hard underfoot now, caked by the summer's sun, threads of grass trying vainly to cover it, shades of the mudflats she called Mozambique, and the chestnut comes into view, the bent umbrella of tangled branches first dark against the silver of the water. The lawn, or is it field, sloping down to meet it with the steep bit where she often tumbled, rolled, catching her skirt between her knees. The trunk rising from the dark cracked earth and the branch, thick enough to be the trunk's extension, arching over the silver waters, so quiet now as to make that perfect reflection, blue or silver sky, black or brown branches. The ropes are gone of course, long rotted and gone, but the bark could never quite grow enough to cover the circular scours they left, scoured by the rope swing, forwards and back, up and down.

The driver of the black Ford took the licence, knowing there would be a thirty minutes' wait, of stepping out of the car and smoking a cigarette. He could see her through the arch, down by the chestnut tree, silhouetted against what he now definitely saw to be a river. Why, he wondered, would anyone return to such a pile, most of all a single woman with no visible male support, no wedding ring, and come to think of it, from what he knew of the world of gossip, not even a rumour of a husband?

He was a practical, venal man with no particular imaginative interior, but as he smoked and allowed his eye to travel round the small world of that forecourt, he suddenly and inexplicably knew. He could see the glasshouse, each pane replaced, with the dark green shadows of lush tomato plants inside. He could see a fresh circle of gravel with no intrusion from grass, dandelion and plantain. He could see the walls and windows that soared above him with a fresh coat of pale-green paint. And through the arch, he could see the rough grass that sloped down towards the river now manicured into a lawn, and hanging from the overhanging branch of the chestnut tree, a child's swing. Yes, he thought to himself, it could be a fine place, a very fine place.

She was walking towards him now, departing from the bank of light that was the sun's reflection in the river. She became obscured for some moments by the mound of the field, then re-appeared again, gradually, against the silver glare. She seemed to grow into shadow as she walked towards him, a trick of light he attributed to the halation of the afternoon rays of the setting sun. He smoked and averted his eyes, looked at the light bouncing off the broken glasshouse windows, then heard the soft shuffle of her boots on the grass changing to the clap of heels against cobble.

'Time to go then, Ma'am?' he asked, and when she nodded he stubbed out the butt of the cigarette on the dry-stone wall, ran to the car and opened the rear door.

The black Ford eased its way down the north side of the river Boyne where strings of bungalows dotted the road like fake jewellery, where the cement works trundled buckets overhead to the tankers and where, if she cared to remember, her father once told

her the *Graniauale* had docked. She could see, through the flaring
afternoon sun, the silhouetted figures of boys casting fishing lines
into the brown waters. She could see the driver's eyes flickering
towards her and away as the bustle through the windscreen thick-
ened and the cement works gave way to the Drogheda Quays.

She tapped him on the shoulder then and told him to swing
left, towards the south side of the river, beneath the shadow of
the margarine factory, back towards Mornington. The riverfront
flattened there, became more gentle, as her memory of it was.
She saw a kingfisher rise from the mud banks and flash electric
blue across the water. She saw boys again, and the dark angled
lines of fishing rods. Then trees obscured her view as the road left
the riverbank, made its way through more dotted hulks of bungalows which seemed planned, or unplanned, to obliterate any
memory she would have had of the village itself. She saw the
Protestant church on a mound among leafy chestnuts where the
road forked and the sad remnants of the village began. She saw a
new triangular edifice of glass and concrete where the Catholic
church used to be. And she saw the village melt then, as if under
the influence of some strange new principle, as the necklace of
bungalows began once more. She saw it all, and her eyes
expressed nothing, at least nothing the driver could divine
through the rear-view mirror, or the side mirror which he had
angled to take in more than the retreating road behind.

The bungalows stopped then, as if the sad marshy wasteland
through which the road travelled was deserving of them no
longer. The black Ford bumped its way over a small canal, past a
lighthouse perched among dunes, a keeper's cottage separated by
barbed wire from the twelfth hole of a golf-course. To the left of
that, the knuckles of sand-dunes spiked with that tough reedy
grass the name of which she could no longer remember. Then a
tower came into view on a rocky escarpment where the road
petered to its seemingly inevitable conclusion. There was a low
limestone wall, and the great mouth of the river pushing its

weight of water to the open sea. And in the centre of its path, as if placed there to define the boundary of sea and river, was a limestone pillar, which poked its way toward the horizon like a large finger made of stone.

The driver stopped, where the road lost its definition in a flat-land of pebbles and broken seashell. He stopped and sat in silence until he heard her speak from the back seat, in voice that was at once strange and familiar. Or strange because familiar.

'I'm sorry, Ma'am?' he asked. 'I didn't hear.'

'It's nothing,' she said. And then, as if continuing silence might seem rude, she pointed towards the horizon. 'There,' she said. 'The Lady's Finger.'

The wire-mesh fence traced the boundary of the golf-course past the twelfth hole from the lighthouse to the Bettystown road, where it turned south at a neat angle and encased the greens, fair-ways and roughs to the eighteenth hole. There the fence ended and a complex of clubhouses began. She allowed the car to drive on, through the sand-filled square of the tiny village, past it through the wooden houses and village beyond, told him to turn right along a smaller river where another kingfisher darted into the overhanging brambles; then back on to the Dublin road, and after a time a left turn to the village of Portrane and a final loop around the village to the sprawling edifice of St Ita's psychiatric hospital.

The black Ford pulled to a halt outside the red-brick façade with its barred windows, its lawns whitened by small dunes of blowing sand, sloping down to a nondescript beach with a round stone tower cutting through the horizon between scuffed waters and cloud-blown sky. The driver stepped out, opened the back door and used his hip to keep it wedged as he reached down to help her to her feet.

Her hair brushed off his cheek as she emerged and her perfume drifted past him like a thin veil. He watched her walk then, over the circle of broken cement and drifting sand, towards the large green doors set into the overpowering red-brick cathe-

dral. She seemed too finished, too elegant for her drab surround-
ings. The driver tried to picture her again half-naked in the
Fairview cinema of his youth, but the image stayed elusive. Then
he remembered a phrase, uttered in a perfect Liverpool burr
which had been some years ago part of common currency. 'Sorry
love but I'm off to Bradford.' Nina Hardy with hair of peroxide
blonde, a lipstick-tipped cigarette in one hand, cases at the open
door of a redbrick house, in a street of similar houses which
retreated behind her to infinity.

'Gardening,' she said to the psychiatrist, 'simple tasks that even
George, in whatever state he's in, could manage. Because,' she
said, and forgot his name momentarily, but was saved by the rectangle of plastic clipped to his white collar, 'Dr Hannon, I knew
George since the age of…well, since he was a child.'

'So, you know his condition then?' the doctor enquired. A
large face, somehow feminine, underneath bouffant greying hair.
He would have suited a magician's act, she thought, in a music-
hall, a false-bottomed box and a saw and a girl in the box with
stiletto heels and fishnet tights.

'Yes,' she said, 'well, I know roughly what happened. My
brother was with him when it happened, helped him to safety
and always wondered should he have. But George,' she said, 'like
a lot of people, was never suited to adulthood.'

'We have an outpatients' work-scheme,' the doctor said. 'They
work in the fields, in the market-gardens round here, return at
night.'

'Yes,' she said, 'I know, I've seen them years ago in the fields
around. Dummies, they called them, doctor, I don't quite see the
therapeutic value in that. I was thinking of something more permanent. He has green hands, doctor, always had, he could grow
wallflowers on a sand dune. I have a garden, I have a labourer's
cottage near the garden, I'm in desperate need of labour, so what
could be wrong with…'

'George is institutionalised,' the doctor said. 'He has been in and out of our care for the last twenty years, but always returns.'

'And can that be a good thing?' she asked.

'No,' he said, 'but it is the reality. We are now the only home he knows.'

'Why not ask him then, doctor?'

'Ask him what?'

'Or let me ask him. Tell him Nina is here.'

And that is how she came to sit in the long waiting-room with the tall windows looking out on the round tower over the beach at Portrane, and came to hear the uncertain tread she remembered from her childhood, and turned to see the nurse lead the large-shouldered figure through the miniscule door.

'George,' she said, 'it's Nina.'

And how he came to turn the face to her that she barely recognised.

46

S HE STAYED IN the Neptune Hotel, Bettystown, for a week, an unlikely presence in the autumnal winds, travelling to the house each morning with an architect one day, a contractor the next. She talked to nobody, ate meals alone, walked the long beach to the river's mouth in the evening, walked the opposite direction some evenings, crossed the wooden bridge over the Nanny river as the Dublin trains trundled overhead. At the end of that week, on the Friday morning, the driver of the black Ford collected her once more, placed the three bags in the empty boot and retraced his journey along the riverside, through the Drogheda traffic to the still-abandoned house. There he waited five interminable hours as car after car arrived and their drivers shuffled through the house to confer with her. The last of these was driven by a doctor in a white coat, who parked behind the black Ford and opened his own rear door to lead out a large hulking figure who sat hunched in the back seat.

He stood in the small dusty forecourt, blinking in the October sunlight, staring at the house and the outbuildings behind it with a great sense of recognition. His grey overcoat was too small for his bulk, the laces on his shoes were untied and the skin was like crumpled, tortured paper on his pale, enormous face. He didn't move a muscle, stood like a statue that had been planted there twenty years before, until she emerged from the kitchen, followed by an architect who scribbled on an open sheaf of plans as he walked. And she left the architect standing and walked towards him.

'George,' she said, 'I can tell by your attitude that you remember.'

He lowered his eyes to meet hers, with a movement of the head that was so slow the driver of the black Mercedes deduced he must be blind.

'Hart to the hind,' he said.

She led George by the hand down the long swathe of green towards the river. The psychiatrist followed, watching the large head stare, turn this way and that, as if entering into a remembered wonderland.

'We spent much of our childhood here, doctor,' she said, 'didn't we, George?'

'We did, Ma'am,' said George obediently.

'It's Nina, George, not Ma'am,' she said, adding, as an afterthought, 'if you please. George came from the cottages over there. The river divided us, right George?'

'Yes,' he said, 'the river,' dealing with the problem posed by her given name by omitting it entirely.

'There was a swing there, wasn't there George, on that branch of the chestnut.' George stared at the branch and reached his hand up to touch the decades-old scar on the bark. 'And I thought,' she said, 'all things being equal, if everything works out as planned, that George would use Dan Turnbull's cottage. You remember Dan's cottage, George?'

'Do I ever,' said George.

'Well, maybe you can take us to it.'

He walked, like a child again, along the barely etched path in the grass above the riverbank. There was a tangle of blackberry bushes then, at the bend in the river, and the copse of ash and elder behind it. The woods seemed impassable, but like a child still, he found his old way through it, pushing aside overgrown brambles, breaking off a stick to beat them back, a Hernando Cortez in an imagined Mexican jungle scything his way to an El

Dorado, which, when the brambles gave way to clearance with empty cider cans underfoot, turned out to be the peeling, once-whitewashed front of a two-roomed cottage.

'Dan's,' said George.

'Yes,' said Nina, 'this was Dan's. Could be yours George, if you want it.'

'Let us not be hasty,' murmured the psychiatrist.

'No,' said Nina, 'we will by no means rush. I thought he could start by getting it in shape, three or four hours a day maybe, someone could drive him here, doctor, maybe even you, take him home again at night. And if he makes progress he could begin on the garden, and if the miracle happens, make this cottage his home. There'll be works here, an architect, a building supervisor, he'll never be alone. And when the house is ready, if I can be as bold as to look forward that far, I will have a gardener and George will have, what is the phrase? A life. Yes that's it, George will have a life.' She turned to him and took his hand again. 'Would you like a life, George?

And George smiled, his huge hand closing around hers, and whispered, using, she happily noted, her name for the first time.

'Nina,' he said, 'what larks.'

They emerged into the driver's view again as they had left it, she first, her right arm angled behind her, the hand lost in George's enormous fist, who followed like a child. They stopped by the bonnet of the black Ford.

'Please give it some thought,' she said to the doctor in the white coat, her hand still engaged by the hulk the driver of the black Ford had deduced to be his patient. He noted that the skin of the hand matched the skin of the face and was missing one finger. The pinky.

'My first impressions,' the doctor replied, 'are more than favourable.'

'I shall await then,' she said, 'your second.' She withdrew her hand from the patient, shook the doctor's. And she raised her pert body on the soles of her black bootees, placed a kiss on the patient's left cheek.

'Goodbye, George.'

She moved towards the car. The driver leapt from his seat, almost hit her with the opening door. And as he opened the rear door he thought he saw a tear in the hulk's cornflower-blue eyes.

47

S HE THREW MONEY at the house and the house, as if anxious
to assume the shape that pleased her most, responded. The
interior was stripped bare within a month, the wiring replaced,
the forecourt filled itself with bathroom fittings, tongue-and-
groove pine, floorboards, kitchen sinks, window-sashes. A
Portakabin for the architect and foreman was trundled on to the
front lawn, the copse of trees around Dan Turnbull's cottage
was tidied, the rhododendron and the ash cut back. The cottage
itself was clean within a month, new-painted, a radio installed
in the corner opposite the fireplace, a sofa improvised from the
rear seat of an old Cortina car placed next to it. She came again
in January; a different driver, waiting for her by the arrivals
desk in Dublin airport, led her towards an identical black Ford
car. She stayed another week in the Neptune Hotel, greeted
George each morning on his arrival from Portrane, said
goodbye to him each evening as the doctor took him home. But
the word home was inadmissible to him, since his real home,
now, seemed to be here.

She walked with him through Flanagan's on the Dublin road,
and chose lawnmowers, spades, clippers and secateurs, and gave
him as his first task the renovation of the glasshouse. She left
word with the site foreman to supervise his duties, keep him
supplied with whatever tools he needed, and by her next visit,
in March, the renovation of the glasshouse was complete.

As the chirping of skylarks over the unkempt grasses was
drowned in the dull bass throbbing of earth-movers, the sound

of a JCB reversing, the thump of kango hammers, George, in what was very much like a homecoming ceremony, was installed in Dan Turnbull's cottage. He then took his place among the hard-hats, the drivers of heavy machinery, the plumbers, electricians and carpenters as the house's archivist, the keeper of its memories, the guardian of its restoration, the inheritor of its soul. He relished any responsibility, embraced it like a long lost cousin, began consulting with the works manager on the restoration, remembered every detail of how it was and how it once more could be.

Dr Hannon observed this with a wry sense of failure, and expressed himself one Monday afternoon to Nina, watching George at work among the tomato plants in the re-paned glasshouse, shocked at the futility of the years spent in the St Ita's wards.

'Is it a comment,' he asked her, 'on the uselessness of psychiatry? Three months here has undone what ten years there could never undo.'

'Perhaps,' said Nina, 'it's simpler than you think.'

'How?' he asked.

'Perhaps,' she replied gently, 'he's happy.'

Though whether happiness was the word for such undivided concentration, such relentlessly meticulous care for the utterly inessential, was a question they neglected to ask each other. He was content, definitely, to spend hours with a spliced rope, two sections of an old garden seat and two nuts and bolts.

'What are they for, George?' she asked as he riveted them together with thin strips of metal.

'You'll see,' he said.

And she did see, on the morning she finally left the Neptune Hotel for London, having long tired of the room with its odours of damp, the evening walks on the windblown sand. The works were in good hands, George was in good hands, the house would now define itself at a pace she could hardly influence. And what she saw was this: George, grown to ten times the height he was when he first sat on it, pushing the new-made, empty swing over the empty river, a swing that was an almost perfect copy of the old.

48

THREE YEARS LATER, George woke with the dawn, as always. He boiled some water on the gas-ring in the tiny kitchen. He heard the purring of wood-pigeon outside, the clucking of a stonechat, the irregular chatter of wagtails and sparrows. He took a piece of yesterday's batch bread in his hands while waiting for the water to boil and bent low under the jamb of the kitchen door, went through to the front one, edged it open with his foot. He tossed crumbs of white bread around the stunted rhododendron bushes and waited with the benign patience of a latter-day St Francis till the birds revealed themselves. When the first wagtail came he clucked his tongue off his teeth in symbiotic approval of its jabbing beak, its jerking feathers. A flurry of sparrows came next and he broke more bread and threw it towards them, watching them retreat and advance with each offering. He heard the mechanical thrum of wings off foliage and glimpsed the plumage of a cock-pheasant making a plumb line through the dark green, leaving a trail of broken sunlight in its wake.

Then the kettle sang. He turned from this breakfast of birds without a second thought, bowed low under the entrance to the kitchen, dropped a teabag in a smudged cup and poured the water. He took a bottle of yesterday's milk from the battered fridge, watching the white milk turn the black tea brown. The swirl of milk in the oak-coloured liquid had for him the same intensity of interest as the jabbing, chirruping beaks outside. He looked around his dwelling then, and if there was gratitude for his new circumstances, he gave little sign of it. All phenomena seemed equally worthy of his attention. He lifted the spent teabag from the cup with a spoon and dropped it in the rubbish-bin beneath the gas-ring.

Then he walked, cup in hand, through the low kitchen doorway, through the more generous confines of the front door, past the pruned and stunted rhododendrons, through the copse of trees – ash, elder, birch – to the reconstituted glasshouse.

He had replaced each pane, had hand-sanded the frames of rusting metal, painted them then with a red oxide and a white primer. He had re-erected the tracery of hanging wires that would support the tomato plants when they eventually deigned to grow. He was bringing into being a past that he remembered, a state of enchantment or grace he dimly apprehended, though not with any sense of joy, wonder, hurry, but with a methodical concentration that would have done a three-year-old child proud. The tomato plants were tiny as yet, their stems needed to be threaded to the hanging wires so as to gain enough purchase to grow upwards. George finished his tea then in one gulp, entered the humid interior of glass and streaming sunshine, applied his large scarred hands to the delicate green stems.

Around eleven, he was digging, near the roots of the old apple tree, the one with the large, bowed branches, each year bent permanently with the weight of an abundance of fruit that nobody wanted. The apples stayed till they fell off and small shrivelled frozen remnants clattered round his spade as he dug. The earth was frozen too, of course, he would have needed a kango hammer to really shift it, but he persisted. One root had overgrown and was protruding from the grass like a buried elbow. He had tripped continually on the triangle of bark and was determined to set it right.

Once a task was begun he plied it slowly and methodically to its conclusion, as if the task at hand was the issue, not the end result. So he dug, and by twelve o'clock he had opened a rough solid circle, half a foot down into the open earth. One old tin can, a horse-shoe, three coins from the turn of the century. Each demanded a pause and a cigarette, an examination by those unreadable eyes, then a careful setting aside, among the solid spadefuls of discarded earth.

So it was almost lunchtime when he saw it. The remains of a hem, with the fragments of lace still intact upon it, the cloth about it half-decayed. He edged his spade around it carefully, following the hem further into the frozen ground. He recognised the lace immediately, how could he not? It was Nina's shawl, that he'd threaded through his fingers so often and so long ago. He bent now and held it just so, and felt it disintegrate further under his gardener's fingers. He cut into the cold crumbling earth beneath it and raised this bundle from the past on his spade, laid it to one side among the dampening grass. A line from their play in the glasshouse sang into his brain, he wondered how he'd remembered it, and once it was there he couldn't get rid of it. And so from hour to hour we ripe and ripe and then from hour to hour we rot and rot. From the fool in the forest, he remembered, but he couldn't remember the end. The cloth had glints of the peacock blue surviving the patina of clay or was it mould. Mould, he thought, like the furred surface of ancient meat, and the lines kept singing in his head, we ripe and rot.

The sun above him was well advanced and the grass was steaming gently with the melting hoar frost. He gripped the hem and pulled it through one finger and thumb and the shawl turned in the wet grass. He felt a hard circular ball inside the hem, like a ball-bearing. He pulled the stitches apart and removed a rust-coloured bead from inside the cloth. He rubbed it between his tobacco-stained fingers and saw the shimmering texture emerge beneath, which he only gradually recognised as pearl.

We ripe and rot, the lines sang in his head again and he still couldn't remember the end. But he remembered the day by the Boyne before the conflagration when he had opened the oyster with his army knife. He untwined the hem further then, as if it was a bow, tied by Nina long ago, concealing further riches inside. And the hem unwound and the shawl turned further and revealed whatever riches it had hidden, in the crumbling earth on the melting grass. Fragments of seashell, he thought at first, or the remains of crabclaws. He remembered the crunch of packed shells beneath his feet outside the shellfish factory and rubbed one fragment in his fingers and saw the whitened texture of bone.

The bones of a small animal, he thought then, a rabbit, a stoat, a kitten and he tried to remember a pet that Nina would have treasured as she treasured her doll Hester, or as she had treasured this bundle, to wrap it so carefully in her shawl, with the pearl he had given her. But he could remember no pet, the only loved, tiny object being the doll, with its puritan bib and smock. Yet Hester had been given to the waters, he recalled, and waked with orangeade and biscuits in a china teaset. He tried to imagine what Nina would wrap with such protective care in her shawl that had been peacock blue, that had the pearl inwoven, what she would swaddle like an infant and bury here beneath the apple tree. And the word infant then sang in his brain with the words ripe and rot, and he would have buried all three words then, infant, ripe and rot, in the earth here the way Nina must have buried her shawl when he was on that transport was it, moving towards the seething bullets or on the burning hill with Gregory dragging him or on the corpse-riddled beach, maybe, burying his own finger. But he couldn't bury words, no more than he could drive them from his singing brain and so he stood and paced, as if to escape them, he walked from the apple tree to the glasshouse, but there was no escape, they were inside him the way those tiny, barely formed bones on the rotting shawl were once inside Nina. And he remembered the whole line then, of the fool in the forest. And so from hour to hour we ripe and ripe and then from hour to hour we rot and rot and thereby hangs a tale.

It was a fool's tale, he knew and it hung round his neck like a fool's bauble, visible to everyone but him. He had always been the fool and had dragged his fool's tale with him, ignorant of its secrets, unaware of its plot. It was collapsing now with the weight of impenetrable years and he collapsed with it, down to the roots of that apple tree, where his head sagged forwards onto his knees and his tears flowed down the frayed corduroy and could have washed those bones beneath his boots clean of earth, there were so many of them. He cried, from the awful realisation, somewhere deep inside him, that all those years could have been different. He cried for the infant he imagined buried by Nina below him, for the cries that might have come from its tiny mouth were it not for the suffocating clay. He cried most of all to drown out those words, still crying out inside him. Infant, ripe and rot.

Then, and he couldn't have told how many hours later, he gathered the bundle of rotting shawl replaced it in the hole and filled in the earth again, the earth which was by now unfrozen, crumbling, like the crumble Mary Dagge used to make. He lay over it like a gravestone, with his arms stretched out, and Nina came upon him later and said, 'You'll freeze George,' and he said, 'Maybe, but I'll warm the earth.'

'Are you an Adonis, George,' she asked him, 'an Adonis in overalls?'

And the next day he came upon her in the glasshouse. He held the shears to her neck as she turned and with quite spectacular clumsiness opened a moonlike gash on her throat. He mistook her loss of consciousness for death, then brought the world back to her while he dragged her through the roses, the world with its scudding clouds above. He realised she was still living while lowering her into the septic tank, then spent one energetic minute severing the head from the body that he had known, in one way or another, since his early childhood. And so her last sight was not of sky, sea or river, but of his blood-spattered watch on his jagging wrist and the time on that watch read twenty past three.

49

THE DAY OF my funeral is a languorous, cloying one, hot, without a breath of wind, sodden precipitation in the air, a humidity that makes people sweat while they are standing. A day that seems designed for different latitudes, Mozambique, maybe, or Zanzibar or some tributary statelet along the Nile. Thunder was promised, but it never comes. The sky itself seems to bulge with immobile, dark-tinted clouds waiting, just waiting to spill their guts onto the church below, its slated spire in turn waiting to prick whatever membrane holds the rains in check.

The dramatis personae is minuscule, much to the disappointment of the supporting cast from the parish who have got news of the event. Yet they sweat together like a multitude. And perhaps the central players in any life would be comparably small, but the unseasonable skies above them seem to emphasize their fragility, the arbitrary nature of my absence and the lack of a centrifugal focus to their grief. What they're missing, of course, is a coffin, the arrival of the hearse, the salving embarrassment of the ritual of hefting my weight onto whatever men would have been chosen for the task. Buttsy Flanagan and Gregory, though they could hardly have carried it between them; maybe Janie could have borne the foot-end helped by Bertie on the other side, wheezing from his emphysemic lungs. But the question doesn't arise.

The church itself seems bound in a girdle of peace. The dust raised by the feet of the mourners beneath the yew-trees forms an umbra or a penumbra, I can't be sure which, and lends the graveyard behind an aspect and a beauty that would have me believe in eternal rest, had my condition itself not implied otherwise.

The sky bulges lower and seems even to shrink. Any hint of infinity has been compressed into its immobile, humid folds, like a blouse concealing a large, sweating bosom. Come on clouds, burst. Drench them all. Janie, with her greying hair wrapped in that elegant mantilla, that black suit with the short hobble skirt, lavender silk stockings and high heels. Do her crying for her, quench that cigarette she's smoking, underneath the yews. Throw a rivulet down Gregory's elegant profile, a cascade of drips from the brim of his sober black hat. Allow the retired Miss Cannon to unfurl that golf umbrella she is holding and spatter her ancient, everlasting tweeds. The scene cries out for umbrellas, for some forced communion underneath a downpour. So the Moynihans, mother and daughters, could meet Dr Hannon, from Portrane.

The priest comes late from the blessing of a meat processing plant in Slane, and his motorbike peppers the damp air with suspended globules of exhaust. His presence does at last what a coffin should have done, gives some shape to the event. They troop behind him into the thin, triangular interior with its single window, behind the altar, looking out upon the waters of the Boyne. And there is a strange relief in the fact that the tiny church is filled, that the event will have an audience after all, quite respectable in numbers. They genuflect and kneel, and cough and wait, while the priest vanishes behind the altar, to emerge after an infinity, his damp soutane covered by a greying chasuble, an altar boy in purer white behind him, carrying the bell and the cruets.

The drama begins then, intoned in toneless Latin, a celebration of another death, a long time ago, another body never found. There is some confusion round the gospel. Gregory has requested a reading, but doesn't, of course, know when it should come. The Latin ceases for a while, the priest waits, then nods impatiently to the front pews, and Gregory rises, a prayer book in his hand. He walks to the lectern, coughs and reads, in slow,

Shade

deliberate cut-glass tones, the lines of a hymn, 'There is a balm in Gilead', and manages to keep to himself his suspicion that in fact there is none. There was none in Jeremiah either, for the virgin, the daughter of Egypt. In vain shalt thou use many medicines, for thou shall not be cured.

But there is balm of kinds for him, if not in Gilead, and it arrives midway through his reading. A slim gentleman, in early middle age, in an Astrakhan coat and a Homburg hat, who genuflects uncertainly and blesses himself badly. Jonathan Cornfold, actor's agent, of Gregory Hardy Associates, my half-brother's balm and the other love of his life.

Gregory kneels by the front pews, Jonathan by the back, a bell rings out and between them the inhabitants of both banks of the Boyne river bend their heads in consecration.

A sacral hush descends, the coughing ceases and it is suddenly there, the event.

> There is a balm in Gilead
> To make the wounded whole.

The heavens open, the rain cascades on to the triangle of slates above and water drips onto the altar boys starched, startling white. That hole in the roof, the priest muses, though he shouldn't, needs mending, and with Mr Hardy's donation, he can now afford it. The sound from above is like the fluttering of wings, and I remember it again, the delicious patter on the corrugated roof of Janie and George's bedroom, the three of us curled up in the blankets below, each raindrop like a falling angel, the beating wings of a dove. The congregation rises and those who want to receive the unburied one walk forwards and receive. And the wings ascend now, or descend from the wooden, dripping rafters, and my mourners gradually go forth, as the dove demands, in peace.

There is more rain outside, and a different sound, and each of them feels, as they meet the rain in their various ways, some with

313

unfurled umbrellas, some with cowled overcoats over their heads, that they have been released from inside an echoing drum. This rain is almost tropical and the diffuse mist the down-pour raises over the bulrushes of the riverbank could equally inhabit the bulrushes in Egypt's land, contagious, as the song says, to the Nile.

They gather in cars and the cars drive off, since the rain won't allow for funereal conversation, to the house, now wrapped in curtains of water, on the river's north side. Neither Gregory nor Jonathan knows whom to exclude or include, and Janie, who does, seems beyond caring, sipping as she has been from a baby bottle of Powers concealed in her handbag. So the entire dripping congregation floods the house, making short work of the Moynihan sandwiches and the trays of whiskey, sherry and Guinness Extra stout.

When the bottles on display are empty, Janie volunteers to go for more and is driven, to her quiet delight, by Buttsy Flanagan to the nearest pub, the Nineteenth Hole in Baltray. Buttsy sinks two pints in the wood-panelled interior, one for each of Janie's double-whiskies, while the bar staff fill the back seat of the police-car with more supplies. Their return is delayed further by not so much a detour as an intermission, near Mabel Hatch's barn, where Janie wants to listen to the sound, of a thousand watery hands drumming off the car's metal roof. Buttsy lights a cigarette and mistakes Janie's knee for the gear-handle, a mistake Janie suspects is no mistake at all. And the principal outcome of their subsequent embrace is the entanglement of her mantilla in the steering wheel.

They rejoin the party, for party it has become, flushed with alcohol and a passion they imagine they can keep concealed. A song is reaching its conclusion, which warns of, or celebrates, 'goodwill and hospitality, including false acquaintance'. And Janie starts up then, with an uncertain rendition of 'The Girl From The County Down', which she misremembers halfway through the second verse. 'A noble call is mine,' she concludes as if she'd sung the whole of it. She spins the half-empty bottle of Powers on the carpet before her and manages to edge it with her toe so it ends up pointing at Buttsy. He rises to his feet and begins the first of seventeen verses of 'The Ballad Of Blasphemous Bill'. And Buttsy, unfortunately, remembers them all. The bottle spins again and elicits from the Moynihan sisters their party piece duet, 'The Indian Love Call', and from the aged Miss Cannon a word-perfect rendition of 'Fair Daffodils, I Weep To See'.

So the living forget the dead, in an orgy of mnemonics. And later, much later in the night, while the persisting rain provides ample excuse for my wake's continuance, while Gregory, downstairs, accompanies Jonathan in his bell-like, plangent account of 'The Fair Maid Of Perth', Janie and Sergeant Buttsy Flanagan provide, upstairs on my virgin sheets, a display of the kind of acquaintance that would make the living blush and the dead rise up, if they only could.

50

T HE RAINS COME down for days, the river rises, bursts its banks,
the tributaries spill into one, not so much a river as a meandering lake, lapping right up to the remade glasshouse. The house
sits beached on the Irish sea, the trees perched on the water's
surface like surprised seagulls. Kittiwakes tread on the sodden
gravel by the kitchen door, the swing idles two feet under water,
an eel winds itself between the ropes. The tides remove the
topsoil, expose the septic tank to the brine, and the brick of the
old Victorian orb collapses inwards like a crushed egg, the effluent merges effortlessly with the silt and the mud of Mozambique,
releasing my maggot-riddled bones.

I'm part of it now, the horizon, that endless line that stretches
from the glasshouse door to Wales and Liverpool. There are
days, endless days when the sun rises, and before it has quite dispersed the morning mists, spreads its equatorial fingers through
a tropical swamp, a bayou. And then it begins its slow retreat and
drags me with it and I am the river now, the seaweed my hair, the
barnacles my bed, the long slow womanly weight of water dragging me towards the house when the tide flows, away from it
when it ebbs.

There are three of us here, one died by drowning, one died by
falling, one died by garden shears. We burble sometimes, we lap,
we sing. We pray for the living who move above us in ships, for
the pilot that guides them, for the harbour that awaits them. For
we know that some day they'll have no more existence than us,
than the tendrils of our hair on the river bed, moving with the
tides, than the horse that wrecked the barley, than the petals of

spring cherry that detach themselves from the tree in the monastery garden, drifting downwards towards the bald pate of the
bearded Abbot, still sleeping, dreaming of them.

Acknowledgements

Grateful thanks to my mother, Angela Jordan, born in Mornington on the Boyne river, whose stories of her father, painter and some-time shellfish exporter provided some kind of imaginative template; and to Jacintha McCullough, born in Baltray, nanny to my youngest children, whom I pestered with questions over a two-year period.

The following books proved invaluable in the writing of *Shade*: Kathleen Tynan, *Twenty-Five Years Reminiscences* (Smith, Elder & Co., 1913); Sir William Wilde, *The Boyne and the Blackwater* (Kevin Duffy, 2003); James Garry, *The Streets and Lanes of Drogheda* (Drogheda, 1993); John McCullen, *The Drogheda Steampacket Co.*, in *Journal of the Old Drogheda Society*, 1994, No.9; Myles Dungan, *Irish Voices from the Great War* (Irish Academic Press, 1985); Robert Rhodes James, *Gallipoli* (B.T. Batsford, 1965); J.B. Lyons, *The Enigma of Tom Kettle* (Glendale Publishers, 1983); Alice Curtayne, *Francis Ledwidge: A Life of the Poet* (Martin Brian & O'Keefe Ltd., 1972); N.E.B. Wolters, *Bungalow Town: Theatre and Film Colony* (Shoreham, 1985); Michael Holroyd, *Bernard Shaw, vol. III: The Lure of Fantasy* (Chatto & Windus, 1991).